JUSTICE MAKES A KILLING

A Bobby Earl Novel

Chickadee Prince Books
New York

To my sons
Jason and Jedidiah

CHAPTER 1

California Highway Patrol Officer Randy Phillips had been following the red Jaguar for the last twenty minutes, making sure to stay a safe half-mile back. Under his Kevlar vest, the tee-shirt was stuck to his back with sweat. "Christ," he mumbled to himself. "Where are they?" He reached down to give his holster a reassuring tug then nervously fingered the lock mechanism on his pistol's hammer.

Keeping the Jaguar in sight was easy. Highway 5 ran ruler-straight across the scrub brush desert toward Los Angeles, two hours away, and the asphalt lanes ahead were empty under the blistering afternoon sun. But this waiting had his gut in a knot. He clamped his eyes shut for a moment to ease the tension. When he opened them, sweat stung his eyes. "Come on, come on," he whispered. "Let's do this."

Suddenly his radio squawked. "Car 2-5-9. We have visual." He bent forward to look up into the cloudless sky. A black and white helicopter was above, keeping pace with the Jaguar like a kite being pulled on a string.

He stomped on the accelerator. The big cruiser quickly closed the distance and roared up within inches of the Jaguar, red lights flashing, siren shrieking. The Jaguar slowed immediately and rolled to a stop on the gravel shoulder. There was no movement from inside. The cruiser halted a cautious ten yards back. The helicopter swooped down and hovered loudly just above, kicking up a swirling cloud of sand and dust around the cars. The cruiser's door flew open, and Officer Phillips rolled out to crouch behind it. His breath came in short pants. He gripped his Smith & Weston in both hands and pointed it through his open window frame at the silent Jaguar.

"Raise your hands, so I can see them," he shouted into the din of the helicopter's engines. "Show your left arm out the window." After a moment an arm appeared out the driver's window. "Now step out of the car. Keep your hands in the air and lie face-down on the pavement."

The driver's door opened, and an elegant woman wearing a fashionable dress stepped out. She shielded her face against the sting of the churning sand with one hand and pushed down her billowing skirt with the other. She yelled over the roar of the helicopter. "There must be some mistake. My name is Kathleen Carlson. I'm a lawyer. What's the meaning of this?"

One Hour Earlier

The howl of the siren frightened the pigeons off the roof of H Block. The birds rose as one and circled frantically in the California sky above Haywood State Prison. A voice barked over the loud speaker, "This is not a drill. Lockdown. I repeat. Lockdown." On the exercise yard, the clusters of inmates in orange jumpsuits stared up at the gun tower. Below the rifleman's perch, a sign read, *WE DON'T FIRE WARNING SHOTS.* The men turned and sullenly trudged back inside, grumbling among themselves.

Rows of cell doors clanked shut in a rolling chorus of slamming steel. Once locked in, the inmates erupted in a thunderous clamor of defiance and complaint at the loss of their yard time. In the East Wing, a guard trotted along an empty cement hallway, breathing hard as he lumbered toward the visitors' room. The thudding of his steel-toed boots echoed off the walls. When he reached the sally-port to the visitor's room, he stopped abruptly and stared in alarm. The steel barred gate was open. The gate was never supposed to be left open. He moved cautiously to the edge of the entrance then darted a look around the doorway.

Inside the small entry room, a black guard sat slumped against the wall, his legs stretched out before him. His head was bowed as if looking down in disbelief at the red stain spreading across his khaki green shirt. A few feet away, Sergeant Clyde Rattner stood with one boot planted firmly on the neck of a prone inmate who lay motionless on the cement floor. The inmate's face was pressed down into a slowly widening pool of blood. The smell of cordite hung in the air.

"Don't just stand there," Rattner shouted. "Help Travis." The guard stood rooted to his spot at the gate, staring down in wide-eyed panic. "Johnson! Move, Goddamn it!"

Startled into action, Johnson went to the fallen figure. He knelt down, then he hesitated. He looked up at Rattner, who glared back at him. He turned back and slowly reached out to press two fingers against the black man's neck. After a moment, he rose and stumbled backward with a stunned look on his face. "Jesus," he said softly starring down at the stricken guard. "I think he's dead. Oh my God. Travis is dead."

"Johnson, listen to me!" Rattner yelled at the frozen guard. "Look at me. Snap out of it. Call for the ambulance and the medical team."

Just then the inmate on the floor breathed out a moan. Small bubbles formed at the corner of his mouth and floated out onto the smooth red pool. One half-open eye stared dully as the blood slowly expanded outward.

"What about him?" the guard asked.

"Fuck this asshole," Rattner spat. "Take care of Travis."

"SERGEANT RATTNER," THE lawyer said in a subdued voce, "why don't you just tell me what happened today?" The two men were alone in the carpeted reception area outside the Warden's Office. The lawyer sat on a desk chair opposite the uniformed guard who was sullenly perched on the room's stiff-backed couch. It had been three hours since the "incident."

The lawyer had a pudgy face, wispy blond hair and an ill-fitting grey pin-striped suit. His ample stomach strained against the buttons of his white dress shirt. "As I told you," he continued, "I'm a lawyer from the legal staff of your union. I'm here to protect you. Your union rep is right outside if you have any questions about this."

Rattner sat hunched forward, elbows on his knees, glaring into the distance as if willing himself elsewhere. His lean work-hardened frame and grizzled hair seemed out of place in a prison guard's uniform. The corners of his mouth were drawn down as if in the grim certainty that life's odds were unfairly stacked against him and he would inevitably end up being cheated. He shifted his gaze and locked eyes with the lawyer. "So," he said in disgust. "You're saying I need protection. I need to lawyer-up."

"No. No. That's not what I meant. We always provide a lawyer for our members whenever there's an incident." The lawyer slid his chair closer and leaned forward. "Look," he said more softly. "I know it's tough anytime you lose a colleague. But we need to go over what happened before you go next door with the cops and the DA. Just to make certain your recollection matches up with the facts. Sometimes people forget things or misremember them."

Rattner sat staring down at a Styrofoam cup of coffee cradled between his hands. "What did the little asshole say happened?" he finally asked.

"The inmate? He died on the way to the hospital."

Rattner took a sip of coffee then drew a deep breath. He set the cup on an end table next to the couch and turned to the lawyer. "Okay," he said in a flat voice. "Here's how it went down. I was a prowler."

The lawyer gave him a questioning look.

"I wasn't assigned anywhere," Rattner explained. "I walked the grounds looking for strays. Inmates in unauthorized areas, that kind of shit. I also filled in when an escort was needed."

"Now, you were unarmed, right?"

"Of course." He furrowed his brow in annoyance. "Nobody carries inside. These fucks would take it away from you in a second." He looked off, a heavy breath whistled through his teeth as he slowly shook his head.

"Right. Just checking."

"So I get a call to escort an inmate from the visitors' room. When I get there, Travis is standing next to the inmate."

"Travis Miller, the officer that got shot?" the lawyer asked.

Rattner nodded. "Except, it don't look right. The inmate's way too close to Travis. So I say something. 'You okay?' or something like that. I don't remember."

"That doesn't matter," the lawyer said. "Go on."

"Then I see it. The fuck's got a gun jammed in Travis's ribs."

The lawyer reached into a folder next to his chair and handed Rattner a photograph. "Is that the gun you saw?"

"I guess. It happened so fast. But it was small like that."

"That's the one they found on the floor next to the inmate."

Rattner shrugged an acceptance and continued. "When I challenge him, he turns the gun on me. And that's when it all jumped off. Travis made a grab for the gun. Then...." Rattner paused and shook his head in disbelief. "Then the fuck just pulls away and shoots Travis. Just like that. I couldn't fucking believe it."

"Then what happened?" the lawyer asked.

"By then I was already moving. I jump the prick and start wrestling for the gun. All of sudden, it goes off. Bam! For a second I thought I might'a been hit. But then he drops. So I pushed my emergency button." He tapped the small black transmitter hooked to the shoulder of his uniform.

"Let me show you something." The lawyer reached into the folder again and pulled out another photograph. "You ever see this before?"

Rattner examined the photo. "No, what is it?"

"It's a photocopy of what was found on the floor. It's a map that shows the prison layout. The vehicle yard is circled. We figure he was headed there to get a truck and force Officer Miller to drive him out the gates."

"But how the fuck did he get a gun?"

"That's the unbelievable part," the lawyer said, his eyes wide in amazement. "This woman who was visiting him. A lawyer of all things. She must have slipped it to him in the visitors' room."

At the same time, one hundred miles away, in the Los Angeles Criminal Courthouse, the court reporter in Department 102 straddled her stenotype machine, patiently waiting for Judge Winkler to take the bench. Her gaze was fixed on the defense lawyer seated at the counsel table. Bobby Earl. She knew him, that is, she knew of him. She had seen him on television when he got that safecracker off who was charged with killing a cop. Even before that, she had known he had a certain reputation in the courthouse. What was it that people said about him? Oh yes, he was the trial lawyer you called when it was time to fix bayonets. But he was known for more than just fighting for his clients. It was said he won the cases you weren't supposed to win.

She studied him. Late thirties, with short tousled brown hair, his broad clean features were divided by a broken nose, which gave him a roughhewn look, more masculine than handsome. It was a face to trust, rather than admire, and apparently juries did just that.

But this was not a jury trial, she reminded herself. This was a preliminary hearing, the stage in a case when the prosecutor had to show a judge there was enough evidence against the defendant to allow it to proceed to trail. As the judge often intoned, he only had to find there was a strong suspicion to believe the defendant was guilty, not proof beyond a reasonable doubt. One lawyer had told her this meant the prosecutor's case had to have just enough life to barely fog up a mirror. This thin measure was one she had yet to see Judge Winkler fail to find.

Bobby Earl leaned back, at ease in his chair, and clasped his hands behind his head. He calmly looked around and let his mind wander. A courtroom was probably the one place Earl felt most at home, where he was most himself. He counted himself fortunate to have found his proper place in the world. He was a trial lawyer. It was the only calling for which he truly felt suited. But not just any type of trial lawyer. Defending the pockets of insurance companies or chasing after personal injury cases had no appeal for him. No, he was a criminal defense lawyer. Something in him needed the intensity, the adrenalin surge of a competition with someone's life at stake; the solitary feeling of standing up alone to authority; the clear determination of who won or lost. There was a hunger in him that only being a trial lawyer satisfied.

And he was looking forward to today's contest. There was a look of confidence in his eyes, like a seasoned commander staring down on a battle field having gained the high ground. As he organized his thoughts, a hint of a smile emerged at the corners of his mouth.

The middle-aged woman in the Chanel suit seated next to him was his client. Caroline Morgan was charged with hiring someone to murder her husband during a messy divorce. That someone, Joe Carrelli, had allegedly gotten a pang of conscience and instead ran to the District Attorney. The detective on the case had finished testifying just before the lunch break. When the voters passed Proposition 15, it removed many of the historic protections built into this hearing. Now the detective could repeat what Carrelli had told him about the plot without Joe having to take the stand to answer any questions. The detective testified that Carrelli said the plan was to quietly make off with the husband's car during the night, drive it to the airport, wipe it down for any fingerprints, and leave it there as if the husband had left on a trip. Joe was then to return, overpower the husband, take him into the desert, kill and bury him. However, according to Joe, after leaving the car at the airport, he got cold feet and backed out. After a couple days, he went to the DA.

Judge Winkler took the bench and looked at Earl over the glasses perched on the end of his nose. "Submitted, counsel," the judge said, anxious to drop his gavel and send the case on to the trial court.

Earl rose, wearing a custom tailored English wool suit with a pale blue window pane pattern; a matching silk tie lay on his white Egyptian cotton shirt. It was a suit no jury would ever see, even though it hung well, having been cut to camouflage his thick body. At six feet, 195 pounds, he was not exactly built like a store window manikin. From the age of 12 he had spent every weekend and summer on the end of a shovel working alongside the crew in his father's asphalt paving business. By the time he was 16 he was as strong as a man and worked like one. As a result, he had the thick muscled back and shoulders of a stevedore.

"If the court please," Earl said. "I'd like to call Mr. Morgan."

"Objection," the young prosecutor yelped, catapulting himself out of his chair.

"The defense is not allowed to call any witnesses. The only exceptions are if the testimony would establish a defense or impeach a prosecution witness."

"Mr. Morgan's testimony will do both," Earl replied pleasantly.

The judge shot a look at the clock. "I would normally hold a hearing to determine whether the testimony qualified. However, it's probably more efficient just to hear it and if it doesn't qualify, I'll disregard it."

"Thank you, your Honor," Earl said. It was always helpful, he thought, to be friendly and respectful to court clerks. It was from that source he had learned that the judge had an early tee time and would undoubtedly allow him to proceed without having to prematurely reveal his questions to the witness at a hearing, before repeating them at the prelim.

Mr. Morgan took the stand, indignantly adjusted his sport coat to accommodate his ample girth, and glared at Earl with eyes filled with resentment. Morgan had inherited a multi-million-dollar bottling company from his father, which the plant managers ran while he sat in the corner office and made lunch dates with his fraternity buddies. These winners in the parental lottery, who pretended they had somehow earned their high perch, were a prime target for Earl's disdain. He had an overwhelming urge to knock them on their ass.

Earl's questions quickly disposed of the preliminary facts. The Morgans married ten years ago, when he had Caroline sign a prenuptial agreement; they were currently separated, contemplating divorce; Caroline and the children lived in the family home, he in a penthouse apartment.

"It's curious, isn't it Mr. Morgan, that of all the crimes that Caroline could be accused of, soliciting the murder of a spouse is the one crime that has the greatest financial benefit for you."

"I don't know what you're talking about," Morgan scoffed.

"Didn't your divorce lawyer discuss with you that if Caroline is convicted of this crime, this specific crime, the California Family Code provides you with very significant monetary rewards?" Earl held up his hand and started to count off with his fingers. "First, by law, you do not have to pay spousal support, *and* she can't touch that retirement fund you have offshore, *and* you automatically get custody so you don't have to pay child support. It's all right there in the statute."

"I guess she should have thought of that when she tried to kill me," Morgan said looking quite pleased with himself.

"More importantly, your prenuptial agreement has a clause that nullifies it if either spouse commits or attempts an act of domestic violence."

"She's the one who asked for that."

"I'm sure she did," Earl said knowingly. He paused, putting his hand on a document on the counsel table, like a chess player contemplating a move. "Are you absolutely sure," Earl asked, adopting a tone of disbelief, "that your car went missing on Thursday night, June 15?"

"Absolutely," he said with a smirk.

"You're absolutely sure? It couldn't have been some other day? "

"No way. I couldn't use it to get to work on Friday. I first thought my neighbor had it towed. He's always complaining about me blocking his parking spot," he said mockingly. "By the time I figured it out it was Sunday, and I reported it the next day."

Earl paused to appreciate the moment. This delay in reporting would have allowed Morgan some wiggle room as to when to claim his car was taken. That answer had been the one point at which Morgan might have saved himself. Usually, controlling a hostile witness during cross-examination was a battle, a contest to force the witness to admit something that, before conceding it, he would prefer to gargle battery acid. Such a witness had to be badgered, coerced, intimidated and finally maneuvered into the box, before the lid could be snapped shut. This had been too easy. From here on the questioning would proceed as any cross-examination should, tantalizingly slowly, with a sense of quiet inevitability.

"That makes sense," Earl said in a conversational tone, nodding in agreement. "Carrelli told the detective he took your car, wiped it clean of fingerprints and left it at the airport on Thursday." Earl picked up a clear plastic bag containing a small rectangular paper. He gave a copy to the prosecutor and placed the plastic bag on the witness stand. "Do you recognize this, Mr. Morgan?"

Morgan's eyes warily darted from Earl to the plastic bag and back again.

"Please take your time," Earl suggested calmly.

Morgan seemed transfixed, as if afraid to pick it up.

"Mr. Morgan?" Earl asked politely. Earl glanced over at the prosecutor, trying to determine how much he understood. Not enough, Earl concluded. He looked like someone prepared for a setback, but not a disaster.

"Let me see if I can help you," Earl said and picked up the plastic bag. "It's a ticket for a parking structure at the airport. The one where your car was found. It's time stamped on the back for Thursday night, June 15 at 9:13 PM."

Morgan's eyes narrowed with apprehension. "Where did you get this?"

"Your dry cleaner returned it with the cleaning to your house, along with some pocket change he found in your clothes. Apparently, he didn't know you'd moved. It seems it was left in your coat pocket." Earl paused, as if waiting for a response. "Mr. Yang is seated in the hallway, if you have any questions."

"So what?" Morgan said. "This doesn't prove anything."

"Except for one thing. There is a very clear thumb print in the middle of the ticket made when the ticket was pulled from the dispenser." Earl made a gesture, pressing his thumb on his curled fingers, as if taking a ticket.

Morgan stared down at the ticket in disbelief.

"It's your thumb print." Earl paused for a response, then continued. "It would appear, Mr. Morgan, that it was *you* who drove your car to the airport, not Mr. Carrelli. You apparently took the ticket as you drove through, put it in your coat pocket, wiped down the car for fingerprints but forgot about the ticket."

"It's not mine. It can't be," Morgan said as if trying to convince self.

"Actually it is," Earl said with quiet conviction. "Mr. Louis Spenser, erprint expert, is seated next to Mr. Yang out in the hall. He compared umb impression with personal items in your house."

Morgan sat in stunned silence.

"If you're going to make up a lie, Mr. Morgan," Earl said, "it's est if a good part of it is actually true. When you made this deal lli to frame your wife, you should have trusted him to drive your car. So he at least drove the car to the airport and went through

through answering your questions." Morgan exclaimed and t the judge in defiance.

Judge Winkler stared back, his eyes filled with astonishment. He seemed befuddled, unsure how to proceed, so by habit he turned to the prosecutor for guidance. Receiving none, he said, "I think you should go upstairs and discuss this case with your supervisor. This matter is adjourned till tomorrow." The judge leaped up and scurried off the bench.

Earl stepped back and sat next to his client. "What just happened?" she exclaimed.

"I think you're about to become a witness for the prosecution."

CHAPTER 2

ONE WEEK LATER

The Haywood City Jail was a nondescript three-story modern building that served many functions. It housed the police department, the probation offices and the jail. One might think, even for a town of twenty-five thousand, that didn't seem to leave much room for many inmates in the town's only jail. But the judges of Haywood had solved that problem. They sent everyone they could to state prison. As an added bonus, this policy meant that the state, not the Haywood County taxpayers, would have to pay to house them.

Bobby Earl exited the elevator on the top floor, crossed to a steel door and held up his Bar Card to a small barred window. After a moment, keys rattled on the other side. The door swung open, and Earl approached a heavy-set deputy seated at a grey metal desk. The desk top was bare except for an old-style cradle phone and a small tin of Renegades snuff. Earl handed the deputy his Bar card and driver's license.

"You're a long way from home, aren't you, counselor?" the deputy said with a disapproving tone.

Earl expected that. In any small town, there was always resentment, even among cops, when a defendant felt the need to bring in an out-of-town lawyer, rather than hire one of their own. This "buy local" prejudice persisted apparently even when the defendant was facing two first degree murder charges. "Gotta make a living, my friend," Earl said. "Have pen, will travel." The deputy directed him with a toss of his chin to a worn wooden interview table that ran the length of the room with a low divider running down the middle.

Earl had left LA before sunrise in order to arrive at the jail when it first opened. Not surprisingly, the interview room was empty. The morning sun shone through a frosted glass window high up on the far wall, casting a column of light in which dust mites slowly danced. Earl took a seat, adjusted his "meet the new client" suit and looked about. All jail interview rooms had the same general feeling. It didn't matter if it was a big city "correction center" or a small town "slammer." There was a heavy atmosphere that immediately enveloped you. Maybe it was the stale air, the drab paint on the walls, the hard cement floors, but whatever its source, it was palpable. This interview room, like all the others, reeked of defeat and wasted lives.

A door opened across the room, and an attractive woman in a drab jail gown entered. She had intelligent eyes and a determined chin. A bit on the short side, but the confident way she carried herself made her seem taller. Her hair was reddish, the color of a fox, cut fashionably short, framing a face that seemed to be in a struggle with itself to maintain its composure.

Earl had checked her web site when he got the call. She was about fifty, judging from the year she graduated at the top of her class at Stanford Law School; currently a partner at Arnold & Mellon, a prestigious old Los Angeles law firm that occupied three floors of a downtown high rise; head of the corporate tax division, with clients that included multinational corporations and individuals in the Fortune 500. She probably billed at an hourly rate that equaled the weekly salary of most school teachers.

She had recently left Horgan & Cooley, another venerated old-line Los Angeles law firm. Earl could imagine the sumo wrestling that erupted between these two legal titans when she presumably took some of her gilded clients with her. Lately she had entered the political arena as the spokesperson for a voter Initiative on the November ballot. Proposition 53, popularly known as SOS, for Save Our Schools, would prohibit the state from paying to incarcerate inmates in private for-profit prisons and use the money it saved to fund public schools.

As she approached, her expression seemed to struggle between hope and despair. That did not surprise him. Her world had just been upended. She had been yanked from a position of respect and prominence only to be thrown into a cement box with an open toilet. He could only imagine how jarring it must have felt the first time those metal handcuffs bit into her skin or when she heard the finality in the sound of a slamming steel door. What might lay ahead must terrorize her thoughts.

"Mr. Earl," she said as she sat down across from him. "I'm Kathleen Carlson. Please call me Kate."

Earl nodded and smiled. "Then call me Bobby," he said.

"My friend, Judge Jefferson, spoke highly of you," she said. "He described you as someone who knows how to try a case. And that's what I badly need."

"Judge Jefferson is a first rate trial judge. I wish we had a few more like him." Jefferson's court was where he defended Sydney Seabrooke, the master safe cracker, charged with killing a cop. Every trial took a piece out of Earl, and that case had taken a fair sized chunk. But now, three months later, he had rested enough. He could use another big case. Who was he kidding, he *needed* another big case. It was like an addiction. He was a trial junkie. It was ironic, but descending into the dark world of murder was the only time he felt truly alive; fully engaged. The rest of the world just floated away as he focused on the next witness, the next question. The high was worth the pain; that is, as long as he won. And sure, a big pay day never hurt. But it wasn't the main thing. The money was more a validation, a confirmation of his worth as a trial lawyer.

"Jefferson's a fine recommendation," Earl continued. "But I'm sure your partners had a few other names to suggest."

She nodded appreciatively. "You're right. Let's just say they weren't overly enthusiastic at the mention of your name. They arranged interviews with some defense lawyers known to them. Former US Attorneys from large firms. But they all seemed to be reading from the same hymnal. The concluding verse was always the same. Let's make a deal." She paused and looked away. When she turned back, there was a not-quite-controllable quiver to her lips. But her words, when they came, were flat and level. "It was very disappointing, to say the least."

"You know," Earl said, "making a deal is not always a mistake. It depends on what happened."

"But that's the point. I know what happened. I didn't do this." She pleaded, then closed her eyes. "Oh God," she mumbled to herself. "This is a nightmare." After a moment, she seemed to gather herself, but when she refocused there was a look of resignation in her eyes. "Bobby, I need your help. I really do."

Earl understood that, for a woman like her, such an admission must be a frightening realization — she was in a free fall without a parachute. She came from a very competitive world. The practice of corporate law at her level was still an old boys club. A woman not only had to be smart, she had to be tough and able to command a place at the table. This meant she was accustomed to being in control, absolute control, calling her own shots, taking her own risks. To lose that control, to be dependent upon the decisions of someone else must only add fuel to her sense of despair.

"I know how scary this must be. To be charged...."

"You don't understand," she said interrupting him. "Not only am I innocent, I was set up! This was all orchestrated to make me look guilty."

This Earl had not expected. The '*I was framed*' defense was on the same page of the defense playbook as the murder victim committed suicide by shooting himself three times.

"And who would do that to you?" Earl asked, careful to avoid a dismissive tone.

"The prison guards union."

Earl raised an eyebrow at her.

"Bobby," she said, giving him a purposeful stare. "I understand that this sounds crazy. But in my particular case it happens to be true."

"Go on, I'm listening."

"I am the spokesperson for Proposition 52, the SOS Initiative. Are you familiar with it?"

"Of course," Earl said. "It would ban the use of private prisons to house state inmates and put the money it saved into our schools."

"The main opponent of the Initiative is the prison guards union."

"Why would prohibiting private prisons put you in the cross-hairs of the guards union?"

"Because the state requires private prisons to only hire union guards. Eliminating private prisons means the loss of a lot of jobs."

"So they would do this over the loss of a few jobs?" Earl asked with a hint of skepticism.

"It's more than a few, it's a couple thousand. But it's bigger than that. Our prisons are so overcrowded that the US Supreme Court has ordered California to reduce its state prison population. In order to meet that court order, the state shuffled inmates from the *state* prisons into these *private* for-profit-prisons. If the inmates in private prisons are transferred back to state prisons they will have to start paroling inmates"

"In the past," Earl said, "they found a simple solution to all that. They built more prisons."

"But there isn't the money anymore. As a state, we now spend more on prisons than on all the University of California campuses and the Cal State Community College system combined. Nearly ten billion dollars a year. In California it now costs more to house an inmate for a year than it does for a year at Harvard. $75,000."

The raw starkness of the numbers gave Earl a pause. The prospect of imprisonment was a daily consideration in court, with years being bargained over like dollars between rug merchants, but he had yet to hear even an afterthought of the financial burden on the taxpayers.

"And that is what worries the union. If they start paroling inmates, fewer inmates means you need fewer guards, which means less union dues, the very money that buys the political influence that pumps up their salaries and perks."

"But the last time I checked," Earl said, "the chance of getting paroled was about the same as finding a movie star without Botox."

"Look," Kate said. "Given the Supreme Court order they'd have no choice, and there are reasonable ways to do it. One out of five inmates is serving a life sentence, many for non-violent drug crimes. Most are eligible for parole." She looked at Earl who nodded in agreement. "Another twenty percent are over fifty. By just paroling the older inmates and the drug offenders would shrink the prison population, which would reduce costs. Particularly medical costs. Without forcing the state to consider parole opportunities, our prisons will become old age homes with the only population in the country guaranteed free medical care."

Earl nodded. He had gone to UC Berkeley on a baseball scholarship but was aware of the whopping tuition increases over the years. Making college more affordable seemed a better use of tax dollars than teaching inmates to make license plates. He recalled receiving alumni contribution requests from the Berkeley Law School, pointing out that they only receive twenty-five percent of their funding from the state.

"By spending less on prisons," Carlson continued, "we could invest in our schools and universities."

Unsure of what to make of all this, Earl moved on. "So who was Adam Hartman to you? Why were you visiting him?"

"Adam said he had information about the private prison system that we could use in our campaign. I was there to discuss it with him."

"And did he?"

"I don't know. He needed time to get it, he said." She paused. "Time he didn't have."

Earl sat quietly trying to absorb it all.

Kate recognized his hesitation. "I did not smuggle in a gun to Adam. It's ridiculous. But what better way to discredit the Initiative than to implicate its spokesperson in a prison break." She paused to study Earl's reaction. "Look, they have a lot on the line here. Between the union and the private prison industry there are millions and millions of dollars at stake. To protect all that, do you think they would hesitate to try something like this?"

Earl sat in silent contemplation, unwilling to docilely agree with her, since it seemed a bit improbable. Yes, he needed a new case, but was this a case worth pouring himself in to? Because that what it would mean. He was not like those lawyers who saw the law as a business, the ones with Rolex watches and titanium briefcases who regarded defendants as commodities. They could distance themselves from the outcomes as if they had no skin in the game. That's why they lasted longer. But Earl knew himself. Once he was in, he was all in. That meant sleepless nights, nagging worries, and a focus that ignored everything else. He took his cases personally. So was this one worth all that?

"Okay," she said, guessing at Earl's skepticism. "You probably think this sounds a bit farfetched. So why don't you go talk with State Senator Sanchez? He tried to get a bill passed to stop the state from using private prisons. The union and the private prison industry went after him in the next election and he was defeated. Maybe it will help you to get another perspective."

"All right," Earl said. He needed time to think, so he steered them to a different subject. "So how did you get involved with SOS in the first place? It seems a bit far afield for a corporate tax lawyer."

"You think?" she said with a wry smile. "Let's just say, my whole professional career has been focused on enabling major corporations and some very wealthy individuals reduce their tax obligations. It was intellectually challenging and financially rewarding, but in the end there was something missing in my life." She shrugged her shoulders. "I just felt I needed something more substantial, I guess you could call it a purpose. So I carefully studied our prisons and saw how the private prison industry has attached itself like a parasite on our penal system." She looked deeply at Earl. "They make a mockery of our justice system by turning prisons from a punishment into a profit-making center. Their profit margin is the difference between what they actually spend on inmates and what the state gives them to support and treat inmates. There's a built in incentive to cut addiction programs, education classes or teaching trade skills. Their wardens even earn a yearly bonus based on how much they cut their costs. And their treatment of the inmates is needlessly brutal."

Earl figured her studious approach was expected in a lawyer of her caliber. She had undoubtedly had him checked out well beyond his trial record and reputation, probably down to his shirt size. But there was something about her account that just didn't ring true. There were plenty of worthy causes that would first occur to a well-connected woman before prison reform. It had to have been something personal, deeply personal, to drive her to carve out the time from an all-consuming law practice and invest the energy needed to jump into the political arena on behalf of prison reform. But that was a discussion for another day.

What he did know was that there were cases that seemed to come with a warning label on the file. And this was clearly one. It had trouble written all over it; a defense that was only good for a laugh over drinks, a smart lawyer for a client and an unfamiliar courthouse where he would be as welcome as poison ivy at a nudist camp.

But there was something else. Maybe it was her. Maybe it was the challenge or just the fact that he wanted another big case. Whatever it was he could feel himself being drawn in. He just hoped he wasn't making a mistake.

Kate stared at him, seeming to follow his thoughts. "Well, Bobby, will you help me?"

Earl was not surprised at her abruptness. He knew she was afraid he might walk away and wanted the reassurance of an answer. "Kate," he said. "This is a big decision. Maybe the biggest of your life. The lawyer you choose will have your future in their hands." He paused to give his words time to sink in. "So if you want to think about it or talk to some other lawyers, you should."

She fixed him with a determined look. "If you're the trial lawyer people say you are, you're the one I need."

Earl met her stare, then drew a deep breath. "All right then," Earl said with finality. "It's you and me."

"Thank you." For the first time, she shot him a confident smile. "And actually, Bobby, I think it's 'you and I,' " she said correcting him.

Earl gave her a nod of acceptance and a slight grin. He recognized that this grammatical hairsplitting was her reflexive need to reassure herself that she still had a say in things. It must horrify her to face this sense of dependence, so she gave him a slight tug on the reins. He only wished any future conflicts could be confined to the pages of Strunk and White's *Elements of Style.*

"Now, let's talk business," Earl said. "This is a first degree murder case, two counts, in a distant county. It's going to be expensive. I charge a fixed fee, paid up front. That amount covers the whole case, including trial. No hourly charges every time I turn a page or pick up the phone. You know what it will cost going in. That way we get the money out of the way and can just concentrate on the case."

"Just name a reasonable number and send the agreement to my assistant at the office." She paused then spoke with more feeling. "I can always make more money, Bobby. But I've only got one life. I don't want to spend it in places like this."

CHAPTER 3

When Earl left the jail he squinted in the glare of the morning sun and walked to his car, where the heat had converted the interior into a rotisserie oven. In the short drive through town, Haywood seemed untouched by the homogenizing effect of the national retail chains. On Main Street, Jones & Sons Plumbing and Robbins Hardware stood shoulder to shoulder with other family named stores. On a corner, the late morning sun gleamed off the shiny new farm equipment in the John Deere sales lot. Down the street, in front of Wilson's Feed Store, men with sun-leathered faces, in faded coveralls and frayed baseball caps, sat on a wooden bench talking and laughing, while next door, Emelio's Bodega advertised "tortillas by the inch."

To Bobby Earl, it seemed a quiet, prosperous town as he drove the length of the three traffic light street. It reminded him of growing up in San Cabrera on the California coast. He knew that like all small towns, there was another Haywood, the one to which an outsider would never be admitted; the one where the secrets were kept and grudges were nurtured.

Earl turned onto a side street. He had arrived that morning before the jail opened and had a cup of coffee at the Rooster Cafe, where Bea, the owner, had insisted on giving him directions. The old courthouse, she proudly explained, wasn't used anymore. It had been judged out of date by the City Council and sold. Earl drove past the stately old building with its marble façade and terrazzo lobby. It was now a warren of antique stalls and craft booths. It was disheartening to Earl to see the proud old edifice suffer these indignities for the sake of progress.

The new courthouse, on the next block, was a cement and glass cube with all the dignity and solemnity of a State Motor Vehicle office. Earl pulled into the parking lot and found an empty space at the end of a row of work-worn pickups with a collection of gun racks and NRA stickers. His pale blue 1971 Mercedes convertible with glove leather seats looked as out of place here as a tuxedo at a barn dance. The car, affectionately known as Old Blue, had been his first indulgence when he started to make some real money. He got out and ran his hand over its contours like the flanks of a fine racehorse.

The court appearance for Kathleen Carlson was not scheduled until 10:00 AM, but Earl had come early for a reason. He hated out-of-town cases. It was the same feeling that he had playing baseball for Cal when they were on someone else's home field. He didn't know the ground rules, he didn't know the players. This courthouse was somebody else's home field.

Sure, the rules of evidence came from the same book, but judges, just like umpires, didn't always call the balls and strikes the same way. He needed to know which judge left you alone in trial and which stepped in to dictate the outcome; which DA held back evidence and which always got the close calls. All the trade secrets that were second nature to him in LA. The things that showed up in the win and loss column. He needed a scouting report.

The elevator stopped on the second floor and Earl pushed through a door labeled *"Public Defender."* A scarred wooden counter separated the waiting area with its rows of theater seats from the clerical staff at their county-issue desks. A Hispanic woman with lumpy hips encased in black stretch pants heaved herself up and walked to the counter. He asked to see the Head Deputy and followed in her wake to an office down a hall.

Earl knew that Public Defenders, with their heavy caseloads, were a constant presence in the courts. Unless they were burned out or on automatic pilot, they usually had a pretty fair read on the judicial landscape. And Earl was not too proud to ask for help if it might benefit his client.

The name plate on the open door read *Matthew Stevens*. The small office was made even smaller by the stacks of case files balanced on every surface. In the room's center was a pile of papers, under which Earl assumed was a desk.

"You must be Bobby Earl," the man behind the mound said. "We heard you might take on the Carlson case." He had a tired face with a closely trimmed beard.

"Guilty as charged," Earl said with a grin.

"I made a call to a PD friend in LA. He said you knew your way around a courtroom, so I expected you'd drop by."

"I was hoping you might give me a rundown on the lineup," Earl said. "Normally, I tell clients they're better off with a local guy. But with this one, I figured she should probably have someone from outside."

"You're right about that one," he said with a bemused smile. "Our local brethren haven't exactly queued-up to represent your girl. "Probably worried some dinner invitations might get canceled." He gestured to a cluttered chair. "Take a seat."

Earl carefully transferred a teetering stack of files to the floor and sat down.

The Head Deputy gave Earl a mischievous look. "You want the PG version or the X-rated?"

"Take off the V chip and let me have it straight."

"All right. You're fucked. No other way to put it."

"That good, eh?" Earl said.

"Well, let me enlighten you on a few things about Haywood," Stevens said. "There are two things that support this county: cotton and that private prison. Your girl is charged with the murder of a prison guard and the prison guards union controls our courts. So how would you peg your chances?"

Earl could tell the Head Deputy welcomed this opportunity to expound on the handicaps he labored under. It was like the perverse pride some people take in describing the terrible weather they endure. "I don't quite follow," Earl said.

"The system is quite brilliant in its simplicity really. The union selects a candidate for DA. They put their money and endorsement behind him, so he gets elected. If he plays ball, when the next judgeship opens up, they run him for that or maybe State Senator. Then they pick another candidate for DA. And on it goes. Your arraignment will be in front of the presiding judge, Farley Robbins. He'll keep the case. He's the former DA. The union backed him for judge when he ran. Which way do you think Ol' Farley's going to rule?"

Upstairs, the Haywood courtroom seemed oddly sterile to Earl; a grey carpet with matching grey walls; a pale oak jury box; a plain unvarnished judge's bench; and a Danish Modern counsel table with cushioned, chrome chairs. It seemed more like a sales floor model for office furniture than a citadel of justice. The murmur in the courtroom quieted when Earl entered and walked down the center aisle past the crowded spectator benches. The khaki green of guard uniforms stood-out among the checkered work shirts and starched white blouses. Some local lawyers were huddled by the bailiff's desk like a high school clique sizing up a newcomer.

A young woman with straight, shoulder length blond hair was seated at the counsel table, reading a file. She had prominent cheek bones, a wide mouth with full red lips and ivory skin so pale it seemed almost translucent. Her beauty, though undeniable, seemed remote, somehow untouchable, as if it were only for display. Earl walked over and introduced himself. She turned slowly, folded her arms and gave him an appraising look. Her green-framed glasses rested on a nose she kept tilted upward. Her lips parted in a hint of a smile, as if pleased that her expectations had been met. It was the confident look, Earl thought, of a gambler who had just recalculated the odds and decided to double-down on the bet.

"Lauren Taylor," she said. "Your discovery's at the other end of the table. The judge already knows we're going to the Grand Jury, so we'll just set it for motions. By the way, up here the judge picks the date."

"Thanks for the heads-up," he said.

She nodded and turned back to the file on the table.

Her brusqueness did not surprise him. To her he represented a stereotype; a big city lawyer who probably looked down on her as a backwater legal plodder whom he expected to just roll over in trial. It was understandable that she would armor herself and raise the drawbridge, even though Earl never made the mistake of dealing with an opponent based on a preconception of their abilities. That was a sure way to get caught flat-footed. However, it seemed certain that going forward they would be operating under Taylor's assumptions.

Earl's relationship with any prosecutor on a case usually took a while to develop. He tried to keep it congenial in the beginning, because you got more that way. Normally it wasn't until somebody's nose got bloodied that the gloves came off. It was clear, however, with Lauren Taylor they wouldn't be wasting any time on the preliminaries.

"There is one thing, though," Earl said. "I was wondering whether the autopsies had been completed."

She slowly turned back. "The inmate's been done. They're doing Officer Miller later this morning. Why do you ask?"

"I'd like to attend."

"You have a court order?" she asked.

"No. But I suppose I could ask the judge for one. That is if you really think it's worth being the first thing you decide to fight over."

They locked eyes, then she smiled smugly. "Want to see if he had a heart attack before he was shot?"

"Something like that," Earl said.

"Joe," she said over her shoulder. "Could you join us, please?"

Earl noted that, although barely in her thirties, she had already acquired the command voice.

A short, thickset man in a rumpled brown suit stood up in the front row. He squeezed his bulk past his seat mates, crushing an old fedora hat to his chest. His limbs almost seemed to be of equal length, like a tough lumbering animal, a badger, perhaps, who would fight silently, without relenting, but only if forced to.

"Joe, this is Bobby Earl, Carlson's lawyer. Our out-of-town guest apparently has an interest in corpses and would like to attend Officer Miller's autopsy. Will you take care of that, please?"

Joe Carter," the man said with a smile, and stuck out his hand. "I'm the detective on the case. Nice to meet you." He looked about forty but could have been older. A band of white skin on his forehead marked where his hat brim rested. His eyes held a childlike curiosity, as if he met the world with the expectation that it could still surprise and amuse him. To Earl, it was an unexpected rarity to encounter a homicide detective who was able to hold onto the poet's view that life was a human comedy rather than wrapping himself in a protective shell of cynicism.

Earl shook his hand. "Thanks for the help."

"Glad to do it," Carter continued. "I'll meet you after court."

Taylor nodded to the bailiff, who went through the lock-up door and returned leading Kathleen Carlson. She took a seat next to Earl at the counsel table. Judge Robbins took the bench. He looked young for a judge, with black hair thick enough to repel water and a politician's practiced smile.

"Mr. Earl, welcome to Haywood," the judge said. "I've had a request from the press to take some photographs, which I granted, so let's get that out of the way before the arraignment."

Earl stood as several photographers scurried past the rail to squat on the carpet and click away at Carlson. "Your Honor, I'd like to be heard on that request."

"But I've already ruled, Mr. Earl," the judge said.

"Your Honor, my arguments may not always be acknowledged as the equal of Justice Cardozo, but they do on occasion raise some issues that perhaps the court had not considered on its own. That is why before the Court decides...."

The judge interrupted him. "Of course you should be heard, Mr. Earl. Just not right now. At the end of our session you can put whatever objections you want on the record."

Earl sat down and stared hard at the judge. Ol' Farley had not disappointed. He might be wearing a robe, but he was still a prosecutor.

"Now," the judge continued, as the photographers retreated back to their seats. "Let's proceed with the arraignment."

Earl had briefed Kathleen on the procedure, so she spoke in a clear, firm voice when she entered a plea of not guilty. The judge picked a future date for legal motions and was off the bench.

Kathleen turned to Earl. "Doesn't waste any time, does he?" she said. "Are they all like that?"

"No, we just got lucky." Earl gave her an ironic grimace. "At least we found out early. This is one guy we do not want to end up in front of." He put a reassuring hand on her shoulder. "It's too early to start worrying. I'll see you before I leave town."

As he stepped outside into the bright sunlight, the spectators flowed by, shooting him disparaging looks and mumbled insults. Off to one side, a group of brawny prison guards circled together, like bison seeking the protection of the herd. Standing silently in the center was a tall, lean man in a crisply pressed captain's uniform, his iron-grey hair in a military cut. His mirrored sunglasses were leveled at Earl.

The news reporters, who had clustered near the courthouse entrance, moved toward him. Earl had checked the local news coverage when he got the call and it had been exhaustive; daily headlines with photos of Officer Miller's wife and son; nightly TV reports recounting the crime in graphic detail; eulogizing testimonials from friends and colleagues; editorials and

TV commentary that skipped over the presumption of innocence and went straight to advocating for the return of various medieval punishments. While this type of pretrial publicity would certainly poison any potential jurors, Earl realized it might also provide the necessary justification for the case to escape the Haywood courthouse. If he was ever to contend that the corrosive impact of such coverage had deprived Kate of a fair trial, he certainly couldn't contribute to it. So when the reporters corralled him, they received a disappointing "No comment."

As the crowd thinned out, a tall young man in a light grey suit and an open smile approached. "Mr. Earl," he said. "My name is Harris, Robert Harris. This is my colleague Leslie Garley." He motioned to an attractive young woman in a dark blue business suit with blindingly white teeth. "We're from Horgan & Cooley, Ms. Carlson's former firm. We were wondering if we might have a word."

"Of course. What can I do for you?"

"More to the point, Mr. Earl, we're here to see what we can do for you."

Earl noticed that Harris spoke with the confidence of a young associate convinced he was fast-tracked for a partnership. "And what would that be?" Earl said mildly.

"You're probably aware that Kate was a valued partner at our firm before she went over to Arnold and Mellon. We pride ourselves at H&C that we are more than just a law firm. Our loyalty to one another makes us a sort of family. Despite her recent departure we still consider Kate a part of that family." Harris smiled and turned as if for confirmation to his associate whose smiling face nodded vigorously in agreement.

Earl knew a little about the ethos of large competitive law firms and a more apt description would probably be *Game of Thrones.*

"We're naturally concerned about Ms. Carlson," Harris continued, "and anxious to help. I needn't tell you that a complex case such as this could overwhelm a sole practitioner, such as yourself. We are a very large firm with tremendous resources and I'm authorized to put those resources at your disposal. Paralegals, clerical staff, investigators, whatever you need. Our associates can read and summarize all the reports; support staff can digitize all the documents in the case so they can be retrieved on your computer and projected during trial." He paused to study Earl for a reaction, which was not forthcoming.

Earl could not imagine putting such distance between himself and the case. It would be as if he were looking at it through someone else's eyes. The act of meticulously reading every report, categorizing it and placing it in its appropriate binder was how he learned the case; how he committed every fact, every statement, to memory. Without it he would be lost.

"This is obviously your case," Harris continued, "but as a former Deputy US Attorney, I tried my share of criminal cases and would be happy to sit as second chair. Ms. Garley could pitch in and do research, draft briefs or do any leg work." Ms. Garley gave Earl a coast-to-coast smile.

Earl wondered what 'leg work' Harris had in mind, but let it go. He stood thinking, deciding on how to reply. The assumption that he wasn't capable of handling a capital case chaffed a little, but he realized he was just speaking to the messenger. He decided on a conciliatory tone. "I appreciate the offer. But it's just not the way I try a case. But thanks, anyway."

The young man seemed suddenly anxious. "Look," he said. "Maybe I'm not the right fit. We could put you in touch with one of our senior litigation partners. Someone with your level of experience."

Earl was surprised to hear a faint tone of desperation in his voice. "Look, it's not you," Earl said. "I just prefer to put together my own team."

After a moment of seeming indecision, he handed Earl his business card. "Please think about it, we could be a big help." Harris stood rooted, as if reluctant to leave. Finally, he and his associate turned and slowly walked away.

As Earl followed their path, he saw a solitary black woman standing at the curb smoking a cigarette, pensively staring into the distance. Earl recognized her from her photo in the paper. Celia Miller, the guard's widow. He found it strange that none of the guards had come over to speak with her. Normally, Earl did not want to think about the victim in a case or their families. He found it took his edge off. But there was something about the woman, standing there alone, that demanded some gesture of common decency.

"Mrs. Miller, I'm Bobby Earl."

She turned to look at him. "I know who you are."

"I just wanted to offer my condolences on your loss. From what I read, it sounds like your husband was a fine man."

She stared at him as if undecided on how to respond.

"I didn't mean to disturb you," he said apologetically. "I just thought I should say something." Earl turned to leave.

"I got nothin' against you or that woman. She had nothin' to do with my man's death."

Her words seemed to hang in the air. Earl turned to face her. "You come see me," she said and darted a nervous look at the group of guards. "Wait till' next week. I'll tell you what really happened." She flicked her cigarette into the street and walked toward the parking lot.

CHAPTER 4

"Always wear a tie clasp to an autopsy." A gruff old detective had once told Earl this, but only after Earl had leaned over the body and dipped his new silk tie into the gooey run-off along the edge of the autopsy table. It was a sticky crimson baptism into the world of criminal law that he never forgot. He still did not own a tie clasp, so today he was using a paper clip.

Detective Carter met him at the entrance to the County Coroner's Office with a Styrofoam cup of coffee and an apology. "The coffee helps the smell," he said. "Old Doc Watson used to let us smoke in there, but this new one," he grimaced. "He's a real by-the-book type."

The examination room had the sterilized appearance of an operating room, which always struck Earl as ironic given the condition of the patients. Officer Miller was laid out on a stainless steel table, his head resting on a metal block. His clothes had been stripped off and bagged in plastic. The necessary photos had been taken to be used at trial to properly inflame the jury. From the side, Miller looked almost peaceful to Earl, as if he had fallen asleep and might wake up at any moment. Earl found himself foolishly wondering if the cold steel felt uncomfortable.

"Shall we begin?" the coroner said. He was dressed in green scrubs with a surgical mask, as if what he was about to do required him to hide his identity. He was speaking into a tape recorder hanging from the ceiling. "The body presents as a well-muscled male negro, approximately thirty years of age, measuring 75 inches in length and 210 pounds in weight. There is a visible gunshot entrance wound to the right zeugmatic or cheek bone."

Earl moved around to the coroner's side and focused on the neat round hole. There was no gunshot residue around the wound, the dark "sooting" on the skin from powder burns that came from a close discharge. That was what he had come to see. A photograph did not always capture the true extent of the pattern left by the small particles of gun powder emitted from the gun barrel. At some point he knew he would need to reconstruct how the shooting occurred; where everyone was positioned; what direction the shot came from. The absence of any GSR at least gave him one objective fact from which to calculate. It was a start.

He was stepping back when he saw it. Bristles of hair on Miller's chest. A faint stubble. Earl knew the old myth about hair continuing to grow after death was not true. Dead was dead. The hair just appeared that way because the skin around the hairs receded from the loss of fluid. The emergence of these hairs could mean only one thing. Miller had shaved his chest. Earl casually walked back around the table, trying not to alert the others to his discovery.

"Yeah, I noticed that too," Carter said. "I got this nephew who shaves his chest. Says the girls like it. Go figure."

Earl did not share the egotistical conceit of those who believed that small town cops and lawyers were not as smart or savvy as their big city cousins. There were many reasons people chose to stay in small towns. Being afraid to compete in the city was usually not one of them. Earl wasn't fooled by Carter's good old boy routine. It was a good try, but no sale. Carter was thinking the same thing he was. Officer Miller had been wearing a wire.

In the parking lot of the Coroner's Office, Detective Carter sat in his car smoking and thinking about murder. It was his profession, as normal, in his mind, as any other. Murder had always been a part of the human condition. Cain killed Abel, after all. We all had it in us. Restraining it was what made society possible.

But seeing the victim was always intensely personal for him. In a town this size he generally knew the victim. Not the gang bangers who were suspects one day and victims the next, but the "everyday people." So he knew Miller. Not well, but he had seen him around with his wife and kid. Miller wasn't just a name on a file to him.

He had thought Miller's case was open and shut. But now he had been dealt a wild card. He didn't like wild cards; you could never tell how they would play out. He needed to talk to someone to bounce ideas off, clear away the underbrush in his mind and help him get his thoughts in order. Taylor was too impulsive; she would send him off in a thousand different directions. His chief had made a career out of not ruffling anyone's feathers. He pulled out his cellphone and called Delores, the one person with whom he discussed all his cases.

He had been in bed with Delores when he first got the call. They had been together for five years and everyone in town considered them a couple. She owned the Half Moon Café on Main Street. He had repeatedly asked her to marry him, which she just as steadfastly refused. "Let's keep things the way they are, Joe," was all she'd say. Her history of a failed marriage, raising a daughter on her own and a couple of roaming boyfriends made her caution understandable to him. And Joe Carter was a patient man.

Joe trusted her judgment. She had a world view that had not been formed by sitting on the sidelines, yet she had not let life run her over. She shared Joe's faith in life's appeal, that it was still capable of hatching surprises. But when Delores picked up his call she explained she couldn't talk. Lunch was her busy time. He lit another cigarette and went back over the steps of the investigation, like a card player reviewing a past hand looking for a "tell" he had missed.

He remembered driving straight to the prison, only to find the guards had all "lawyered-up." It happened every time. The prison's first call was always to the union, which would promptly dispatch their lawyers. "It's in our contract," was their programmed response when asked why. It was nightfall by the time he and his team had been notified. When he was finally granted access to the witnesses, their statements had been so honed and polished they fit together as neatly as a completed jig saw puzzle, all ready to be framed on the wall. That was on full display when he interviewed Officer Rattner. Here was a guy who had just witnessed the murder of a fellow guard and then had to struggle with the killer for his own life. Yet, he recited the events in precise order, as unemotional as if he were reading a bus schedule.

Normally that would have tripped his suspicion switch but it was routine up there whenever outside law enforcement was called, so he had come to accept it as part of their culture. The union's overwhelming need to protect and polish their public image made them insist on filing any rough edges off their guard's statements. Besides, the case had seemed so straightforward that he could have tied a bow around it the first night.

But wearing a wire was not business as usual at Haywood Prison. Miller must have worried that pulling out his chest hair each time he took off the recorder taped to his chest would eventually leave a couple bald patches. Pretty obvious give away. So he shaved his whole chest. Maybe this time the guards had more to protect than just the union's sterling reputation. He turned on his car engine and headed back to the station. He wanted to read through the file again.

Lauren Taylor stood staring out her office window on the DA's floor in the courthouse. A phone message in her hand read that her older sister Rebecca "wanted her to call." Taylor knew what to expect, it was pathetically predictable. Rebecca's husband had lost his job — again. And the payment on their double-wide was overdue — again. Back in high school, Rebecca had gotten pregnant, promptly dropped out and married her boyfriend with the hot rod pickup. That was ten years and three kids ago. Lauren's once vivacious teenage sister was now worn and tired.

Watching her sister meekly surrender to her life and sink under its weight had caused Taylor's sisterly sympathy to turn to resentment. Rebecca's resignation ignited a determination in Taylor to never accept what others decided was her due. She refused to just settle for a commonplace life. She needed to be a person of consequence, one who wielded power, to be the hammer not the nail. Her frustration over the delay in being recognized for her real worth had fueled a simmering anger that focused on anyone or anything she perceived as blocking her path. At times her anger bubbled to the surface and flared up, forcing her to bank the flames, but they were never extinguished.

Now her chance had arrived. This case would be her springboard up. Winning the case would guarantee the union's backing and her career would really take off. She didn't intend to be just a big fish in a small pond. But first she had to win the case — no matter what it took. No one was going to steal this from her without a fight. If some rules had to be ignored, so be it. If some people ended up scarred, too bad. This was her one shot. Besides, the bitch was guilty so what difference did it make?

Taylor drew a deep breath and turned to pick up the phone. She might as well get this over with.

Business had improved when Earl returned to the attorney room of the Haywood Jail. He was not alone this time. Two lawyers sat at the end of the long interview table, talking quietly to each other as they waited for their clients. Neither acknowledged his presence.

Earl had told Kathleen he would see her before he returned to LA. This was the kind of promise you kept. To someone in jail, trapped all day with her own thoughts, a promised visit was a command performance.

"Well," Kathleen said as she sat down. "Today was certainly a cold dose of reality."

Earl nodded. "I know," he said quietly.

"But why didn't you bring up bail?" she asked pointedly. "Right now there is no bail. We should've at least tried for it. It is absolutely horrible in here. And the thought of prison, my God." She paused, her eyes wide in alarm. "I never realized how frightfully horrendous it would be in here."

Earl had not anticipated such an early test of his judgment. If one thing was essential, it was that Kathleen had to trust him. There would be times in the heat of a trial when he would need that trust. Times when hard decisions had to be made, ones that rested on nothing more than Earl's gut instincts. Some lawyers took the easy way and approached this connection with their clients with a condescending attitude. They painted a rosy picture of the client's prospects and appeased their every whim in order to tranquillize them into a sense of security. They then pretended to be shocked at the adverse results. Earl felt the best way to earn a client's trust was to treat them with respect, which meant they deserved a straight answer, an honest answer, not just the one they wanted to hear.

"Kate, there's no way this judge is going to set bail. The law in California says in a capital case, which this is, the court doesn't have to set bail if the DA has enough evidence so that a 'presumption of guilt is great'," Earl said quoting the statute. "This language is vague enough to give this judge the leeway to deny bail, and he will."

She looked dismayed. "But those other lawyers said we at least had a chance."

"I wish that were true, Kate." He paused to gauge her frustration and saw she needed convincing. "I could certainly make the motion. But all that would accomplish would be to allow this District Attorney, in the guise of arguing against bail, to parade her version of the case before the media, broadcasting all the things she would never be able to get into evidence, the lies and innuendo that will poison the jury against us. And judging by my brief exposure to this DA, she would love nothing more than the chance to metaphorically lock you in the public stocks and hurl garbage at you."

Kate sat in glum silence. Earl took her silence as tacit acquiescence, so after a moment he broke the silence with a change of subject. "After court I had an offer of assistance. Robert Harris, an associate in your former firm, said that Horgan & Cooley were offering their resources to help us on the case. He even suggested he could try the case with me."

She smiled a grim smile. "That was Leland Bain, LB as he's known, the firm's managing partner. He represents the firm's largest client, PCA, Prison Corporation of America. Haywood was actually one of PCA's prisons.

"If he represents a private prison corporation, he must have been none too pleased at your efforts to put an end to the use of private prisons?"

"That was why I left the firm. My involvement with SOS gave the appearance of a conflict at the firm. So I left and took some of my clients with me."

Earl was aware that a lawyer moving from one firm to another out of necessity, rather than to take advantage of a more lucrative offer, was always fraught with difficulties. This fact only added to his belief that there was a more personal motivation behind Kate's involvement with the Save Our Schools Initiative.

Kate narrowed her eyes and gave Earl a skeptical look. "This offer, you know, was merely a way for LB to get someone on the inside, angling to steer things to protect his client, PCA. I'm sure he's concerned I might use the case to highlight the abuses at private prisons, the beatings, sexual assaults and general mistreatment. I hope you turned it down."

"I did, as a matter of fact. I'll be putting together my own team which we'll discuss later, but now tell me about Adam Hartman, the inmate you were visiting."

Kate paused to gather her thoughts. "Adam Hartman was a doctor, well respected and successful. His wife was apparently quite good-looking and Adam was ... well, not so much. They were a '*what's she doing with him*' sort of couple. He discovered she was having an affair, so one afternoon he surprised them. Stupidly, Adam brought along a gun, which I'm guessing was because Adam was not very fit and rather meek. A struggle ensued over the gun and the lover was wounded, but not seriously. Adam swore the gun discharged accidently, but the wife and her lover told a different story. He was convicted of attempted murder, which carries a life sentence."

"Sounds rather harsh," Earl said.

Kate nodded. "Adam contacted me saying he had information that could help our campaign. He gave me just enough, along with his professional credentials, to convince me he was credible. I hoped if I could shift the media spotlight onto the union it would inevitably reveal the real reason they were opposing Prop 52. So I started to visit him."

"Why did it take several visits?" Earl asked.

"Adam needed time to gather the information. He was very cautious. He was convinced that if it leaked out that he was the source of information that threatened the private prison industry his life would be in danger. I realized he was in a private prison, but at the time I thought he was being melodramatic." She gave Earl a bitter smile. "I actually grew to be quite fond of him. I enjoyed our visits and we often corresponded. I never thought...." Her voice trailed off. After a moment she gathered herself and looked earnestly at Earl. "He was an odd little man. Quite bright and very witty. Never bitter about his situation, just spoke of it matter-of-factly. Like diagnosing a medical condition."

"Call your office and have them send over your correspondence with Adam. I should probably read it."

Kate nodded in agreement.

"What was in it for him?" Earl asked, acknowledging the old adage that "nothing comes for free," particularly in prison.

"He wanted my help in securing a parole date and reinstating his medical license. He also wanted the promise of a job at the hospital where I served on the Board."

Earl knew that an attempted murder conviction was not a "straight" life sentence and parole was possible after seven years. But rarely granted. However, Hartman's demand to reinstate his license caused Earl to raise his eyebrows in mock admiration.

"Actually," Kate said, "with Adam's background and good behavior record, this was all possible. His crime had nothing to do with how he practiced medicine."

"But you never got the information."

"No," she said and stared off, her thoughts elsewhere.

After a moment she turned back to him. "Do you think we can ever get a jury that will listen to us?"

"That's where I'm headed right now. To find out just that," Earl said.

She scrunched her face into a question.

"I'm going to get a haircut," Earl said.

Nobody would mistake Harry's Barber Shop for an upscale hair salon. A barber pole rotated its red and white stripes above the entrance. Two old fashioned barber chairs sat heavily on a checkerboard linoleum floor, facing a wall of framed photos of the local high school teams, past and present. The man sweeping the floor was wearing a white cloth coat with "Harry" stitched over the pocket.

Earl had learned there was no better place to take the pulse of a small town than at the barber shop or hair salon. For men in particular, there was something about sitting in a barber chair, looking at themselves in the mirror, which somehow convinced them that their opinions needed to be aired. It was as if they confused the barber's white sheet with a Roman Senator's toga and they had a civic duty to hold forth on the pressing issues of the day.

"Come on in, my friend," the barber said and brushed his hand over the leather seat of the nearest chair. Earl sat down, and the barber floated a white sheet over him, which he fastened behind Earl's neck.

Earl's eye focused on the photo across from him. A line of boys with too-large football pads and serious expressions stood behind a row of beaming cheerleaders kneeling in the foreground. Earl remembered his own high school days, when he would lose himself in sports. The rawness and excitement of competition, the certainty of a clear winner and loser, all shaped by a set of unbending rules. Too bad life wasn't like that.

"You just looking for a place to rest, or you want a haircut?" The barber's words jerked Earl back to the present.

"Oh, sorry. I was just looking at the photographs," Earl said.

"Yeah, we're pretty proud of our little town."

"When I was driving through, it seemed something was going on down at the courthouse."

"Is that so," the barber said and turned the chair around so Earl was facing a mirrored wall. The barber stood behind him, looking at Earl in the mirror with a knowing smile. "Wondering about that were you?" he said. "Would that be because you're representing that Carlson woman and want to know which way the wind's blowing?"

Earl grinned, and gave a nod of respect. "How'd you figure it?"

"Come on. How could I not? You're not from around her, you're wearing a suit that didn't exactly come from mail order, and you don't need a haircut."

"All right, Harry, how 'bout I pay you for a haircut I'm not going to get, along with a very appreciative tip, and you just tell me how things sit around here?"

"Deal," Harry said as he directed a thumb over his shoulder at the chairs along the wall and released Earl from the white sheet.

Earl passed him some bills, which Harry pocketed.

"It's like this," Harry said, and he mounted the barber chair to face Earl. "That prison is the largest employer around here. That's why we wanted one up here. Worked hard to get it, too. Signed petitions, knocked on doors up at the capital, made some contributions. Our town was dying, the young people were leaving. We figured a prison would save us. But the state turned us down. Thirty-three prisons are enough they said. Shit, the government doesn't care about folks like us." He waited for Earl to agree.

"I'm listening," Earl said.

"Then that prison corporation came along. PCA. They offered to build a prison if we donated the land. They're a private business. They operate private prisons all over the country. They said they could house those inmates cheaper and more efficiently than the government and still turn a profit. People up here like that idea. So we went for it."

"So how do they get the inmates?"

"They sign a contract with the state. The state sends 'em. It's like a hotel; they get paid by the day for each one of those clowns."

"I see," Earl said.

"Now, half of the people here depend on that prison for their living. Providing the food, repairing the facilities, sundries, you name it. And the staff all live here. All nine hundred of them. This is where they spend their money, buy houses, school their kids, get haircuts. Everybody either knows somebody who works up there or they're related to one."

"Sounds like prisons are good business."

"Not just that, they count those inmates as part of our county population, even though they can't vote. So we get another seat in Sacramento."

He stopped talking and fixed Earl with a look of mild astonishment.

"A big time lawyer like you?" He slowly shook his head. "You really needed somebody to tell you what people around here think of that bitch of yours that killed Travis?"

CHAPTER 5

During the drive home, Earl had to fight the urge to pull over and start reading the stack of case reports, the legally required "discovery" he had received in court from the DA. He had even taken the precaution of putting them in the trunk of his car so he would not be tempted to read them as he drove the long straight highway stretching across the dusty flat land to LA.

But there was one thing he had to do. He needed an investigator. Earl had never kept a full-time investigator on retainer. He recognized that every case was different and required a different set of skills to pry open the facts and flush-out witnesses. No one investigator was right for every case. They were like racehorses, some were good for a short burst of speed, others could hold their focus over a distance, still others were steady in the bump and tussle of the pack and, finally, there were always the "mudders" when things got messy. So Earl tried to match the investigator to the case. And when it came to a cop killing, or their distant cousin a prison guard, there was only one guy, Arthur "Manny" Munoz, the former head of LAPD's Robbery Homicide squad. Earl reached him on his cellphone. He would be in Earl's office on Monday.

Two hours later, he pulled up in front of his house, a wood-frame California bungalow, two blocks from the ocean and Venice Pier. It was, as he described it, the house that murder built, paid for with the accumulated fees from four murder trials.

He had made good time for a Friday evening. At the door, he was met by his saggy-jowled hound dog with the lamentable name of Henceforth. The big dog's tongue flopped out to one side as his broomstick tail happily banged against anything foolish enough to be within range. Earl realized the dog's name was an unfortunate choice. When he first got the dog he had taken care over the choice of a name, so much so that each evening when he returned home with that day's inspiration, he would solemnly announce to the young dog, "Henceforth, your name shall be...." After several days of these reversals, the only name to which the dog would respond was "Henceforth."

With a guttural *humph*, the dog wheeled excitedly, urging Earl to follow him toward the kitchen, as if he had personally prepared a homecoming surprise. Earl paused at the kitchen doorway to enjoy the view. There she was, Samantha Price, Deputy District Attorney. The soft light of sunset that fell through the window caught a mischievous glint in her eyes as it danced over her strong, clean features, giving a sheen to her auburn hair. She was bent over the counter, concentrating on opening a bottle of wine and pretending not to have noticed his arrival. Henceforth cast his sad eyes up at Earl seeking approval as if her presence was all his doing. Earl played along and thanked him with a good scratching behind his droopy ears.

Earl had met Sam six months ago when she was part of the team of DAs who prosecuted the Seabrooke case. When the trial was over, he finally allowed himself to act on the feelings he had been keeping in check. Now she was a part of his life. Just how much of a part they were both trying to figure out.

Earl thought back to the first time they were truly together, the night she opened her arms wide and took him inside. From that moment on, he knew something had changed. In the past, after such a night, he had always gotten up early and started to make breakfast as if to mark a break from the night before. He understood why. He felt guilty. He knew the night had probably meant more to the women than it had to him. This morning ritual seemed an easy way to make clear his emotional boundaries. But with Sam it had been different. He wanted to stay in bed. To hold her, to be with her. He felt his interior walls, built to maintain his distance, were starting to crumble. He knew then he was in trouble, but somehow he didn't care.

From an early age, Bobby had learned to rely on himself and only himself. His family had been worse than some, better than others. His father was a hard man who drank too much and had a ready back hand, while his mother lived in a dreamy haze, believing that the privileged world of her upbringing still swaddled her. Earl senior was a silent, sullen man, who resented the attention his mother gave Bobby, not knowing this focus was just as unwelcome to Bobby. So Bobby learned to keep his own counsel and make his own decisions. His ex-wife had told him he never unlearned those lessons from his past, that he always held back a part of himself. With Sam, he was trying hard to fight against those instincts.

Earl knew that being with him was more complicated for Sam. She was more cautious and with good reason. For one, there was his past. After his divorce, he had spent the next few years as a serial monogamist. One girlfriend after another; some lasted a few weeks, others a few months. Each finally rebelled against his self-imposed distance, his all-consuming absorption in his cases, his not being "completely there." For another, there was her job. She was a prosecutor. They came from two different worlds. The members of her tribe would never understand such a pairing, never be able to completely accept her as one of their own. She was sleeping with the enemy. From the beginning, she had wanted their life together to remain private, but lately that had become something of a burden. Besides, it no longer felt to her like the right thing to do.

Earl walked up behind her and folded his arms around her strong, athletic body. He nuzzled her hair, whose fresh scent always reminded him of a pine forest. "Home is the hunter, home from the hills," he said in a forced deep voice.

"Well," she said without turning around. "I hope the mighty hunter bagged something big, because I'm starving."

"Big? Are you kidding? She told me to name my own number."

Sam turned to face him with a wry smile. "She obviously was unaware of your legendary reputation for avarice."

Earl gave her a lingering kiss. "You know I only take advantage of widows and orphans."

Henceforth nudged Sam's leg with his wet muzzle and whined plaintively. Sam leaned down and tug on his jowls affectionately. "Don't worry sweetheart. You're still my favorite boy." Henceforth curled his lip in what passed for a grin of contentment. "Would my second favorite boy like to watch the baseball game with me tonight?"

"You know," Earl said drawing her back up to face him. "It's like a drunkard's dream. Chinese take-out, wine and a woman who'll watch baseball with me. How could it get any better?"

"That part comes later," Sam said. Her face lit up with a playful smile.

At the same time, in downtown Los Angeles, Leland Bain sat behind an ornately carved Brazilian cherrywood desk in the coveted corner office of Horgan & Cooley. The firm occupied the entire 25th floor of the Chase Building, as well as the two below it, to house the 150 lawyers in their Los Angeles office. Bain was a lean man, nearing fifty, with thinning hair that was in a rapid retreat from his forehead. His elongated face with its thin lips gave him the calculating demeanor of a man who expected every encounter to be a contest. He was wearing a pale grey tailored suit of soft Italian wool, a crisp white shirt with gold cuff links and a grey silk tie. In his buttonhole was a small, blood-red Dragon's Mouth orchid. An identical fresh one was delivered to his home each morning.

As he sat staring ahead, his mind drifted through his ever present roster of grievances. His thoughts rolled like a Buddhist prayer wheel over all the past remembered slights, perceived insults and imagined injustices that he had endured on his way to his current position of prominence. He kept this list, waiting for a chance to exact his revenge.

When Bain joined H&C, ten years ago, he had been an unusual hire. He had none of the credentials normally required for consideration by a top tier law firm: a degree from an Ivy League law school, Law Review, and a clerkship, preferably with a federal judge. In contrast, Bain had attended a second tier law school and transferred over from a midsize firm in the Rust Belt. This perceived deficiency in his accomplishments always felt like a stigma that followed him in his dealings with his colleagues. He was ever vigilant for any hint of condescension or a dismissive tone, convinced his opinions were ridiculed behind his back.

But Bain had one distinction that had brought him to the firm — he came with a promise. He assured the firm he could land a huge client, one that would spawn a steady stream of billable hours. And, to every one's astonishment, he did. Private Prison Corporation. PCA, was now the LA office's largest client, accounting for over thirty percent of its revenues.

Being responsible for such a revenue stream had earned him a seat on the firm's compensation committee. H&C was a national firm with offices around the country, but only one partner from each of the three largest offices sat on the committee. The Three Wise Men. They set the draw for every partner in the firm. Controlling the purse strings made him a very powerful person in the firm. A prominence of which he made sure everyone was abundantly aware

But now his thoughts were focused on the return of a young associate, Robert Harris, whom he had sent to imbed himself in the Carlson camp. He already knew the result. If it had been successful, there would have been a phone call. Knowing of this failure would have normally afforded him a glowing sense of satisfaction. Just as all failures in other people brought him immeasurable comfort. But this mission had been one of his own design. Any sense of vindication quickly vanished and was succeeded by a simmering enmity toward the tool that had proved inadequate.

The intercom buzzed. His assistant announced that Harris had arrived, and Baine told her to send him in. The door opened, and Harris walked into the vast office, past the green granite meeting table with its silver coffee set and calfskin armchairs, across the large Oriental rug that covered the polished wood floor and stopped at the back of the green leather client chairs. He was not invited to sit.

"I met with her lawyer, and he's thinking about our offer," Harris said with forced conviction. "He seemed...." Bain quietly held up a hand, his hard eyes fixed on the young lawyer.

"You know why I picked you for this assignment, Harris?" Bain said mildly. "First, because you're young and wouldn't appear threatening to a lawyer of the caliber of Bobby Earl. He'd know you were only there to carry his briefcase."

"I offered...." Harris said. Bain shut his eyes and slowly shook his head, and the young lawyer stopped talking.

"Secondly," Bain continued, "because I thought you were smart enough and hungry enough to be able to convince someone to accept something valuable that was absolutely free. Not exactly what I'd call a tough sell, would you?"

"Mr. Bain, I'm going to take another run at him."

"No, Robert. I don't think so. I'll find something for you to do that's more in keeping with your talents." He paused to let the import of his words sink in. "You're in the litigation department, aren't you? That's where you're supposed to be able to sell our client's position in court. Probably not a good fit."

"Mr. Bain, please. I can do this, I know I can."

Bain turned his chair away. "That's all, Robert," he said. He sat looking out the steel-framed office window at the orange glow of dusk and regretted the absence of the heavy layers of smog that used to add a rich scarlet hue. After Harris left the room, Bain buzzed for his assistant. Chris Kinder appeared immediately. She was a heavyset, middle-aged woman with large black-framed glasses and short blond hair. There was a quiet air of competence about her.

"Tell my driver to bring the car around," Bain said. "And tell Patterson I want that Phoenix Prison brief on my desk in the morning."

"I'm sorry, Mr. Bain. But when you told me you'd be working late, I thought it was okay to let Frank grab a quick dinner."

He gave her a surly look. "When the hell, did I start paying you to think? Tell him I'll be out front in five minutes."

She rushed from the room to make the calls. They had been together for five years and their working relationship fit a pattern — never an expression of gratitude, frequent tirades of abuse and the complete absence of any personal connection. But she was paid well. A heck of a lot more than the other assistants. So what was she supposed to do? She was a single mother with a teenage daughter and an elderly mother to support. But there were times she wondered what toll this was taking on her.

Chris picked up the phone. "Frank, I'm really sorry. This is all my fault."

Earl spent the entire weekend with Sam. He didn't know where they were headed but he knew he wanted to take the journey. This time he was determined to make room in his life. So he vowed to himself that for the entire weekend he would deny his craving to dive into the reports on Kate's case. Like a reformed smoker demonstrating his will-power by keeping an unopened pack in his pocket, Earl placed the papers prominently on the kitchen counter. They remained there until Sunday when he and Sam returned from a run on the beach and she unexpectedly asked why he had not read them. When he expressed his concerns, she quickly brushed them aside reminding him they were both trial lawyers and it would be interesting to discuss the case. For once, she pointed out, there was no fear of a conflict because her office was not handling the case. He gratefully accepted. How could he refuse the chance to discuss his case with a smart trial lawyer with a keen tactical sense?

When Earl drove to work on Monday morning, he still felt the contentment of a weekend with Sam. He parked his car behind an old two-story California Craftsman. The old mansion had been divided into offices, and Earl rented space on the ground floor. He loved the feel of the old building that seemed to promise secrets with every creak of its wooden floors.

He stepped in the back door where he entered the domain of his secretary, Martha Sullivan, a lean, older woman with short grey hair, who swam at the YWCA every morning and did the New York Times crossword puzzle in ink. She had come as a package with his office-mate and mentor, James McManis. After twenty-five years together, they still addressed each other as Miss Sullivan and Mr. McManis. She was unmarried and he a recent widower. Earl suspected that she had once dreamed of this opportunity, but now it seemed too late. She ran both men's lives with an autocratic confidence, secure in the belief that they could never function without her. Whether true or not, it was an assumption that Earl did not want put to the test.

"Well, Martha, the cupboard is no longer bare. You may add the name of Kathleen Carlson to our stable of clients and give the crew an extra ration of grog to celebrate."

"Bobby Earl, you had better not be talking about hoisting that bottle Mr. McManis keeps in his desk drawer. I have told you it's not good for his health."

"I am aware of your edict, Martha. It was just a figure of speech."

"Well, fine. You can just take your figure of speech into your office and answer these phone messages," she said, indicating the notes in her hand. "I gather someone did not spend his weekend in the office." She arched her eyebrows at Earl and waited for an explanation. Earl gave her a wink, took the notes and stepped into his office.

The room was furnished more for his own satisfaction than to impress his clients. The hardwood floor was covered with a Persian rug. A large mahogany desk occupied one side, where it faced two high backed client chairs. An overstuffed leather chair sat next to the brick fireplace. On a table sat his antique nickel slot machine, which each new client was urged to try in order to remind them of the role that luck played in the judicial process.

On the wooden mantle were two framed photos of athletic teams, both with a younger Bobby Earl when he played baseball and club rugby at Berkeley. While he had gone to Cal on a baseball scholarship, he was never a real threat at the plate. But he did know the art of catching. He called each pitch and moved fielders into position depending on the tendencies of an opposing batter. He made it his job to study opposing hitters and learned how to spot their "tells," like the way they adjusted their feet between pitches that telegraphed where they expected the next one, or if the mark the ball left on the bat after a foul was on the barrel, the hitter might square-up on the next one. The details that would give his pitcher an advantage.

After rushing through a few phone calls, he stood up and went looking for his office-mate. When Earl had first started to practice, James McManis had been his mentor, almost a surrogate father. Back then, Earl used to watch him in trial and admire how he would slowly take control of the courtroom. Always the consummate professional, McManis was known for his unquestioned integrity, acerbic wit and good natured sense of humor. He could eviscerate a hostile witness with the deftness of a surgeon, yet maintain an air of civility, as if he regretted having to expose them as a fool and a liar. And when he spoke to the jury, they could sense he trusted them and that he expected them to do the right thing. In the end, no jury ever wanted to disappoint James McManis, even when they had to. That was back when the newspapers dubbed him the Lion of the Courtroom, the Dean of the Criminal Bar.

But trial work is a young man's game. When his wife Ellie died three years ago it seemed to hollow out his world. She had been a calming counterbalance to the intensity and pressure of the courtroom. She had seemed to know, even welcome her position as the citadel in his life, the strong place that could not be taken. James would not show hurt or fear unless she acknowledged hurt or fear. He seemed at a loss on how to fill the void she left, unable to refocus himself. He had once confided to Earl that he now lined-up pillows on her side of the bed so if he awoke in the night he had the illusion that she was still there.

Now in his late seventies, McManis spent most days among his law books, using his still-keen legal mind to draft legal briefs and appeals for other attorneys, rarely going to court. And that was where Earl found him, upstairs in the library with his head bent over an open book. His hair was snowy white; as if signifying he was in the winter of his life. As always, he had on his suitcoat, tie firmly in place, but now his once broad shoulders were a bit stooped, and he had to hold the book a bit closer to see the print. But he still had that square jaw and firm chin that people associate with generals.

Seeing McManis surrounded by rows of uniformly bound law books reminded Earl that, in this computer age, such books were mostly ornamental in other law offices. But Earl knew this was not the case with James McManis. His deep respect for the law meant that appellate decisions deserved a place of permanence on the printed page. To McManis the analysis of a well-crafted opinion demanded an intimacy that could be achieved only by holding a book and running your fingers over the page. A computer screen seemed too remote to permit his immersion in the author's reasoning.

"Jim, have you got a minute?" Earl asked.

"For you lad? Always," McManis said, putting down his book.

"I've got a business proposition for you."

"That's good, because I just told Martha to contact the phone company to see if my phone had stopped working."

Earl smiled and took a seat at the long library table. "You know that new case of mine? The one I told you about? The lawyer charged in the prison break murders."

"Of course. Tough case."

"Well, it's set in Haywood County," Earl explained. "There is not a chance in hell of my getting a fair jury up there. Half the people work at the prison or depend on it for their livelihood. The other half is either married to a prison guard or a relative of one. I've got to get out of there."

"So you need a change of venue to another county," McManis said. "Which just happens to be my specialty."

"Exactly." Earl smiled, acknowledging the old adage of the Criminal Bar that whatever problem a prospective new client brought in was always the lawyer's specialty.

McManis pulled over his yellow pad. "Now, how do you spell venue?"

"Jim, I'm serious. I want you to handle it. The hearing, the witnesses, the experts, the appeal, the whole works."

McManis stared at him, his shaggy eyebrows arched in a question. He still had the eyes of a younger man, alert and bright as the eyes of an eagle.

"Look. I'm going to lose the motion in front of this judge," Earl said. "That's a given. So my only chance is to present the kind of evidence that will stand up on appeal. And nobody is better at shaping legal arguments than you."

"Bobby, that's kind of you. But...."

"No buts," Earl said interrupting. "I will lose this case if it stays up there. The client knows that and has budgeted for this." He paused. "Jim, the case hinges on this. I need your help."

McManis stared off in thought. After a few moments, he turned back to Earl. "It's been a while since I shouldered that kind of responsibility in a major case. You're sure about this?"

"Never been surer."

McManis drew a deep breath. "All right lad," he said after some thought. "I suppose I could chip the rust off and add something to the proceedings."

Earl could see the gleam return to the eyes of the old war horse. "Good," Earl said. "I'll leave it in your hands."

McManis nodded purposefully and stared down at his yellow pad, already assembling his thoughts for the motion.

As Earl walked back to his office he had a warm feeling of fulfillment. It was not simply that he was able to do something to repay his old mentor. Bringing McManis on board was clearly the best thing for the case. Earl did not indulge in self-delusion. He knew he was not the consummate practitioner of each of the myriad of skills required to mount a well-honed criminal defense. It was a rare lawyer who was. He, in fact, had never met one. Earl knew his strengths, and they had been tested on the anvil of high pressure trials and had not been found wanting. But the case needed McManis on that motion. It would require a deep dive into the arcane law of venue changes. Besides, there was an added sense of confidence in knowing they were a team. Together. It just felt right.

CHAPTER 6

It was a short drive from Earl's office to the New Politics Foundation. The liberal think tank was housed in a modern glass and steel high-rise with spare chrome furnishings, polished marble floors and Jackson Pollack rip-offs. Earl followed the young intern off the elevator and down a hallway. The office of former State Senator Carlos Sanchez was a bit out of step with the building's minimalist decor. It looked as if his old office in Sacramento had been carefully dismantled and reassembled here on the third floor. The contrast with its surroundings made it seem like a museum diorama or a zoo's attempt to duplicate the natural habitat of an exotic creature. The office walls were crowded with framed photographs of the senator with once-prominent politicians. His large wooden desk was littered with engraved mementos commemorating events in his former life.

"I was sorry to hear about Kathleen Carlson," Sanchez said shaking Earl's hand. He offered him a seat. Sanchez's broad face was open and at ease. "I met her when she was considering getting involved in prison reform. I can't believe she would do something like this. The papers are calling it a prison romance. It just doesn't sound like her."

"She seems to think the prison guards union had something to do with it," Earl said. "She was hoping you might fill me in about them."

"I guess it's fair to say I know a little about them," Sanchez said with a rueful smile. "I have them and the private prison industry to thank for all this." He made a sweeping gesture to the surroundings.

"She told me," Earl said.

"I sponsored a bill to prohibit the state from contracting with private prisons to house State inmates. Their lobbyists killed it in committee. Then the union went after me in the next election." Sanchez paused, shaking his head as if discarding a bitter memory. "Anyway, what can I do for you?"

"I'm interested to know why the guards Union would be interested in the Initiative campaign to ban private prisons."

"Well, that requires a little history," he said settling back like someone who enjoyed recounting a good tale and had the time to indulge it. "You see, the union is really a creation of one man. Buddy Wright, its current president. A former prison guard, as was his father before him."

"I've heard of him," Earl said. "Big guy. Wears a hat. Always chomping on a cigar."

Sanchez nodded his assent. "Buddy figured out a scheme that twisted our criminal justice system into a tool for him and his members to make a whole lot of money."

Earl tilted his head in a question.

"Buddy merely recognized what everyone already knew. That in politics, money is power. And the union had money because every prison guard paid dues. So he took that dues money and put it to use. He started by putting his own Initiative on the ballot. That was the Three Strikes Law. He hired one of those companies to gather the signatures and found a crime victims group to front as the sponsor. He bought media spots to promote it, using the victim group as the public face of the Initiative. I guess Justice Kennedy of the Supreme Court put it best when he said, and I quote, 'the three-strikes law sponsor is the prison guards union and that is sick!'"

Sanchez paused for Earl to respond, but he sat silently thinking, a bit overwhelmed at his own lack of awareness of the politics behind this watershed law.

Sanchez continued. "When Three Strikes passed, Buddy just repeated the formula with other crimes. Longer and longer sentences. More and more life sentences." Sanchez paused to see if Earl was following him. "It was simple arithmetic. If the inmates stayed inside longer, when the new ones started coming in, the population would rise until they were overcrowded. More coming in and fewer going out. So you needed to build more prisons, and that meant more guards. When Buddy took over, there were about ten prisons in California, now we have 33. There were 2,600 guards, now there are 27,000. We have the largest per capita prison population in the country. Each year we spend over ten percent of the state's *entire* general fund on the corrections system."

"You know," Earl said, "I never understood the belief that increasing sentences acted as a deterrent. As if someone contemplating a crime would go through a sentencing calculus, willing to do it if they *only* got ten years if caught, but for fifteen or twenty years they wouldn't risk it. Hell, these guys never contemplate getting caught in the first place. Now it seems a political necessity for every politician to be able boast they increased the punishment on some crime."

"Which brings us back," Sanchez continued, "to our old friend money. Remember, each of those 27,000 guards pays union dues. That amounts to over $30 million a year, which Buddy uses to buy friends in high places. The union makes huge campaign donations to our state legislators, who just happen to be the ones who set the salaries of prison guards. Not surprisingly, they are the highest paid guards in the nation. A prison guard makes more than an assistant professor with a PhD. at the University of California. Base salary of $72,000, with overtime, it's over $100,000 a year. Buddy has converted our criminal justice system in to a machine to print money for him and his members. They're making a killing."

"Siphoning off tax dollars that could go to other uses," Earl said.

Sanchez gave him a nod of approval. "It's an accepted fact in Sacramento that the prison guards union is the most powerful lobby in California. They even had the clout to require Union guards to be used in any private prison the state contracts with."

"Do you really think Buddy Wright considered Kate and this Initiative a credible threat to their interests?" Earl asked.

"Well, just a few years ago, the union was able to beat back any Initiative that threatened to reduce sentences. But it seems the public in California is losing its appetite for lengthy incarcerations. Several initiatives have passed that eased up on these long sentences. The union has been sitting back, waiting for public sentiment to swing back. Then this initiative comes along. We have eight private prisons that employ several thousand Union guards. That's a lot of jobs to lose.

"But why go after Kate, rather than concentrating on the Initiative?" Earl asked.

"Kate Carlson is a very effective spokesperson. She's intelligent, articulate and comes across as believable, not like some raving left wing radical. Plus, she's well-connected and can get the endorsements of some very prominent people." He paused and pursed his lips as he thought. "Maybe Buddy figured the union couldn't wait anymore and decided this is the one where they make a stand. Maybe they were a little desperate. That's usually the point when people overreact. So would they view her as a threat?" He gave Earl a shrewd smile. "You bet they would."

Before he left to see Sanchez, Earl asked Martha to make copies of the reports he had received in discovery from the DA. Upon arriving back at the office, he went upstairs and placed a copy on the library table that McManis was populating with small towers of stacked law books. Without disturbing the old lawyer's concentration, he went down to his office and dropped a copy of the Carlson reports on one of the client chairs then settled in at his desk. He had read the reports on Sunday when he discussed the case with Sam, but his mind was reshuffling things after his talk with Sanchez. He flipped open the file and looked again at the mug shot of Dr. Adam Hartman. He had a chubby face and a receding hair line. He stared, clear-eyed, straight into the camera with the confident look of someone who expected his words to be heeded. Was this the face of a murderer? Earl had looked into the eyes of dozens of such men. And he had learned one thing. You could never tell.

Earl was returning his second phone call when he heard Manny Munoz tease Martha in the outer room. Martha excitedly said that "Mr. McManis" was working on the case. When Munoz appeared at the door, Earl waved him in and silently pointed at the stack of reports on the chair.

Munoz was a bear of a man with a tree stump neck and the kind of strength that said "don't test me," but none of the macho bravado that came with his size. Instead, he had a friendly and goodhearted demeanor that was completely disarming. Witnesses opened up to him because Manny felt familiar, like slipping on an old pair of house shoes. And he was one hell of an investigator. They had worked together on several cases. Earl trusted his instincts and respected his smarts. More than that, he was genuinely fond of the big man.

Manny carefully eased his girth into a client chair and began flipping through the reports. After Earl had finished his fifth call Munoz tossed his copy onto the chair beside him and gave Earl an incredulous look.

"Smuggle a gun into prison?" Munoz asked. "Who does she think she is? Harriet Houdini?"

"She says she didn't do it," Earl replied.

Munoz gave him a skeptical look. "Pretty big coincidence. Guy's got a gun right after her visit."

"Unless somebody set her up."

"Now it's sounding worse," Munoz said.

"You think I would waste you on an easy one?" Earl said with a grin. "You've only got so much tread left on you." Earl was not worried about Manny's questioning attitude. In fact, that was what he wanted. He did not need a cheering section. Seeing the problems was the key, the ones he would worry about in the middle of the night, the ones he could not afford to miss. Recognizing the defense strengths was the easy part.

"They're going Grand Jury on this one, so we'll learn more when we get the transcript," Earl said. This maneuver was a familiar tactic the prosecution used in big cases. It allowed DAs to put on their witnesses in a secret proceeding without the presence of the defense, so there was no cross-examination. In the common parlance, these handpicked jurors would indict a ham sandwich if asked to do so by the DA.

"But let me fill you in on where we're at so far." Earl gave him a sketch of his interview with Kate and Sanchez.

"Well, if they did set her up, they're doing a damned good job," Munoz said, with a look of certainty. "It's not just that a gun pops up right after her visit, but they found a map of the prison on the floor. That sure makes it look that at least *he* was expecting something to happen with her visit."

"Yeah, that doesn't help," Earl admitted. "And we can't trace the gun because there's congressional legislation that won't permit a national gun ownership registry."

"But she's got her own problems as well. It says when they searched her car they found a loose round under the seat. And not just any cartridge. It was a 25. The same caliber as the gun the inmate had."

"I know, I know," Earl said glumly. "That hurts, no question,

"And a .25 is not your everyday caliber. Plus, what's this about gunshot residue on her hands?" Munoz looked incredulous. "Man, all that's missing is a confession and you could put a ribbon on this one."

"Okay, but how could she smuggle in a gun in the first place? You know they have a metal detector up there. Hell, they've even got them in schools now."

"I'm sure they do. But I know this particular gun. It's called a Baby Browning. It's just 4 inches long. Let's be honest, there is a place a desperate woman might hide it. I've seen the narcs' recover some pretty big dope pouches from up in there."

"Oh, come on, Manny. Kathleen Carlson is a partner in a big white shoe law firm. I don't see her dropping down to that level. Besides a metal detector would pick that up anyway. That's our strongest defense."

"By the way, who was this inmate, anyway?" Munoz flipped through the reports. "Yeah, Adam Hartman. Who was he to her? Why was she visiting him?"

"She says he was just a guy who had information that would help the Initiative," Earl replied.

"Long drive for a busy woman." Munoz mused, then flipped through the reports until he came to a particular page. "It says here he needed to be escorted by an officer back to his housing."

"Right," Earl said. "Which means he was probably in protective custody. So he must have reported that somebody threatened him in order to get himself removed from the general population. Let's subpoena his prison file. I'd like to know who he was afraid of. And see what else you can turn up on his background. I don't want any surprises at trial."

Munoz wrote in a small notebook nestled in the palm of his hand. "I'll make some calls. See what I can learn."

"Good, Manny. But the one we really need to take a look at is that guard," Earl said. "Clyde Rattner. You know, the one who says Hartman had the gun and shot Officer Miller. The hero who saved the day. If Kate is right and she was set up, then he's right in the middle of it all. So let's start by subpoenaing his personnel file. Maybe that will give us something."

"I wouldn't hold my breath on that set-up theory, but I'm on it," Munoz said as he wrote another note.

There was a courtesy knock as the door swung open and McManis stepped through. "Manny, good to see you. Martha said you were here."

Munoz got to his feet. "Mr. McManis. It will be a pleasure to work with you."

"Same here, Manny, and that's exactly why I popped in. I'd like you to get the record of the guards union's contributions to any political campaigns in Haywood County in the last ten years."

Munoz looked as if he had been asked to calculate the square root of pi.

"It's just an idea I'm kicking around," McManis said. "They're easy enough to find."

"Easy for who? Remember, I'm a tired old cop."

"By law, in California," McManis explained, "every campaign has to report the source of their contributions. You can get them from the Secretary of State."

"Will do," Manny said and sat down to make a note.

"I'll leave you gentlemen to it," McManis said and left.

Munoz squeezed out of the chair and gathered up his copy of the reports. "This is going to be a tough one, Bobby," he said.

"They all look that way at first," Earl replied. "But at least there's a joker in the deck."

"A joker is always good," Munoz said with enthusiasm.

"When I was up there, I attended the autopsy of Officer Miller. I didn't know this coroner, so I didn't want to worry about something getting left out of the report. Anyway, it looked to me as if Officer Miller had been shaving his chest."

Munoz widened his eyes. "That *is* interesting. Unless he was on the player's circuit, it seems someone was going to tell secrets out of school."

"That's exactly what I figured. He was wearing a wire and wanted to avoid those tell-tale barren patches."

"There's a dear diary I bet a lot of people would like to get hold of," Munoz said.

After Munoz left, Earl tipped back in his chair and thought. It was a strong case against Kate Carlson. A very strong case. But in a strange way, maybe too strong. Why the hell would she do it in the first place? Where's the motive? Some torrid prison romance? And why would a woman as smart as Kate possibly think she could get away with this? She wouldn't. It didn't make sense. She would know that she would immediately be a suspect. It was just not her kind of play. It was too obvious, too clumsy.

Earl was beginning to think what he didn't want to think. Kathleen Carlson might be innocent. Earl much preferred guilty clients. It had nothing to do with how much effort he expended, because he performed according to his own self-imposed standard, whether or not the client was guilty. He was driven by pride in his professional skill and a personal sense of obligation to always give his best effort. He knew what was required in a case and set himself a pretty high bar. An innocent client didn't make him work harder, it just added to the pressure.

CHAPTER 7

Earl lay in bed in that half-awake state where he rummaged through his thoughts. His mind drifted back to his high school days in San Cabrera, where everyone in town attended the school's basketball games, whether or not you had a kid playing. Even his father and his father's brother John, a local deputy sheriff, would attend. Uncle John's daughter, Mary Ellen, was a member of the school's Spirit Team. Unfortunately, his cousin stood out alongside her bouncy, frenetic teammates with her hefty body that seemed stuffed into a too small uniform which strained in protest. Always one step behind the other girls routine, she was more adept at dodging her falling baton than at twirling it.

Earl was fond of his cousin. Mary Ellen was a shy girl, who always seemed to have her face in a book. He rarely saw any of the other girls with her, as if they feared their status in their little cliques might suffer if seen in her company. During the noon recess she normally sat off by herself with a book in her lap. On the occasions that Bobby joined her, she seemed genuinely grateful that the school's baseball star would eat his bag lunch with her. Even at his age, Bobby understood the courage it took for someone like Mary Ellen to put herself up on a public stage to perform.

During the school's first home game a student in the visitor's bleachers started to belittle Mary Ellen, mooing like a cow, to the delight of his friends. After a bit, Bobby quietly walked over and tried to reason with the husky farm boy, only to be sneered at and ridiculed in turn. When Bobby invited the boy outside, the invitation was gleefully accepted. When they returned, both wore the signs of the conflict, but the mocking stopped.

Earl's father and Uncle John took note of the episode. From that night forward, they would sit in the stands with the other parents and wait to see if some loudmouth student on the visitors' side would start heckling Mary Ellen. Then his uncle would elbow Earl's father and yell loudly, "Bobby, you going to let them talk to your cousin that way?" That was the signal for Bobby to invite the heckler out to the parking lot and give him a lesson in comportment.

Bobby had little choice in the matter. If he had ever ignored his Uncle's challenge, his father would have considered it a public humiliation. This fear of shame was what his Uncle counted on. A part of Bobby actually relished these socially sanctioned fights. It gave him an outlet for the undefined simmering anger he felt living in his father's house. Whether Bobby prevailed in these rough and tumble sessions or not, they were effective. There were few requests for a refresher course.

Over the years, whenever he puzzled over his instinctive aversion to authority, his meandering thoughts always ended up back at the memory of his father's unspoken command and his uncle in his Sheriff's uniform, leering down from the safety of his perch as he goaded Earl into action.

Earl roused himself awake and rolled on his side. He found himself staring into the sleeping face of Henceforth, who had settled himself during the night on the adjoining pillow. Henceforth slowly opened one droopy eye and flopped out his tongue to slather Earl's face with a greeting. Earl rolled over in the other direction wiping a hand across his face and nearly toppled onto the floor. Apparently, as he slept, Henceforth had succeeded in confining Earl to a narrow strip of the bed while claiming the other three-quarters for himself. Earl pushed at Henceforth, who had promptly gone back to sleep. The big dog was an immovable lump and merely grunted his annoyance at being disturbed. It was clearly time to go to the office.

Earl arrived at the office, poured himself a cup of coffee and asked Martha if she needed any help on her crossword puzzle. She gave him an expected smirk as he fled into his office. Within a few minutes there was a courtesy knock on the door as it swung open.

"God damn, there's a lot of money in locking people up," McManis said stepping into Earl's office.

"How's that, Jim?" Earl was familiar with how McManis' quick mind often jumped ahead like a moving train, forcing one to jump aboard in mid-journey.

McManis sat down, a legal pad in his hand. "I've been looking at that private prison in Haywood in connection with the venue motion. Did you know that PCA is a national corporation with ninety for-profit prisons around the country? They had over a billion dollars in revenue last year. Their stock is traded on the New York Stock Exchange, for Christ sake." His mouth curled in disgust. "PCA has four private prisons in-state and two out-of-state to house California inmates. They're paid a fixed amount per day like a hotel. They're making millions. And they're not even the biggest private prison corporation in the state."

"Yeah, Kate explained to me how it works. The Supreme Court ordered us to reduce the *state* prison population because they were so overcrowded it constituted cruel and unusual punishment, so they pay *private* prisons to house the overflow."

"It's like in that movie," McManis said. "If you build it they will come."

"And they're not the only ones making a killing off the justice system," Earl said. "You can add the prison guards union to the list. They campaign for longer and longer sentences so more guards are needed. More

guards means more union dues, which means more money for pc
contributions and the guards end up with higher and higher salaries. It'
a Ponzi scheme."

"Well, the private prison industry must have taken a page from t
play book, because they shamelessly lobby the legislature for long
sentences with big campaign contribution."

"And you can bet," Earl said, "the judges handing down these
sentences haven't a clue how they've been played."

"While the guards and private prisons are siphoning off tax payers'
dollars," McManis said with a tone of dismay, "there's a bunch of others
joining the party. Each year there's a national convention for the private
prison industry. Everybody has a booth there, AT&T, Proctor and Gamble,
IBM, companies making metal doors and toilets, you name it. You can't
believe the number of people making a buck off prisons. They're bigger
than the porn industry."

Earl had heard of the prison-industrial complex, but had always
thought it was just overblown rhetoric.

McManis stared off in thought and then turned back to meet Earl's
eyes. "To my way of thinking, there's something immoral about making a
profit out of incarcerating someone. Taking away a citizen's freedom is one
of the weightier decisions the state can make. It just seems wrong to turn it
over to someone to make money off it." McManis heaved a sigh. "Well, I'll
climb down now from my high horse, but I'll tell you this. With all that
money involved, it's hard for this old Barrister not to imagine that PCA
didn't have their greedy mitts in this somewhere." He tapped his nose and
gave Earl a knowing look. "Remember, never ignore the smell of money."

Earl sat thinking after McManis left. He knew it was never wise to
ignore it when real money made an appearance in a case. Money or the fear
of losing it had a way of loosening the constraints on lawless behavior. But
where would PCA fit in among this cast of characters? Earl couldn't even
determine who among them was a predator and who was prey. He shook his
head, got up and went to the file room to pour himself another cup of coffee.

When he returned, Martha was waiting for him. "This just came in
on that Powell case," she said. "It's a good opportunity for you to work on
your computer."

Earl rolled his eyes at the papers in her hand. Martha had embarked
on a campaign to make Earl at least semi-literate on his computer. She had
been surprised to discover someone from Earl's generation who was so inept
at technology.

Earl had grown up in a house without a computer. His father used
one in his asphalt paving business, but it was kept in his office at the
equipment yard. His mother sought refuge in her books and corresponded on
vellum paper in a florid hand. All through school, Earl took notes by hand.

Over time he realized the process had value as a learning tool and preferred it. In high school, when a typed paper was required, the local librarian, who had observed his study habits, agreed to type it for him in exchange for his shelving books. In law school it made more sense just to pay someone and devote the time to his part-time job.

Earl, for his part, regarded his computer not as a tool but as an adversary. He was convinced it was not a machine, but an animate object, one that subsisted by "eating" his documents. It was a creature that randomly sabotaged his efforts for no other reason than to expose Earl as a fool.

"Bobby, you can do this. You have to learn. I won't be here forever, you know. Just insert this into the file that you've been working on." She turned back to her desk. Discussion over.

Earl trudged into his office and glared at his back table. There he sat, Son of Hal. His original laptop had been named after the runaway computer in Stanley Kubrick's film, *2001: A Space Odyssey*. Hal had been stolen, replaced by his progeny.

Earl approached warily, not fooled by the computer's complacent air. He opened the file, put the cursor on the right spot, punched the *Insert* key and started typing summaries of the reports he had received on the case. When he finished thirty minutes later, he carefully saved his work as instructed by Martha. That's when he noticed for the first time that these new entries had typed over and replaced all the prior material in the file, obliterating all his earlier work. He spat out a string of curses, then an ear-shattering bellow for Martha that was loud enough to be heard out on the street.

When Earl returned from the walk he took to calm down, he felt guilty about his outburst. He apologized to Martha who had, of course, repaired the damage. Earl made a mental note to send her flowers the next day.

When he stepped into his office, Manny was wedged into one of the client chairs, cradling a cup of coffee in his baseball mitt hands.

"I sent out those subpoenas for Adam Hartman's inmate file and Rattner's personnel records. But I found out something that I thought you would want to know."

"Intel is always welcome," Earl said.

"Remember, we were wondering about Hartman being in protective custody and who might have threatened him?"

"I do indeed," Earl said.

"Well, I went to the favor bank and made some calls. Seems our man Hartman was a popular dude with the other shut-ins. He worked in the infirmary and had a rep of trying to get proper medical care for people."

"Not always at the top of what a for-profit prison wants to spend its money on," Earl observed.

"Right," said Munoz. "Plus he was willing to write letters for the inmates who couldn't. Half the guys in there can't read. So he was like a town ... What do you call it?"

"A scribe," Earl suggested.

"Yeah, we had one in my father's village. Mexico had this rule that you had to wear shoes to go to school." Munoz shook his head in dismay. "You know how quickly kids outgrow shoes and how expensive that is for poor people. You would see little girls wobbling to school with high heels taped to their feet. So lots of older people couldn't write. There was this one old woman, 'la amanuense,' who would write letters for them for a small price."

Earl knew that Munoz's mother had been sent north so Manny would be born in the States, then they returned to Mexico. He had seen Manny quietly collecting used shoes to ship to his village. Now he knew why.

"You know," Manny continued. "Being a prison scribbler, or whatever you call it, is a good way to pick up information. Gossip is a full time occupation in prison. Lot of time on their hands. Maybe our man learned something he wasn't supposed to know."

"Good point," Earl said. He sat, thinking. What if this *was* a setup, but Kate wasn't the target. What if Hartman had learned something that certain people didn't want to leak out? What if Hartman was the one who needed to be eliminated and Kate was just thrown in as a convenient bonus or maybe a misleading distraction? And what about the dead guard, Travis Miller? Wearing a wire was one sure way to end up on someone's hit list. Earl ran a hand over his face. There were too many moving parts to piece together. He needed more information, and that was exactly what he hoped to get tomorrow when he drove up to Haywood.

The black Lincoln Town Car slipped smoothly in and out of the downtown Sacramento traffic. In the back seat, Buddy Wright, President of the prison guards union poured himself a drink from the liquor cabinet and loosened his tie. He was a thick-shouldered, beefy man whose jowls were beginning to sag, giving him a face like a bull dog. But a bull dog that relied more on its bite than its bark. His trademark Panama hat rested on the console between the front seats. He took a swallow from his drink and placed it in its holder.

To his right sat a man in a modest grey business suit, with short-cropped salt and pepper hair and shrewd penetrating eyes. Jerry Reynolds had been with Buddy Wright since the beginning as an indispensable partner; in Godfather terms, his *consigliere*. He was the author of the strategy that had built the union from a second-rate stepsister of law enforcement to the most powerful force in California politics. It was so simple. Just convince the public and the legislature to punish criminals with longer and longer prison terms. Their partnership had been a successful one because each was satisfied with his role. Buddy with his Panama hat and outsized ego was the face of the union. Reynolds worked the back halls off the Capital's rotunda commandeering votes. Depending on which legislator you talked to, Reynolds would be described as either an extortionist, piggy bank dispenser, cagey horse trader, loyal friend or blood enemy. But behind his back everyone agreed on one description — Buddy's Brain.

"Got a call from that lawyer for PCA, the corporation that owns Haywood," Buddy said.

"Leland Bain. I told him to call you."

"He was banging on about getting me to tell the DA to send him and PCA's corporate counsel everything she gets on the Carlson case."

"Yeah, he told me."

"I told him I'd think about it." Buddy smirked. "What's in it for us? Hell, I'm the one who got the Governor to make sure they hired our guards. I even got them their fucking contract, for God's sake, by sending that letter of ... whatcha' call it."

"Letter of concern," Reynolds said.

"Yeah. When I got hold of that confidential memo their competitor wrote, the one where they admitted they were shortchanging the pension fund for those guards in Mississippi, that was enough for me. We were gonna back PCA." Buddy turned and silently stared out the window.

After a pause, Reynolds spoke. "You know, it might not be such a bad idea to do them a favor. PCA leaves our guards alone to run their prisons. They're just interested in turning a profit. Which is fine with us as long as they keep building prisons. And remember they agreed to coordinate their campaign contributions with us. That gives us access to some pretty deep pockets.

Buddy reached for his drink, took a sip and sat thinking.

"Besides," Reynolds said. "We don't want them going off the reservation on this Carlson case and making trouble. It's best if they follow our lead and stay in line."

Buddy took a swallow from his drink and placed it back in its holder. He nodded in agreement and pulled out his cellphone.

"Let me speak with the District Attorney, this is Buddy Wright."

A voice on the other end picked up immediately. Buddy listened briefly and said, "No thanks necessary, Bob. We're always willing to stand with someone who has the guts to demand justice for the victims of crime." He paused for a moment to listen. "We'll talk about it another time, Bob, right now I called about something else. I want you to tell that DA of yours to send a copy of everything she gets on the Carlson case to the lawyer for that prison corporation, PCA, and their corporate counsel." He listened. "That means *everything*. My girl will give you their contact info."

Buddy listened. "Good. Now that I've got you, give me a status report on the case. It's a top priority, Bob, so pull out all the stops on this one."

He took a sip of his drink while he listened. "What's a change of venue motion?" he asked.

He listened briefly then interrupted. "Hold it. I don't want the case moved. When's this hearing?"

Buddy tapped the driver on the shoulder and jabbed with his finger to indicate a different route.

"What's the name again of that lawyer of yours who's handling the case? Yeah, right. Lauren Taylor. She up to this? This is too important, Bob. I don't want this getting fucked up."

He swallowed the rest of his drink as he listened then suddenly sat forward. "I don't give a shit if she's a ball buster. I don't care if she's got fucking fangs on her pussy. I only care that she wins this thing. Remember, you picked her. I'm holding you personally responsible." He paused then lost patience. "Which judge is handling this thing?" He paused. "Fine," he said and abruptly hung up to call another number.

"This is Buddy Wright. Let me speak to the judge." His eyes widened with impatience as listened. "Well, tell him to get *off* the fucking bench. I want to speak to him. Now!"

"We wanted you to know, Kate, how sorry we all are that you're in this situation. No one believes for a minute that you did anything wrong," Laura Goodman said. She was a senior associate at Horgan & Cooley, and her group had selected her to deliver a message of support. She spoke for the dozen or so young women lawyers whom Kate had taken it upon herself to mentor when she was at the firm. Kate championed them at partnership meetings, discussed their legal questions and advised them on navigating the treacherous waters of the firm's politics. It was a rare day without at least one closed-door counseling session.

Kate gave Laura an affectionate smile, but she was tired. Her eyes burned and her limbs were leaden. The nightly chorus of shouted conversation from cell to cell, along with her anxiety over the case, made sleep merely an intermittent refuge. She knew she looked a mess but, given the circumstances, she had come to accept it.

"Thank you, Laura," Kate said, "it was kind of you to come."

"Is there something I can do for you? Bring you anything?"

"No, I have what I need," Kate said.

Laura sat silently, considering what to say.

"It's all right, Laura," Kate said with a grim smile. "I'm sure my absence has presented certain opportunities for others at the firm."

Laura pursed her lips then heaved a sigh in resignation.

"It's LB," she said. "He's sending out some of the partners to try to poach the clients you took with you to your new firm."

Kate looked away. She felt as though she were falling. Her throat was constricted with emotion. On top of all the pressure she was facing, LB pulls this. What a bastard. All her tamped-down anger and resentment flared up like hot coals in the pit of her stomach. The canon of survival at any firm was "you eat what you catch." Without a client book, no matter the outcome in her case, she would be out at her new firm. What more could be heaped on her? Her anger started to dampen under a flood of self-pity. She immediately jerked herself back, frightened by such self-indulgence. The next stop on that train of thought was resignation, and she was not about to give in and accept her fate.

She turned back to Laura, worried that her voice might crack. The thought of breaking down before Laura was unthinkable. "He certainly makes his priorities clear," she said.

"But to do it now. So quickly. It seems heartless," Laura said. "I understand it's just business. But it seemed personal by the way he's talking about you. What does he have against you, anyway?"

Kate considered the question for a moment, considering how much to reveal. "It started some time ago. I refused to kiss the ring, and then I made the mistake of trying to replace him on the compensation committee. It seemed to me that he was using his authority more to sustain his seat than to fairly compensate the partners. I underestimated how much his self-esteem depended on his place in the firm. It was as if I had threatened his very existence. He never forgave me."

"Well, none of the other partners could ever be accused of standing up to him. When he approaches, most just take out their knee pads."

CHAPTER 8

"Thanks for agreeing to meet me this early, Mrs. Miller," Earl said. "Like I told you, I'm due at the courthouse this morning."

"That's okay," she said. "I don't sleep much lately, anyway."

They sat in her small, uncluttered living room. The widow of the dead prison guard stared off as if imprisoned in her own thoughts. Earl held a coffee mug between his palms and waited patiently. He glanced over at a framed photograph on a well-polished table. A younger Travis Miller stared back, dressed in his formal dress blues. He had a permanent part in his hair that seemed carved with a chisel. There was a look of pride on his face and a confident set to his square jaw.

She followed his gaze. "Travis served two tours in Iraq. Got wounded twice and went back each time."

"He sounds like a very brave man."

She sat silently for a moment then spoke with more feeling. "Travis was a very decent man. He treated people with respect and expected the same for himself. That's why he couldn't stand the way those guards behaved."

A small, cocoa-colored boy, about 6 or 7, appeared in a doorway, dressed in jeans and a Spiderman tee-shirt. "It's all right, Lamont," she said. "I just need to talk to Mr. Earl here. You go back and finish your breakfast."

The boy turned and left.

"He was just checking on me," she said with a sad smile. "Each time Travis left he would say to Lamont that now he was the man of the house and he should take care of his mother." She paused and pursed her lips together.

"I know this is a hard time for you, Mrs. Miller. But you were saying something about the guards."

"That's why I asked you to come see me. That woman of yours didn't kill my Travis. Those guards did."

"How do you know that, Mrs. Miller?"

"Those inmates are no angels, but them guards." She paused, her lips curled in disgust. "They treated those prisoners something awful. Strut around and beat down inmates for no good reason. Just to show they could. They actually shot guys on the yard for getting into a fist fight. A fist fight! And that captain up there, Gunther's his name. He's the one tellin' them to do it."

Earl remembered the tall man in sunglasses around whom the guards huddled outside the courthouse.

"It made Travis sick. Said he didn't go fight no war to be a party to that."

"Travis told you all this?"

"Of course. Travis even went to the head of the union. What's his name, Buddy something. Told him. He said he would look into it. Told Travis to let him handle it. But nothing came of it."

"That must have taken some courage," Earl said.

"You didn't know my Travis. When he thought he was right, there was no backing down. He said those inmates had to do their time for breaking the law. He was fine with that. But that didn't give those guards no right to make some inmate their own whipping boy. Like the inmates were there for their amusement. Do anything they wanted to them. So he went to this state lawyer."

"A State Attorney General?" Earl asked.

"That's it," she agreed. "But nothing happened there either."

"Mrs. Miller, do you know if your husband ever wore a recording device. Something he would tape to his body?"

She nodded slowly. "I saw it once. He didn't want me to. It was something he taped on his chest."

"Do you know what happened to the tapes?"

She shook her head. "By then, Travis didn't want me being involved. Said it was for my own good. That was when the threats started."

"What do you mean?"

"He didn't want to tell me about all of them. Didn't want me to worry. In the beginning it was just stuff like notes on his locker, spitting on the ground when he walked by. They knew better than to say it to his face. Then one day there was an alarm call about a gang fight and a guard needed help. He ran and jumped right into the middle of it. Then he looks around and sees he's all alone. There was no guard in trouble. They had set him up. And nobody came to back him up. Nobody. He nearly got shanked. That's when he put in for a transfer."

"To another prison?"

"Right. It was approved in one week. One week. No transfer gets approved that fast. They wanted to get rid of him." She fixed him with a defiant stare. "I'm a Christian woman, but I'll go to my grave before I forgive them for taking my Travis."

"By any chance do you know the name of the Attorney General that Travis went to?"

"I sure do. I found his card in Travis' things."

Earl stepped off Mrs. Miller's front steps and headed toward his car. He glanced up and down the street. He had been aware since he reached

Haywood that he was being followed. The sparse traffic in town made it nearly impossible not to notice a tail. The same blue Honda that had followed him since he pulled off Highway 5 was parked three houses away. He walked up to the Honda and tapped on the driver's window. It slowly lowered. The driver gave Earl a blank stare.

"I'm headed to the courthouse," Earl said. "You can follow me, unless you know a short cut we could take." The window silently went back up. Earl smiled to himself and went to his car.

The driver reached for his cellphone as he watched Earl drive away and punched in a number. "Captain," he said when someone answered. "It's Billy Krandle." Pause. "Yes, sir. I did. And you were right, he visited that Miller woman." Pause. "Yes, sir. He's on patrol duty today. I'll call my brother right now. He'll take care of it. He's more than willing to help us."

After leaving Mrs. Miller, Earl stopped at the Clerk's office in the Haywood County Courthouse to look up certain records that McManis wanted to use for the change of venue motion. After finding what he was looking for, he took the elevator up to the DA's office to pick up some more discovery material at the reception desk, happy not to have to deal with Ms. Taylor. She was rationing out case reports at a miserly pace, as if each page had to be printed on currency from her own wallet. Then he drove out of town and onto Highway 5 heading to LA. The asphalt ahead shimmered in the heat and in the distance the fiery sun made the road look like pools of water.

It was Friday afternoon, and Sam would be coming over to spend the weekend. He shoved a Dire Straits album into the CD player and settled back for the long drive home. He could use the time to think about what Celia Miller had told him. If there were guards that preyed upon the inmates, it sounded like they had found out that Travis was trying to put together a case on them. A criminal prosecution would cost them more than just their jobs and pensions. It meant a possible prison sentence. Stripping abusive prison guards of their badge of impunity, then dropping them in among inmates, would be like tossing chum fish into a shark tank. Maybe Kate wasn't the target after all. Maybe it was Travis Miller and she was just a convenient patsy to divert suspicion.

The red lights flashing in his rearview mirror startled him. He looked at his speedometer. A little over the limit, but not enough to warrant a stop. He slowed and pulled over to the shoulder.

A paunchy policeman approached and leaned a meaty forearm on the open driver's window. His eyes seemed small, as if squeezed in his fleshy face and set too close together. The insignia on his shoulder read Haywood Police Department.

"In a hurry to get out of town, Mr. Earl?" he asked.

"Not particularly." Earl glanced at his name tag. "Officer Krandle."

"I just thought after your little chat with the widow you might be in a rush."

Earl gave him a knowing smile. He could guess where this was headed, so he stared silently ahead as he handed over his driver's license and car registration. The cop straightened up and carefully examined them. Then he took a lighter from his shirt pocket and lit the corner of one, then the other. Holding them daintily between his fat fingers, he watched them burn until he had to drop them to the pavement where he calmly rubbed out the flame with his shoe.

"Seems we've got a problem here, Mr. Earl," he said. "We take driving without a license or registration real serious around here. Not to mention that high speed chase you led me on." He stared down at Earl with a look of feigned regret. "You want to step out of the car for me."

The interview room at the Haywood Police Station was a cement box with a small window in its metal door. No two-way mirror, no video camera, no hidden microphones. Just a plain wooden table with cigarette burns and four straight back chairs. Bobby Earl sat in one of the chairs, his hands cuffed behind him, his legs extended out with his heels supported on the seat of another of the chairs. In the gap between the two chairs, Officer Krandle straddled Earl's outstretched legs, his full weight pressing down on the knee joints.

Krandle leaned forward, leering into Earl's face. "It's called the hobby horse. Hurts like hell, don't it. But it don't leave no marks."

Earl stared straight back, his eyes filled with pain and raw hatred. His face was bathed in sweat, his breath coming in short, tight bursts.

"Man," Krandle said. "You're pantin' like a dog shitting peach pits. You got a problem?"

Earl hissed out words between breaths. "You fucking tub of lard. Take off these cuffs and let's see who has a problem."

"Why you getting' so huffy?" Krandle said. "It's your own damn fault. Nosin' around town, talking to people you shouldn't. Listenin' to a pack of lies that don't amount to a gob of spit."

The door suddenly slammed open. Detective Carter stepped in, his face flushed with anger, his dented fedora pushed to one side. "Krandle, you dumb son of a bitch. Get off him."

Krandle gave a startled look then shrugged in disbelief. "Come on, Joe. We were just having a little fun. Weren't we, Mr. Earl?"

"Get up and uncuff him," Carter barked.

Krandle reluctantly stood up and reached for his keys.

Carter watched Earl who slowly, painfully lowered his legs, then stared up at Krandle with a savage look. "No," Carter said. "You better give me your keys and get the hell out of here."

"I can do it," Krandle said.

"Let lard ass do it," Earl interjected, breathing hard. "We've got some things to discuss."

Krandle handed Carter his keys, winked at Earl and left. Carter uncuffed Earl and helped him to stand up. "Come on," he said. "I'll drive you back to your car."

They drove out of town and onto the Highway without speaking. Finally, Carter broke the silence. "Krandle has the IQ of a baseball score. Whole family's that way. My mother used to say a Krandle couldn't pour piss out of a boot if the directions were printed on the heel."

Earl stared ahead in silence.

"His brother is a guard up at the prison." Carter glanced over at Earl. "I'm not excusing what he did. If you want to file a complaint, I'll back you up with what I saw." He paused. "But I'm asking you not to. Krandle may be a bit dim, but normally he's an okay cop. It's just this case. It's got people a little worked up."

"I'm not filing a complaint," Earl scoffed, staring ahead. "Never intended to." That's all I need, Earl thought. He could envision the small town news coverage. *Out of town lawyer complains about police treatment.* The TV clip of the DA in high moral dudgeon defending Haywood's finest against this big-city lawyer. There was already enough local prejudice against Kate without him stepping into the lime light.

"Officer Krandle and I will have our day." Earl said. "He's down on my dance card. Besides he was just the messenger."

On the drive home, Earl was still seething. He pulled off the freeway when he reached Santa Monica and within a few blocks was parked in front of Tito's Batting Cages. A tall chain-link fence surrounded the open lot. Inside that perimeter, a series of individual lanes were screened off. In each a pitching machine was hurling baseballs at a batter who was trying, with varying degrees of success, to hit the ball.

Earl stepped out of his car and listened. After years behind the plate, the sound from each whack of a bat played a different note on his baseball musical scale, telling him if the batter had connected for a solid hit, fouled it off or was just pushing his bat out there hoping to make contact.

After the hobby horse affair, Earl choked with anger. He knew all that rage would bubble just below the surface, looking for an outlet, any excuse to erupt. When that red curtain of fury dropped over his eyes he was blind to the consequences. That was something he was not willing to risk bringing home to Sam. He remembered that when he was married to Cindy and this anger gripped him, he would bring it home. She once tearfully told him that she never knew who to expect when he came through the door. Would it be her sweet Bobby or a sullen angry imposter? The way he had behaved around her was at the top of his guilt list. Now he understood why she walked out the door. At the time he had been oblivious to the cloud he forced her to live under.

He shed his coat, rolled up his sleeves and grabbed his old wooden bat out of the trunk. There was no better way to ease that pressure than to turn the pitching machine up to max and smack the shit out of some fast balls.

When Earl got to his house, he found Sam sitting on the back steps, wearing a pair of shorts and a tee-shirt, holding a glass of wine. Another full glass waited on the step beside her. Earl took a moment to look at her. Before Sam, Earl had always felt alone, even when he was with someone, which is the greatest loneliness of all. He had always lived with a sense of his own unconnectedness, which he accepted as his natural condition, as fixed as the color of his eyes. Until Sam entered his life.

Earl sat down next to her and picked up his glass. The sinking sun gave the horizon a pink glow that slowly reddened until it bathed the clouds in a deep crimson. Henceforth lumbered about in the yard, performing all his imagined feats of agility to impress Sam's dog Beauty. Her dog's name had always struck Earl as somewhat ill-chosen for a scraggly toothed black mutt with a perpetual bad hair day. But who was he to comment with a dog named Henceforth?

Beauty ignored Henceforth and sniffed in the flower beds. Losing patience, Henceforth went for his "closer." He flopped down on the grass, extended his front paws like a sphinx statue, then lifted his head to the sky and started to bay. It was a sound that was both as forlorn as a funeral requiem and as grating as a donkey's bray. His saggy jowls swayed from side to side as he strained for the high notes. When he thankfully stopped, it was heartrending for Earl to see the look of disbelief on Henceforth's face as Beauty continued to examine the foliage.

Earl put his arm around Sam and nodded toward the big dog. "Where did I go wrong?" he asked.

"I guess you never taught him any of your famous opening lines," she said.

"Then I better get back out there and work on a few."

Sam elbowed him in the ribs and they went back inside. Earl changed into jeans and a tee-shirt then padded back barefoot into the kitchen. A small TV on the counter was turned to the evening news. Earl had Sam laughing at a self-deprecating tale when, early in his career, an old judge had dismissed one of his more imaginative motions by questioning whether Earl had gone to law school, adding that if he had, he should demand a refund.

Suddenly something on the TV caught their attention. The news anchor adopted a somber tone. "Kate Carlson, the former spokesperson for Prop 52, the Initiative to prohibit the state from using for-profit prisons, was recently indicted in connection with death of Officer Travis Miller, who was killed in a failed escape attempt from Haywood prison. The polls have shown a significant drop in public support for Prop 52 since this incident." After a pause, he said, "Stay tuned, we'll be right back with the weather from our crack meteorologist, Doctor Steve. But first, a quick break."

A grainy black and white video filled the screen showing a riotous scene. A churning mass of prison inmates locked in furious combat, violently attacking each other. Men being savagely beaten, stabbed, stomped unconscious. A world out of control. Over the video a deep authoritative voice was speaking. "There is a storm headed toward California. If Proposition 52 passes, these men will be back on our streets. Vote No on Proposition 52." The picture changed. A middle-aged woman from the Victim's Coalition spoke of her murdered son and urged a *No* vote so none of the viewers would have to get the fateful phone call she received. Finally, a uniformed prison guard appeared. "We walk the toughest beat in California. We know. Vote No."

CHAPTER 9

"So how'd you find me?" the Deputy Attorney General asked.

"Mrs. Miller found your card among her husband's things," Earl said. They were in the Public Corruption section of the California Attorney General's Los Angeles office. Seated across from Earl was Frank Corbett, who had his shirtsleeves rolled up, his tie undone and a sullen look on his face. It was clear he resented this meeting, but what Earl couldn't figure out was why he was there at all. The usual bureaucratic solution to this unwanted situation was simply to have some minion announce they were "currently unavailable." But there he sat.

"Okay," Corbett said as if he were about to dive into freezing water. "Here's the deal. I'm going to tell you about Travis Miller and what he was doing for our office. But let's be clear about some things." He fixed Earl with a resentful stare. "It's not because I feel I'm required to tell you. I'm not. It's not because I give a flying fuck about your case. I don't. And it's not because I can stomach helping a defense lawyer earn a fee. I can't."

"All right," Earl said. "Your game. Your rules."

Corbett nodded curtly, as if settling an argument, one with himself. "I'm doing this for Travis. I owe him that. Even if it means dealing with...." His voice trailed off.

"Understood," Earl said. He didn't take Corbett's remarks personally because he suspected he knew the inner turmoil that was producing them.

"Travis trusted me," Corbett said looking away as if he were speaking to himself. "He was one of my guys and I let him down. I'm responsible for getting him killed." He turned back to Earl with his jaw firmly clenched and a fierce challenge in his eyes. Earl understood this reaction because he shared the same uncompromising sense of responsibility and felt the same guilt when he thought he hadn't measured up. Corbett's confession was his way of doing penance, a public acknowledgement. Earl's role in this was just to bear witness, which did not grant him the right to comment.

"Travis came to me," Corbett continued. "He hated the way the inmates were being treated. These private prisons are notorious for how they abuse their inmates, but Haywood was the worst. They called it the Gladiator School because the guards staged fights between inmates so they could bet on them. Beatings were the standard punishment for the smallest infractions. Shooting was the response for the slightest disturbance on the yard." He paused, as if it were beyond his comprehension. "And they call themselves law enforcement."

Earl nodded his understanding.

"Travis was the first prison guard who ever broke the code of silence," Corbett said. "I had heard talk about what happened up at Haywood, but I could never get anyone to step forward. You can't build a case on inmate testimony alone. It would never hold up in court."

"Coming forward like that took some balls," Earl said.

Corbett nodded. "He told me about this clique among the guards. A gang, really. They were the ones who dealt out the punishments. Their leader was the captain up there, Ernst Gunther. Called themselves the Sharks."

"You're kidding. Like some prison version of *West Side Story*?" Earl said.

"Believe me these guys never saw a Broadway musical. They thought the name fit because they attacked without warning." He smirked.

Something suddenly clicked in Earl's memory. Among the crime scene photos were some of Rattner, the guard who shot Hartman, documenting any physical evidence of his struggle. Rattner had a tattoo on his wrist. A shark with a toothy grin.

Corbett continued. "I told Travis we needed proof. Hard evidence. So I convinced him to wear a wire."

"Did he do that?"

"He did. And it was even worse up there than I thought. Indiscriminate beatings. Just senseless brutality"

"That sounds like enough to put the cuffs on some people," Earl said.

"Wait," Corbett said raising a cautionary hand. "I wrote up a report. Took it personally to the top, the Attorney General himself. He said he'd look at it. I was anxious to get going, but I waited. And waited. I didn't hear anything. Finally, the AG said to send over my file. All of it. Including every copy of the report. A week later, I'm told to drop it. Some jurisdictional bullshit about a pending federal investigation."

"You think there's any truth to that?"

Corbett looked at him with skeptical eyes.

"So what do you think happened?" Earl asked.

"You never heard this from me," Corbett said. "Agreed? Because I'll just deny it."

"Agreed," Earl said.

"A month later the AG announced his run for the governorship and the prison guards union endorsed him. And I'm sure they made a healthy contribution to his campaign."

"So you think the AG showed the report to Buddy Wright, the union president, and made a deal to drop the investigation? And that's how the guards at Haywood found out about Travis."

"That's why I feel responsible. In a way I'm the one who exposed him. And that's why I'm willing to tell you all this. I think those guards were afraid Travis was going to make a case on them. So they killed him. Your woman was just a handy scapegoat. Which means we're after the same thing. You need to uncover evidence to show someone else is good for the killings, which may be the very proof I need to go after the Sharks. Travis deserves that."

"A good place to start would be those tapes Travis made. Have you got them?"

"No, he wouldn't let me keep them. He was afraid of a leak. And once the threats started, Travis didn't trust me anymore. He didn't trust anybody. Can't say I blame him."

On the drive back to the office, Earl called Munoz and told him to drop a subpoena on the guards union for the report that Corbett had written to the AG. He knew the union would never admit seeing it, but he wanted to see what it might flush out when they were aware he knew of its existence. It was a lesson he had learned as a boy watching an old owl. Each night it would perch in a tree next to the field behind his house. With loud screeches it would announce his presence to the mice hiding in the field. If they didn't move, he couldn't see them in the tall grass. But eventually one would panic and run. Maybe a subpoena would force someone into a move.

The lawyers at Horgan & Cooley spent such long hours at work that their offices usually contained some reminder of their other life; framed photos of family and friends, a child's "art work," some object of personal significance. Leland Bain's office contained no evidence of any outside interest, no rival for his devotion to H&C.

Seated at his desk, Bain scrutinized a spreadsheet of the firm's billable hours for his client, the Prison Corporation of America. PCA had prisons all over the country whose legal problems were handled by lawyers in other H&C offices. While other lawyers might do the work, Bain made sure all the billing went through him, issued over his name. It was his client, his book, he got the credit. It was the very size of those billings which enabled him to maintain his prominence.

The intercom buzzed.

"Mr. Bain, Mr. Bowdeen is here to see you."

There was a pause, then Bain said, "Chris, come in here."

Bain was annoyed. Enoch Bowdeen was Corporate Counsel for PCA, and Bain knew why he was here. Bain had hoped to delay this meeting until tomorrow when he could announce a favorable result he was expecting in a sexual harassment suit against a PCA warden in Florida. When his assistant appeared he motioned her to step to the side of his desk and spoke in a low voice. "I assume you've already told Mr. Bowdeen that I'm here, haven't you?" He gave her a benign smile, but there was bitterness in his voice. "You didn't tell him I was in a meeting, or away from the office or any other reasonable excuse that a congenital moron would have come up with."

"No. I mean yes, I told him you were in."

"Looking at my calendar I don't seem to see that Mr. Bowdeen has an appointment. Did I miss something?" he said in mock astonishment.

"No he doesn't, Mr. Bain. But I thought since PCA was such an important client you would want to see him," she said, involuntarily stepping back. "I'm sorry, Mr. Bain."

He glared at her in annoyance. "Show him in. We'll talk later."

She fled to the door, opened it and stepped aside as Enoch Bowdeen strode past. She quickly shut the door behind her.

"LB, you ol' son' bitch. How's it hangin'," Bowdeen boomed as his cowboy boots thudded on the polished wooden floor. This was a routine Bowdeen had perfected over the years, preferring to come off as an oilfield roughneck, just a good ol' boy. He had found it an advantage in business when others assumed he was the product of generations of inbreeding. In reality, he graduated Phi Beta Kappa from the University of Texas, was law review at Harvard Law and had an MBA from the University of Chicago. He was known to have an extraordinary talent for numbers, especially the kind that followed dollar signs. Bowdeen plopped down in a client chair, adjusted his rumpled but expensive business suit and loosened his tie.

"Can I get you a drink, Enoch?" Bain asked.

Bowdeen nodded once as he fixed Bain with an angry stare. This was no longer good ol' Enoch from the Hill Country of central Texas. This was the Corporate Counsel of PCA, the man responsible for steering all of PCA's legal business to Leland Bain and, as Bain had anticipated, Bowdeen was not happy.

Bain put a cut crystal glass of bourbon on Bowdeen's side of the desk and resumed his seat with a glass of Perrier water.

Bowdeen took a swallow of his drink while maintaining eye contact with Bain over the rim of his glass. "LB," he said. "Looks like you got us knee deep in a hog wallow, didn't you, boy?"

"I don't understand, Enoch." Bain's eyes held steady, but his cunning mind was spinning. "I'm talking about that little filly of yours," his voice taunting and nasty. "The one that kicked her traces and ran off with all those clients."

"Yes, Kathleen Carlson. What about her?"

"Yeah, that's the one," Enoch said with a tone of sarcasm. "The one who's trying to put us out of business. The one you said a lawyer of yours was going to represent and be able to rein in. Yeah, that one."

"She wouldn't accept it," Bain said, as if that would explain it.

Bowdeen snorted through his nose and clamped his lips together, shaking his head. "Well, don't that just beat all, now that she has the one thing that always gets the public's attention. Notoriety. Now she can use her time in the limelight to spout off about the evils of private prisons, and we don't have anybody inside the tent to stop her."

"Nobody is going to give her a soap box. She's responsible for the murder of a prison guard. It's not going to happen."

"Well, I don't like it. But more importantly, Leland, the Board's not happy. If this Initiative passes it means the end of us doing business here. But that's not even the real kick in the balls, because California is just a small percentage of our business. The true danger is that, for some God forsaken reason, this state seems to be a harbinger of change. California started the Three Strikes movement and it spread across the country. If they change course and this Initiative passes, other states may follow. Then we're not talking about a drop in the bucket, we're talking a tsunami."

"Enoch, believe me, I know. I do know," Bain said, attempting a tone of appeasement. "But, with this indictment, the Initiative is dead and she's history. The poll numbers are dropping every week. It'll never pass."

"That's what I originally thought would happen. Now I'm not so sure."

Bowdeen stared down as he swirled his drink. "The Board's been asking questions, Leland." He stared up under raised eyebrows. "Like why have I got all our business at just one law firm?" He gave Bain a wry smile. "I been sort'a asking myself the same thing."

"Enoch," Bain implored. "I promised if you came on board, I would get you a State contract for every one of your California prisons. And I have."

Bowdeen made a slight gesture, conceding the point.

"And you've personally done very well," Bain continued. "I've made sure of that." There was no need for Bain to mention the hefty referral fees paid into an offshore account. "And your son was just awarded a scholarship by the firm which will pay for his tuition at the Exeter Academy."

Bowdeen's face grew stern. "Leland, let's understand each other. When you say you'll take care of something and then you don't, I start thinking about changing horses."

"Enoch," Bain beseeched.

Bowdeen threw back his drink, put his glass on the desk and shifted his mood as if it had been a passing storm. "I gotta skedaddle. Busier than a cat burying his shit on a marble floor. Need to talk with the warden down in San Diego. He's bellyaching about the size of his bonus for cutting costs. Greedy bastard." He got up and walked to the door, then said over his shoulder, "You best hope this doesn't go south, Leland. It could cost you a lot more than just a client. So don't get too comfortable in that chair."

CHAPTER 10

Earl had been waiting 30 minutes. He accepted it for what it was. A petty gesture to put him in his place, like seating a negotiating opponent in a lower chair or sending an assistant to an important meeting. He glanced at his watch, and reminded himself not to get distracted.

The lobby of the Haywood State Prison was institutional green; lifeless green walls, drab green linoleum floors and a green wooden counter that separated the staff from the public. Inside the barrier, a hefty guard planted a haunch on a county-issue metal desk and complained about his lack of overtime to a guard eating a pizza. Others stood about talking or pecking with their fingers at computer keyboards. Against the back wall, a potted plant on a file cabinet drooped from lack of water.

A side door opened. Lauren Taylor walked through, followed by the tall captain in his crisp uniform and Detective Carter in his weathered fedora. The absence of the captain's mirrored sunglasses revealed a pair of pale grey eyes that seemed washed out, devoid of emotion. He looked directly at Earl. His stare was as steady as Earl's but much colder. Lauren Taylor's green-framed glasses could not conceal her sullen attitude at being ordered to perform what she clearly considered an unwelcome task.

Before meeting with Earl, she had sat down with the captain. There were a few things about which Lauren Taylor was not sure; whether she wanted to be married or single, whether her next step up should be the DA's job or whether she should shoot higher, and whether she would ever meet a defense lawyer that she did not detest. But one thing she did know for certain: she had to win this case. The first step on that road was to hold back as much information from the defense as possible. She was surprised, but reassured, when the head of her office relayed that certain interested parties would be grateful if particular items in the case were conveniently overlooked and not passed on.

Like all prosecutors, she was aware of the strict requirement to reveal any evidence that was uncovered that might be helpful to the defense; a constitutional duty designed to ensure that innocent people were not convicted. But at the same time, everyone knew prosecutors were never punished for failing to do so, and appellate courts were loath to reverse a case for such a violation. Schooling the captain on this "realpolitik" view of the rules of discovery was unnecessary; he could have taught the class.

Taylor approached Earl with all the enthusiasm of a petulant teenager forced to hug her funky-smelling great aunt. She perfunctorily introduced Captain Ernst Gunther and reminded Earl he knew Detective Carter.

"So," Taylor said, "the judge agreed that you were entitled to a tour."

Earl welcomed her lack of a greeting. No feigned civility. No phony cordiality. Earl liked the footing they were on, it was honest, no need for pretense. They were in a fight. It may be one with rules, in a courtroom, but it was still a fight. So why pretend otherwise?

"I assume," she continued, "that you just want the highlights. Unless, that is, you've acquired an interest in scatology as well as corpses and want to see the toilets."

Earl was silent. He saw no need to reply.

"All right, then. Captain Gunther, if you would, please." She gestured to the steel frame that contained the metal detector.

Gunther had a bemused expression, as if being asked to explain that rain fell from the sky. "Mr. Earl," he said. "I assume you've been to court and gone through security. Been through airport screenings. This is the same thing." He paused. "Any questions?"

"How high is it cranked up?" Earl asked. "Will it alert on shoes with mental insoles, or a ball point pen?"

"If you had any lead in your pencil, it'd go off."

Earl ignored the crude taunt. "And everyone goes through, no exceptions?"

Gunther looked over at a trustee working behind the counter. "Phillips. Get Mr. Earl one of our pamphlets on the visiting rules." The inmate disappeared into a back room.

"Read the pamphlet, Mr. Earl. If you have any questions, call me. But to answer your question. Everyone gets screened. No exceptions."

"How about the guards?"

"As I said. Everyone gets screened."

Earl noticed Carter glance at Taylor, who glared back as if warning him against engaging with the enemy.

The inmate returned and handed Earl a glossy pamphlet with a picture on the cover of a smiling mother with her children.

"All right," Taylor said. "Let's see the visitors' room."

They followed the captain down a cement hallway and onto the exercise yard. It was filled with inmates, talking in huddled groups, playing basketball, lifting weights. Against the wall on their left were two closet-size wire cages. In each, an inmate stood inside gripping the wire with clawed fingers, staring out with dull eyes, their clothes still wet from last night's rain. A graphic reminder for the other inmates of their powerlessness.

The captain stepped outside, and an unnatural silence fell over the yard. He put on his sunglasses and walked calmly into the crowd. Inmates parted before him like the Red Sea. No one made eye contact. Inmates turned away and remained motionless, blending into the background of blue work shirts, like birds seeking safety amidst the flock in the presence of a hawk.

The group followed him across the yard and through a metal door. They entered a large open room with an array of small tables and folding chairs. At each table, a single couple was seated. Inmates were huddled close to their women visitors, holding hands or entwined in some form of embrace. Children ran gleefully back and forth to a line of vending machines along the wall. The din of conversations and squealing children insured privacy for any quiet exchange. A guard sat at a desk next to a metal door and scanned the room with bored eyes.

"So you allow contact visits for the families," Earl said.

"They're not allowed to pass anything or take off any clothes. Just kissing," Gunther explained.

"Surveillance cameras?"

"Two," Gunther said. "Covers the room, but not the bathrooms."

Earl turned to Taylor with an inquiring look.

"You'll get the video tapes today," Taylor said.

"Lawyer visits, I understand, are behind Plexiglas and over a phone," Earl stated. "No contact,"

"The Department," Taylor said, "must figure that the girlfriend of a drug dealer is more trustworthy than a defense lawyer." She smiled in amusement. "Shall we move on to the inmate entry room?"

They stepped through the metal door and into a small, cement-walled room. Earl recognized it as the sally port from the crime scene photos. For some reason, it was unsettling to Earl that not a trace remained to mark that a man's life ended here, as if what had happened was as ephemeral as a passing shadow and about as noteworthy.

"When an inmate's visiting time is up, he steps in here and gets searched." Gunther explained. "Then he's sent back to his cellblock,"

"This was where Officer Miller was stationed according to the reports," Earl said. "So Miller would have searched Hartman when he came out of the visitors' room into the sally-port?"

Gunther nodded. "Or tried to."

Earl turned and looked at the bare cement walls as if they held some answer. "But Adam Hartman had to have an escort. Which means he was in protective custody, right?" Earl looked at Gunther for confirmation. "So why was he in PC?" Earl asked.

"I don't know," Gunther said. "He was probably afraid of someone on the yard. You'd have to check his file."

Earl turned to Taylor.

"Send a subpoena to Corrections," Taylor said. "I'm not doing your work for you."

"Just checking to see if there was a thaw," Earl said and turned back to Gunther. "And Rattner was Hartman's escort?"

"That was part of his assignment. He was a rover, which includes escort duty from the visiting room. He was the one who got called."

"So why call Rattner? There must have been other rovers," Earl said.

"Rattner was called because he was the only one willing to work with Miller."

"What do you mean?"

Gunther looked at Taylor who gave an unconcerned shrug. "The other guards thought Miller was soft," Gunther said. "That he wanted to be friends with the inmates. Which is dangerous. It can get you, or somebody with you, killed. Rattner was the only one willing to take that chance."

Earl said he had seen enough. Captain Gunther led them back to the lobby where Taylor produced a banker's box of more discovery, containing additional police reports, laboratory results and video tapes. On top was a transcript of the testimony given before the Grand Jury. "Pleasant reading," she said and insisted he sign a receipt. Taylor turned and was followed by Detective Carter as she stepped back through the same side door.

Captain Gunter remained, staring at Earl as if they had unfinished business. "I understand you paid a condolence call on Travis Miller's widow. Very considerate of you."

"I'm sure it's nothing compared to the support she's received from that little service group of guards you head up."

"Rumors are a very dangerous thing, Mr. Earl. You never know who might get hurt."

"Like Travis Miller?'

Gunther's eyes narrowed with contempt. "Grief sometimes causes people to lash out without thinking clearly. So I'm sure you wouldn't want to start repeating baseless rumors. That could result in some very unfortunate consequences."

"Thanks for the advice," Earl said. He picked up the box of materials and headed out the door. He had something to do.

There are certain promises a defense lawyer must always keep; give the jury what you pledge to do in your opening statement; keep your word to a prosecutor; and visit a client in custody when you say you will.

Kate looked tired. There were dark smudges under her eyes. But she held her shoulders back as she walked toward Earl with a smile on her face. He mentally applauded her effort to put up a good front. She would need that grit for the long road ahead.

Earl smiled a greeting and followed her lead by deliberately avoiding any enquiry about her jail conditions. Earl had seen too many clients fall into despair when they allowed the wretchedness and misery around them to break their inner resolve. Why risk inviting her to give voice to her fears and daily humiliations, knowing where that path might lead? He needed her to stay strong-willed and clear-headed to withstand the shock waves ahead that inevitably came with a jury trial.

Earl brought her up-to-date on the state of the prosecution's evidence and what he had learned so far. She was shocked, then angry, over the presence of a matching bullet in her car and gunshot residue on her hands. He tried to reassure her it was early yet and they had just begun to work. Besides, he told her, the fact that the murdered guard, Travis Miller, was wearing a wire was certainly something that would resonate with a jury.

He let her ponder all this for a moment, then said, "There's a couple other things we should discuss. Let's go over again why you were visiting Hartman. The DA is going to argue that you're the head of the tax department of a large law firm. Lots of important clients. You're busy, yet take time to visit a guy in state prison. And not just one visit, but several. Why?"

"Adam wrote me a letter a couple months ago. He had seen me on television talking about Prop 52. He said he had information that would help the campaign against for-profit prisons."

"And you believed this?" Earl asked.

"Not at first. Then he wrote me again and gave me some of his background. I checked him out and thought it was worth a try."

"So what did you do?"

"He would only speak to me, so I went to visit him to determine if he really had useful information."

"Did he give you anything worthwhile?" Earl asked.

"Yes and no. At first he told me he had proof that the guards were smuggling cellphones and drugs into the prison."

"Smuggling?" Earl's attention was wrenched into focus. "He said the guards had a way to sneak contraband into the prison? Did he tell you how? Which guards? Anything?"

"No," she said.

Earl exhaled in disappointment. If a guard could smuggle a cellphone, he reasoned, why not a small gun. "Why wouldn't he tell you?" Earl said in frustration. "He's the one who contacted you."

"Because I told him I wasn't interested. A few corrupt union guards wouldn't change voters' minds. I needed something that attacked the private prison system itself." She paused. "And then I made a mistake."

Earl's question was in his glance.

"I told him I would be willing to report these guards to the authorities, if he wanted." She grimaced in regret. "He was astounded that I didn't realize how dangerous it was for him if any of this came back on him. After that he was wary of me."

"You can't really blame him," Earl said. "There's more than one way to get your time card punched in prison."

Kate nodded. "After a time he calmed down and told me he had something else. He could give me facts that would expose violations by private prisons that would put them out of business in California."

"So what happened?" Earl asked.

"I told him if he could give me credible evidence of that, I'd help him with what he'd asked for. He said he needed time to gather the material. I took that to mean he still wasn't sure he could trust me. He was afraid his identity as the source might get out. That's why I was visiting him, to prove that he could trust me."

"But why use the visitor's room? You're a lawyer, why not the lawyer's booths?

Kate shrugged. "In the lawyer's booths you speak over these telephones which the guards listen in on. Like I told you, Adam was very distrustful. He didn't want any mention about prison conditions that might be overheard. Besides, at the time, I wasn't his lawyer of record, so I figured why not use the public visitors' room. It's a much friendlier atmosphere. Talking over a phone behind a Plexiglas screen puts you at a distance, psychologically. I was trying to build trust with Adam."

"So in the visiting room you sat at one of the tables, I assume."

She nodded.

"The guard," Earl continued, "the one on the desk that day, said you two were acting in a suspicious manner." Earl made quote marks in the air. "I don't know what that means because it's not described in the report."

"I have no idea what he's talking about. We might have leaned close to one another because it was noisy in there. But that's it."

"Okay," Earl said. "Another thing. Do you know why Hartman requested to go into protective custody?"

"I don't. I just assumed he was afraid. Prison is such a dangerous place and Adam was no hardened criminal."

"But he had been in Haywood for several months before he requested PC. Did he ever mention any inmate or group he was afraid of? Anyone he was having trouble with? Fights, threats, anything?"

"No. And I never asked. I didn't want to embarrass him. Requesting PC is a touchy subject in prison," Kate said.

"I understand," Earl said, aware that rape was an ever-present danger in prison. "By the way, we're not the only ones who will have to explain some evidence to the jury. That metal detector you had to go through is going to be defense exhibit number one. Apparently it was so sensitive it could detect if you were born with a silver spoon in your mouth. Let them try to explain how you could have smuggled a gun past it."

Earl's smile slowly faded as he saw a troubled look creep across Kate's face.

"There's something I should tell you," she said.

Earl's heart sank.

"All right," he said forcing himself to sound calm.

"I didn't go through the metal detector," she said.

Earl felt as though he had been punched in the gut. His mind was in free fall, desperate for something to hang onto. "What are you talking about? Everybody has to go through it."

"Not if you have a metal implant. I had a skiing accident. There's a metal rod in my leg. So they would use a hand scanner instead and a pat down."

"Okay," Earl said, scrambling to recover. "We're still all right. Even a hand scanner should be able to detect a gun, for Christ's sake."

"The trouble was the hand scanner would always go off because of the rod in my thigh. So they would have to do a pat down."

"Okay, tell me exactly what they would do."

"They would pull me aside and a guard would take me to a back hallway, where we would wait for a female officer." She paused and drew a heavy breath. "It could take up to an hour to get a matron there. The same guard usually had this duty. Phil was his name. I liked him. We would sit and talk as we waited. The matron was a different story. It was the same one each time. Denise Wallace. A real nasty piece of work. She would take me into this room and search me. I was forced to stand there while she rubbed her hands over me. It was just humiliating." She searched Earl's face for some sign of understanding. "I know I should have told you. It's just...." Her voice trailed off.

Earl didn't ask her why she had hidden this from him. He knew the answer. Denial. What was the saying? "Denial is not just a river in Egypt." It seemed a universal trait, not just one reserved for the simpleminded. Even intelligent, sophisticated clients indulged in this irrational, self-destructive behavior. Earl had seen fear shave plenty of IQ points off the smartest of minds, make them trade reality for wishful thinking, believing that, somehow, if they didn't acknowledge it, the truth would never come out.

Earl assured her they could work around it. Why pile on, he thought. She knew well enough that this was a problem. A big one. Getting patted down was not the equivalent of having to go through a metal detector. Half the inmates in prison were walking around with a metal shank shoved up inside them that no pat down would detect. He wished sometimes that he too could fall back on magical thinking. But there was no ignoring this one. Their case just took a hit. He just hoped it wasn't below the water line.

After his visit with Kate, Earl needed time to sit and think. Selma's Cook Shack at the end of Main Street seemed like a good choice. He parked in the lot in back and left his coat in the car. When he stepped into the restaurant the murmur of conversation died down as people nudged each other and looked in his direction. It was reassuring, he told himself, to see that he was as popular as ever in Haywood.

He took a seat in a corner booth facing the window onto the street and ordered a cup of coffee and a burger then settled down to read the pamphlet on the visiting rules. After a few minutes, the restaurant door opened. Earl glanced up at the reflection in the window and saw two husky men walk in, dressed in jeans and work boots. One wore a sweatshirt with cut-off sleeves that displayed bodybuilder arms, the other wore a Pendleton and had his back to Earl. They slid into a booth a couple behind his. The sweatshirt faced Earl and seemed to regularly glance in his direction. Earl's radar flashed concern. After a minute, he scoffed at himself. Was he getting so edgy that every stocky guy he encountered should be considered a potential threat? That was not a view of the world he wanted to live with.

He turned back to the pamphlet and continued reading. Finding no great revelations, he turned to the last page. Tucked inside was a small folded paper that slipped out and floated down to the floor. He picked it up. On it was hastily written, "GET HARTMAN 602s." Earl put down the pamphlet and stared in confusion at the note. Looking up, in the window's reflection, he saw the sweatshirt staring at him, then whisper something hurriedly to the Pendleton who turned to look at him.

Recognizing the Pendleton sent a jolt through Earl. It was Deputy Krandle. Pig-eyed, hobbyhorse Krandle. He didn't need a crystal ball to see where this was headed. He calmly put down some bills, clenched his right fist around the salt shaker on the table and casually walked out the door without making eye contact.

As he moved toward his car, he could hear the crunch of boots on the sandy asphalt behind him. He didn't look back over his shoulder or increase his pace, but he did listen intently. When he judged they were right behind him, Earl spun swiftly around and using that momentum, drove his right fist into the startled face of the nearest man. Mr. Sweatshirt. With a fist made rock-hard from the salt shaker and shoulders muscled on his father's road crew, he delivered a crushing blow. The man crumpled to the ground.

Suddenly, something crashed into Earl's skull. His ears rang and lights danced in his eyes. He staggered back, fighting to stay conscious and not go down. He knew another blow was coming and instinctively raised his left arm. He saw the club coming and felt it slam into his forearm. He swung wildly, not connecting with anything, then kicked out and did. Krandle backed off and eyed Earl warily. It gave Earl the time to clear his head. Krandle's expression switched from doubt to fear.

"Don't even think about it," Earl said deliberately. "I'll run your ass down."

Krandle blinked and drew several deep breaths, gathering himself to charge, hoping to knock Earl to the ground where the club could do its work.

That was when everything seemed to slow down. Suddenly Earl was calm. He knew what to do. He had faced this before, back when he was a baseball catcher. He was often called on to block the plate, by standing in the path to home plate, waiting for a throw from the outfield as a runner from third bore down on him determined to deliver a blow that would slam him to the ground and knock the ball loose. Earl knew how to play this. The secret was not to absorb the impact, but to yield to it.

Krandle charged and plowed into Earl who sank back, pulling them both to the pavement. Earl quickly rolled back up as he had been trained to do. He launched a series of punches as Krandle tried to struggle to his feet. He never made it.

Earl limped to his car and drove off. He knew as soon as the adrenalin wore off he would start to feel the blows. He just hoped his arm wasn't broken. In the rearview mirror he saw the sweatshirt stagger to his feet and spit something onto the ground. Earl hoped it was some teeth. That would send a fitting message back to Captain Gunther.

This encounter with Krandle, like his last one, he told himself, would have to stay in the memory file. Technically he threw the first punch, so Pig-Eyes could claim self-defense. It would be his word against theirs. He could see the headlines, *Carlson lawyer gets in brawl in parking lot*. Without witnesses, it would be a pissing contest with a skunk, and Kate's case would suffer the stench. Best savor the victory and get home before he started to stiffen up.

The cell door slid open with a clank. An inmate lay on the bottom bunk reading a book. He cautiously rose and slowly backed up to the rear wall. Captain Gunther stood just outside the cell, his eyes hidden behind his mirrored sunglasses. Two guards stood behind him wearing helmets with darkened plastic visors that covered their faces. Each guard held a heavy night stick which they tapped lightly against their open palms.

"Hey, Captain. What's going on?" the inmate said with a quiver in his voice.

Gunther stood silently staring at the inmate. After a pause, he slowly removed his sunglasses, revealing eyes without depth or viciousness or gentleness or anything else. "I'm very disappointed, Phillips. I didn't expect this from you. Thought you were smarter than that."

"What'a you mean, Captain? I didn't do nothin.' "

"I suppose you missed your old cellie. I can understand that. But to act so foolishly? So recklessly?"

"Me miss Hartman? Oh, Captain. He was just my cellie. That's all. You know, guys come and go. No big deal."

"It must have mattered, Phillips. Why else would you send a note to that lawyer? Did you really think I wouldn't find out?" He shook his head in disbelief. "What did you think was going to happen?"

"It wasn't me, Captain, honest. I wouldn't do somethin' like that," Phillips pled.

"Actions have consequences, Phillips."

"No, Captain. Please. I swear to God. I never."

Captain Gunther stepped aside and nodded toward the cell. The two guards sprang forward and wrestled with the flailing inmate, who eventually sank limply to the floor in desperation. Each guard grabbed an ankle and dragged the screaming Phillips out onto the walkway. Their night sticks rose and fell methodically as Phillips screamed in pain. After a few moments, the only sound was the rhythmic thud of their clubs.

CHAPTER 11

"So you knew about this report on those guards up at Haywood," Enoch Bowdeen said angrily, his jaw stiff with outrage. He stood holding a sheaf of papers in his upraised hand, his eyes wide with astonishment.

"Yes, I did," Bain said calmly.

"Well, goddamn it to Hell!" Bowdeen bellowed and slapped the papers down on the desk in front of Bain.

He sat down heavily in one of the client chairs.

Bain leaned forward, resting his elbows on the desk. "And I took care of it," he explained mildly. "The Attorney General buried the report and put a stop to the investigation. It's a non-issue."

Bowdeen glared at Bain as he considered. "Who else knows about this?" he challenged.

"I spoke with Buddy at the union. He already had a copy of the report. He'll make certain it never gets out."

"He goddamn well better," Bowdeen said, emphasizing each word. Then he took a deep breath and sank back into his chair, squeezing his eyes shut in frustration. "Those fucking *union guards*." He made the words sound like an incurable disease. Looking up, he glowered at Bain. "You stuck me with 'em and they've been nothing but trouble. They're expensive and you can't fire 'em. And now this," he said in disgust and flicked his hand at the papers.

"Enoch, the Governor required that you hire them as a condition for giving you the contracts," Bain said with a faint undertone of frustration.

"Yeah, yeah, I know," Bowdeen said with exasperation. "But *these* yahoos. What do they call themselves, Sharks? What are they, some kinda' fucking street gang? Christ Almighty. Is there any criminal law they didn't break?" His breath whistled through his teeth. "If this shit goes public it could cost us our contracts."

"I understand, Enoch. I do." He leaned forward, elbows on his knees, and stared down at the carpet. "California is no place to do business. Not like Texas, not like half the states I deal with. California has a regulation on everything, from what slop we give them, to rehab programs for junkies. Hell, they won't even let us use them for labor."

"It's a waste, I know, but using prison labor is against the law in California. There's nothing I can do. But remember, you also house California inmates in two of your out-of-state prisons where convict labor *is* allowed. And we just renegotiated a new contract for you with Microsoft to use those California inmates to assemble parts in your Mississippi facility"

Without looking up, Bowdeen said, "Get me a drink."

Bain got up and returned with a cut-crystal glass half full of bourbon, which he placed on the desk. He retook his seat. "Enoch, the contract we negotiated with the state doesn't require anywhere near the regulations that the state prisons operate under. You're free to run your operations."

Bowdeen sat silently, sullenly staring down. After a moment, he looked up and fixed Bain with a determined look. "Leland, it's time I explain something to you. And you had best get it and get it good." He took a swallow from his glass, keeping eye contact with Bain over the rim. "California constitutes a small revenue stream for us. Less than ten percent. We're here because of one thing and one thing only. You've got a border with Mexico." He paused and raised his eyebrows to emphasize the point. "The big money, the fuck you money, is in housing illegals for the feds. This new administration has turned out to be very good for us. That's why our stock price is up. That's why we invested so heavily in the campaign." Bowdeen took another swallow of his drink. "You following this, Leland?"

"I'm following," Bain said, trying hard not to reveal his irritation at being subjected to a lecture.

"No more catch and release. Now every crosser gets charged with illegal entry and detained. It's called Operation Streamline. Under federal law, ICE is required...." he paused, "you got that, *required* to either fill or pay for a national daily bed quota of 34,000 detainees. Rain or shine. Currently half of those detainees are either housed in one of our facilities or one of our competitors. The rest are in federal lock-ups. But the new administration has proposed an increase in the bed quota to 80,000 a day. The feds don't have any more capacity. Those are the contracts we want. They'll be worth millions."

"Those are the impressive numbers," Bain said and meant it. That would represent a substantial increase in H&C billable hours.

"But the feds also have requirements on how we run things, not many, but kicking the shit out of inmates is a hard one to work around. So let's be clear, I will not permit some knuckle draggers to put those future prospects in jeopardy. You best explain that to Buddy in no uncertain terms. If he doesn't rein in his cowboys, I most certainly will." Bowdeen threw back the last of his drink and put the glass on the desk. He leaned forward and his eyes grew menacing. "Leland, if any of this goes public it's gonna get ugly for some people. You hear me?" His jaw stiffened. "You just remember what you've got at stake here. I don't need to spell it out. There'll be blood on the floor, Leland. And it ain't gonna be mine."

Earl walked into Jimmy's Diner the next morning around nine. Most of the regulars had already left. He was stiff and sore and moving slowly from the brawl in the parking lot. There was a knot on his head that he hoped his hair hid, and his forearm looked like a Picasso painting during his blue period. But with it all, he still felt the buoyancy that came from being the last man standing after a fight.

In the red vinyl booths, solitary figures sat hunched over breakfast plates and coffee cups. A stout, middle-aged waitress circulated through the restaurant, holding a pot of coffee, joking and chatting with the customers. She wore a brown shapeless uniform; her rhinestone name tag read *Millie*. She greeted Bobby by name as he passed. Munoz sat at the back; his large frame covered the vinyl bench. His thick forearms lay on the table like two fallen tree trunks. He grinned as Earl approached. They had arranged to meet that morning, so that Earl could give Manny a copy of the new case material.

Earl briefly told Manny about his conversations with Mrs. Miller, the widow who thought the guards murdered her husband, and the Deputy Attorney General who confirmed Miller was wearing a wire which he suspected the Sharks had found out about. As Manny put it, he had seen lesser motives for murder.

Earl said nothing about the fight when he told Manny about the note mentioning Hartman's 602s. Manny said it sounded like the number of some prison form, so they agreed it should be subpoenaed. Earl also wanted the inmate interviewed who had slipped him the note, but they both knew a visit from Kate Carlson's investigator might put him in danger. So Earl reluctantly consented to Manny's niece visiting her "uncle" at Haywood State Prison.

Finally, Earl gathered himself and told Manny that Kate had not gone through the metal detector.

"So what are you telling me?" Munoz asked. "She didn't bother with just sneaking in a gun, she smuggled herself in?"

Earl explained that Kate had a metal rod in her leg that limited the inspection procedure to a pat-down.

There was a moment of silence, then Munoz said, "That hurts. There are pat-downs and then there are *pat-downs."*

"Christ, don't I know it. That was going to be the centerpiece of our defense." He paused as the gravity of this fact hit him again. "I'll just have to wait and see how this matron plays it on the witness stand. But it's their procedure and it's her job on the line. Let's see if they try to water it down and make this a semi-skim pat-down. It wouldn't be the first time I've watched a DA put on a cop he knew was whistling Yankee Doodle out his ass. Which" he grimaced, "would force me to put Carlson on."

"I'll try to have those prison files on Rattner and Hartman when we next meet."

Millie appeared at the table to offer a refill. "No thanks Millie, gotta run." He turned to Munoz as he got up, "I'll call you after I go through what I got from the DA."

Munoz watched Earl walk rapidly away, then stared down at his coffee. This case was a tough one, he told himself. Maybe too tough. He hoped Earl didn't start believing his client. Knowing Bobby, to lose a case thinking his client was innocent, would eat his guts out. Manny stood up and put some money on the table. He had to move. Lack of effort on his part was one thing Earl would not have to worry about.

When Earl got to the office he got another cup of coffee. Last night he had been too banged up to sleep much. He eased gently into his chair. Each ache reminded him that he was being sent a message. But from whom? Was Captain Gunther just lashing out at him because he was worried that Earl might expose the Sharks and their abuses? Or were the Sharks frightened he would discover that they had killed Travis Miller to stop him from betraying them? And, of course, there was Kate's belief that the union set her up to defeat her Initiative, so maybe Gunther was just following Buddy Wright's orders. All of which brought to mind McManis' warning about big money. If Kate's Initiative to ban private prisons passed, then PCA was out of business. That would certainly have put her on their radar screen.

At the center of all these thoughts was Officer Clyde Rattner, the only one left alive to tell what happened in that sally-port. How convenient. What was his role in all of this? Was he the real shooter? If so, who was he working for? The Sharks? The union? PCA? Earl needed some background on him to build a profile, a character sketch, something that might point him in the right direction.

And then there was Hartman. What if he had been the target all along? Maybe Munoz had been right when he suggested he might have learned something he wasn't supposed to know. His mind was spinning, lost in calculating the various combinations. It was like playing three-dimensional chess. But one thought kept pushing its way to the front. The one he couldn't shake. He was starting to believe Kate Carlson was innocent.

He forced himself to stop brooding and think in concrete terms. The rest of this week had been set aside for him to try and buy time in his other cases. He needed to clear the decks so he could dive into that box of new material he had just received from the DA. It was only noon and he knew he would feel guilty if he left early when there was work to do. But he needed a long stretch of concentrated time with those new reports, reading them piecemeal was pointless. Still he needed an excuse to leave. Then he remembered he was low on dog food. For centuries, Henceforth's ancestors had survived on table scraps and kitchen leavings, but not Henceforth, the gourmet. A former girlfriend had earned the hound's affection by exposing him to an haute cuisine mix which promptly became a dietary necessity. This favorite concoction was only sold at a market off Melrose Avenue. Earl convinced himself that his duty as Henceforth's attendant was a legitimate excuse to skip out.

It was time to get out Old Blue and take Henceforth for a ride.

Earl spent the next three days racing from courthouse to courthouse, where he promised, cajoled and haggled with prosecutors and judges to continue his other cases. He needed time to prepare a defense in the Carlson case. Or rather to find a defense. He envied DAs who were given the time to concentrate on a big case without the distraction of other cases.

It never ceased to astound him how each judge assumed they were the bright sun of the judicial galaxy around which all else revolved. Most seemed consumed by one aim that eclipsed all other considerations -- the need to dispose of their cases as quickly as possible. This obsession was driven by an overriding fear that their case count would build up, causing the presiding judge to diagnose them as suffering from an "inability to manage their calendar." For such a condition, a treatment of "freeway therapy" would be prescribed, which meant the delinquent judge would be banished to a courthouse that was the furthest, most arduous journey possible from their home. This was a threat of no small consequence in a county with over 45 courthouses, spread over 500 square miles, with freeways that were parking lots in the morning rush hour.

By the end of his campaign to pry out continuances, Earl was convinced he had contracted type 2 diabetes from a constant diet of honeyed appeals to clerks, cloying apologies to judges and saccharine compliments to DAs.

But it was now Monday and after a weekend with Sam he felt fortified. Over the next week he came to the office in jeans and a sweatshirt, devoting himself completely to studying the contents of that cardboard box. Martha held his calls, allowed no appointments and supplied endless cups of coffee.

The foundation of his preparation on any case was always built on mastering the facts, every line in a witness' statement, each detail in a report. Some facts were solid blocks and had to be accepted, others might be shaved or shaped to appear differently, while others might disintegrate under cross-examination. This included the prosecution facts, which must be taken on board or skirted around or plowed right through, but never ignored.

At this early stage, he normally started to formulate his final argument to the jury. A view of the case that he could summarize clearly and simply in a few words. The facts of the case must fit cleanly and harmonize with each other within the framework of this argument. The demands of the final summation guided every decision in the case: which lines of investigation might supply support for the argument, what questions needed answering during cross-examination, what evidence to attack and what to embrace.

To Earl, a persuasive final summation presented the defense through a story. It should take all the disparate facts in the case, separates out the trustworthy from the unreliable, the truth from the lie, and assemble them into a narrative that tells a story. One with a bold beginning, a well-formulated middle and an inescapable conclusion. Such a story gives the jury a framework within which to organize the chaotic collection of facts and assertions thrown at them into something comprehensible. Such a story had to be painstakingly constructed until the justness of the conclusion was overwhelming. But right now he had no story to tell.

Earl wrote his case notes by hand, because the act of writing helped him to remember. In the heat of a cross-examination, there was no time to reflect on an answer or go back to check it against the reports. A skilled cross-examination had to have a certain rhythm, a momentum that built until Earl felt as if the wind was at his back, that he was one with the jury and they were urging him on. To do that, the facts, statements, contradictions, all had to be at his fingertips, embedded in his memory, as if written on the inside of his eyelids.

Earl's handwritten notes themselves were like a second language or code that spoke to him. A heading meant one thing if it was underlined, something else if it was starred or color-coded or given a page citation or a question mark in the margin. Each symbol carried a message that jumped off the page at Earl. By the time of the trial, his notes were as familiar to him as the hand signals sent from the third base coach when he had stood in the batter's box.

The last step was to organize this material so a document could be easily found when needed. Unlike most lawyers who entered their case documents and impressions into a computer, Earl used three ring binders, divided into sections. A section for each witness, one for the physical evidence, the autopsy reports, investigator logs and so on. Binder after binder, section after section. As the binders began to line the shelves in his office, he derived a sense of calm and control from this image of orderliness. The only problem was that the section for defense evidence was empty.

He needed a defense and not just any defense. Earl knew that for juries the legal standard of proof beyond a reasonable doubt was in reality a sliding scale. The more serious the offense, the less proof they required to convict. In a murder case like this the standard would slip to "we're pretty sure she did it." This erosion was not because juries consciously abandoned their duty, but rather from a fear that their decision might set a dangerous person free. Earl was going to have to prove that Kate was innocent and the only way to do that was to give them the real killer. He needed to put someone else in her chair or he would be living a defense lawyer's worst nightmare — standing next to someone he was now convinced was innocent, as she was sentenced to spend the rest of her life in prison.

There was a tap on her door, and Lauren Taylor looked up from her desk. The lights in her office reflected off her green-framed glasses and hid the look of annoyance in her eyes.

"Come in, Joe," she said. "Have a seat."

Joe Carter entered and sat across from her. He looked incomplete without his rumpled fedora.

"Something has been bothering me, and I thought we might talk about it."

"Sure," she said. "Shoot."

"I don't think we were exactly playing it straight with that defense lawyer during the walk-through up at the prison."

Taylor fixed him with a condescending stare. "Joe, that's really not your call, now is it? I'm the lawyer on this case. I decide what we need to tell the defense and what we don't."

Carter pursed his lips and nodded slowly. After a moment he said, "Do ya' mind if I tell you a story?"

Taylor leaned back in her chair and folded her arms.

"My old man was a carpenter. A good one. But slow. He got paid by the job. But he never rushed a job so he could move on to the next one. Everything had to be done right. So he didn't make a lot of money. Not like guys we knew who cut a few corners and slapped things together. My mother would argue with him about it, and he always said the same thing. There's a right way to do something and then there's something less. And something less is like cheating." He looked at her, hoping for understanding. "He would say he wanted to be able to look anyone in the eye after a job and know he didn't owe them a damned thing."

"That's very interesting, Joe. I'm sure you were very proud of your father. Now if you'll excuse me," she said and leaned forward to pick up some papers.

"My point is this. I want to convict this woman, but when it's over I want to be able to look her and that defense lawyer in the eye."

She gave him an impatient look. "Listen. I *am* going to convict the bitch. You can count on that. Which is all you should be concerned about. Now, I've got work to do."

"DELORES, CAN YOU HEAR ME?" Carter stood in an empty stairwell that led downstairs from the offices of the DA. He was amazed that he had cellphone reception. "You got a minute? It's about this DA, again." Carter explained to her how Taylor had withheld from the defense that the guards did not go through the metal detector at the prison and how that was "sort of important."

"She didn't exactly lie," he told her. "But she let that captain up there get away with a pretty slick answer. It certainly created a false impression."

Joe's girlfriend had heard, on more than one occasion, of his resentment over the Ice Queen's ethical lapses. "Joe, honey, we've been over this before and I told you what I thought. If she wants to play it that way, then it's on her."

"But that's the thing. She's involving me. I was there and I knew it wasn't true, so it's like she's got me lying, too."

"Joseph," she said sternly. "This is not your problem. Sometimes you are just too darn straight. You're a stickler for what *you* think is right. It's a messy world, honey, you got to learn to let things go sometimes."

Carter was silent for a while then said: "I hate this case. There's something about it that's just not right. And she's adding to it."

"I know. So just put your head down and get through it." She paused for a response that was not forthcoming. "We'll talk about it tonight, okay? But I gotta go now, Ella had to leave early."

From his office Earl heard Martha laughing, so he knew that Manny Munoz had arrived. But minutes passed without his appearance. Earl was impatient. He had read and reread the police reports, practically memorized the Grand Jury testimony and all he had from it were questions.

He had suspects. Ones with real motives, but he had no proof. As it stood, he would not even be allowed to present any of it to a jury because of the Third-Party Culpability Rule. In California, the law did not allow him to even tell a jury that someone had a motive to set up Kate, or to murder Officer Miller, unless he had concrete evidence that actually tied them to the crime: a witness, a statement, something tangible. It was not enough that someone had a motive and the opportunity.

Manny Munoz appeared with a grin on his face. "I've been with Mr. McManis," he said in response to Earl's look of irritation. "I gave him the guards union's political contributions to our brethren in the black robes. Justice may be blind, but it ain't cheap."

"That should help," Earl said. "He's really dialed in on that change of venue motion."

"The old campaigner sure seemed fired up. It was good to see. Man, I remember when I first joined the Department you would hear cops all the time, coming back from court, cursing his name."

Earl smiled at the reminiscence. "So if you're handing out the fruits of your labors, what have you got for me?"

Munoz tossed two files onto Earl's desk, each imprinted with the California Corrections Department logo. Earl picked up the one on top. "Clyde Rattner's personnel file. Good work, Manny. Let's see what this gives us," Earl began to read through the file as Munoz carefully squeezed into a chair, as though he were backing a semi into a tight spot.

After a short interval, Earl looked up. "Well, he was certainly qualified to be a prison guard. His previous job was repossessing cars and driving a tow truck. Did you see anything in here that would help?"

"Sorry," Munoz said, shaking his head.

"Rattner is right in the middle of this, Manny, I just feel it. Hell, if Hartman didn't shoot Miller then Rattner did. If we find out where he fits in, I'm convinced the other pieces will start to fall into place. Right now we're drawing a blank."

"I know," Munoz said nodding in agreement. "But it's tough because none of the guards up there will ever talk to us about one of their own. The code of silence up there is hard and fast. But there is a guy I know who might fill us in."

"Great, we could use a break." What Earl didn't say was that he was convinced that Kate Carlson was innocent. And Munoz would never ask. Manny was like a bloodhound on the scent, he followed the facts to wherever they led him. Whether it was good for Earl's case or not. Which was just the way Earl wanted it.

Earl picked up the second file which was labeled "Adam Hartman." After a few minutes of reading he dropped it back on the desk with a look of disappointment. "Nothing," he said. "Nothing about why he went into protective custody. Nothing about who he was afraid of. Nothing." Earl looked off in frustration. "There must be some documentation at the prison when an inmate requests protective custody. So let's subpoena it."

Manny flipped open his small notebook, nestled it in the palm of his hand and wrote. He looked up and said, "I checked into the note you got from that inmate. It is the number of a prison form. A 602 is what an inmate fills out to file a complaint. So I subpoenaed it like we said."

"That could be something," Earl said hopefully. "Hartman sure wasn't complaining about the thread count of his sheets. So where are we on that?"

"Not so good. The complaint apparently had something to do with his treatment by the prison staff. So the record clerk notified the union. It's in their contract, he told me. I guess the guards want to know which inmate complained about them so they can go and adjust his memory. Anyway, now the union is fighting the subpoena. So get ready for some delays."

"Goddamn it," Earl said in disgust at the prospect of another hurdle. "Fine," he said with resentment. "I'll deal with the union. But I need to find out who Hartman was afraid of."

"Well, the inmate who passed you the note isn't going to help," Manny said.

"Phillips? He wouldn't talk to your niece?" Earl asked.

"Couldn't talk is more like it. He's in the hospital. The official version is he fell down the stairs. Cracked his skull. Possible brain damage."

"Those lousy bastards." Earl fell silent, thinking that Deputy Krandle must have told Captain Gunther about seeing a note fall from that visitors' pamphlet.

Munoz brought him back. "I've read all the new reports and took a look at the video of her visit."

"Good," Earl said, getting refocused. "The DA is going to argue that she didn't use a lawyer booth because she needed a contact visit to pass the gun. But when I watched it, the video sure doesn't show that."

"Well," Munoz made a reluctant grimace. "Not exactly. If I was a suspicious DA, here's what I might see. It shows Kate going into the bathroom. No camera in there. She removes the gun from wherever. Remember it's small, you pretty much can conceal it in your hand."

"Maybe in those mitts of yours, but Kate's hand?"

Munoz shrugged. "It's pretty small, 'compadre,' " he said and gave Earl a skeptical look. "Anyway, then they both go over to the vending machine. She puts in the money and reaches into the tray. She leaves the gun there and takes the candy. She pays again and Hartman reaches in and retrieves the gun, but leaves the candy."

"Jesus," Earl said. "I guess it's possible, but there's nothing on the video to prove it, and I don't see the DA even thinking of that."

"I don't know about her, but I checked out that detective of hers. Joe Carter. He's no dummy." He paused and studied Earl, who seemed lost in thought. "Hey cheer up, remember, you've got Officer Miller wearing a wire. That's gotta start people wondering."

"Yeah, and Corbett the Deputy AG can confirm it. But nobody seems to know where the tapes are."

"Too bad," Munoz said. "And there's no mention in the reports of finding a recorder on his body, either."

"Corbett told me he wrote a report about the guards' abuse of the inmates that included Miller's statement and explained that the tapes would confirm it. He took it personally to the Attorney General. If Corbett is right, the report was leaked to Buddy Wright, the union president, which would be how the Sharks knew about Miller."

"That would sure have put a target on his back," Munoz said. "You know, what really gets me about those guards is how chickenshit it is to beat up somebody who can't fight back. Any inmate who defends himself would get charged with assaulting a prison guard. That carries a life sentence." He shook his head in disgust. "But I've got a question. What's up with the gunshot residue? The reports say they swabbed her hands at the station right after her arrest, and it came back positive for GSR."

"Yeah, I know," Earl said grudgingly. "The DA will probably argue she test-fired the .25 in the desert on the drive to the prison. And dropped one of the cartridges when she reloaded. That would account for the round in her car."

"The funny thing was they didn't find that much GSR on Adam Hartman," Munoz said. "Just a small amount on his palm. Strange for the guy who's supposed to have shot Miller."

"I noticed that. They'll probably claim most got rubbed off handling the body." Earl rolled his shoulders as if to ward off getting dispirited. "All right, let's see where we're at. Hartman told Kate the guards were smuggling in cellphones and drugs. So let's say they smuggled in the gun and Rattner is the shooter. Who's the target?"

"Officer Miller is at the top of my list," Munoz offered. "If those Sharks thought Miller was putting a case on them, they were facing a wardrobe change from uniforms to prison blues. So they use Rattner to get to Officer Miller. Hartman provides them with a convenient fall guy, so he gets eliminated and Kate Carlson is collateral damage."

"Okay. And what if Kate is right and the union set her up?"

"I thought about that," Munoz said. "If Kate was the target, why run the risk of pulling off two murders. Why not just plant the gun on Hartman and claim she passed it?

"It wouldn't work. Remember, Miller was on duty at the sally-port. It was his responsibility to frisk the inmates when they left the visitor's room. Rattner was only called because Hartman was in protective custody and needed an escort. Miller would never have gone along with something like that."

Munoz nodded. "Yeah, he was definitely a stand-up guy."

"You know," Earl said. "McManis thinks we shouldn't ignore the smell of money."

Munoz squinted his eyes in a question.

"Jim, explained to me how much money that private prison corporation, PCA, makes off their facilities, like the one in Haywood. Maybe they saw Kate's Initiative as the start of a movement to pull back from this mass incarceration."

"That brings us back to Rattner," Munoz said.

"And Captain Gunther. I don't think anybody up at Haywood scratches their ass unless he tells them which hand to use."

"Which just leaves Adam Hartman," Munoz said. "Maybe we're looking at this the wrong way. Maybe Rattner wasn't doing the heavy lifting for somebody else. Maybe he had his own agenda. Maybe Hartman learned something about Rattner he shouldn't have. If Hartman was the target, Miller was just eliminated as an inconvenient witness."

Earl was numbed into silence, overwhelmed by the tangle of possibilities, unable to see a clear path. After a moment, he looked at Munoz. "You're right about Adam Hartman. He is a big question mark. For starters, why was he was afraid to stay in the general population?"

"Maybe he just didn't want to get married to one of those tattooed beauties around the weight pile," Munoz said with a grin.

"Thanks, Manny," Earl said with good-natured derision. "Just get me Hartman's request for protective custody.

CHAPTER 12

Kate Carlson approached Earl with a forced smile, but moved as if slowed by weariness. She was not built for this type of fight. Her mind might keep battling, but her body was failing. Life as a jail inmate was starting to take its toll. Her normal air of confidence now had an edge of bitterness. She now understood that this was not going to be a sprint but a marathon.

Kate was seldom at ease with the other inmates. Most saw themselves as victims, and they often were. They started life with nothing and went down from there. Some were bright, several were actually entertaining. But when she got to know them, sooner or later she came up against a character defect so deep and wide that crossing over was impossible: lying, an explosive temper, a misperception of the world that could not accommodate normalcy. After a while, she just kept to herself.

"We came a day early," Earl explained. "Mr. McManis wanted time to prep our witnesses and organize the exhibits. Get everything lined up for tomorrow. He and Manny Munoz are working on it right now back at the motel."

"I met with Mr. McManis a couple weeks ago when he briefed me on the motion. He seemed very conversant with the law and well-prepared. I'm confident he'll put our best case forward, but . . .," she gave a shrug of resignation. "That Judge is never going to give us a change of venue,"

"We know that. Our appeal brief is already written. This hearing is just about putting on the kind of evidence that an appellate court can't ignore."

"I hope to God you're right," Kate said. "I could use a change in scenery."

Earl smiled. "There's something we should discuss. I have information that Hartman filed an official complaint about his treatment by the prison staff. Did he ever discuss that with you?"

Kate thought for a moment. "Not that I recall. I know he was frightened of the guards, almost paranoid. But he never said anything specifically other than he didn't want to speak over the phones in the lawyer's booths because they might listen in."

"Did he ever mention a guard by name or a group called the Sharks?"

"The Sharks?" She wrinkled her face in bewilderment. "No." She paused, then fixed Earl with an intense look. "If Adam was worried about the guards, then the union and Buddy Wright were behind it. Bobby, I'm telling you the bastards set me up."

THE PHONE RANG in his room at the Welcome Inn Motel just as Munoz was getting into bed. He thought it would be Mr. McManis reminding him for the tenth time to pick up their expert in time for tomorrow's court hearing. But it wasn't.

He dressed quickly and stepped out into the motel parking lot. A dusty Ford pickup was parked off in the shadows, away from the lights. He walked over and got in the passenger side. Detective Carter was behind the wheel, his hat pushed back on his head.

"I didn't figure you for the cloak and dagger type," Munoz said.

"Neither did I," Carter said. "But things keep changing."

"So what's up?"

"I made a phone call to a friend of mine in LA. Used to go deer hunting with me. Works in your old Department. Says you're somebody who can be trusted. Is he right?"

"Depends on what you've got in mind."

"I want to set you straight about some things, but I want my name kept out of it. Can I count on that?" Carter asked.

"If that's it, you've got my word."

Carter nodded and squirmed around in his seat to face Munoz. "I think your man, Earl, mighta' got the wrong idea about something when we took that walk-through the other day up at the prison."

"About what," Munoz asked.

"Captain Gunther told him that when the guards report for work they get screened like everybody else. Now, that's sorta' true, but I think Earl assumed that meant they went through the metal detector."

"And you're saying they don't?"

"The Department of Corrections says they can't afford it," Carter said.

"What's that mean?" Munoz asked.

"The union contract says they go on the clock the minute they get to the front gate and sign in. So they get paid for the time it takes to get to their post and relieve the prior shift, which, in a facility that size, takes a while. It's called walking time. To put them through a metal detector would require each one to take off their steel-toed boots, belts, everything. That would take too much time. Too much walking time."

"So the guards aren't screened at all?"

"No, but it's just random checks. Occasional lunch box searches, a few get pat-downs. That sort of thing."

Munoz sat thinking. If that was what they considered screening, it was about as porous as the border with Mexico. Which meant it was quite possible one of the guards could have smuggled in a gun. Jesus, this puts a nice big hole in the prosecution's case.

"Joe, why are you telling me this?"

"Yeah, I know. I'd wonder too if I was in your place. But their contract is a public record. There's nothing secret about it. You can check it yourself."

"But why are *you* telling me?"

Carter pursed his lips and squinted as if considering the question for the first time. "I guess it's because of a friend of mine. Bill Winslow. He was the DA here a few years back. A good man. In fact, the union backed him when he ran. A couple years into his term, the captain up at the prison, a guy named Ernst Gunther, arranged a welcome party for a busload of new inmates. He wanted to make sure they understood who was in charge. As they got off the bus they were made to run through a gauntlet of his guards. Handcuffed. They lit em' up pretty good." He paused to let it sink in then continued. "Bill made the mistake of empaneling a Grand Jury to investigate. The next day a flyer attacking him was in every mail box in the county. That was followed up by personal phone calls to every registered voter. He lost the next election to the union candidate, our current DA."

"I'm sorry to hear that," Munoz said.

"The union pretty much polices its own up there. We only get called when they shoot an inmate on the yard. So be it, it's their turf. But this is my case and I don't want them fucking it up by hiding stuff." He turned and started up the engine.

Munoz returned to his room and picked up the phone. Earl could use some good news. Carlson may have bypassed the metal detector, but maybe Earl would find some consolation in learning she wasn't alone.

It was late, but everyone was still at the office. Martha had waited to hear how the change of venue motion had gone in court. Now her eyes sparkled with pride as she watched Mr. McManis trying not to preen under Earl's praise.

"Now, now, lad. Let's not get carried away," McManis said, rebuffing the compliments while, at the same time, clearly enjoying himself.

"Martha, you should have seen the judge's face when James introduced the union's contributions to his own election campaign," Earl said.

"And to all the other judges," McManis said trying to introduce a more sober tone, but failing when he started laughing.

"Judge Robbins looked as if he had just seen his publicity photograph with the Governor and discovered his fly had been open."

"And what about that public opinion poll?" McManis reminded Earl.

"Oh, God. That was great. James had a telephone survey conducted on residents in the county."

"A representative sample of our potential jurors," McManis explained.

"Not one person said they thought she was innocent. Ninety percent said they were sure she was guilty and the other ten percent said she probably was. So the judge jumps in to question our statistician. Robbins takes this incredulous tone and says he can't believe that not a single person in the survey doubted her guilt. Our expert said that actually there were a few. Where upon the judge gave this triumphant smile to the DA. Then our man explained that he threw out those responses because they came from a couple of mental patients who were on a home visit but were confined in an institution in another county." Earl pounded the desk as he laughed.

"How was the print and electronic media coverage received?" Martha asked. "Did it help?"

"Miss Sullivan, you get full marks," McManis said, addressing her in their accustomed formal manner. "Your work was enormously effective. Those big banner headlines just jumped off the page. Even the prosecutor was stunned at the volume and tone. I read some into the record and put all the rest in as an exhibit."

"But the best," Earl said, "was the demographics expert who estimated the percentage of the county residents who worked at or did business with the prison. Eye-popping numbers. Then James asked the judge about his father-in-law who owns a huge farming operation that sells produce directly to the prison. I thought I actually saw smoke drift out of his ears."

"And the judge's ruling?" Martha asked.

"You know how he ruled, Martha," Earl said. "We file the appeal tomorrow."

"Well, congratulations," Martha said. "Mr. McManis, it sounds like you did a splendid job. Now I must take myself off home." She turned at the door. "I expect you two feel you've earned a celebration. With which I heartily concur. However, a measure of restraint should be observed. Don't you agree, Bobby?"

"Of course, Martha," Earl said.

They all said good night and she left.

McManis turned to Earl. "You know, of course, that she's taken the precaution of marking the level on my bottle upstairs. So be prepared. Tomorrow morning it's every man for himself."

The inmate walked with a heavy limp. One leg was stiff, inflexible, as if he had shoved a shot gun down his pant leg. As he clumped across the floor of the visitors' room, the occupants at each table he passed fell silent. Manny Munoz understood why. No one wanted to risk that an offhand comment or laugh might be misconstrued as directed at Tomas Soto. There were easier ways to commit suicide.

"I didn't expect to find you here at Haywood," Manny said. He had stayed behind after the venue motion when a search of the inmate registry showed Soto's location.

Soto took a seat at his table, extending his rigid leg out to one side. He stared at Munoz with a face as emotionless as ice.

"I thought they had you up at Q," Munoz said into the silence.

"I am. But I came down to defend my hand ball championship," Soto said with a smug smile.

Manny knew this was an inside joke. Soto was the *consejero*, or *consigliere* to the leaders of La Eme, the powerful Hispanic gang that operated in every State Prison in California. Making contact from San Quentin with the gang's lieutenants in these other prisons was difficult. Normally, he communicated through wives, lawyers, code words in letters or smuggled cellphones. But relaying abbreviated messages from one to the next on important matters, such as someone's demise, could lead to misunderstandings. Face to face was better. And the Department of Corrections provided this opportunity when they sponsored a prison-wide hand ball tournament that included the private prisons. For obvious reasons, despite his lack of mobility, Soto never seemed to lose a match. So the Department was forced to ship Soto from one prison to the next to defend his title and incidentally maintain his chain of communication. Inexplicably, the Department had determined this was the first and last year the tournament would be held.

"Thanks for seeing me," Manny said. "I'm here to ask for a favor."

"You got some balls, Munoz. You helped put me in here."

"You're right. I was part of that task force. You were a big fish, *el jefe*. But I was also the guy who stopped them from using your wife against you."

"And how's that?" Soto said derisively. He leaned back and folded his arms.

"The DA wanted to charge that young wife of yours. Rosa, wasn't it? Make her a party to the conspiracy. Then offer to cut her loose if you agreed to cooperate." Manny paused to get a response. "Come on, you've seen it before. You never wondered why they didn't use her?"

"So why didn't they?"

"I told the DA I didn't play that game. Families were off limits. We either had a case on her or we didn't. And everyone knew you were too smart to trust a young girl like her. We could never make a legitimate case against her. So I told the DA that I planned to write it up that way."

Soto stared silently at Munoz. His face was empty, but it was clear he was searching his memory for events against which to assess Manny's claim.

"Does Rosa still visit you with the boy?" Manny asked.

Soto slowly nodded, then spoke. "What's this favor you're asking?"

"A couple things," Manny said.

"So now it's a couple," Soto said sarcastically.

"Let's just take it a step at a time and see what you think."

Soto sat blank faced and waited.

"Talk to me about the Sharks," Manny said.

"That bunch of maricons. Fuck 'em."

"I understand they beat people down for no good reason."

"Shit, the guards in all the joints do that. But these faggots, here in Haywood, they cross the line."

"How so?" asked Munoz.

"Say some dude pisses them off. A ding acting crazy or some complaint writer. They snatch him up and lock him down with the Booty Buster."

"Who's that?"

"This big faggot in J Block. He uses the dude until they let him out."

"You mean they let him rape the guy? Like some form of discipline?" Manny asked.

"Shit, who's to stop them? Captain Sunglasses? Hell, he's the one who sets up the gladiator fights."

"What's that?"

"They take a La Eme veterano and put him out in an empty exercise yard. Then they toss in somebody from Nuestra Familia. They know what's gotta go down. Then they bet on the fight. They think it's funny."

"And Officer Rattner is a member of those Sharks, right?" Manny asked.

Soto gave him a knowing smile. "I figured you were headed there. You're on that case where the guard got shot, aren't you?"

"That's right," Manny said.

"You shoulda' just asked, bro. Yeah, he's a Shark. I'll tell you about him 'cause he works with Nuestra Familia. Sooner or later we're gonna have to throw down with them. So why not?"

"What do you mean he works with Nuestra Familia?" Manny asked.

"Man, he's their packer. Don't you guys know anything? Shit, he's the one who brings in their cellphones and drugs."

"He smuggles them in? Don't the guards know?"

"Jesus, you really are lame. Know? You think that could go down without Captain Sunglasses knowing about it? Man, he probably takes a piece of the action."

"Why would the captain go along with that?" Manny asked.

"Why not? It's not his problem. The drugs help keep the inmates quiet, more manageable, less trouble. And if there's a turf war, it's inmate on inmate. As for the cellphones, they're used mostly for outside business, street sales, staying in control, shit like that."

"So it's a win-win," Manny said. "Do you know how Rattner does it?"

Soto gave Munoz a menacing look. "There's a lot of cars on that highway, homes. They all don't belong to Nuestra Familia. I wouldn't start trying to play traffic cop, if I was you." He pushed himself upright. "I think you just used up your favor."

Earl was on the phone when he waved to Munoz to come in. He mouthed "Be through in a minute." For the last several days, Earl had been busy with his other cases, assuring clients their turn would come and coaxing prosecutors to continue cases. Now with some breathing room, he had called Munoz to come in for a progress talk.

"There's one piece of the puzzle you can put in place," Munoz said when Earl hung up the phone. "Rattner is a member of the Sharks and was smuggling in cellphones and dope for the Nuestra Familia. If he can do that, a small gun is no problem."

"How'd you find out?" asked Earl.

"It's a solid source. We just can't use him as a witness."

"Did your man tell you how Rattner does it?"

"No, because he also runs a dope business up at San Quentin and probably uses the same method with a different guard."

"Jesus," Earl said. "That puts a whole new spin on things. Remember, Hartman promised Kate he had information on the smuggling of drugs and cellphones by prison guards. Maybe he had found out about Rattner's little enterprise and that's who he was talking about. If Rattner thought Hartman was going to lay him out that would sure as shit put Hartman in his crosshairs. Prison guards don't do so well in prison as inmates."

"Maybe we've been looking in the wrong direction?" Munoz said.

"If Hartman was afraid of Rattner, it makes sense to go into protective custody to get away from him. Maybe Rattner wasn't acting on behalf of somebody else. Maybe he had an agenda all his own and Officer Miller was just an unfortunate witness, not the target. Plus, handing the union the spokesperson for Prop 52 as a suspect would ensure the prison authorities wouldn't be too anxious to look anywhere else."

"Which makes it even more important," Munoz said, "that we get hold of that 602 form and see who Hartman named as a threat."

There was a rap at the door. McManis stepped in with a pleased look on his face. Over his shoulder, Earl could see Martha beaming with anticipation.

"You two look like you just won the Irish Sweepstakes," Earl said.

"Better than that lad," McManis said, flourishing a paper in his hand as if he was about to announce an Oscar winner.

"You want me to do a drum roll?"

"You should," McManis said. "We just won our appeal. We got a change of venue."

"Goddamn! That's great! I knew you could do it, James. Where'd they send us?"

"You won't believe it. Los Angeles. With 33 state prisons in California, most small counties have one. So to avoid the same problem as Haywood, the court decided they had to send us to a large city. LA is the closest and most convenient for the witnesses."

"So Lauren Taylor will have to set up shop down here and try the case on our home court," Earl said.

Martha stepped forward. "And it seems some of Mr. McManis' success has reflected onto you. Here's an email that I printed out, since you refuse to check them regularly." She handed it to him. "A lawyer from the guards union wants to meet with you."

"That's interesting," Earl said as he read the email. "She probably wants to discuss our subpoena for Hartman's 602s."

"Or take your measure," McManis said. "Maybe you're making somebody nervous."

CHAPTER 13

The envelope lay open on her desk, the offending contents had been crumpled into a ball and thrown against the wall. "Those stupid fucking assholes," she murmured. Lauren Taylor squeezed her eyes shut and sat fuming. After a minute, she got up and retrieved the letter. The Appellate Court had transferred the case to Los Angeles. Their decision was conveyed in the same bland language that would be used to announce a change in the hours at the local library. She returned to her desk and flopped down in her chair.

Why did this, of all things, have to happen, she asked herself? This could completely ruin her plans. This case was exactly what she had been waiting for. Her springboard up. Once she won the case, it would solidify the union's backing, and her career could really take off.

Now she felt as if she was in the grip of an icy hand and it was choking her. It was hard to breath. She had counted on a compliant court in Haywood County, where the judges faced reelection and all the jurors valued the prison for what it brought them. Trying the case in Los Angeles frightened her. She knew no one there, and no one knew her. She could never count on having a leg up down there.

This could rob her of her big chance. She had never envisioned spending her life as a big fish in a small pond. Her overriding need was to be become someone of consequence. To occupy a position of power. Becoming a prosecutor had been only a first step. Sure, being a DA gave her the power to pass judgment on people, hold their futures in her hands, deciding who should be locked away for decades and who should be granted a plea deal. But it wasn't enough.

She drew a deep breath and gathered herself. Nothing had changed, she told herself. It was still the same prize, the road had just gotten a little rougher. All that mattered was to win the case. She *must* win the case. Whatever it took.

Her mind pivoted to the cause of this change in her fortunes — Bobby Earl. Her general contempt for him as another defense lawyer, one of that unprincipled breed who would represent anyone for money, had shifted. Now it was personal. She hated *him*, with his aloofness and arrogance. His refusal to acknowledge that she held the winning hand and had the ability to play it. She would show him. Her anger built into a cold fury. She was going to crush him and that rich bitch of his.

But first she must refocus on the present and what needed to be done. She picked up the phone, and dialed the union's number. Buddy

Wright should hear the news from her first, so she could explain how this move to LA didn't really matter.

The union's headquarters were on J Street in Sacramento, four short blocks from the Capitol and the offices of the legislators who set the guards' salaries. The union owned the ten-story historic Beaux Arts building. The directory in the lobby listed 25 lawyers in the euphemistically named Union Legal Department, who were undoubtedly more familiar with the dining preferences and campaign bank accounts of each legislator than any provision of the Administrative Code.

Barbara Kipler met Earl as he stepped off the elevator on the top floor. She wore a drab business suit and a closed expression, like a kid in class hoping to go unnoticed so as not to be called on.

"Thanks for coming," she said. "Hope the flight was okay. Just follow me." She led him down a long hallway to a corner office. The sign on the door said President Bryan 'Buddy' Wright. She opened the door, stepped back for him to enter and closed it behind him.

It was a spacious office, larger than Earl's living room, with views on two sides overlooking Sacramento. A desk the size of a pool table was centered in front of a wall filled with photos of prominent politicians smiling with the man who was currently seated behind it. Buddy Wright wore an open-collared dress shirt and suspenders that pictured a chain of circus strongmen. On the desk his trademark Panama hat lay next to an unlit cigar. With the phone pressed to one ear, he waved Earl to a seat.

"Senator, it's our pleasure," he said into the receiver. "Those sky box seats are just sitting there unused." He listened and rolled his eyes in annoyance. "Of course they're not a gift. They're going to waste. Got a calendar conflict. Jerry will drop them off this afternoon."

Earl noticed a man with steel grey hair in a blue suit and rep tie, sitting to one side, silently studying Earl. His eyes were steady as a snake's.

Wright hung up the phone. "Mr. Earl, glad you found the time. I wanted to meet you. This is Jerry Reynolds, our Vice President." Buddy gestured toward the grey haired man who slowly nodded.

"I thought I was here to discuss our subpoenas with your legal staff."

"Oh, we'll get to that." Wright tipped back in his chair and picked up his unlit cigar. "That was pretty impressive, moving that trial to LA. I admire talent. Like to surround myself with smart people."

"Then you should be talking to James McManis, he handled the motion."

"I like that. It's good to give others credit. But I wanted to talk to *you*. We've got a first-rate legal department here. Could use a bright young man."

"I like being my own boss," Earl said.

"Understood, understood." Wright nodded in agreement. "Then maybe you could do me a favor. There's this commission looking into conditions at the port. The chairman asked me to find him a lawyer. Doesn't take much time, pays real well."

"Not my field, Mr. Wright. So tell me, why am I really here?"

Wright stared at him for a moment. "Why do you think?"

"Well, you probably figured I was going to bring up the fact that your union is backing the fight against Prop 52 and wouldn't be exactly inconsolable if their spokesperson disappeared off the scene. So I suppose you wanted to check out the opposition."

Wright curled his lip into a sneer. "My opposition? Son, look around you. You really think I'm concerned about some backstreet defense lawyer? I can pick up this phone and call the Governor. You got that? And you know what?" He thrust his face forward. "He'll take that call." He snorted smugly and eased back in his chair. "And you know why. This prison system that you're so worried about, who do you think runs it? The wardens? The Department of Corrections?" he scoffed. "You really think I'm concerned about somebody like you?"

"Then you tell me, why am I sitting here?" Earl asked.

Wright leaned forward, the veins in his neck bulging out. "Because I want to know who you're fronting for! In the middle of the campaign over Prop 52 you start bringing up the union's political contributions." Wright tossed a copy of Earl's subpoena across the desk. "Asking about some report, claiming our guards abuse prisoners, smuggle contraband. Who are you working for?"

"My client," Earl said.

"That asshole bitch that killed Miller? "Bullshit!" Wright shouted.

"You mean the same Officer Miller who came to you about the abuses at Haywood, thinking you'd do something about it? The same Officer Miller who ends up getting murdered and the only guy left alive is one of your union guards? That Officer Miller?" Earl cocked his head and frowned in mock bafflement. "And by coincidence, the person who gets blamed just happens to be the spokesperson for the Initiative you're fighting."

Wright sat staring at Earl, as if seeing him for the first time.

Earl locked eyes with him. "So what's it going to be?" Earl asked. "Do I get the records?"

Wright made a disgusted smirk and slowly shook his head. "You're a real fucking piece of work, you are. But guess what, hot shot? There is no report from an AG about Officer Miller. Never was. And I never met Miller. Never spoke to the man." Without taking his eyes away from Earl's, Wright snapped his fingers and reached out toward Reynolds who handed him a manila envelope. Buddy tossed it across the desk at Earl. "That's Hartman's 602 and his request for protective custody. Knock yourself out. Now get the fuck out of my office."

Earl took the file and stepped to the door, where he stopped and turned back. "Nice view from up here. Too bad the windows don't open. It could use some airing out."

Wright gave Earl a dismissive wave as he left.

After a moment, Wright turned to the man at his side. "What do you think, Jerry?"

"I think he's trouble," Reynolds said.

"Yeah, me too. I'm glad we decided to give him the records. He's the kind who doesn't give up. Sounds like he's starting to sniff around about what we might'a done to stop that Proposition. Hopefully, those records will send him in a different direction."

"It would help if we gave him a nudge in that different direction. Something to keep him occupied."

Wright sat thinking, chewing on his cigar. After a moment, he said, "Get hold of that Deputy DA in Los Angeles. What's her name? The one who wants us to make her a judge."

"Rosealee Martin," the man said.

"Tell her to dig up something on Earl that Lauren Taylor can use against him. Something personal. And tell her, no excuses. Tell her we want to see if we can count on her."

Outside the union building, Earl stopped on the sidewalk and tried to hold his expectations in check as he tore open the envelope. He pulled out two pieces of paper. The first was Hartman's request for protective custody. There was a line on the form designated for the "person or persons who constitute a threat." In it Hartman had written "The Aryan Brotherhood," a notorious white supremacist prison gang. "Shit" Earl murmured. He had been so sure that Hartman would have said he was afraid of Officer Rattner. It would have made so much sense: Rattner learned that Hartman knew he was smuggling drugs; he was concerned Hartman might expose him; Rattner threatened Hartman who then asked for protective custody; but Rattner got to him anyway. It all fit so nicely and a written statement by Hartman would have been the first piece of evidence to prove it.

Earl was deeply disappointed, but he tried to buoy himself with the hope that the second form might still give him an opening, a chance for a defense. The 602 form was designed for an inmate to complain about his treatment by the prison staff. Perhaps Hartman had used it to complain about Rattner. Earl quickly focused on the handwritten entry: "I have been subjected to numerous unwarranted cell searches and my personal property has not been returned." What the hell is this? Earl thought. He had subpoenaed these documents to provide some answers and all they did was raise more questions. Hell, he had enough questions, in fact, all he had were questions. He ran a hand over his face. Why would a bunch of tattooed skinhead racists threaten a timid hospital aid? In prison they moved in two different worlds. And what were the guards looking for in Hartman's cell? Maybe he did learn something that made somebody nervous enough to kill him. Earl stared off in bewilderment. "Jesus," he grumbled. "What a case."

Early Sunday morning, Earl and Sam ran along the beach, staying in the hard wet sand just above the surf line. Sam's fluid strides seemed effortless, barely disturbing the sand. Her pony tail bounced rhythmically on her back like a metronome. Earl labored, like he was carrying a sack of rocks across his shoulders, pounding into the sand with each stride as if trying to punish it.

Sam's dog Beauty trotted along beside her, accustomed to this routine. Henceforth loped a distance ahead. He turned suddenly and dropped onto the sand, his head resting on his paws, his eyes bright with anticipation. He had positioned himself directly in Beauty's path. When she neared, he leaped up and excitedly lumbered away, expecting her to chase him. Beauty trotted straight past, head raised, as if mystified that Henceforth could so confuse the courtship ritual that he would expect *her* to chase *him*. When Henceforth discovered he was not being pursued he stopped, cocked his head in puzzlement, then, holding steadfast to his plan, raced ahead to once again repeat the exercise, his confidence undiminished by yet another failure.

When their route brought them back to the Venice Pier, Earl and Sam stopped. Earl bent down, hands on his knees, his chest heaving, gasping for air. Sam stood upright, drawing deep, even breaths, calmly pulling her hair back to adjust the fastening on her pony tail. After a couple minutes, they started the walk back to the house, holding hands.

"I just got a curve ball on that Kate Carlson case," Earl said. They often talked about the case, grateful for the opportunity, free of complications, to discuss an aspect of what constituted such a large part of each of their lives — trial work. "I got the records from the union on Hartman, the inmate who was killed. The reason he listed for requesting protective custody was that he was being threatened by the Aryan Brotherhood." Earl lamented how this fact blew a hole in his theory that Rattner had killed Hartman to prevent him from exposing Rattner's smuggling activities.

"The AB?" Sam said. "Couldn't he have picked a less dangerous group? Didn't they just get indicted up north for shanking a prison guard? No wonder he asked to go into PC."

"Which plays right into the prosecutor's theory that this was an escape attempt," Earl said. "Being threatened by the AB sure sounds like a good reason to want out of there."

"Afraid so," she said with an apologetic tone. "A jury is probably going to see it that way, as well."

"But something bothers me. The AB and a guy like Hartman lived on two separate planets in the joint. Hartman wasn't even in their orbit. So maybe the AB was acting for someone else. But who? If the AB had been concerned about Hartman for themselves, they would have taken him out before he ever got into protective custody."

"Have you got any way to check out this AB threat?" Sam asked.

"That's the problem. I don't. The AB is really disciplined. There's not a chance any of them will talk to me."

They reached the house, and Henceforth shouldered his way past them to be first at the door, anxious to get on the couch for his morning nap. Sam turned to Earl. "He's your romantically challenged boy. So you get to hose him off. Last time he turned the couch into a sand box. Rubbing my bum with sandpaper is not exactly a turn-on."

"Yes," the man said into his cellphone. He lay on his back on a bed in a roadside motel room, wearing a military green tee-shirt and boxer shorts. The mirror on the opposite wall had a spider web crack in the corner and reflected a room that was well past its "use by" date. The veneer on the once stylish night table had peeled off the leg and the worn carpet had long ago defeated any attempts to remove an accumulation of overlapping stains, making it impossible to decipher its original color.

"I understand," the man said mildly, "you didn't want any further contact. But it has become necessary that I speak to you." His face was as expressionless as a waxen death mask. There was a remoteness in his eyes, as if they had seen things that caused him to withdraw inward, severing any connection with life. Perhaps he had been seared by the carnage of war, but more likely it arose from the icy heart of a professional killer.

"Our friend Rattner contacted me. I thought you should know." He paused to listen. "That's correct. He reported that a lawyer from the Attorney General's office visited him. This apparently has alarmed him." He paused again. "Yes, it is unfortunate. As you know," he continued, "when I accepted this assignment, we both understood my options were limited as to who I could use for this operation. It required someone with access inside the prison. That circumstance did not allow me to use a professional. For a civilian, our friend's reaction is not an unexpected occurrence. It's natural in someone who lacks experience in these matters and the necessary self-discipline."

He sat up effortlessly as he listened and swung his legs to the floor. "It's difficult to assess the level of fear in a civilian, but I didn't sense such a panic that he might do something foolish."

The man stood up as he listened, and stepped to the window that overlooked the parking lot. He used a finger to part the curtain a crack and stared out. His eyes were grey and steady, the eyes of a marksman. "I would set the risk of him tipping over at maybe twenty percent. That would normally be on the high side, but in this case it's probably acceptable."

The man dropped the curtain and listened. "Of course he doesn't know your identity. That was a foolish question," he said flatly. He stopped talking and listened. "This is your decision. You're certain then. You must be clear on this. You want the relationship terminated. Do I understand that correctly?"

The man walked back to the bed and sat on the edge as he listened. "Yes, it will look like an accident. I will have to find a suitable operational site and calculate the degree of difficulty. I'll send you a price by the normal channels." He started to end the call but stopped when the other party kept talking.

"No," he said calmly. "'Just do it' is not a contract. We will follow the proper procedures. You'll hear from me in the agreed manner." He hung up and tossed the cellphone onto the bed. He sat thinking for a long minute then stretched and rotated his neck. He ran his hands through the bristles of his buzz cut hair and stripped off his tee-shirt. His lean, well-muscled body bore several prominent scars, the by-products of a history of violent encounters. He nimbly dropped to the floor and did a long series of push-ups until a sheen of sweat showed on his back. Satisfied, he sprang up and walked to the closet. He hoisted out a tall padded rifle case with familiar ease and placed it gently on the bed.

CHAPTER 14

Bob Bishop's office was as simple and straight-forward as the man who occupied it. As Head of Felony Trials for the Los Angeles DA's Office, he felt no need to promote an image by covering his office walls with citations and awards. His reputation in the legal community was well established as a formidable trial lawyer and a man whose word you could trust.

Sam entered, shut the office door behind her and took a seat across the desk from him. Bishop, as usual, was coatless, his shirtsleeves rolled up and tie loosened. He tipped back in his chair and folded his hands behind his head.

"I've got a question," she said.

"Only one?" Bishop asked with a smile.

"I'd like you to keep this just between us."

"All right," he said.

"I have a relationship with a defense lawyer."

"Yeah, Bobby Earl. There's been talk."

"I know there has," she said unhappily. "Anyway, Bobby represents the defendant in that prison guard killing. The Haywood County case that was transferred down here."

"I'm familiar with it. We're providing their DA with an office. Luckily that's all we have to do with it. It's their show," Bishop said.

"Well, an issue has come up in the case. It would help Bobby to clarify things if he could talk to somebody on the inside of the Aryan Brotherhood. Jimmy Rappaport has this AB dropout who had been housed at Haywood. Jimmy's been trying to turn him, but I think he's finally given up."

"I know," Bishop said. "He talked to me about it. Jimmy was hoping the guy would 'come-to-Jesus' and help us make some cases, but the guy won't cooperate. He's been on ice for a couple years up at Pelican Bay. Jimmy has been threatening to drop him back into the general population at San Quentin. That would probably be a death sentence given the AB's oath of blood in and blood out, but the guy still won't budge. He's a real hard case."

"Since we're not involved in the prosecution of the Haywood case, do you think it would be proper for me to pass on the AB's name to Bobby?"

"What does Jimmy say? Is he completely through with the guy?"

"He says he is," Sam replied.

Bishop sat silently, staring up at the ceiling. After a moment, he started to reason out-loud. "Let's think this through. Letting Earl interview this guy won't compromise his value to us because he's refusing to talk. So the guy is up for grabs. At this point he's just another possible source of information. So I don't see a problem. But it's Jimmy's call." Bishop tipped forward and met Sam's eyes. "But out of fairness, if his name is passed on to Earl, the Haywood DA should also be told about him. And you should tell Jimmy what you plan to do with the information before you ask for the name. You don't have to give him Earl's name, but that it's going to the defense. If he's okay with it, I'm okay."

"Thanks Bob. I just needed some advice," Sam said.

"Well then, let me give you some more. You know that this relationship of yours poses a real problem for your career." He gave her a frank look and pursed his lips. "There was a time, when I first started, that DA's and defense lawyers considered themselves members of the same tribe. We were all trial lawyers. We had one side of a case and they had the other. We fought hard, but after it was over we'd have a drink, rib each other and go to dinner together. That's when your father was the top trial lawyer in the office, the prosecutor we all tried to model ourselves after." He gave her a comforting smile. "But that was then. I guess what's missing today is trust. We've become like the Democrats and Republicans in Congress with each side trying to claim the moral high ground over the other." Bishop paused to study Sam. "That's today's reality, Sam. Being with a defense lawyer, no matter how well respected, means your colleagues will always question your loyalty. They'll never completely trust you. It may not be fair and they may not even be right, but that unfortunately is the world you live in."

Sam was chatting with Martha while she waited for Earl to finish with a client. It surprised Martha how much she liked this young woman. Sam could have been the daughter she never had. If only she could talk to her like one. She would give Sam one simple piece of advice. When it came to men, don't let your heart make you settle for dreams about the future. Bobby Earl may be an honest, decent man, one whom Martha was deeply fond of, but she had seen his women come and go. She hoped that this time it would be different. Martha certainly knew something about these things. There had been a time she thought she could wait for Mr. McManis. But time has a tendency to run out.

Earl's client, a dumpy little man with hunched shoulders and thick glasses, left without a word, like a kid released from after-school detention. Earl pulled Sam into his office and gave her a hungry kiss. It was Friday and they had the weekend ahead.

"Slow down, big fella, I've got something to tell you."

Earl dutifully took a seat. She told him about her colleague's unsuccessful efforts to flip an Aryan Brotherhood drop out. He was no longer of any use to her office, so Bob Bishop had signed off on her releasing his name to Bobby. She had also sent a message to the Haywood DA that they were passing on the name.

"Maybe you can convince this guy to tell you why the AB was threatening Hartman?" she said.

"Sam, I really appreciate it, but you didn't have to do that."

"I know that," she said.

Earl reached out and took her hand between his. "I know how hard that was for you. Hell, just being with me creates problems for you in your office. I hate you being in that situation."

"Bishop knows about us. He said there's been talk in the office."

"Sam, I'm really sorry. It's not fair. You're the one who gets all the heat. I wish I could take some of it off you."

The intercom buzzed. It was Martha. Mrs. Miller, the guard's widow was on the line. Earl and Sam exchanged questioning looks. Earl picked up the line.

"Mr. Earl, somebody broke into my house. Went through all my drawers, closets, everything. Whole place is a mess. Do you think it was them guards?"

"Is anything missing?"

"Not that I can see, but I can't really tell."

"They were probably looking for money or jewelry," Earl said, knowing full well that was not the case, but not wanting to worry her.

"Well, good luck on finding any of that lying around. I was afraid it was them guards, looking for those tapes you mentioned."

Earl knew that was exactly what they were looking for. "Mrs. Miller, call the Haywood police. Ask for Detective Carter. I'm going to call him right now."

"But what if they come back? It's just me and my boy. I'm going to stay with my sister for a while. Lamont can finish the school year up there. Goodbye, Mr. Earl. I gotta go."

Earl sat in one of the Plexiglas visitor booths in Pelican Bay, California's super-max prison, reserved for inmates considered too violent to be placed in any other state prison. He was the room's sole occupant. After passing through the initial screening in the lobby, he had walked down a series of lengthy cement corridors without seeing a single person. At regularly spaced security gates, a disembodied voice over a speaker questioned him, and then the gate opened electronically. The visitors' room, like the corridors, was as sterile and lifeless as a test tube. No life-affirming graffiti or debris was visible to confirm any prior human presence.

The room was eerily quiet. Finally, Earl heard the scrape and jingle of chains. Four guards appeared escorting an inmate in an orange jumpsuit who shuffled slowly, in mincing steps due to ankle chains. His hands were cuffed behind his back and attached to a thick waist chain in what the inmates called a "three-piece suit." The slow procession eventually arrived at the Plexiglas door to Earl's booth.

Tommy "The Beast" Thompson was barn-door wide and thickly muscled. His dirty brown hair hung down in clumped strands to his shoulders and his hermit's beard was more like a bramble bush. The guard nudged him inside, and the door locked behind him. He backed up against the door and extended his bound hands through a slot to be un-cuffed, just as he had done earlier through his cell door to be manacled. Thompson was never allowed to be in the presence of a guard when his hands were free.

He stood and stared at Earl with the cold interest of a curator paused before a glass display case. Finally, he sat down and picked up the phone on his side. Earl saw the shamrock tattooed on the back of his hand. The Brand. The symbol earned by those who killed at the direction of the Aryan Brotherhood.

"Thanks for agreeing to see me," Earl said. "I've got nothing to do with the cops or the DA. I'm a private attorney defending someone charged with killing a prison guard. I hoped you might help."

Thompson sat silently for a minute studying Earl. In his world he was a predator and he was sizing up Earl as prey. Earl could feel his contempt as he calculated Earl's meager chances on the survival scale.

"First, go make a phone call for me. Then we'll see," he said in a voice made raspy from disuse.

Earl knew where this was headed. The Aryan Brotherhood, like all prison gangs, used pliable lawyers to pass seemingly innocuous messages. The trouble was they contained code words. A birthday greeting could, in reality, be someone's death sentence.

"You know I can't do that," Earl said.

"Can't or won't?" Thompson asked.

"Won't," Earl said.

"So why should I talk to you?"

"The better question is why not? I'm not asking you to be a snitch. What else have you got on your busy schedule? You live in a windowless cement box the size of a parking space, 23 hours a day. If they remember, they let you out to exercise by yourself in a dog run. You have no human contact. Your food is shoved under the door to you on a tray. So why not sit and shoot the shit with somebody for a while. What do you have to lose?"

The skin around Thompson's eyes crinkled in amusement. "You talk like you've got some brass, but then again, you're on the other side of this screen, aren't you?"

"Look, this place crushes people. I know that. Solitary confinement plays with your head after a while. I'm only stating the obvious. No disrespect intended. Why not take a break?"

Thompson sat silently for a moment before giving a faint nod as if finishing an internal debate. "You know," he said, "an old con once said this place was like being sealed in a capsule and shot into space."

"Good description," Earl said.

Earl knew he had to start slowly with Thompson to get him to talk. "So why'd you drop out, anyway?"

Thompson seemed surprised by the question at first. Then he shrugged his shoulders and said, "All right. Why not? You seem harmless enough." His arrogant gaze affirmed that Earl was here at his sufferance. "I liked carrying the Brand. Always did. I liked the power, the respect. I even liked the violence." His eyes gleamed with the memory. "A knife fight is really like a dance with moves and counter moves. In a way it can be beautiful. Sort of a dark and brutal moment of truth." He paused to see if Earl understood. "See, in prison we live in a different kind of society, one where violence is accepted as justified. And I was good at it. It gave me stature. And it felt righteous. In the beginning we were like Holy Warriors, protecting our tribe."

Earl did not find this flow of words unexpected. Men in prison spend years and years doing nothing but reading and talking. They develop a patter; a certain fluency.

"So what went wrong?" Earl asked.

"I was a member of the Green Light Committee. Nobody got hit unless we sanctioned it. If we agreed, his name went in the hat and we all drew to pick who would do it. Then one day this snitch gets moved to where we can't get to him. So our chief puts the name of the snitch's wife in the hat. He says people had to know what would happen if they snitched. That if we couldn't get to them, we'd get to their family. We'd use brothers on the outside." Thompson furrowed his brow in disgust. "Man, we were never about making war on women and children. So I dropped out."

"Did you know Adam Hartman when you were at Haywood?"

"Sure. Little do-gooder dude. All the cons talked to him. He was grapevine central. He would write up complaints for them. Even wrote letters for them. He was an okay dude. Never had much to do with him."

"Did you know a guard named Clyde Rattner?"

Thompson's eyes turned wary and he gave a slight nod.

"Look, I know that Rattner was packing for Nuestra Familia," Earl said. "Do you think there was any way that Hartman may have known what Rattner was doing?"

Thompson hesitated for a moment. "There are always rumors in prison. It's the coin of the realm, so to speak. Hartman could have heard something or somebody could have told him. They told him everything else."

"Look, I assume Rattner may have done some work for the AB, as well. I don't want to know and I don't care."

"I'm greatly reassured," Thompson said facetiously. "That takes a great weight off my mind."

"I understand," Earl said with a grin. "Let's just say, hypothetically, that Rattner found out that Hartman knew he was smuggling drugs and cellphones. Suppose Rattner got afraid that Hartman might rat him. Do you think the AB would have helped Rattner?"

"What do you mean helped?"

"If Rattner came to the AB and asked them to take care of Hartman, would your people have been willing to do that?"

Thompson pursed his lips in derision. "What the fuck for? That's his problem. Look, even if Rattner was doing some business for *us*. And I do mean *if*," he said sternly. "That's a lot different than us taking care of business for *him*. We would never put ourselves in a spot where he could turn snitch on us."

"So the AB never threatened Hartman? Put out a hit on him?"

"Hartman? No, why would we?"

"I checked his file. He requested to be put in PC. The reason he gave was that the AB had threatened him."

"Oh, that. Dudes do that all the time. It's easier to get PC if you say the AB is after you. We have sort of a reputation." The corners of Thompson's mouth curved slightly upward. "But we never threatened people. Shit, if we wanted you dead, you were dead."

"Do you know how Rattner was able to smuggle stuff in?"

"That's way above your pay grade, little man."

"Well, thanks for talking to me," Earl said as he gathered up his papers. "I know you have to do your time, I just wish it wasn't under these conditions."

"And thank you for not asking how a smart guy like me ended up in a place like this. If you had, I mighta' thrown your name in that hat." Thompson's eyes widened in wild, maniacal delight as his lips curled back from his teeth. It was a nightmarish image. Earl wondered about all the men for whom this sight had been their last.

CHAPTER 15

The wood-sided house was in need of painting. The sun snuck through the branches of a large oak tree to make dancing patterns on the corrugated tin roof and glinted on windows layered with dust. The wild grass in the front yard was fender high on a rusting pickup sitting on cinder blocks.

The screen door slammed open. Clyde Rattner hurried down the front porch steps toward his truck. A thin young man with a week's growth of beard on his hollow cheeks was filling a bucket with water at the side of the house.

"Who was that on the phone, Pa?' the young man called.

"You never mind. Just tend to your chores," Rattner said over his shoulder.

"It was about that government lawyer fella,' weren't it?

"You just get them dogs fed, like I told ya.' "

"Well, where you headed in such a damn hurry? You gonna be home for supper?"

"I gotta meet somebody," Rattner said as he climbed into his truck.

The young man cursed under his breath as Rattner sped off. At the bottom of the drive, Rattner turned onto a dirt road carved into the side of the mountain, which curved down for half a mile before meeting up with the main highway. There was a steep drop over the edge, but Rattner knew every curve and dip of the road, so he hurtled down the mountain, spraying rocks at each turn.

His thoughts were a jumble. "The mother fucker promised me there would be no blow-back," he said to himself. "What'd he call it? A cookie cutter case for the cops. They'd never take a second look, he said. So why'd that fucking lawyer from the AG show up? A fucking Attorney General. I swear to God, this better be made to go away, because I'm not gonna ride this beef alone."

He slowed down as he approached a familiar hair-pin turn. He pulled hard on the steering wheel, skidding into the curve, when he heard a muffled pop, followed by the slap, slap of rubber. A blow-out. The truck veered violently to the right. "Oh, sweet Jesus," Rattner moaned as he plunged over the edge. The truck tumbled down, end over end, into the deep ravine. Halfway down it crashed into a boulder outcropping and caromed off to continue falling, its metal shell crunched and folded like a crushed beer can. At the bottom, it slammed top down onto the floor of a dry river bed, as fixed as a gymnast nailing a landing. Suddenly it burst into flame, sending up an ugly black plume of smoke against the clear blue sky like a signal for help. But it was already too late.

Sitting in her new borrowed office, Lauren Taylor remembered the anxiety she had felt about the transfer to Los Angeles and laughed at herself. One call from the union and the DA here had done everything but adopt her. They gave her this office, use of their clerical staff and access to the books they kept on jurors past performance. Even Detective Carter got a cubical among their investigators.

She stepped to the mirror and passed her fingers through her hair as she admired herself. She liked being attractive, the power it bestowed and the doors it opened. But the mechanics of sex or love itself had never been very satisfying, more a means to an end.

As she reflected, a memory thrust itself forward, elbowing her thoughts aside. It was about her father, the pastor at the Divine Word Baptist Church. After her sister got pregnant in high school, every time Lauren was allowed out with a boy, he would warn her about the foul beast of lust. The poor fool. To think she would ever have been swept up in a tidal wave of passion and let some boy have his way with her. She snorted. She was always the one in control, never somebody's play thing. By the time she was fifteen she had stopped going out with the local farmboys. Grown men were the ones she chose, they were the ones with the money and were surprisingly easy to manipulate. She snickered, remembering how her father would wait up for her to return, as if he were some Hazmat official seeking to detect the presence of sulfurous vapors to confirm that a bargain had been made with Lucifer.

She had left all that behind her now. Left him, left that small town and all those people with their small ambitions. She was not going to settle for some commonplace life. But right now she had to get to court. She had a little surprise for Bobby Earl.

Earl stepped out of the elevator on the ninth floor, commonly referred to in the downtown LA courthouse as Murderer's Row. Any homicide case that involved high publicity, a security risk or a protracted trial was assigned to one of its six courtrooms, each presided over by a judge who always remained firmly in control of the proceedings and could be counted on to steer a case away from an unwelcome controversial verdict. The ghost of O.J. Simpson still haunted these halls.

As Earl walked down the crowded hallway, he passed a TV camera man seated on a bench, reading the sports page. Earl knew that having only one TV camera meant there must be a pool agreement among the local stations. He paused at the door of the courtroom. The sign read, *Department 110, Judge Bonnie Lee Parker.*

It could have been a worse draw. Judge Parker had been a partner in a large downtown law firm, where she specialized in Estates and Trusts. Since she had, as the saying goes, "come from money," preserving rich people's wealth was a comfortable career choice. Reasonably ambitious, her political contributions seemed aimed at securing an appointment to the Appellate Court, so this stint in a trial court was just a first step. On the bench, she had brought with her the calm, deliberate style that her former law practice fostered. It seemed an article of faith with her never to surrender her composure. No matter how lawyers or defendants behaved, she never gave them the satisfaction of an emotional response. She had learned quickly that the prosecution was supposed to get the close calls, but not all the calls. Acknowledged as very smart, she was the consensus choice last year among defense lawyers for the Golden Glove Award, given to the judge who was considered the most difficult to slip one by.

Earl pushed through the door. Judge Parker's courtroom always seemed slightly cooler than any of the others. There was an unhurried, controlled pace among her staff, all of whom were women. The clerk, bailiff and court reporter had all been with her for over 5 years.

Before approaching the DA, before talking to his client in the lock-up, before anything else, Earl went to pay homage to the court clerk. As in every courtroom, there were a hundred ways in which a clerk could either help or hurt a lawyer in front of a jury. She could communicate her opinion about a lawyer by small gestures, such as showing irritation over the way he requested an exhibit, as opposed to cheerfully searching for one when asked. Juries identified with the clerk as a working person just trying to do their job, so they resented any self-important lawyer who appeared to be making it difficult for them.

Equally as important was the clerk's role as the only available off-the-record conduit of information to or from the judge. The clerk was the person who regularly had the opportunity of being alone with the judge in chambers, where she might comment on how a lawyer was treating her and the other staff, voice her impressions about the case or relay conversations she overheard during the recess. All the little things that might have a subtle influence on any judge.

Alice Russell, Judge Parker's clerk, always dressed a bit more fashionably than her colleagues, as if to signal that she was a cut above. Which, as Earl could attest, she was. She sat with her hands folded on top of her desk and watched Earl over the top of her wire-rim glasses as he approached. She pursed her lips together in a failed attempt to suppress a smile, anticipating their usual playful exchanges.

"Mrs. Russell," Earl said with mock seriousness, giving a slight bow with his head. "And how fares the boy genius?"

"He better hit the books a little harder or he's going to end up a lawyer," she said.

"Perish the thought," Earl said, eyes wide with mock alarm.

"So what is this circus you've brought to my courtroom?" she said, nodding toward the reporters.

"You'll have to ask the DA, I'm afraid. I tried to be reasonable. Even offered to settle for a dismissal. But there's just no satisfying some people."

Alice gave him a skeptical look.

"By the way," she said. "She's fired the first salvo in the paper war." She lifted a thick sheaf of papers then dropped them back on the desk. "She's got your copy."

Earl turned and walked over to the court reporter, who was straddling her stenographic machine. He had seen more than one cross-examination interrupted, followed by looks of disdain from the jury, when a court reporter threw up her hands in disgust to complain about a lawyer's machine gun delivery or been found guilty of talking over a witness. When the trial approached, Earl would ask her if she could wait for the recess to tell him if the rhythm of his examinations ever left her without breathing space. On this occasion he assured her he would provide the spelling of any appellate cases he cited, so she wouldn't have to search for them. Then he headed for the DA.

Lauren Taylor leaned back against the jury box, arms crossed, staring straight ahead with a smug expression as Earl approached.

"You're late," she said, not yet looking at Earl.

"I don't think so," he said looking at his watch. "In fact, I'm early."

"No, I was referring to the autopsy," she said. "I assumed you still had that fascination with dead bodies." She smiled to herself, clearly enjoying this.

"I don't follow."

"Clyde Rattner is dead," she said flatly.

Earl was stunned. "What happened?"

"A car accident," she said.

Earl paused, absorbing the information, puzzled by Taylor's reaction to the loss of her main witness. "Sorry to hear it. But that seems to leave a bit of a hole in your case."

"Not really," she said and handed Earl a stack of legal papers. "I've filed a motion to let me use his statement to the Detective after the shooting. That's all I really need. Sorry you won't have a chance to cross-examine him."

Earl started to leaf through the documents.

"Oh," she said. "There's more good news. Your client had a boyfriend. It's always heartwarming when a woman her age finds someone."

Earl was becoming annoyed. "Why don't you stop fucking around and just tell me what you're talking about."

"Mr. Carter," she said over her shoulder.

Joe Carter rose from his seat inside the jury box and sidestepped past the empty chairs. He handed Earl an accordion file folder filled with papers.

"These are copies of the correspondence between Kate Carlson and Adam Hartman and the reports on Officer Rattner's accident," Taylor said. "More like love letters, really. But we'll let the jury decide."

The clerk announced that the judge was taking the bench, so Earl took a seat. He was angry at being ambushed by this news and burning for a way to wipe that smile off Taylor's face. She was too pleased with this development. This could be trouble. Real trouble. He needed to get back to his office and assess the damage.

Judge Parker strode to the bench. In her fifties, she had short grey hair, probing eyes and a confident demeanor. A white collar showed outside her robe and a single strand of pearls hung around her neck.

"Good morning, Mr. Earl. And welcome, Ms. Taylor. I see you're both here on the Carlson case. We should bring out the defendant." She nodded at the bailiff.

Kate took a seat next to Earl. She had been transferred down to the LA women's jail. Earl had arranged for some of her clothes to be deposited there. She was wearing a dark blue Armani pantsuit and a white blouse. The once tailored suit hung loosely. She had lost weight. Her face was care-worn and tired.

"I should divulge to the parties that when I practiced law, my firm had dealings with Ms. Carlson's firm," the judge said. "I never handled any of those matters and never dealt directly with Ms. Carlson on a professional or private basis. As such, I see no need to recuse myself. Do either of you have any questions or comments on that issue?"

The last thing Earl wanted was to roll the dice in hopes of a better judge. The odds were way too long. He and Taylor both answered in the negative.

"Now, I see the People have filed a motion on an evidentiary matter. I assume you'll want time to reply, Mr. Earl, so we'll set that over to our pretrial conference. I expect to pick a trial date at that time, so please have any other motions filed by then. Is there anything further?"

Earl stood. He remembered Hartman's 602, complaining of excessive searches of his cell. "I've just been handed some of the material recovered from Mr. Hartman's prison cell. I am making a formal request at this time for any other material recovered in that search or any material seized in any previous searches to be made available to the defense."

The judge turned to Taylor. "Any problem Ms. Taylor?"

"No, your Honor."

She turned to the clerk. "Alice, give us a four-week date."

Earl sat, staring at the folder. He had driven at a furious pace back to the office, impatient to see if Taylor really had something or was just trying to give him heart burn. But now he hesitated, reluctant to learn any more bad news. Finally, he heaved a sigh and poured out the contents onto his desk.

He first pulled out the reports on Rattner's accident. He wanted to get them out of the way before bracing himself to read the letters. As he read through the accident reports, the facts seemed quite straightforward. Rattner had driven down from his house in the hills above Haywood along a narrow mountain road. He had a blow-out on a hair-pin turn. His truck went over the side and down a deep ravine. The autopsy found he had died of a broken neck and internal injuries. Rattner had been tossed around inside the cab like dice rattled in a cup. A stern reminder to wear a seat belt.

The facts looked straightforward enough. But it seemed like one hell of a coincidence that the main witness in the case gets killed just before trial. He should probably look more closely at this, but not now. The letters had to be faced, it was time.

Earl had asked Kate, in one of their first interviews to have her office send over the correspondence she had with Hartman. The file had been waiting for him when he returned that day from Haywood. One of the perks of working in a large law firm was never having to use the postal service for local mail. You just gave it to the office messenger to hand deliver.

He had originally just skimmed over Hartman's letters and filed them in one of his binders. He went to the cabinet, pulled them out and returned to his desk. Earl arranged both sets of letters in chronological order. The letters from Kate, which the DA had provided, were barely legible copies of the originals. Kate's letters had been handwritten, not typed, in a clear, graceful script. The envelopes all bore a prison stamp of "CENSORED." Like all inmate correspondence, they had been routinely read by the staff before being released to Hartman to insure they contained no contraband or security issues. A police report had been included which explained that Carlson's letters to Hartman had been recovered from his cell after the shooting. Hartman's letters to her were in the nearly indecipherable handwriting apparently taught in every medical school. His were also inside envelopes stamped "CENSORED," because the staff likewise read all outgoing mail.

Earl rearranged the letters. Rather than arrange them chronologically, Earl made two separate rows. The DA only had the letters from Kate to Harman that were found in his cell. The plausibility of Taylor's interpretation of them as "love letters" had to be based solely on the content of Kate's letters. She did not have Hartman's letters to Kate.

As Earl read Kate's correspondence to Hartman, he noted, with some concern, a growing sense of familiarity on her part. She described how much she enjoyed their meetings and was looking forward to the next. She expressed admiration for Hartman's courage, and outrage at his unjust incarceration. The final paragraph of Kate's last letter did nothing to alleviate Earl's unease.

> *You must put your trust in me. I have agreed to help you and will not let you down. But it will take time to gather the material that is needed to help you. So be patient. When you are out, I will find a place for you. And if for some reason that does not work out, there is always Europe. I have lots of contacts there.*
> *Yours, Kate*

Earl knew how Kate's words *should* be interpreted. But that was because he had talked with her and knew what they were referring to. Next, he turned to Hartman's letters to Kate, which the DA did not have. His first letter to Kate set the basis of their relationship. In it he promised information that she could use in the Proposition 52 campaign. But then Earl became alarmed as he read another Hartman letter, written about a month before the shooting.

> *Kate,*
> *I never thought I would get someone like you to help me. You won't regret it. I know this will be difficult, but I know you can do it. I promise I will come through on my end.*
>
> *I hope you now see why, early on, I told you not to register with the prison as my attorney. If you had, we would have been unable to use the visitors' room where it is so much easier to have some privacy.*
>
> *I am glad you understand that I have to be very careful.*
>
> *I can't wait to see you.*
> *Yours, Adam*

Earl always tried to evaluate the weight of any piece of evidence, prosecution or defense, through the eyes of the jury. Coldly, analytically.

Earl leaned forward and cupped his face in his hands. He had to focus, erase everything that he knew outside the contents of Kate's letters. How would the DA portray them? How would a jury see them?

He could hear her voice. Yes, Carlson was in love with Hartman. So, when he told her the Aryan Brotherhood was threatening his life, she agreed to save him. That was the "help" she was referring to — helping him escape. The reason she didn't come right out and profess her love for him in her letters was simply because she knew the staff read all incoming mail and she didn't want to be ridiculed or watched more closely. And the "necessary material" she needed to gather was a gun small enough to be concealed. She even referred to a "place" for him when he got out, meaning she would hide him or, if necessary, get him out of the country with her "contacts."

Earl thought such an interpretation was a bit of a stretch. It made sense on a certain level and each piece could be made to fit, but only if you *wanted* to see it that way. A jury's judgment would depend on the strength of the rest of Taylor's case. These letters were not a knockout blow, but they sure didn't help. Hell, he thought, the DA hadn't needed any additional poker chips, it was the defense that was playing with IOU markers.

The only sure way to refute it was for Carlson to testify. Sure, she could explain that the "help" she was offering was to support his application for parole and to assist in seeking to reinstate his medical license. The "place" she was referring to was on the staff of the hospital where she served on the Board. But her testimony would allow the DA to demand Hartman's letters to Kate; letters that didn't have the tone of a businesslike relationship.

What else could go wrong with this case? It was so frustrating! At almost every turn, what would have normally been a defense advantage had been turned into a point for the prosecution. From not using the attorney's booth in favor of contact visits in the family visiting room; to not going through the metal detector; to only submitting to pat-downs. And now converting a seemingly motiveless act by a respected lawyer into a lover's reckless rescue attempt. It was time to have a talk with Kate Carlson.

Before he left, however, he needed to prepare a formal request to the DA. Earl knew Kate's letters were not all that was recovered from Hartman's cell. He needed to see the rest, and he didn't want to rely on Lauren Taylor's verbal assurance in court. Turning to his nemesis, Son of Hal, he typed a description of the material he wanted access to and the reasons supporting his request. He stopped there. Putting it into the proper legal form would give Hal the perfect opportunity to make a meal of his work. Martha could do that. There was no reason to bait the ogre. Son of Hal would just have to wait for his chance to send Earl into a rage. Right now, he needed a clear head.

CHAPTER 16

Earl never considered himself eye candy, but in the attorney visiting room of the Women's Central Jail, he was drawing a few come-hither smiles. He chalked it up to his looking like a private attorney whom the women believed would be their magic carpet out of there. It was painful to see these women trying to look alluring in their orange jump suits, offering up the only currency they had to spend.

Kate Carlson, on the other hand, was in a far different mood. She was reading copies of her letters to Hartman, which Earl had passed her. When she finished she pushed them aside and raised her eyebrows in a question. "Is there a problem?" she asked.

"It's a problem of interpretation," Earl said evenly. He explained the interpretation the DA would put on these "love letters" and the complication posed if they were forced to put into evidence Hartman's overly familiar reply.

"That's ridiculous," she said and explained again how, in exchange for his information, she had agreed to back his bid for parole and find him a place at a hospital if she got his license reinstated. "The 'material' I needed to gather were affidavits from Adam's colleagues and friends in support of his parole application and documentation proving he had bona fide offers of employment. By mentioning 'Europe' I was merely noting that if his medical license was reinstated he could always seek a position over there and I would help him."

"Kate, you're a very smart lawyer, but this is a criminal trial. We hear all the time that a jury trial is a search for the truth. That's not exactly how it works. In a trial like this, the jury is going to be presented with two competing stories of the why and how this occurred. They are then asked to choose between them. It's black and white, guilty or not guilty. The truth usually lies somewhere in between."

"Well, I'll just explain it to them," she said confidently.

Earl sat thinking for a minute. Putting Kate on the stand was a gamble he had hoped to avoid. There were so many facts she would be challenged to explain -- the use of the visitor's room for "privacy," the gunshot residue on her hands, the bullet in her car, the "coincidence" of the shooting occurring right after her visit. And Earl could just envision Lauren Taylor's mocking derision when Kate offered her explanation that the guards union set her up. Kate would probably grow increasingly resentful under Taylor's scornful questions, allowing the DA to eventually chip away Carlson's image of a level headed, senior law partner and expose the steel underneath. A tough woman is just the kind a jury might think would risk passing Adam a gun.

"Kate," Earl said. "Making a decision on whether or not to testify is very complicated and carries with it immense consequences. Let's discuss that when we get closer to the jumping-off point." Earl was counting on the fact that Kate, like all lawyers, had undoubtedly heard the nightmare tales of clients insisting on taking the stand only to sabotage their own case. These anecdotes were a stark affirmation of the of the old courthouse maxim that the truth alone did not always protect you.

Kate's face turned somber as she silently contemplated Earl's unspoken message.

"What about a boyfriend?" Earl asked and paused when he saw her hesitate. "Look, Kate, I'm not suggesting we put your personal life on display. But I know the DA will try to make this into one of those stories that are featured on the covers of magazines at grocery checkouts. Some kind of desperate prison romance. One way to counter that is to present someone with whom you have a real relationship."

Kate stared off in silence, immersed in her own thoughts.

Earl could see he'd stumbled into a touchy subject. "Kate, I'm not trying to pry into your personal life to satisfy some leering curiosity. Believe me, this is very important to the case."

Kate turned and stared deeply at Earl. She dropped her gaze and heaved a sigh as if bracing herself for an ordeal, then looked up. "I had always thought" she said with a faint smile of regret, "that marriage and a family were in my future. I wanted children, but at the right time, with the right man. As work absorbed more and more of my life, these plans kept getting pushed further and further into the future. I always regarded this as a temporary condition." She looked at Earl and shrugged. "Along the way there were men, of course. A series of liaisons of convenience. Some were married, others were not, but none were ever such that they could claim a place in my life. And now, it seems, I have finally caught up with my future. I'm alone, Bobby."

"Kate, I understand." Earl said flatly. He was determined not to demean her by assuming words of sympathy would be welcome. "But, you must have companions for social events, your firm's annual dinner, Bar functions, award dinners."

"I have been escorted to those types of affairs. But of late I seem to find myself only being invited out socially to even up the number of guests at a dinner party."

Earl nodded his acceptance and felt a bit chastened. To break the mood, he said, "There's something else I need to tell you."

"How much good news can one girl handle?" she said with a feigned smile.

"That guard, the one who shot Hartman. He was killed in a car accident."

Her eyes widened in surprise. "I won't pretend I'm sorry, but doesn't that help us. The DA won't have his testimony."

"The DA has filed a motion with the judge to use Rattner's statement to the detective."

"But that's hearsay. She can't do that."

"Well, she's got a theory for its admission. I'll file a brief in opposition. But there's something about that accident that seems sort of odd. Could be nothing, but I'm going to take Manny and go up there to have a look."

Kate nodded, still enmeshed with her concerns over these developments. "You know, I got involved with the Initiative in order to try to solve real problems, ones that mattered. It sounds idealistic, even a bit naive, I know. But it's the truth." She gave Earl a bitter smile. "Ironic, isn't it? Now my most immediate problem is keeping a very amorous lesbian from crawling into my bed at night."

The cherry red Mustang gave a low rumble when Munoz downshifted to start up the narrow mountain road leading to Rattner's house. Bobby Earl sat in the passenger seat, Henceforth in back. Rattner's address, listed in his personnel file, had only been a P.O. Box, but the postmaster at the general store had given them directions. On the drive, Earl had taken the precaution of putting Henceforth in the back seat because of the dog's insistence on sticking his head out an open window. As the air rushed by, his saggy jowls fluttered in the breeze, sending a steady spray of drool behind him.

Earl's mind was a jumble of the loose pieces to the puzzle this case had become. The official conclusion that Rattner's death was an accident was one of them. It seemed too much of a coincidence that just before the trial the sole living witness to what happened runs his truck off a road he had driven down safely a thousand times before. Earl didn't believe in such coincidences.

But just as nagging was his need to answer the first question that any jury would be asking him. If Kate Carlson didn't smuggle the gun inside, who did? Earl was convinced he knew. It was Rattner. But he needed to prove it. His only evidence came from Manny's "unnamed source." Just saying it might work in a TV drama, but not in a real courtroom. He needed something solid, something with the ring of truth in it. That was why they were here.

Munoz pulled off the road and down a rutted dirt lane. He stopped a few yards from the house and they got out, leaving a disappointed Henceforth behind. The front door opened and a gaunt young man in bib overalls stepped onto the porch.

"You can stop right there or I'll loose the dogs on ya.' What ya' all want?" he asked. The incessant barking from behind the house gave voice to his threat.

"I'm Bobby Earl, this is Manny Munoz. I represent Kate Carlson. I wanted to talk to you about your father."

"I was told not to talk to ya'. So you best git."

"Listen," Earl said. "I don't think your father's death was an accident. I would think you'd be interested in finding that out."

"I already know it weren't no accident."

"What makes you say that?" Earl asked.

"Pa drove that road goin' on fifteen years. He weren't about to drive off the edge."

"So let's talk. I'm willing to try to find out who was responsible. Nobody else is looking into it. The cops sure aren't. They already closed the case."

The young man stared silently at them with suspicious eyes, uncertain what to do.

"Look, just tell me what happened that day. Then we'll leave."

"A damned lawyer started it. Some kinda' General came a few days before wantin' to see Pa."

"You mean an Attorney General?" Earl asked.

"Yeah, somethin' like that. Askin' Pa questions. Got him all riled up."

"Then what happened?"

"That day Pa he got a call from somebody around suppertime. Don't know who. He took off, mad as hell. Said he had to meet somebody. He never come back."

"What do you think happened?" Earl asked.

"We've talked enough. You get movin' or I'll set them dogs on ya.'

Earl and Munoz returned to the car and followed the dirt lane out to the road. They turned right, rather than back down the mountain and pulled off to the side to wait. While they sat, Earl explained to Manny that the AG mentioned was undoubtedly Frank Corbett, the one who convinced Travis Miller to wear a wire and make a case on the Sharks. Corbett felt responsible for Miller's death and was convinced that the Sharks had used Rattner to murder Miller. So he had probably rattled Rattner with questions about the shooting.

After a few minutes an old short bed pickup truck rattled down the rutted lane and swung left onto the road. The gaunt young man inside was holding a cellphone to his ear.

"Looks like dog-boy is reporting in," Munoz said as they got out of the car and retraced their path back to the house.

Munoz walked toward the back of the house, which raised an increasingly frenzied chorus of barking. In the distance they could hear Henceforth baying in reply. Trees groaned in the wind. Earl stepped onto the porch. Dry leaves scampered across the wooden planks. He knocked on the door. Not expecting an answer, he already had a credit card out and began to slip the flimsy door latch. After a minute, the door swung open and he stepped inside.

The room was dark. Sunlight struggled to penetrate through the dust-covered windows. The air smelled of boiled vegetables and someone with an aversion to bathing. A tired couch faced a television console backed up against one wall. On the kitchen counter, flies hovered above a stack of dirty dishes like planes circling to land. An old refrigerator, plastered with stickers, jolted into life and hummed grumpily.

Munoz returned. "Seems that young man wasn't bluffing about the dogs. There's a whole kennel of them out back. And judging from their size and attitude, they weren't bred to be show dogs."

"He's raising fighting dogs," Earl said with disgust.

"You got it. You ever see one of those matches? We busted one once. My guys wanted to take the bastards out back and give them some bare knuckle tattoos."

"I'll call it in when we get back," Earl said. "But right now, let's get to work, no telling how long we've got."

For the next thirty minutes they methodically searched the house, returning everything to its original place. Finally, Munoz called to Earl from the front room. Next to him on the kitchen counter was a small plastic lunch cooler with its top hinged open. On the side *RATTNER* was printed in black marker.

Earl walked over. Inside, resting on the top tray was an array of photographs. The nude women posing in them were not shy about displaying their wares.

"Porno for lunch?" Earl asked.

"Porno's not allowed in prison," Munoz said. "But everyone has it for their dates with Rosey Palm and her five sisters. Rattner probably put his sandwiches on top of the photos. Remember the guards don't go through a metal detector. Let's say he gets picked for a random search when he shows up for his shift. They'll find the porno and won't look any further. Figure the old guy's just supplementing his pension with some harmless contraband. So they just have a good laugh and let him through. Pretty slick, I'd say."

"I'm not with you. Why is that so slick?

"Lift up that top tray."

Earl did as requested, but the bottom portion was empty. "Manny, we don't have time for this. What's the point?"

Manny took out his pocket knife, tipped the cooler on its side and slipped the blade along the inside bottom edge. The bottom popped out, revealing a hidden compartment.

"Jesus, Manny. Good work. How'd you spot it?"

"Its dope stashing One A. You just measure the inside wall against the outside. Doesn't add up."

"Let's get some photos of all this and include the house," Earl said. He'd worry about the legality of all this later.

Munoz got out his camera and Earl returned to the car, where he dug out Rattner's accident file. When Munoz joined him, they drove back down the mountain. Earl held the police photos of the accident scene in his hand, looking for the location. When he spotted it they stopped. The edge of the road was scarred with deep drag marks and an ugly oil spill where Rattner's car had been winched up from the ravine and dropped on the road.

Earl got out and shaded his eyes against the hot sun to study a rock outcropping on a ridge directly across the steep ravine. When Earl opened the car's back door, Henceforth tumbled out and immediately lifted his leg on a nearby rock, like a conquistador stepping ashore to proudly claim newfound territory. Earl poured water from a plastic bottle into his cupped hand, and Henceforth noisily lapped it up.

They returned to the shade of the car and continued down the road to a turn-off and parked. The descent from the road at this point was less arduous. Earl tossed his coat into the car, rolled up his sleeves and indicated they should head for the distant rock formation. Manny led the way down, slipping on the loose gravel and awkwardly maneuvering his bulk over the rocks.

At the bottom, they pushed off through the dust covered scrub brush and creosote bushes, scaring up sand flies and swatting sweat bees off their arms. The still-hot air weighed on them like a heavy blanket and smelled like turpentine from the scent of desert sage. Henceforth lumbered off, his nose close to the ground, propelled by some genetic code to frighten and chase any small mammals in the vicinity.

Twenty minutes later they reached the rock formation on the ridge. Earl was breathing hard and wiped sweat out of his eyes. His shirt stuck to his back, his forearms were scratched and his pants were coated in dust. Manny was sucking air like a winded draft animal. Earl put a thumb and forefinger to his mouth and whistled for Henceforth.

Behind a flat boulder, the grass was matted down as if someone or something had lain there. Several branches on a bush in front of the boulder had been cut and tossed aside. Earl knelt down and peered through the opening. It was a clear view of the turn in the road where Rattner met his death. Then they both saw it, a black v-shaped smudge on the edge of the boulder.

Manny put a name to it.

"It's a muzzle flash from a high powered rifle," he said.

Earl nodded. At least this answered one question. Rattner didn't have an accident. Someone had shot out his tire. Rattner must have constituted an unwelcome link to someone who decided to sever that chain. Permanently.

"Hell of a shot," Manny said, his hand shading his eyes as he stared back at the road. "Must be 500 yards straight across, at a moving target."

Henceforth whined in frustration behind them and scratched at a crevice in the rocks. Earl stepped over and saw something shiny in the crack. Henceforth apparently assumed any cylindrical metal object must be a source of food since his gourmet meals came in a can. Earl lifted out the object, speared on the end of his pen. A rifle shell.

"Let me see that," Manny said.

Earl handed him the pen and he carefully examined the cartridge. "I'll be damned," Manny said, holding the bottlenecked cartridge up close to his eye in order to read the stamped lettering. "It's a point .338 Lapua Mag."

"What's that mean?" Earl asked.

"A .338 is a shade less than a .34 caliber bullet. Manufactured by Lapua Magnum. It's a high-powered, long-range rifle cartridge. Rimless, center fire. They were used in Afghanistan and Iraq by our snipers. Nowadays you can get these anywhere."

"Why'd the shooter leave it?"

"This ammunition is only used in powerful long range rifles, which are all single-shot weapons, probably a Remington, 700 series. These rifles can only hold one bullet at a time in the chamber and the bolt action does not automatically eject the cartridge."

"What's that mean in 'firearms for dummies'?"

"Okay," Manny said. "Our shooter was in a prone position, based on the matted grass. He steadied the rifle on the boulder." Munoz pointed to the rifle's discharge mark. "He lined up his shot in advance because he knew exactly where the truck would pass. After he fires, he stays in position, keeping his eye on the target, in case he needs to take another shot. He pulls back the bolt. Without looking up, he uses his fingers to take out the expended cartridge and reloads. This cartridge just rolled away."

"So there should be fingerprints on this," Earl said hopefully.

Manny nodded and grinned.

Earl told Manny to take pictures, then took out a doggie bag which he always carried for any unexpected offering by Henceforth and dropped in the cartridge. "How do you know all this, Manny?"

"I do a little hunting." Manny said. "Now it's only the animal kind."

CHAPTER 17

When Earl and his companions climbed back up to the road, he was just as tired, scratched and dusty as before, but he felt buoyed. The cartridge in his pocket had at least the potential to provide some answers and knowing that Rattner was murdered certainly reshuffled the deck of suspects. A fresh draw always held out the possibility of a better hand.

They all got in the car and started down the mountain.

"I was wondering," Manny said, "if we should tell Detective Carter what we found and explain our theory about Rattner's so-called accident."

"Yeah, I know, I was thinking about that. But I don't think so. The only hard evidence we have is that some hunter fired a rifle out here. That's not enough for them to open up a closed investigation. All it would do is tip off the DA."

Manny nodded in agreement as he drove, and the discussion turned to what needed to be investigated in light of this new information. "Get hold of Phillip Jones, the fingerprint guy," Earl said. "See what he can get off this bullet casing." Earl leaned over and put the doggie bag in Munoz's shirt pocket.

"You know," Manny said. "That was a very difficult shot. I imagine any marksman capable of that kind of shooting would first want to calibrate his sites for that distance. Why don't I check the local shooting ranges? I bet a guy with that type of rifle would probably make an impression."

"Good idea," Earl said. "And I'm curious about that phone call the kid said Rattner got just before he took off to meet someone. His cellphone might have gotten torched when the car blew, but it isn't listed with his property in the coroner's report," Earl said, running his finger down a paper in the file. "I wonder if they recovered his cellphone from the wreckage."

"I'll check with the tow company that recovered his truck."

When they reached the bottom, a prison transport van was parked across the road, blocking the way. Captain Gunther was leaning back against it, his legs crossed at the ankles, arms folded. The sun gleamed on his mirrored sunglasses. At both ends of the van a prison guard stood with a shotgun resting in the crook of his arm. Munoz stopped the car a few yards away.

"Now we know who Rattner's kid was calling," Earl said.

"And the cavalry has arrived," Munoz said. He unbuckled his seat belt and reached for the door handle. "I'll handle this."

Earl put his hand on Manny's forearm. It felt as tense as a steel cable. "Manny, let me," Earl said earnestly.

He walked down the road and faced Gunther. "You setting up a private toll booth?"

"Mr. Earl," he said pushing himself off the van. "It's time you and I had a talk."

"I thought you already sent me a message with Jack and Jill?"

"Ah, yes," Gunther said with a hint of amusement. "But apparently you didn't get it."

"Some of it must have gotten lost in the translation. I wasn't in much of a receiving mood."

"That's why I'm here," Gunther said. He removed his sunglasses, revealing his cold grey eyes. "To make certain we understand each other."

"Most generous of you."

"I've learned that people sometimes stumble unintentionally into situations because they fail to see things from the other's perspective. By not foreseeing the consequences their actions might have on others, they force people to react in a way neither wants."

"And what is it that I don't understand, Captain?"

"That I run a prison, not a boarding school. Simple as that. Men are sent to me because society says they're too dangerous to live among civilized people. They want them caged. Once that's done, they think that's the end of it." He shrugged as if stating the obvious. "Never a thought as to how I'm supposed to deal with them. How my guards, unarmed and outnumbered a hundred to one, impose order among these violent predators? Perhaps they feel an appeal to their spirit of cooperation will prevent them from attacking their keepers? Not likely, is it?" He gave Earl a condescending look. "The hard truth is there is only one thing such men understand. Fear. Fear of certain, uncompromising, bodily harm."

"With you as judge and jury," Earl said.

"That is the only choice I'm left with, Mr. Earl. These men can smell weakness. If they ever do, we're finished. Fear is our only weapon."

"So when your guards randomly beat inmates, sanction rape as a punishment or arrange gang fights for their amusement, they're actually just doing their job. But if I bring it up in court, we have a problem."

"The fact is the public does not want to know such ugly truths. They want us to handle their human garbage but not be forced to see how we do it. They would prefer to stay ignorant of the measures required to pen up these savage creatures." He looked at Earl under raised eyebrows. "Being made to face these harsh truths might cause them to look for someone to blame. A human failing rather than a systemic problem. Which brings me to the point." He fixed Earl with a steely look. "My men are easy targets. Such accusations would threaten their livelihoods, perhaps even their liberty.

That's the problem you're creating, Mr. Earl. And I can't allow that. It's best to let the public sleep. Which is why we're having this conversation."

"You mean that's why you're threatening me," Earl said.

Gunther gave a slight shake of his head as if in disappointment. "There's a saying, Mr. Earl. Anyone can choose his friends, it's only a wise man who chooses his enemies." He paused, locking eyes with Earl. When he spoke his voice had a tone of finality. "I'm offering you a choice."

"Since you're so intent that we understand one another, let me ask you something. I can understand what happened to Officer Miller. He was an honest man who wanted to put you and the Sharks where you belong. Out of uniform and behind bars. But why Rattner? He was one of yours. How did his existence suddenly become a threat?"

Gunther's jaw muscles visibly clenched and his cold stare turned venomous. "Have a safe trip home, Mr. Earl. These roads can be dangerous."

The hallway on the first floor of the District Attorney's Office in LA was lined with equally spaced doors leading to equally small offices. Deputy DA Rosealee Martin stepped out of the office being used by Lauren Taylor and looked furtively up and down the hallway. Martin took out her cellphone as she walked away and scrolled down her address book for the number of the prison guards union. She was anxious to report she had done what had been asked of her.

A minute later, Lauren Taylor walked out into the hall and down to a nearby office. The door was open. Sam sat at her desk reading a case file and sipping a cup of coffee. Taylor knocked on the open door to get Sam's attention.

"Hi, I'm Lauren Taylor. I'm on that case from Haywood County. Have you got a minute?"

Sam looked up and hesitated for a beat, then said, "Of course. I'm Samantha Price."

Taylor took a seat facing Sam. "Do you know Judge Parker? I need to get an idea of what kind of evidentiary rulings she makes. See, I've lost my main witness and I want to get in his prior statements. Do you think...."

"I don't really know Judge Parker," Sam said interrupting her. "But Jim Barnes, just down the hall, has had some cases with her."

"Okay," Taylor said and paused a beat. "What about this defense lawyer, Bobby Earl? I heard he was on one of your cases. What do you think I can expect from him on cross-examination?"

"He's a good lawyer, so I'd prepare my witnesses if I were you."

Taylor pursed her lips as if in thought. "There's also a bunch of forensic evidence. You know, gunshot residue, ballistics, fingerprints, that kind of thing. How sharp is he on that stuff?"

"You know, I'd like to help, but I've really got to go." Sam looked at her watch and stood up.

"That's too bad," Taylor said, making no attempt to leave. "I understood you knew Bobby Earl quite well."

Sam fixed her with a hard stare. "Did you Lauren? Well, imagine that? If you're really interested in his trial abilities, why don't you talk to a few of the other DA's who've lost a case to him. You shouldn't have any trouble finding one."

"Sounds like you sort of admire him."

"Let me ask you something, Lauren. When you were rooting through the trash cans, doing your research on me, did you learn about this condition I have? I suffer from AAD, Asshole Aversion Disorder. Whenever I'm around one I lose my equilibrium and I spill things. Like this cup of coffee that I'm holding. So you better take those teeny-bopper green glasses of yours and keep the fuck away from me. Because I feel an attack coming on."

Taylor gave her a knowing grin and stepped to the doorway. She turned with eyes lit with malice. "Say hello to Bobby for me."

Seated at her desk, Martha filled in the last entry on the day's crossword puzzle and tossed it aside. Friday's puzzle was usually difficult, but never as demanding as Saturday's. Midweek's puzzles never posed a challenge for her, so she handicapped herself by only using the "down" clues. She was reaching for her cup of tea when Earl pushed through the back door.

"Did you attend the computer class?" she asked.

Earl saluted. "As ordered, Sergeant Major."

"Good. Go set up a file on your computer where you can save your briefs and motions. Then you won't need to reinvent the wheel each time. I've already saved a motion from the Wellington case on your computer as a Word document. You can start with that."

Earl stepped into his office and walked directly up to Son of Hal. Allowing himself too much time to think would only erode his newfound confidence. Besides, he was convinced the computer could detect fear. Any display of timidity would encourage it to do something to sabotage his efforts -- corrode some electronic impulse, cause a short, blow a fuse. He clicked Son of Hal awake and mechanically followed the steps he had been taught in the class. After five minutes, the document emerged on the screen with enormously wide margins on each side, leaving a narrow column of words running down the center of the page like the divider strip on a computer highway to nowhere.

There was a perfunctory knock on the door, and Manny Munoz entered. Earl sat glaring at Son of Hal and slowly hissing every oath he could string together. The computer sat complacently, as if this outcome had been predetermined.

"You talking to computer screens, now? You look sorta' unhinged," Munoz said.

Earl spun around, his face scrunched in resentment. "This fucking thing," he said gesturing over his shoulder. "Shut the door. Martha is already convinced I have the IQ of a cucumber."

"Then calm down," Munoz grinned. "Let's talk about the case."

Earl nodded, breathing deeply to calm himself.

Munoz laid a manila folder on Earl's desk. "Here's the rest of what they recovered from Hartman's cell. That DA seemed pissed that you filed a motion. Made me sign a receipt. Something about her word in court not being good enough for you."

Earl eagerly opened the file, which contained copies of rumpled and soiled papers. He flipped through the contents. One by one he laid the pages aside; prison Complaint Forms filled out for other inmates; drafts of letters to the editor of a local newspaper decrying prison conditions; notes scribbled on scraps of paper with names and addresses of inmates' family members. Earl pushed these aside when he came to a letter from Hartman to his sister asking about some relative and enclosing a KenKen numerical puzzle he had solved.

"There's a note attached to this letter from our favorite prosecutor," Earl said with a grin. "This letter and puzzle were found in a puzzle book. If you want a copy of the book, come to the office and copy each page by hand."

Earl passed the puzzle over to Munoz. "This mean anything to you?"

Munoz gave it a cursory look and shrugged. "I've seen guys in the joint play chess by correspondence. I don't know, maybe he and his sister exchanged puzzles trying to stump each other?

Earl put it aside and pulled out a California Public Records Form with words crossed out and others written in the margins. "This is interesting," Earl said. "It's obviously a draft, but it appears Hartman was requesting a copy of the contract awarded to PCA by the state to house inmates at Haywood." Earl read further. "He was also asking for the bidding package PCA submitted to win the contract." Earl handed the form to Munoz.

"Yeah," Manny said examining the form. "It's the same as the Freedom of Information Act on the federal side. Any average Joe is entitled to learn how the state government is conducting business."

"Right," Earl said. "And look at this." He held up an official looking pamphlet. "Here's a copy of the state regulations governing the treatment of inmates." Earl leafed through the pages. "It stipulates standards on health care, nutrition, exercise, a bunch of things."

"I thought the wardens and The Department of Corrections were in charge of all that."

"These are the minimum standards. They don't set a very high bar, but they do have the force of law and have to be met." Earl reached out and picked up the Public Records request. "I wonder what Hartman was up to? What was he looking for?"

Earl pulled open a desk drawer, propped up his outstretched legs and stared up at the ceiling. He felt frustrated. He didn't know what he had expected to find, but this wasn't it. And he couldn't see how any of this fit into the case, let alone give him a hint of a defense.

"Well," Manny said, pulling Earl back. "After our death march up that hill, we can at least scratch off one theory. Rattner apparently wasn't acting alone. He didn't murder Hartman just because he was afraid Hartman would snitch him off for smuggling drugs."

"But even if Rattner didn't have his own agenda, who murdered him? And why? Say he was doing his duty as a Shark to get rid of Miller, or working for Buddy Wright to frame Carlson, or for PCA to stop Hartman, each of them still needed Rattner around to testify at the trial. Rattner is the one who could put the gun in Hartman's hand. Make it look like Carlson slipped it to him in the visitor's room. Rattner's version would have been unchallenged. The only other witnesses are dead."

"Good point," Munoz said. "My guess is that whoever was using Rattner got worried that he might flip on them. That AG pressuring him at his house might have spooked him. I've seen how fear makes a lot of people talkative and I bet somebody else was thinking the same thing."

Earl sat considering all this until he reminded himself that now was not the time to cast about for answers. He was facing a deadline. The pretrial conference was in ten days. Before then, the Code required he submit to the prosecutor his list of witnesses and the documents he planned to introduce. If they weren't on the list, they couldn't testify or be used. So who should he include? Without a clear idea of a defense, he would have to use a shotgun approach, just so he didn't leave anyone out.

Earl lowered his legs, pulled out a yellow pad and began to write. "Okay," he said. "I'll prepare the witness list and when we get a trial date you take care of the subpoenas. Let's include Buddy Wright the union

President and I'll give notice I intend to use the campaign finance reports that show the union is bank rolling the opposition to the initiative."

"I'll get them from the same place I got Mr. McManis' campaign filings for the venue motion," Munoz said as he made notes.

"And put down that former State Senator that I talked to, Carlos Sanchez. He can explain how the guard jobs are tied to maintaining an inflated prison population and that Carlson's initiative would reduce those numbers. Then there's Corbett, the Assistant AG. He can testify that Officer Miller was wearing a wire to help make a case against the guards for their treatment of the inmates and the time the guards were facing if they were convicted. Add Captain Sunglasses, of course, for a discussion of penal philosophy and the benefits of the Fraternal Order of the Sharks. And Denise Wallace, that matron who gave Kate the pat down."

"Sounds good, Bobby."

Earl nodded and gave Munoz a cheerless smile. Earl knew these efforts fell well short of "good." He had nothing that connected Clyde Rattner or Buddy Wright or Captain Gunther and the Sharks to the actual killings. A possible motive was never going to cut it. Besides, under the rules of evidence, the judge probably would not even allow him to present any of this to the jury. Without some concrete evidence of their involvement, it was a real stretch. And Judge Bonnie Lee Parker didn't strike him as that limber.

"Okay," Earl said. "What about any physical evidence we might introduce? Where are we on prints from that bullet casing we found?

"The print man recovered a partial. But it's not enough to establish a positive ID and you can't run a partial through any data base."

Earl grimaced. "Any luck in finding Rattner's cellphone from the wreck?"

"I did," Manny said. "I went to the tow yard. Those guys scavenge wrecks before they get crushed into scrape metal. Luckily his phone got tossed into a box. It was a little charred from the fire, but you never know. I gave it to my tech geek. He'll see if he can recover the last number that called him."

"How about the shooting ranges? We have to get something out of all this."

"I checked. There are three within driving distance. All three also sell guns, so they'll all have security cameras." Earl looked him a question. "Any type of gun store is a prime target for robberies because a stolen gun can easily be sold. They put in cameras hoping they're a deterrent. I'll need a subpoena to get their video film."

"You'll have it before you leave. And make copies of all this and get it to Kate." Earl gathered up the papers on his desk and shoved them back in the manila folder. "Maybe she can figure out what Hartman was after. I sure can't."

CHAPTER 18

It was Saturday morning and the lawyers visiting room was nearly empty when Earl walked in. Off in a corner, a harried looking public defender in yoga pants, sat facing a Hispanic woman with teased hair as puffed up as cotton candy — ideal for her boyfriend to stash his drugs.

Earl took a seat opposite Kate Carlson. "You called and left a message that it was urgent," Earl said. "So I'm all ears."

"I think I found something," Kate Carlson said, her eyes bright with excitement, as if she knew a tantalizing secret that she could barely contain.

"Well, let's hear it," Earl said with a good natured grin.

"Manny brought over the material from Adam's cell."

"I know. I was hoping it might mean something to you."

"And it did," Kate said. "Now I know what the information was that Adam promised would help our Initiative campaign."

"Really?" Earl said. "What was it?"

"This is it," Kate said, holding up a copy of the KenKen puzzle that Earl recognized from Hartman's letter to his sister.

"Enlighten me," Earl said, repressing any hint of the impatience he felt after being pulled from his bed on a Saturday morning. He reminded himself that to those inside, the press of time did not exist.

"Adam was keeping track of the medical care the prison was providing the inmates." Kate held up the state-issued pamphlet that had been among Hartman's effects. "This is a copy of Title 15 of the California Code of Regulations that sets forth the legal standards for the care of inmates. I studied this when I was deciding whether to get involved in prison reform."

"I'm familiar," Earl said.

"The law requires that inmates receive any and all necessary medical care." She pointed to the puzzle. "Adam has listed the number of that statute in the margin on the left as if he was doing some calculations. See 3350. The numbers in the boxes next to it must be some kind of code, probably designating certain types of common medical conditions that you would expect to encounter in a prison population the size of Haywood's. Heart conditions, diabetes, cancer, that sort of thing." She glanced at Earl to see if he was following. "The numbers beside those must refer to the number of patients treated for this type of condition. As you can see there are a lot of zeroes." She looked expectantly at Earl. Seeing no reaction, she explained. "There are no zeros in a KenKen puzzle."

"How does any of this help our case?" Earl said.

"Don't you see?" she said with a hint of frustration and again held up the paper. "Look. This number in the margin on the left is the section requiring mental health treatment by a clinical psychologist." She ran her finger over to the corresponding box. "Zero. This next number requires an off-site contractor for medical treatment that's not available at the prison. Zero." She looked over at Earl to see if he understood. "And these numbers are for just a two-week period."

"Seems Haywood had some very healthy inmates," Earl said.

"You don't get it," she said in exasperation. "It is not *possible* in an inmate population of this size not to have some of them with serious medical conditions. Particularly among those old lifers." She waited for Earl to respond.

"So they were cherry-picking the inmates they accepted. But how would this help your Initiative campaign?"

"Bobby, listen to me. The state has made clear they're not going to spend the money to build more prisons. But they've been ordered to reduce overcrowding. So California solves this overcrowding by putting inmates into *private* prisons. The state bought the PCA line that they could do the job on the cheap. But the cost comparison is not apples to apples. PCA doesn't take inmates with expensive health conditions or mental problems." She gave Earl an eager look. "And that's not all. Adam has listed the statutes and the corresponding number of inmates offered vocational training, drug abuse programs, educational programs, even whether meals meet the minimal nutrition standard. PCA doesn't provide any of the required rehabilitative programs or even proper food. PCA cuts out whatever they can get away with in order to increase profits. They are nothing but a warehouse for prisoners."

Earl sat silently absorbing this while Kate anticipated his next question.

"See," Kate said. "If private prisons are not really cheaper and they don't provide the care and rehabilitation the law mandates, there's really no legal justification for using them."

Earl now understood what the guards had been looking for when Hartman complained about excessive cell searches. The prison staff must have learned that Hartman was collecting these statistics. It was easy to envision what PCA might think if they were passed to Kate for her campaign — they could lose their contracts and any public airing of these practices would inevitably led to an examination of PCA's lobbying efforts and political donations. Such a development would not be welcome news in the board room of PCA. And if the state dropped the use of private prisons, that would eliminate a lot of union guard positions.

Kate held up the scribbled copy of the Public Records Request Form. "And, I bet that's why Hartman made this request for the PCA contract and bid package for Haywood. He probably wanted to see how they were able to select these inmates. But no matter how they managed it, these statistics show they don't follow the law and they're not cheaper than state prisons."

"If these statistics were coded," Earl said as if reasoning with himself, "then he must have been mailing them to his sister. He must have been afraid that if they were found the guards would confiscate them." Earl fell silent as he searched his memory. "You know, when I looked at Hartman's prison file, I think he listed his sister as an emergency contact person. She lives somewhere up north."

Kate smiled, pleased that Earl finally grasped the impact of her discovery.

"I'll tell Manny to subpoena Haywood's inmate medical records to see if they back up these numbers." He stared intently at Kate. "I'll contact Hartman's sister. This may be the break we were waiting for. Good work, Kate."

It was late Wednesday night when Munoz pulled up next to the curb on the arrival level of the American Airlines terminal at LAX. Bobby Earl maneuvered toward him through the swarm of released passengers who were wheeling luggage, pulling along fatigued children or simply standing, frozen in place, busy with their cellphones. He tossed his briefcase in the back seat, slipped off his suit coat and dropped into the passenger seat.

"So how did it go?" Manny asked over his shoulder as he cautiously inched into the traffic leaving the airport.

"She's going to testify," Earl said with obvious relief. "You can add her to the witness list." He had spent the day with Polly Hartman on her houseboat in Sausalito, across the bay from San Francisco. The grey haired woman still wore her "love beads" as a homage to her former life as a flower child in the Haight Ashbury district. The incense in her cabin was as thick as the morning fog off the bay, so Earl asked that they sit on deck "for the view." Through it all, he liked the woman with her ungoverned spirit and the courage to chart a life path without a compass.

"She never believed her brother was killed in an escape attempt. She wants to help find his murderer."

"What did she say about Hartman's code?" Munoz said as he leaned on the horn and forced his way into traffic.

"Kate was right. Hartman worked in the prison's hospital and kept a running tab on the medical conditions they treated, or more accurately didn't treat. Other inmates gave him the information on the lack of drug rehab and educational classes. He wrote to her every couple weeks and enclosed a KenKen arithmetic puzzle. The statistics were disguised as numbers in the puzzle. They had a code so the prison censors wouldn't catch on. Each medical condition was assigned a number and the code sections were always placed in the margins. She can explain the whole thing."

"So she kept all the records?"

"You bet. They're right in my briefcase. I'll file a motion at the pretrial conference to allow their admission at trial. She can lay the legal foundation. Those, plus the prison medical records to support them, should be enough for the judge to let me argue that PCA and the union would have been damn worried that Hartman might pass them to Kate. That's why they kept tossing his cell looking for them. And why an employee of PCA and a Union member shot him."

"So," Munoz said, "you'll be able to put on the evidence that they're the ones who might be good for the murders." He darted a quick look at Earl. "And finally get around that . . . what'a you call it rule.

"Right. The third-party-culpability rule."

"Then maybe Hartman was the target after all," Munoz said, keeping his eyes on the road as he swung onto Lincoln Boulevard heading toward Venice.

"Between the PCA contract and the union jobs, there was certainly a lot of money at stake," Earl said. "You know, I keep thinking of the McManis rule: Never ignore the smell of money."

Kate sat in the visitor's room to wait for her visitor to be admitted. It was a visit she always welcomed. Rosa Jimenez was one of the people to whom Kate felt a deep and enduring attachment. Rosa was ostensibly her cleaning lady for the last fifteen years, but that description diminished her importance in Kate's life.

Kate's mother, June, long divorced from her father, had been living with Kate when it was discovered she had lung cancer. During her battle against the disease Rosa had been her caretaker, sat with her during her chemo treatments, bathed her and prepared her meals. Rosa's quiet faith had been her mother's tether to hope. There was an ease and openness between the two older women that had been both heartwarming and remorseful to Kate, whose relationship with her mother had been distant and contentious. Her mother, a bright woman, blamed the conventions of her generation for denying her a career and ironically resented her daughter's easy ascendance. This past history did not prevent Kate from feeling a deep gratitude and admiration for Rosa.

Each morning Kate would sit with Rosa and talk for a few minutes over coffee before going to the office. It was during these times she learned that Rosa had come from Guatemala, was granted asylum and given a green card that permitted her to work. Her husband, Gilberto, however, was from Mexico and was undocumented.

One morning Rosa was uncharacteristically late and arrived in tears. Gilberto had been arrested by ICE when they raided his workplace. Kate immediately called an immigration lawyer and learned that a bail bond could be posted securing his release until his deportation hearing. Kate immediately agreed to put up the bail. The paperwork took two days, after which Kate accompanied Rosa to pick up Gilberto. ICE had housed him along with other immigration detainees in a private prison in San Diego.

When they arrived they were told that Gilberto was unavailable. He was in the medical clinic because Gilberto had "assaulted a guard and had to be restrained." It sounded inconceivable to the two women that Gilberto, with his sunny disposition, would have instigated such a confrontation. They returned to Los Angeles. Two days later the call came. Gilberto was dead.

When they recovered his body, his face was broken and battered as if from a savage beating. The prison report stated that he fell during the attempt to restrain him and smashed his face against the cell bars. An "unfortunate accident" was the conclusion. Kate never spoke of this when promoting the Initiative to ban private prisons, but it was never far from her thoughts.

The clank of the gate drew her attention. An older, sturdy Hispanic woman sat down across from her. Her grey hair was pulled back in a bun and a small gold metal cross hung from a thin chain around her neck. There was a quiet dignity in her wrinkled face.

"Rosa, you were just here last week. You shouldn't come so often. Spend that time with your family," Kate said with a warm smile.

"This different, Miss Kate," the woman said with a heavy Spanish accent.

"Is anything wrong?" Kate asked.

"No," she said then hesitated for a moment. "Your person, she come to get the mail, when I clean."

'Yes, Jennifer, my assistant."

"Si. She upset. Tell me how others make things bad for you at your work."

Kate already knew that LB was sending out some partners to lure her clients back to Horgan & Cooley. Then last week the other shoe dropped. Brandon Moss, one of the senior partners at her new firm, Arnold & Mellon, had come to assure her that the firm was behind her "110 percent." But for business reasons they had to make it appear they were distancing themselves from her, "just until this whole mess gets cleared up." He explained that the other partners were stepping up to service her clients and persuade them not to jump ship, but of course they would be hers again when she returned. Kate knew this was the equivalent of the mafia kiss that sealed your fate. She was finished there.

"Yes," Kate said. "She came to see me too."

"Your person, Jennifer, she tell me not to worry. Alejandro's school would get paid. At first, I no understand. Then I think. It was you. There is no scholarship," she said, dividing the word into segments.

Kate had been paying to send her son to college, telling the proud older woman that he had won a scholarship. "Alejandro is a very good boy, Rosa. He deserves to be in college. Jennifer should not have said anything."

"No be angry at her. She upset." She paused to control her emotions. "You a very kind lady, Miss Kate. You always good to me. Now, you help my Alejandro. I thank you. May God bless you. I go to church now and pray for you."

"That DA sent me the defense lawyer's witness list in the Carlson case," Enoch Bowdeen said with a tone of disgust. "Hartman's sister is on it. And, of course, he's subpoenaed the inmates' medical records from Haywood."

Leland Bain looked warily at Enoch, not knowing how to react.

"This is exactly what I was afraid of." He snorted in derision, then spoke as if to himself. "The staff up there had told me when Carlson started to visit Hartman. Recognized her from TV as the bitch trying to take away their jobs. Didn't think much of it at the time."

"I remember, we discussed it," Bain said.

"Then one of Gunther's snitches told us that Hartman was collecting statistics on the medical care at Haywood. I was afraid he would pass them on to her and she'd use them against us in the campaign.

"But I thought you took care of that?" Bain said.

"I thought I had!" Bowdeen snarled. "I ordered the guards to start tossing his cell, looking for them. Never found them. Figured he must be mailing them outside, so I had the Warden personally read his correspondence. Said there was nothing. So I had the guards persuade him to ask for protective custody. Reckoned I had him safely tucked away. But then our snitch said Hartman was still collecting those statistics." He paused and drew a deep breath, clamping his eyes shut as the memory returned. "Goddamn it, the threat of those numbers getting out was like an axe over my head." Bowden stared off and fell silent.

After a moment Leland spoke to break the silence. "How could he still be getting information in protective custody? Isn't he isolated from the rest of the inmates?"

"Oh, Christ," he waved dismissively, "those yahoos can get a message anywhere to anyone. Call them 'kits.' Can't stop them."

"I still don't understand," Leland said mildly. "Why couldn't the prison just cut off his correspondence, like I suggested."

"Because of those fucking California laws." His voice snappish, irritated. "Title fucking 15. One of the regulations *you* let them put in our contract." He glared at Bain. "You're supposed to be a lawyer, for God's sake. You should know this crap." His voice turned mincing. "Those poor benighted criminals have an 'uninhibited' right to correspond." He snorted his revulsion. "If we had confiscated his letters, I would have had the ACLU crawling up my ass. Once they started, no telling what they would have found."

Bain nodded to appease him, quickly banishing the mental image of the ACLU rummaging about in Enoch's body cavity.

"Then the DA sends me this motion that defense lawyer filed." He held up some papers. "Seems the little shit was sending the statistics to his sister, disguised in a Goddam KenKen puzzle. Some kinda' code the sister says she can explain. Slipped 'em right past the fucking Warden."

"Well, at least you're protected under the contract," Leland said in an effort to assuage him. "Remember, I stuck a clause in there that gives you the right to reject any inmate the state sends you that has a 'serious medical condition.' That's vague enough to justify not taking somebody with a bad cold."

"Jesus and His Nails. If dumb was dirt you could cover a fucking acre." Enoch fixed him with a look of incomprehension. "Our business model is that we can house inmates cheaper than the state prisons. That's why they use us. You got that?" He gave Bain a contemptuous look. "If they ever catch on that we're only taking the healthy ones and sticking the state prisons with the bill for the sick ones, then our numbers no longer hold up. And if they see how we avoid spending on all that drug rehab for hypes' and education for retards. Well...." He waved a hand in frustration.

"I understand," Leland said.

"You Goddamn better, Leland! It is absolutely critical, you hear me, *fucking critical*, that those statistics do not get aired in public." Bain saw his jaw muscles bunch and harden. "There's no coming back if they get publicized in a trial. We'll lose our prison contracts and our chance at housing those illegals. That kind of revenue loss has consequences. Heads will be on the chopping block."

"I will personally see to it. I'll represent PCA at the pretrial hearing. Those statistics will not be admitted. Guaranteed."

Enoch gave him a disgusted look. "Get me a drink," he said.

Leland returned and put Enoch's usual glass of bourbon on the edge of the desk. Enoch took a hefty swallow, then drew a deep breath and slouched back in his chair, like a taut wire uncoiling.

After a time Bowdeen spoke, this time in a more conversational tone. "You know," he said, "that Hartman was like a dog with a bone. He wouldn't give up." Enoch took another long drink. "He even put in one of those Public Record requests for our bid package on the Haywood contract. Can you believe that shit?"

"I know," Leland said. "Buddy warned me that some brain dead bureaucrat even included the union's letter of concern in the response.

"That was the memo somebody sent to Buddy, right?"

"Yeah," Leland said. "I told him he had to use it."

"Damn right he had to. Hell, the union sending in that memo was what won us that contract." Enoch snickered in amusement. "I was happier than a two-peckered dog when I saw it. Imagine, GCCA put in *writing* their strategy to cover up sexual abuse by their guards. Christ, how stupid can you be? I don't care if it was a confidential memo. Stuff like that can get out." Enoch shook his head. "They even included how they avoided funding the prison guards' pensions."

"That material" Leland said, "was still in Hartman's cell when they searched it after the killing. The DA has been told not to turn it over,"

"Well, I gotta go." Enoch stood and downed his drink. "But I want to make sure we understand each other." His voice turned nail hard. "If those statistics get used at the trial it crosses my drop dead line. I've handled my end, you better handle yours. Or you will have seen the last piece of PCA business you're ever going to see.

"Enoch," Leland said in an agitated tone. "Calm down. You don't mean that. You can't."

Enoch turned when he reached the door. "Leland, do you know why a dog licks his balls?" He paused and stared coldly at the other man. "Because he can, Leland. Because he can."

CHAPTER 19

Earl and Sam were flopped on the couch. The evening news was on the television, recorded earlier so they could watch it when they returned. This was part of their Friday night routine — dinner out, maybe a movie and the news when they got home. They had reached a comfortable place, one where they welcomed not having to make a decision about what to do at the end of the week. It was enough just to be with each other.

A space had been cleared in Earl's closet and even a drawer or two for Sam to keep some clothes. This was a first for him since his divorce. And it just seemed to happen. A step taken without any acknowledgment that it had any meaning. Earl, for his part, refused to allow himself to attach any significance to it because that would require him to think about the place Sam occupied in his life. He just wanted to delude himself into believing that things could stay as they were. Unexamined and unnoticed. Why not, he was happy.

Sam sat leaning back against Earl, her legs curled under her. Henceforth rested his large head on her thigh. His eyes drooped half shut as she scratched his head. "What'a *gooood* boy. Are you my best boy?" Sam cooed. "Does he have an itchy ear? *Oh yesss*, he has an itchy ear."

Earl enjoyed watching her as she pushed her hair back over one ear and grinned down at the comatose dog. Her smile came so naturally, it was as much a part of her as her throaty laugh. But what lay below that surface? Would he ever be capable of understanding this intelligent, complex woman? He knew she was many-layered and, like everyone, had secrets that she guarded. To be admitted to this inner world of hers would demand trust. To earn that would require him to have the courage to peel away a protective layer in return for each of hers. And therein lay the rub. He was afraid. Afraid to be vulnerable, of course, but it was more than that. Afraid that if he opened up, what she would find would not be like Pizarro discovering the dazzling Pacific Ocean. It would be more like wandering into a barren, emotionless desert, buffeted by occasional gusts of anger. So he sat silently and watched.

But Earl was not the only one watching Sam. Her dog Beauty sat on the floor staring at her, slit-eyed with jealousy. Suddenly Beauty raced to the front window and stood up on her skinny hind legs, her paws on the window sill. She began to yip.

Beauty's alarm was like a trumpet call in Henceforth's ears — man the ramparts, your house is under assault. He immediately rushed toward the window, emitting a deep guttural growl and jammed his muzzle against the glass. He peered into the night then exploded into spasms of chesty barking. After a minute, he looked back over his shoulder to check whether his audience appreciated his efforts, only to find that Beauty had stealthily taken his place. She was curled up in Sam's lap, eyeing him smugly.

"Henceforth," Earl chastened. "You fall for it every time." The big dog walked dejectedly over to Earl and nuzzled his hand. "So now I'm the consolation prize?"

Suddenly Earl reached for the remote control and turned up the volume on the TV. Lauren Taylor was on the screen, seated at a library table before a background of shelves packed tightly with sober looking law books. A setting, no doubt selected to give mute testimony to her legal acuity. Behind her, flanking the California and American flags, were two square jawed, ram rod straight prison guards. She apparently was holding a press conference.

"We are appealing to anyone who traveled on Highway 5, between Los Angeles and Haywood on June 29th. If you saw a car stopped on the side of the road or saw any suspicious activity along that route, please contact your local police department. Such information may be important in the prosecution of Kate Carlson, the mastermind behind a failed prison break, during which an unarmed Corrections Officer, Travis Miller, was murdered." The screen was filled with a black and white photo of a uniformed officer Miller.

Earl clicked off the television and stood up. He cautioned himself to stay calm. After a moment he said, "I guess I don't have to wonder whether or not to expect low blows during the trial. Now, I'll just have to worry whether she bites in the clinches."

Sam sat tight-lipped and stared disgustedly at the blank screen. "Makes you question whether she's trying a case or running for office. Probably both." She paused and looked up at Earl with sympathetic eyes. "I'm sorry Bobby. She's obviously trying to reach your future jurors."

"Yeah, I guess she figures she's at such a disadvantage that she needs to reach out to all those potential jurors who approve of prison breaks and murdering guards."

The man was doing pull-ups on a metal bar twisted into the wood frame of the bathroom doorway when his phone chirped. His movements up and down were slow and fluid like a well-oiled piston. The soft evening light filtering through the drawn curtains sketched the muscles in his back as they bulged and stretched under his sweat glazed skin.

He gracefully dropped onto the rug of the motel room and picked up his phone. "Yes," he said flatly, then listened.

"Slow down and speak clearly," the man said quietly. "I don't need to know why. It doesn't matter. All...."

He was interrupted.

When he could, he spoke slowly, calmly emphasizing each word. "I don't care. It does not matter why."

He paused.

"You are saying there is an individual that you want terminated, is that correct?"

He listened.

"No. You must be definite. You want this person terminated. Is that your decision?"

He waited patiently.

"All right, let's start with her name and location. Give me the proper spelling of her name and a physical description."

He listened without taking notes.

"Is Polly her proper name?"

He shrugged.

"Don't worry, I'll get a photograph through my sources. It may...."

He was interrupted again.

"When is she due at this hearing?"

He nodded to himself.

"Then she's probably already in transit. In what courthouse is this scheduled?"

He listened.

"I understand. You want this termination to appear random. But given this deadline, I may have to take the first window of opportunity regardless of the circumstances. Is that agreed?"

He held the phone away from his ear to avoid the shouting on the other end. His face remained impassive. "It is either agreed or not. It's your decision," he said evenly, unconcerned. "All right. Because of the spontaneous nature of the operation I cannot give you a price in advance. Is that also agreed?"

He waited.

"I will contact you after the operation by our agreed method."

The man ended the call.

The sun snuck narrow fingers through the window blinds and traced pale bands of light across the desk. Earl rose and stepped over a row of trial binders standing at attention on the floor, conveniently within reach of his chair. He crossed the room and flicked on the lights. Returning, he took care to avoid the other binders which lay flopped open on the rug as if exhausted from their labors. He had combed through these notebooks for days, and now his desktop was covered in a snow flurry of paper. Earl was absorbed with writing and rewriting the motions he needed to file in time for the pretrial conference. He always wrote his legal briefs by hand on lined legal pads because he was convinced that without a pen in his hand he couldn't think clearly.

There was a knock on the door, and Munoz thrust his head in. Earl looked up, irritated at being interrupted.

"There's something I think you should see," Munoz said. He walked around the desk and inserted a flash drive in Earl's computer.

"What's that?" Earl asked. "Dinner for Son of Hal?"

"I went back to those shooting ranges with that subpoena for the footage from their security cameras. Got talking with this one fella' about amazing rifle shots. He was bragging about this one guy who set up his target at the far end of the range. Had to be 500 yards, he said. So I went through his footage around the time of Rattner's supposed accident until I found this and down-loaded it."

Munoz opened the drive and a clear picture filled the computer screen. A view of a small shop filled the screen. On top of a wooden counter sat an old brass manual cash register and a display of handguns. On the wall behind the counter, a line of rifles stood upright on a rack above shelves stacked with boxes of ammunition. "That's the owner," Munoz said, stabbing a thick finger at an older man in a worn denim work shirt. He was talking to a younger man with an athletic build, wearing a green army tee-shirt and a grey baseball cap with a pair of dark glasses wedged above the bill. The younger man was autographing a bulls-eye paper target that had been pinned to the wall next to a line of other notable perforated targets. Except there was no bulls-eye in his target. It had been shot out

"You can tell from the date and time," Munoz said, "that this was recorded two days before Rattner's death."

"Who's the guy?" Earl asked excitedly.

Munoz retrieved a folder and produced a folded paper target in a clear plastic bag. Earl peered closely at the signature. "Daniel Boone?" he asked incredulously.

"Yeah, guy had a sense of humor. I talked to the owner about his rifle. A Remington 700 CDL with a scope. I'd bet my daughter's Baptism Rosary he's our shooter."

"Run the video again," Earl said. They watched until Earl said, "Stop it. Look there. He braced his hand against the target before he signed it."

"That's why your crack investigator has it in a plastic bag," Munoz said with a grin.

"Good work, Manny. Get it over to our fingerprint guy to see if he can get any prints off it and compare them to the partial on the bullet casing we found on the ridge."

"See," Munoz said. "I told you our luck was bound to change."

CHAPTER 20

Kate sat hunched forward, staring down at the cement floor. She was alone in the holding cell next to Judge Parker's courtroom. It was early. Court had not started. In the silence she could hear the bailiff and clerk laughing. It felt so disorienting to hear the ordinary sounds of life going forward when her world was in ashes. It seemed a parallel universe, unconnected and unaffected by her troubles. She understood that the lives around her were not caught up in her personal maelstrom of fear and tension, but facing such normalcy made her ache for a release from this constant torment.

The door out to the courtroom opened and Earl stepped inside. He had been waiting in the hall when the bailiff opened the doors that morning. He needed to meet with her before the pretrial hearing started. He pulled over a folding chair and sat down next to the bars of her cell and faced her. There were dark smudges under her eyes, as if sleeping were an option she had neglected to sign up for.

"Is she here?" Kate asked immediately.

Earl knew she was asking about Polly Hartman, who was scheduled to testify today about the statistics her brother Adam had gathered about Haywood's treatment of inmates. She would establish the required legal foundation so Earl could use them later in the trial. Earl had put her travel arrangements in Martha's capable hands. As he expected, Martha had also guided Polly in the proper courtroom attire, which did not include her favorite peach colored Shalwar Kameez, a traditional Indian dress.

Polly Hartman was currently sitting in the Tierra Mia Coffee Shop on 7th, a few blocks away, where Munoz had deposited her after picking her up at her hotel. It was a precaution against the DA approaching her in the court hallway and frightening her into not testifying by lying that she might be charged as a conspirator in her brother's escape attempt.

"We've got her on ice and ready to testify," Earl said.

"Thank God, I was so worried she would back out."

There was a knock on the lockup door, and the bailiff stuck her head in. "You're wanted in chambers."

"I am afraid I am duty bound to report to the court a most serious ethical violation. Unfortunately, the guilty party is Mr. Earl," Lauren Taylor solemnly intoned. "This breach of the rules is of such an egregious nature that, regrettably, it will require that he be removed from the case."

Earl had just lowered himself into one of the leather chairs facing Judge Parker at her desk. He took a moment to assure himself that he had heard Taylor correctly, before deciding which was more impressive, the audaciousness of her accusation or her contrived portrayal of disappointment.

"This ethical breach is such, your Honor," Taylor continued, "that I feel Mr. Earl's client should be present to hear this."

Earl started to push himself out of his chair. Judge Parker held up her hand and nodded for him to keep his seat. Her calm expression did not change. Still wearing her robe, she gestured to the court reporter seated beside a wall of law books to start recording.

"Let's take this a step at a time, Ms. Taylor. What's this ethical violation you're referring to?"

Taylor leaned forward in her chair, eager to tell her tale as if she were about to share some choice piece of gossip with a friend. "You see, the office I'm using here is just a couple down from a woman DA named Samantha Price. I'm alone down here, so I would stop by her office from time to time to talk. And like lawyers everywhere I would end up discussing my case." She smiled as if admitting a truism with which they were all too familiar. "I told her what witnesses I was worried about, the weaknesses I saw in my evidence, my trial strategies, all the things one prosecutor would share with another." She paused, then continued sounding aggrieved. "I have since learned, to my great surprise, that Ms. Price is Mr. Earl's girlfriend. She apparently concealed her relationship so she could pump me for information to pass along to Mr. Earl."

"All right," the judge said cutting her off. She turned her gaze to Earl and raised her eyebrows in a question. "Mr. Earl?"

Earl's first thought was that he had underestimated Lauren Taylor. She was a gutter fighter. A no-holds-barred, gouge out your eyes, bite off an ear, brawler. He stared hard at Taylor, wanting to make eye contact so she would feel his contempt. Taylor looked straight ahead avoiding his gaze, as if she were just a reporter of the facts.

"Mr. Earl?" the judge repeated to draw him back.

Earl turned to face the judge. His jaw was set and when he spoke his voice was tight, as if someone had a hand around his throat. "I do not, under any circumstances, intend to discuss my personal life for Ms. Taylor's amusement. Period. However, I will say, as an officer of the court and under oath if required, that I have not received one goddamned piece of information from Ms. Price regarding the prosecutor's case."

"Language, Mr. Earl. We're on the record," the judge said matter-of–factly, then turned back to Taylor. "Specifically what confidential information regarding your trial strategy do you believe the defense has been made privy to?"

"I'd rather not say in the presence of defense counsel," Taylor said.

"But if your claim is that the defense has already acquired that knowledge, what difference would it make if he stays?"

Taylor paused. "Well, maybe she didn't tell him everything I disclosed to her."

"I see," the judge said and stared hard at Taylor before drawing in a heavy breath. "All right," she said with finality. "First of all, I don't think, at this point, the defendant needs to be present. Secondly, what I need now is to hear from Ms. Price."

"Judge, wait a minute," Earl said. "That's not necessary. I said I would testify under oath. Answer anything you want. Don't drag her into this."

"Mr. Earl, these are serious accusations. Infiltrating an adversaries' camp, stealing their work product, all made on the record. I have no choice. I will hear from Ms. Price." She picked up the phone and asked her clerk to contact Samantha Price.

"Now," the judge said. "I think this would best be handled in chambers. I would like to question her alone, without counsel present. Is that agreeable to you both?"

"Your Honor," Taylor said. "I would like to be present. Perhaps assist the Court in questioning her."

"I understand that you may be a more seasoned trial attorney than I, Ms. Taylor. But for these purposes I can probably manage it alone. The session will be on the record."

Back in the courtroom, Earl sat at the counsel table, his mind a blur of emotions. He was seething with anger at Taylor, knowing at the same time, she had done this to get that exact reaction, hoping to throw him off his game. Make him think more about revenge than about the case. Start him spiraling down into a personal game of tit-for-tat. But mostly he was dreading the effect this would have on Sam.

The door to the courtroom opened and Sam walked in. She gave Earl a quizzical look as she walked by and went into the judge's chambers.

The minutes passed slowly as Earl waited, reviewing a parade of horribles in his mind. The door to chambers finally opened and Sam walked out, her face clouded with fury. She shot Taylor a withering gaze and continued straight out the doors, never looking at Earl. He started to go after her but the judge came out onto the bench.

"I have concluded my examination of Ms. Price and find there has been no improper conduct. There is some dispute as to the nature of the conversations between Ms. Price and Ms. Taylor, but no matter what transpired, I am satisfied that no confidential information was passed on to

Mr. Earl. I am ordering that the record of these proceedings be sealed. I see no need for them to be made public. Now, let's move on to our other issues. Madam Bailiff, please have the defendant join us."

Earl willed himself to rein in his emotions and concentrate on the case. These upcoming motions were too important. He breathed in deeply and evenly, calming himself.

Kate joined Earl at the counsel table. She sat twisted in her seat, looking out at the audience. "What are they doing here?" she asked.

Earl turned and saw three men in business suits seated in the front row. He recognized the grey haired man that had been in Buddy Wright's office when they had met, Jerry Reynolds. "One is the union president's man. Who are the others?"

"That's Leland Bain with the flower, he's the managing partner at my old firm that I told you about. The other is Enoch Bowdeen, Corporate Counsel for PCA, the firm's biggest client. The woman behind them is Chris Kinder, LB's assistant, poor woman."

"Your Honor," Taylor said pleasantly, seeming unaffected by the court's ruling. "I received the defense witness list last week and on it is an Assistant Attorney General named Frank Corbett. There is a representative from that office here who wishes to address the Court."

A middle-aged man in a dark suit and drab tie stepped forward. His stooped shoulders and disheveled hair gave him the academic look of a "book lawyer," probably from their appellate department. "If it please the Court," he said looking down at the notes he was spreading out on the table. "I am John Winslow from the Attorney General's Office. One of our attorneys, Frank Corbett, has been listed by the defense as a witness in this case. It is our understanding that he will be asked to testify regarding an ongoing criminal investigation being conducted by our office."

"Mr. Earl?" the judge asked.

"Officer Miller, one of the victims in this case, was working undercover for Mr. Corbett in an investigation of the prison guards at Haywood Prison. However, that investigation was closed some time ago. So I do intend to question him about it."

"Counsel's information is incorrect," Winslow said. "That investigation has been reinstated and is currently ongoing. Any information concerning it is obviously confidential and to make it public would compromise the investigation. As such, our office is invoking the government secrets privilege of section 1040, and Mr. Corbett will be instructed to refuse to answer any questions on that subject."

"May I inquire when this investigation was reinstated?" Earl asked.

"Objection," Taylor said. "It's irrelevant."

"I'll allow it. Mr. Winslow?" the judge asked.

"Yesterday."

It was clear to Earl that reopening the investigation had nothing to do with a renewed interest in uncovering the abuses of Haywood prison guards. It was merely a further payment by the Attorney General for the union's endorsement of his run for Governor. The union did not want any discussion of the Sharks' mistreatment of inmates to be aired in open court, so the AG obliged. "Your Honor, this is clearly a sham whose only purpose is to assist the prosecution in preventing us from presenting a defense."

"That may be one of the consequences, Mr. Earl, but it does appear that the government secrets privilege applies." The judge took a book from a shelf on the side of the Bench and turned the pages. After some time, she shut the book. "And I don't see any applicable exception."

Earl sat down in frustrated silence.

"Hearing nothing further, I will uphold the privilege barring his testimony. Now," the judge said holding up a sheaf of papers. "The People have a motion that they be allowed to introduce the statement that Officer Rattner made to Detective Carter after the shooting."

Earl felt a jolt of adrenaline. This was a pivotal juncture in the case. Denying Taylor's motion would gut the prosecution case. Earl had spent long nights in the library honing and polishing his brief, hoping to do just that. Without Rattner, the only way Taylor could present her version of events to the jury would be if she were allowed to read his statement. Without it there was a good chance she wouldn't be able to prove her case. She would be left with two dead bodies and Rattner next to the murder weapon.

"The statement obviously violates the rule against hearsay," the judge said.

"That's correct, your Honor," Earl said. "And the defense objects to its admission."

"Ms. Taylor?" the judge asked.

"It fits under the spontaneous statement exception to the hearsay rule under Evidence Code section 1240. The rationale of this exception is that when a person sees or experiences a traumatic event and makes a statement while still under the stress and excitement caused by such an event, the statement is considered trustworthy. The People's position is that Rattner made the statement while still under the stress and excitement of the shooting and thus was not in a frame of mind to fabricate a story."

"Your Honor," Earl said. "This exception properly applies only to an emotional utterance in the heat of the event and not later during a police interview. There was a lengthy gap in time between the shooting and his interview. Enough time for him to give careful consideration as to what he should say. And it's important to note that this statement was the product of police questioning, not something he blurted out while under the shock of the events. Moreover, reading his statement to the jury without the ability to cross-examine him about the truthfulness of his story, places the defense at a great disadvantage because Rattner is the only surviving percipient witness to these events. If allowed, his untested version of these events will be the only one the jury will hear."

"This presents a very troubling issue," Judge Parker said. "I carefully read your briefs and gave it considerable thought. It's a close call. Very close. But on balance, I'm going to allow it. It's true that some time had passed before he gave his statement and that it was in response to questions. However, the emotional trauma of seeing a colleague murdered and then having to struggle over a gun to save your own life would certainly endure for some time. I feel he was still under the force of those emotions when he made the statement and unlikely to speak a calculated lie, which fits the rationale behind this hearsay exception. That will be my ruling. Rattner's statement can come in."

Earl sat back and squeezed his eyes shut as he absorbed the blow of this defeat. He had hoped, on a ruling that could go either way, Taylor's little stunt about Sam might cause the judge to lean in his favor. He should have known better. Parker was too much in control of her emotions to tip the scales because of her opinion of the lawyers. And to expect a judge to take the legs out from under the prosecution in a high-profile case before the trial even starts was asking too much.

"Next in order," Judge Parker said, "the People have a motion to introduce pieces of correspondence from the defendant to Mr. Hartman. Copies of which are attached to the motion. These likewise are hearsay." She turned to Taylor. "The People's position?"

"Yes, your Honor. These letters constitute admissions by the defendant under Evidence Code section 1220. Particularly when read in the context of the relationship between the defendant and Hartman and the circumstances of the crime. There is no problem due to a lack of cross-examination, since they are the defendant's statements and she can explain them if she chooses to testify."

Taylor paused and looked directly at Kate. "The People contend that the defendant, a busy lawyer, repeatedly visited Hartman, who lured this much older woman into a romantic relationship. Hartman was being threatened by a very violent prison gang. In fear for his life, he requested to be placed in protective custody. They conceived this escape plan because Hartman was in danger and put it into action immediately after her last visit. When read in this context, the wording in her letters becomes clear."

"Mr. Earl?" the judge asked, turning to him.

"Judge, the People admit these letters need to be interpreted. There is no admission of guilt anywhere in the words themselves, no declaration of love, no plans for an escape. To allow the use of these letters will permit the jurors to attach to them whatever meaning they want to conjure up, no matter how illogical or ill-founded. Such wild speculation is not the decision-making process that should be permitted in a court of law."

"You are absolutely correct, Mr. Earl," the judge said. "These letters are open to interpretation and that is exactly why we have juries. I am confident that both sides will ably present their own version of the proper meaning of these words. It is the role of the jury to decide whatever meaning they find most plausible and give the letters whatever weight they feel they deserve. I will allow them in."

Earl sat down. He felt numb. Allowing Rattner's statement and Kate's "love letters" permitted the DA to put on her entire case without giving Earl a chance to question anyone. Taylor would have Rattner's uncontradicted statement that Hartman had the gun and shot Miller immediately after his visit with Kate. And by allowing Taylor to put her own spin on the letters, she could create the motive for Kate to help Hartman.

Earl wiped a hand across his face. Hell, he thought, now he wouldn't even have Corbett, the deputy AG, to testify that Miller was investigating the guards and maybe Rattner shot him to protect the Sharks. Without Corbett's testimony, how could he even prove the Sharks existed? He could call Mrs. Miller to say she saw her husband with a recording device, but anything Travis told her about the Sharks was hearsay. Even if he could show that Miller was wearing a wire, there was nothing to prove he was after the Sharks. So how could he establish they had a motive to kill him? Captain Sunglasses was as likely to cop to it as he was to join Guru Rajneesh's Enlightenment Commune.

Earl turned to Kate. He knew she was too smart not to recognize the damage these rulings had done to their case. He put a hand on her shoulder and gave her a confident look. "None of this takes Buddy Wright and the guards Union off the board. They had a lot to gain by pinning this on you. And remember, we have Hartman's sister," he said earnestly. "With her, we can show that Hartman had collected data that proved that PCA's private prisons were not cheaper than our State prisons. In your hands, that proof would have given a huge boost to the Initiative to put private prisons out of business. That's a pretty good motive to stop him, I'd say." He gave her shoulder a reassuring squeeze. "We're still in this."

"Anything further from the People?" the judge asked.

"There is, Your Honor," Taylor said with a confident air. "The defense has placed Mr. Bryan Wright on their witness list, the President of the prison guards union. They have also given notice," she said as she held up a sheaf of papers, "that they intend to use the reports filed by the union detailing their political contributions. This is just pure harassment. Mr. Wright and the union have absolutely nothing to do with this case. Unless, of course, our goal here is to generate publicity for Mr. Earl and his career."

"Mr. Earl, do you care to share with the court the relevance of this witness?"

"Of course, your Honor. In addition to showing that Ms. Carlson was not the perpetrator of these murders, we intend to go further and prove who was responsible. The prison guards union had a direct financial stake in defeating Prop 52 and discrediting its spokesperson, Ms. Carlson. The prosecution's case against her is based wholly on circumstantial evidence. Evidence that will be supplied by Union members, the very people who would benefit the most by convicting her. I would ...."

"Your Honor," Taylor interrupted as she rose with a peeved expression.

The judge gave her a stern look that caused Taylor to silently resume her seat.

"I would suggest," Earl continued, "that the Court revisit the issue of the witness' relevance after the Court has heard the People's evidence and is more familiar with the facts of the case."

"I agree," the judge said firmly.

Earl had sensed that it had not been the time to ask the judge to rule on a defense that claimed the guards Union had framed Kate. He needed a lot more to fill in that picture and didn't want to risk losing the chance to come up with it.

The judge stood up and gathered her papers. "Let's take the morning recess," she said. "Twenty minutes."

CHAPTER 21

When they reassembled in the courtroom after the break, Earl saw Leland Bain huddled against the jury box with Lauren Taylor. They were too much at ease with each other for this to be a meet and greet. This was clearly not their first encounter. Earl was puzzled for a moment and then it hit him. Of course. He had subpoenaed the medical records of Haywood Prison to back up Hartman's statistics. The private prison belonged to PCA, Bain's client. They were going to fight it.

The judge took the bench and nodded to her bailiff. When Kate joined him she looked discouraged. He was not surprised. If anyone was keeping score, he had yet to put a point on the board.

"If it please the court," Leland Bain said as he stepped forward. The small red orchid in his lapel seemed at odds with his immaculately tailored navy blue suit and crisp white dress shirt. The flower stood out like a member of a harmonious music ensemble who had just hit a jarringly wrong note. "I am Leland Bain, managing partner at Horgan & Cooley. I represent the Prison Corporation of America. PCA owns and operates the Haywood Prison. Ms. Taylor has suggested that I address the court on this issue as we are the real party in interest."

"And what issue is that, Mr. Bain?" the judge asked.

"The defense has served Haywood Prison with a subpoena for the production of the medical records of all the inmates in that facility. We are asking the court to quash the subpoena."

"Is this correct, Mr. Earl?"

"It is, your Honor, if I may explain...."

"I'll hear from you in a moment. First, let's hear the grounds on which PCA objects to the subpoena." She nodded at Bain.

"Haywood Prison, like any institution must comply with the mandates of the federal Health Insurance Portability and Accountability Act. Under HIPAA we have a legal duty to safeguard a patient's right to privacy by ensuring our inmate's sensitive medical information is not divulged to outside parties."

Earl sat fuming and wondering if there was a legal objection for gross hypocrisy. Prison officials were about as concerned with inmate privacy rights as they were with the rate of exchange for the Mongolian *tögrög*.

"The protections under HIPAA," Bain continued, "cannot be skirted by merely issuing a subpoena. The only avenue to overcome these protections is if the court itself issues an order that the records be produced. The defense must prove to the court's satisfaction that the relevance of these records outweighs the patient's right to privacy."

"All right," the judge said holding up her hand. "I understand the issue. Mr. Earl, what's the importance of these records?"

Earl got to his feet. "I am happy to explain that, but I would prefer to do so in chambers, ex parte, without the presence of opposing counsel. Any meaningful explanation will require me to reveal attorney-client communications from Ms. Carlson, as well as disclosing our defense strategy."

"Your Honor," Taylor said springing up. "The People have a right to hear...."

"Ms. Taylor," the judge said interrupting her. "I'm sure you would *like* to hear the defense strategy, but you do not have a *right* to hear it. I'll hear from Mr. Earl in chambers, on the record." She nodded to her court reporter who, along with Earl, followed her through the door next to the bench.

Ten minutes later Earl stepped back into the court room and sat next to Kate. "She wants to hear from Polly Hartman. That's a good sign for us." Earl pulled out his cellphone. During the morning recess Munoz had gone back to the coffee shop to sit with Polly. Earl called him to bring her to the courtroom.

It was a warm, cloudless day in downtown Los Angeles as Munoz and Polly walked up Broadway toward the courthouse. Martha had spoken with Polly about what to wear, and she had on a short sleeve cotton dress with a hummingbird print.

They passed the magnificent old movie palaces that sat forlornly empty or had been requisitioned to serve as evangelical churches. As they approached 3rd Street, the sidewalk became increasingly crowded. This stretch was a popular Hispanic shopping district. Store front windows bordered the sidewalk, filled with billowy wedding gowns and embroidered baptismal dresses. When they reached the Grand Central Market, they inhaled its rich aroma of Mexican cooking, which wafted from a dozen different food counters scattered about the block wide space. Inside were tables stacked with colorful pyramids of fruits and vegetables; long metal counters displaying wide-eyed whole fish on mounds of crushed ice; and booths piled high with pungent herbal remedies. As they neared 2nd Street, on the windowless side of a tall brick building, a gigantic mural of the actor Anthony Quinn grinned down on a parking lot.

A block below the courthouse they waited at the light. When it turned, they started across 1st Street. As Munoz stepped down his subpoena file slipped from his hand and he knelt on the sidewalk to gather up his papers. Polly hesitated in the cross-walk then continued to cross the street. Munoz heard a heavy dull thud and looked up. Polly's body careened along the pavement, her dress pushed above her waist, one arm flapping awkwardly about her head until she slammed up against the curb. When Munoz reached her, she lay quietly amid the trash in the gutter. Her eyes stared unblinkingly up at the sky, frozen in surprise. He looked down the street. The car never stopped.

"Mr. Earl, Ms. Carlson, we are all shocked by this news," the judge said. "Please convey our condolences to Ms. Hartman's family for their loss. I don't know what else to say."

Earl nodded in stunned silence.

"Nonetheless," she said and drew a deep breath, steeling herself. "We have your case to deal with. Without any supporting testimony to interpret these figures," she held up the stack of papers with Hartman's coded numbers, "I have no choice but to grant Mr. Bain's motion to quash your subpoena for Haywood's medical records."

"Thank you, your Honor," Bain said.

"That appears to conclude our pretrial calendar." She paused for affirmation. "Now let's pick a trial date. With discovery completed and witness lists exchanged, I see no reason for any further delay. Today is Friday. I'll see you all back here three weeks from this coming Monday. We'll have a fresh jury panel then, and we can start to pick a jury."

Earl sat quietly as the courtroom cleared, and the bailiff escorted out a subdued Kate. Earl felt numb, completely deflated. One thing was clear, this was no accident, no random hit and run. Munoz had explained, there had been no squeal of brakes, no effort to avoid Polly. The car jumped the light, struck Polly at full speed and just kept going, throwing her broken body aside like a rag doll. Somebody had ordered this, somebody involved in the case. He stared at the three men across the room. Leland Bain, PCA's corporate counsel and Jerry Reynolds from the guards Union. Each spoke briefly with Taylor, then walked out. No one made eye contact with him.

When the courtroom was empty, he gathered his papers, went into the hall and sat on a bench. His mind was a jumble. This was a tipping point. Any chance he had of a defense was in tatters and he was afraid — afraid that he would fail to protect an innocent client. Overall, he felt a deep sadness over the death of gutsy Polly and a sense of remorse that he had involved her. At the same time, a cold anger bubbled up deep inside him as he grasped that someone had made the conscious decision to end her life for their own ends, as if just snuffing out an unwanted candle. He needed to get away, clear his mind and rearrange the pieces that were still left on the board. He couldn't let them get away with this. He just couldn't.

But first, he had to get hold of Sam. He called her cellphone. No response. He left a message to call him. If he went up to the DA's office it would only make things worse. He felt as though he couldn't wake up from a bad dream, as he headed for the elevators.

Back in her office, Lauren Taylor dropped her briefcase on the floor and slumped into her chair. She heaved a sigh and reluctantly reached for the phone.

"Mr. Wright, please, this is Lauren Taylor calling." She nervously tapped her pen against the edge of the desk as she waited. After several minutes a voice on the line brought her to attention. "Mr. Wright, its Lauren Taylor. Yes, sir, I'm fine. I'm just calling to keep you informed as you requested." She paused and wet her lips. "We were in court this morning and, uh," she hesitated. "It's just that, at this point the judge won't drop you from the witness list."

There was a pause as she listened with her eyes closed and lips pursed, as if she were a schoolgirl being chastened by the teacher. "I'm sorry, sir," Taylor said. "But I'm certain I'll be able to get her to agree before you have to testify." Another pause followed as she listened. "Yes, sir. I'll look forward to his call. I appreciate all your help." A buzzing sound in her ear jarred her as the line went dead. Grim-faced, she slowly replaced the receiver.

"Buddy, it's me. Did she call?" Jerry Reynolds, stood in the parking lot next to the courthouse, speaking into his cellphone. Reynolds moved the phone a few inches from his ear to mute the shouting from the other end.

"We know why he wants you to testify. That's why he got our contributions to that victims' group. He wants you on the stand so he can talk about us backing the opposition to the Initiative and accusing you of setting up Carlson to defeat it."

Reynolds held the phone away again and grimaced in annoyance. "I told you I didn't think she could handle it. But it'll be fine. I'll handle it." He paused to listen. "No, not for this kind of assignment. Let me handle it. Calm down. I've got an idea. There's some people I can call."

It was past midnight, and Sam had not called. Earl had gone straight home from court to be by the phone. As he waited, he forced his mind to stop concocting ways to strike back at Taylor for her cruel ploy. Right now he just wanted to see Sam. Hear her say it was going to be all right between them, so he could get back to thinking about the case. By midnight it was clear she wasn't going to call. At least not tonight. He needed to stop spinning the same thoughts about Sam over and over in his head. The best antidote was to go for a punishing run. He quickly got into his running shorts and shoes and headed out the door.

Down the street, two men sat in a nondescript grey sedan, parked deliberately out of the glare of the street light. The one with a broken nose and boxer's scar tissue elbowed his companion when Earl stepped out of his front door. They watched as Earl trotted toward the corner and turned toward the beach. The two men scrambled out of the car and plodded after him, their large bodies moved awkwardly, as if unaccustomed to any pace above a stroll.

There was a cold wind off the ocean. The moon hid behind a leaden sky. The night was black as tar. The waves made a thunderous sound as they pounded against the beach. A foghorn sounded a lonely call. Earl breathed heavily as he ran in the loose sand, pushing himself to numb his mind. He turned finally and headed back. Up ahead, he could see the dark outline of the Venice Pier. A piling loomed in front of him and he reached out for support. He was spent. He bent over, hands on his knees, struggling for air. A dark shape came out of the shadows. He straightened up. Something exploded against his head. It made an ugly, meaty sound. Lights flashed behind his eyes. Then it was dark.

Earl opened his eyes. A fly-specked light bulb hung from the ceiling on a short frayed cord. Bare plaster walls enclosed a narrow room. No furniture. No windows. A small glass panel stared at eye level from a paint-chipped metal door.

Earl lay on his back on a cot in the middle of the room, dressed only in his running shorts. He tried to sit up. A dull ache in his head was quickly eclipsed by a fiery pain in his ribs. He gasped and fell back. He lay panting for several seconds, before carefully raising his head. His wrists were buckled with leather cuffs attached at the waist to a wide leather belt. A braided sheet, knotted at his stomach, pressed him to the cot. Another set of cuffs bound his ankles. He was immobilized.

Each sweat-stained cuff was branded with MSH. He knew what that meant. Metropolitan State Hospital. The County insane asylum located in Norwalk. "Metro" was where the men who eat rats in the county jail ended up.

His shorts looked like they had served a lifetime as a hand towel in a bus station restroom. There was a small puncture wound on his forearm, as if he had been given an injection. Earl knew what he looked like, but he couldn't remember a thing.

A key turned in a lock and the door swung inward. A woman stepped through carrying a folding chair. About twenty-five, she wore a white lab coat under a smug expression. She rattled open the chair and sat next to his cot. A laminated ID card clipped to her coat held a photograph taken before she stopped smiling and cut her hair. The card read — Sharon Bates, Psychiatric Technician.

"You want to tell me what the hell is going on?" Earl said with outrage in his voice.

"Certainly, Mr. Darrow," she said in a condescending tone and flipped open a page on a clip board. She read for a minute then looked up. "Some passing motorists brought you to the Venice Community Health Clinic. They said you were directing traffic at the intersection of Pacific and Venice Boulevard. Dr. Phillips examined you and signed a commitment under section 5150."

"That's a 72-hour psychiatric hold," he said with astonishment.

"That's correct," she said. "I see you've had some experience with that."

"Of course. I mean, not personally, but in my profession."

"I see," she said and turned back to the file. "The police were summoned to transport you but it seems you didn't want to go. My, my, it says here that it took three officers to subdue you."

"Okay," he said. "I get the picture. Have I been given an injection of anything?"

She flipped more papers. "No, do you feel the need for one?"

"No, I just...."

"Good, then you can answer some questions for me," she said. "What color check do you get? Green or gold?"

Earl looked puzzled.

"Do you receive SSI or Disability?"

"Look, Miss Bates, this is all a terrible mistake. My name is Bobby Earl. I'm an attorney. Someone knocked me out and must have given me some type of drug."

She nodded and wrote in the file.

"What are you writing?"

"Just some notes for your file."

"I mean specifically."

"My last entry says paranoid schizophrenia."

Suddenly Earl felt very cold. "I understand how this must appear," he said, trying to sound reasonable. "I was probably acting very crazy. Psychotic, if you will. But I'm sure you're aware that certain drugs, such as phencyclidine, will produce psychotic behavior in even normal people."

"How long have you been using Angel Dust?" she asked.

"Listen to me, damn it. Call my office. James McManis will come down here and verify all this."

She closed the file and stood up. "It's Saturday, Mr. Darrow. Your office won't be open."

"Then call him at home. I'll give you the number."

She folded up her chair.

"Look this has gone far enough," he said. "Take off these goddamned cuffs."

"I think we'll leave the restraints on for now. Perhaps if you show you can control yourself, we'll remove them on Sunday."

"Okay, just one thing. Let me talk to a doctor."

"Certainly. First thing Monday morning when he comes in."

The door clicked shut.

Earl closed his eyes and forced himself to be calm. He had to think. Figuring out who put him in this fix was for another time. It was a long list, take your pick. The real question was why? He would be out in 72 hours. It seemed a lot of effort for such a short respite. Where was the upside for them?

Suddenly the scheme became clear. When the doctor signed him out on Monday morning there would be a reception committee to greet him at the front door. The Press. Tipped off by whoever orchestrated this little farce, the TV cameras would be rolling as the drug-crazed defender of Kathleen Carlson was released from the loony bin. On the news that night, the commentators would remark about the upcoming murder trial and chuckle over the footage, explaining that Bobby Earl, the defense lawyer in the case had identified himself as "Clarence Darrow," when he was found in the middle of the street directing traffic in his shorts.

The rumor mill at the courthouse would grind his reputation down to a punchline. A mere target for mockery. His every court appearance would be accompanied by sidelong glances, whispered asides and muffled snickers.

And what about jurors? His TV image was one no future juror was likely to forget. After such publicity, he could forget about the Carlson jury listening to him, let alone trusting him. That is, if she was still his client by trial time. As for presenting a defense that some powerful shadowy figures were the real culprits in the shooting, he could just imagine the jury's response: *consider the source.*

The crushing fear of shame descended and sat heavily on his chest. A wave of nausea welled up inside him. He clamped his eyes shut, fighting against panic. This was too serious to let emotions paralyze him. There was only one solution. Escape.

Earl was familiar with this place and its layout. He had been here to help the son of a prosecutor who, on a bad acid trip, had insisted on sharing his newfound enlightenment when he stumbled into a crowded church during Easter services. Metro was a temporary holding facility for mental cases who became a nuisance on the streets or were intent on hurting themselves. It was not Patton State Prison for the criminally insane, with its high walls, steel-barred cells and armed guards. Escape was possible. Only two sturdy, locked doors barred the path to the outside. He had to find a way. But there was nothing to be done until they took off these cuffs. Tomorrow he would need to be alert, so he let himself slip into a welcome sleep.

Sunday morning. He had spent all Saturday pretending to be cooperative. Now he was free to prowl D Ward. It was easy enough to do. The ward consisted of one gym size, open room with high ceilings and linoleum floors. Windows, high up the wall, filtered light through wire mesh screens.

Two dozen men and women were scattered about the room or slumped in a haze on vinyl-covered sofas and chairs. A stoop-shouldered man never looked up as he paced hurriedly back and forth along a line on the floor. A woman with dirty grey hair pressed her hands over her ears and shouted "Shut up" at voices only she could hear. The man across from Earl was bouncing his legs, "doing the Prolixin stomp," named after the drug which provided the music.

"It must be Sunday."

A short man with skin the color of fresh asphalt sank into a chair next to Earl. He wore a Giant's cap with an upturned bill and a pink plaid sports coat over his bare chest.

"Levon, he don't work but Sundays," the little man said and nodded toward a glass enclosed office which sat in the middle of the room like an illuminated fish tank. Inside, Miss Bates dropped brightly colored pills into small paper cups. Beside her stood a tall raw-boned man with a long hard-chinned face.

"Other staff won't have Levon, on account of how he treats us. But, Miss Bates, she says she need Levon, her being here alone and all." He leaned conspiratorially toward Earl and whispered. "I think she likes him 'cause he be packing heavy wood in his shorts." The little man leaned back and laughed, a hearty, infectious, pound-the-chair laugh. Earl found himself joining in, surprised at how good it felt, even when he had to grab his side.

"My name's Wilver. But you can call me Scooter."

"Bobby." They shook hands and Earl returned the little man's quick, easy smile.

Miss Bates stepped through the glass paneled door of the office, balancing a tray crowded with paper cups.

"Medicine!" she called.

Earl's little companion sprang from his chair, making clear why they called him Scooter.

Earl spent the day studying the room and learning the staff's routine. The only promising opportunity he saw was a phone that sat invitingly on a desk in the glass windowed office. But during the day, Miss Bates left the office only once, when she administered the medication.

At exactly 5:00 PM, Miss Bates flapped into her coat and walked to the metal door at the end of the room. She rummaged in her purse, then keyed the door and was gone. By 9:00 PM Earl was getting worried. Time was running out. Soon they would be locked in the sleeping barracks to await the morning. Monday morning.

He heard furniture scrape on the floor. Levon was pushing chairs and sofas into makeshift rows. He herded some patients into the seats and flopped down into a chair.

"All right," he announced. "It's Showtime."

Some of the commandeered audience hooted and giggled, others ducked their head and covered their ears.

"Tonight we feature Mr. Bojangles, followed by Miss Emily."

Scooter cautiously crossed the room and started to scuff his feet over the floor in a soft shoe dance while Levon kept time by clapping.

Earl rose to put an end to the little man's humiliation, but then he stopped. Levon's back was to him. Through the glass he could see the office phone just a few strides away. He slipped noiselessly into the room. He quickly dialed Munoz's number, then clutching the receiver he crouched out of sight beneath the desk, turning his back to the door.

On the fourth ring someone picked up, but suddenly a loud buzz filled his ear. The phone had gone dead. He turned slowly. Levon towered above him, his finger pressed on the phone cradle. The door was open. He should have locked it.

"You're starting off real poorly here, son," Levon said. He took the receiver out of Earl's hand. "Now, git."

He nodded toward the door.

Earl left and headed back to his chair.

"Not that way, son," Levon called. "It seems you weren't quite ready to shed those restraints. Let's get you back to the quiet room."

Earl knew that would be the end of all hope.

"Not tonight, Levon," he said.

Levon gave him a faint condescending smile and reached his arms toward him. Earl stepped up inside the outstretched arms, dipped a shoulder and drove his fist into Levon's stomach. The tall man's breath burst forth with a gasp as he hunched over. Earl laced his fingers behind Levon's neck and yanked his head down as he swung a knee up at the unprotected face. Levon jerked to the side, gripped Earl's outstretched leg and heaved. Earl hurtled backward through the air, reaching out desperately to cushion the fall. He landed hard and started to roll as soon as he hit the floor. Even so, the heel of Levon's boot thudded an inch from his ear.

Suddenly a metal folding chair appeared poised above Levon's head. It whistled down, bringing its hard edge crashing into his skull. He crumpled onto the linoleum.

Scooter stood behind him holding one of the chair legs in his hands. He stared down at the fallen figure, eyes wide with astonishment. Then he looked at Earl and broke into a broad grin.

Earl shouldered Levon's body onto its side, dug into his pockets and pulled out a set of keys. He gently took the chair from Scooter and stepped back into the office. He replaced Miss Bate's folding chair and called Munoz to come get him.

"No time to explain, just get down here."

Then he opened the filing cabinet and retrieved his file. When he left the office Scooter was still staring down at the unconscious body.

"Scooter, come on, let's get out of here."

The little man seemed startled to hear his name. He stared back at Earl, seemingly unable to move.

"Come on, move it," Earl said. "When he wakes up, you'll get in trouble."

"He'll never believe I done this," Scooter said. "And all them is too scared or too crazy to tell." He looked over at the others who were either staring off with disinterest or jabbering to themselves. "I'll be fine. Just open the sleeping barracks and I'll get everyone in bed."

"Aren't you coming?"

"Bobby, I got no place to go."

They held each other's eyes, letting the silence speak for them. After a moment, Earl unlocked the sleeping barracks and headed toward the outside door, pausing only to put a hand on Scooter's shoulder.

Outside, he paused and opened his face to the night sky. A pair of searchlights dueled in the dark like fencing sabers. An airliner outlined against a watery moon seemed to hang as motionless as a Christmas tree ornament. After all, Earl said to himself, it had turned out to be a fine night.

CHAPTER 22

When Earl opened his front door, he was met by a bucking Henceforth, delighted at his return. The big dog galloped into the kitchen and nosed his food dish toward Earl, then edged back, poised in eager anticipation. "I'm sorry, big fella.' You must be starved." He poured in a double ration which the dog seemed to inhale without chewing. Earl was grateful, that during his absence, Henceforth had access to the backyard through his over-sized doggie door. As clumsy as Henceforth was around unwary lamps and stray coffee cups, he was quite fastidious when it came to fouling his own living space. He would have been mortified at his inevitable surrender to nature's call if he had been confined inside for two days.

Even the welcome sight of a jubilant Henceforth did nothing to keep Earl from slipping into a dark mood. Having escaped the prospect of a public humiliation, his thoughts were now mired in the wreckage of his case. The court's rulings meant he would be forced to defend an innocent client with only a shadow of a defense, effectively blocked from any attempt to pull back the curtain on the real forces at work behind these events. This was a case he had to win or it would haunt him, bubbling up to torment him in the middle of his nights.

His thoughts moved on to all the innocent lives that had been stolen around this case: Polly Hartman, crushed to death to prevent her from testifying; Travis Miller, shot trying to stop the Sharks; Adam Hartman, attempting to expose the fraud of the private prison system. And Kate Carlson, set up to spend her life in prison.

He squeezed his eyes shut and told himself to snap out of it. Allowing his mind to be flooded with outrage would be like putting on blinders. He needed an unhindered view. In trial, things always changed and changed quickly. An unexpected opening might appear anywhere. If such a chance came along he had to be able to spot it and instantly grab hold of it before it passed by. This was no time to distort his focus. There was a jury trial looming, one that he needed to win.

Earl walked into his bedroom and sat on the bed. He pulled open the drawer to the nightstand. A .38 revolver lay there as if daring someone to pick it up. Earl hated guns. He had seen how they could convert an angry split-second impulse into a life-altering tragedy. Guns were as indiscriminate as cancer in claiming the good with the bad.

He had been forced to carry this gun during the Seabrooke murder trial when his life had been in danger. It was the price Martha had extracted when he insisted she leave town for her own safety. Now, he told himself, he must decide once again whether to arm himself. He was clearly a target. He had just been knocked unconscious, kidnapped and drugged. But to what end? If his assailants had wanted to kill him there had been nothing to stop them. They had certainly shown no such hesitation with others. However, in dealing with him, murder was apparently a notch up the solution scale they weren't willing to risk. Or maybe, he just wasn't worth it, which in a strange way was more deflating than reassuring. At any rate, it seemed a bit premature to start an arms race. He decided against packing.

He discarded any thought of calling the police. He had assaulted a Metro staff member to enable his escape, and he had no tangible proof that he was actually kidnapped and not just out flying on some genie juice. An official report would be too enticing to keep quiet, inevitably bringing to light the whole improbable story, the very thing who ever staged it wanted to achieve. Best leave Clarence Darrow to the pages of history.

He took a shower, slipped on a clean tee-shirt and jeans and padded barefoot into the kitchen. He was enormously hungry. On the counter, the phone was blinking for attention, as if excited to have a voice message. Earl pushed the button. It was Sam.

"I've been calling for two days. Where the hell are you? I didn't want to have to leave a message, but I guess I'll have to." There was a long silence. "After court on Friday, I've been thinking. About us, my job, everything I guess. How it all fits together. Or not. Or whether it even matters. Anyway, I need some time. Just a little. To sort things out." Another long pause. "I'm sorry this comes when you're about to start your trial, but maybe that's a good thing. I know how you get. Anyway, good luck with your case, Bobby. I'm sorry."

Earl was stunned. He had received messages from girlfriends in the past. Women who had grown weary of pounding on the protective shell he built around his emotions. But this was different. Sam was no ordinary girlfriend. He had tried with Sam. He knew at times he had fallen short, that he never matched her courage with his own, never succeeded in knotting his life with hers. But he had tried. Now he felt the wrenching pain of separation, as if a part of him had been torn away, leaving a gaping void. Life without Sam.

He grabbed a beer from the refrigerator, tipped it back and drank deeply. He wiped the back of his hand across his mouth and told himself to settle down. Stop manufacturing a crisis. She said she needed time, that's all. No final goodbye, no fade to black. They both had known this day would come. Her being a prosecutor and him a defense attorney made facing this chasm inevitable. They had to find a bridge they could both walk over.

So he'll wait. And she's right about the timing. The best medicine for him right now was to bury himself in the trial.

Over the next several days, Earl came to the office in jeans and his Cal sweatshirt. Martha held his calls and ran interference with his other clients while he pored over his binders and made endless notes. After the pretrial conference, each day had taken on a quiet urgency. He felt a constant dull anxiety over the looming trial date.

So Earl read and reread the reports. Day after day. Gathering material to prepare a line of questioning for each witness, what to bring out, what to attack, what to get the witness to change or modify. Examining witnesses was a game of attrition played over the facts in a case. Earl's aim was to nail down his facts, the ones that fit the defense version of events and then protect them from any assault by the prosecution. The facts that supported the prosecution theory had to be discredited or outright destroyed. Like pieces on a chess board, he wanted to preserve his facts and sweep the board clean of the opponent's. Those left standing were the building blocks around which he would build his final argument.

Earl picked up his trial notebook. Flipping through the handwritten notes for each witness reconfirmed what he already knew. It was the same with each one. He was preparing to poke holes in the prosecution case, to call their facts into question. But where was his version of these events, one he could argue to the jury and have the facts to back it up? There were certainly candidates he could nominate, such as Buddy Wright and PCA, who had some compelling reasons to set up Kate in order to defeat her Initiative. But he needed something to bridge the gap between a motive and some proof that they actually did it. Without that proof, bare motives were not even admissible before a jury. As for Captain Gunther and the Sharks, without Corbett, the Assistant Attorney General, what proof did he have that the Sharks even existed or that by wearing a wire Officer Miller posed a threat to them?

Without some breaks along the way, he would end up just playing defense, which might be a way to put on a good show, but would never win a murder case.

It was barely six a.m. when Earl walked into Jimmy's Diner, and most of the regulars were already there. In the red vinyl booths were groups chatting over breakfast plates and newspapers. Millie, holding a coffee pot, smiled a greeting at him as she stood joking with a table of customers. Munoz was seated at a booth against the wall, eclipsing the bench on his side.

"Thanks for joining me for sunrise service," Earl said and smiled. "I have to cover a couple courts this morning to explain my unavailability due to a previous commitment to be a 'piñata' in the Carlson case."

"That will be a first," Manny said.

Millie appeared and poured Bobby a cup of coffee. "Where's Sam?" she asked. "I haven't seen you two in a while. Don't tell me you let that girl get away, Bobby?"

"We've both been pretty busy," Earl said, not knowing how to explain their status and not wanting to sum it up with some trite label.

Millie squinted in skepticism at his answer. She had long since made known her approval of Sam, and Earl knew she was about to give voice to her disappointment with him when she was called to pick up an order.

Munoz watched Millie move toward the kitchen. He knew better than to tread into Earl's private life. "Well," he said. "I've got a couple things you can check off your list."

"Okay, what have you got?"

"That target from the shooting range, the one our shooter autographed. Jones did raise some prints off it and, sure enough, they matched the partial he got off the bullet casing we found."

"Manny, that's great."

"Not so fast. Jones called in some favors at our Department of Justice where they keep the criminal fingerprint database for the whole State. They ran it for him. Unfortunately, there were no hits. Which means our man doesn't have a criminal record in California."

"Too bad," Earl said. "But what about the FBI? They collect the prints from every law enforcement agency in the country."

"True. But the FBI only takes requests from law enforcement for a search of their database. Which means we would have to go through LAPD, because Haywood would never do it. And how would we justify a defense request that's based on a hunch about a crash that has already been determined an accident?"

"Damn it," Earl said in frustration. "He's got to have his prints on file somewhere. How about the military? Somebody capable of making that kind of shot probably pulled a hitch in the Army. They keep a database of fingerprints."

"I know, but even if they would do it for us, which I doubt, you need a name for them to do a search."

Earl pursed his lips shut in frustration.

"I did get something on Rattner's cellphone," Manny said. "Remember, it was recovered from his truck at the tow yard. It was a bit crusty, but I gave it to my tech geek. And damn if he didn't pull up the number of the last call Rattner received before the crash."

Earl waited, unwilling to get his hopes up.

"But it was a burner," Munoz said. "One of those prepaid cellphones that comes with its own number. It has a certain number of minutes on it. Drug dealers use them a lot. You pay cash for them, so there's no record of who bought it. They use them for a week or two then toss them. That's what must have happened with this one, because the number is disconnected." Manny handed a paper to Earl. "My guy wrote it up for you, with the number of the call Rattner received, in case it ever turns up."

Earl slowly nodded and smiled ruefully. This was what he had expected. Another dead end. And even if they had put a name to the shooter, there was nothing to show who he was working for.

"Good work, Manny. It's not your fault they didn't pan out. But I'll tell you what. Let's turn all this over to the prosecution: the bullet casing, Rattner's phone, the video tape, the fingerprint report and the bulls-eye target. If we ever catch a break and we can use any of this at trial, we're required to have shown them to the prosecution beforehand. Give them to that detective. I don't trust Taylor."

Earl spent the final two days before the trial in the office idly flipping through his binders. He knew this exercise was brought on by his normal pretrial nerves, for which he had never found a cure and that always vanished as soon as the trial started. A knock on the door drew his attention, and Martha stuck her head in. "I didn't want to buzz. It's Sam on the line." She gave him a concerned look. When two weeks had passed without Martha fielding a call from Sam, she had demanded to be told what was going on.

Martha's announcement had given Earl a jolt. A call from Sam was what he had been waiting for, but now he was apprehensive. There was no guarantee it would be the conversation he wanted. He stared at the phone. He felt the same torment as when a jury filed in with a decision, and he sat waiting for the clerk to read the verdict. A part of him wanted to hear the answer, but another part just wanted to push the pause button and freeze time. He picked up the phone.

"Hey, Sam," he said, trying hard for the right tone.

"Hi, Bobby," she said in a restrained voice.

"I've missed you," he said.

There was a pause on the line before she said, "I've missed you, too."

Earl was tense. He tried to avoid saying too little, but was afraid of saying too much. "How are you?"

"All right. But Taylor made sure her lie got circulated throughout the office. So, I've been getting a few stares. My friends know it's not true, but there are always people who seem to delight in getting in a free jab."

"Sam, I'm really sorry."

"I know, Bobby. It's not your fault. It's our professions. They're a tough match. I just have to figure out a few things."

"I understand."

"But on a lighter note, I thought I'd go by your place and pick up Henceforth. You're starting your trial next week, so I just thought he might stay with Beauty and me. I know you'll be working late, so it'll be one less thing to worry about."

"Thanks Sam. That's really thoughtful. The old hound will be thrilled."

"Okay, then. So good luck with the trial. And Bobby, I hope you kick her ass."

Earl put down the phone. Sam hadn't sounded like her normal self, but she didn't sound as though she were ready to call it quits either. At least not yet. God, he hated this. He felt so helpless, because this was about the one thing he could never change. He was a criminal defense lawyer.

The report that lay on her desk had been as welcome as a bootprint in freshly laid cement. Lauren Taylor had already completed preparing her case, it was buttoned up and air tight, when yesterday Detective Carter had dropped this on her. The defense had turned over this hodgepodge of items that they might possibly use in the trial. Not to her, mind you, but to *him*, and Carter had listed them in this written report: a flash drive with a video of some guy signing a target, a bullet casing apparently with the same guy's print on it and a cellphone.

She remembered how she reacted when she first surveyed this strange collection. It had sent a wave of panic through her, sick to her stomach with fear that she had overlooked something. Her mind immediately started spinning imaginary scenarios in which Bobby Earl had somehow concocted a defense that would defeat her. But then reason reasserted itself and she recognized it for what it was. Earl was merely trying to distract her, make her chase her tail trying to connect the unconnectable. It was a tactic with which she was quite familiar. She smiled with satisfaction remembering her ploy with Earl's girlfriend. This was merely his weak attempt at payback.

It had, however, caused her a certain inconvenience. Buddy Wright, the union president, had instructed her to immediately pass on any new developments in the case to both him and those two lawyers. She hated to do it. It only created questions she couldn't answer and gave those lawyers more chances to second guess her tactics. Nonetheless, she had borrowed a secretary and told her to make copies of the flash drive and photos of the rest and send them to Buddy, Leland Bain and Enoch Bowdeen. Her gaze shifted over to her desk phone and she braced herself for the anticipated calls.

CHAPTER 23

"You've been avoiding my calls," the man said evenly into his cellphone. He stood at the window of his motel room, staring out through a narrow part in the curtain. A fierce morning sun caused last night's dew to sparkle on the windshields of the cars in the parking lot.

"What security video are you talking about?" the man said quietly and listened. "A shooting range? Hundreds of people target practice every day. If that...."

He was interrupted.

"Slow ... down," he said, drawing out each word. "They have a bullet casing with fingerprints. All right," he said calmly. "And they match what?"

The man stepped away from the window and sat on the bed.

"The prints match those on the target in the video, Okay."

He sat thinking for a moment.

"Did they identify these fingerprints? Do they have a name?"

He listened.

"I didn't think so," he said dispassionately. "So there's nothing to worry about. We...."

He was interrupted and listened.

"Let's not indulge in speculation. I took the only opportunity available. You knew that might be necessary. So why haven't you met me with my payment?"

He paused to listen.

"No, I will not meet with a third party. We agreed in the beginning, for our mutual security, that no one else would be involved. We would only deal with each other, face to face. No wire transfers or intermediaries. If I...."

He was interrupted again and listened.

"No one will see us together. You are being paranoid. There is no way that anyone even knows you exist. You must follow the agreed procedures. I will...."

Suddenly there was a buzz on the line.

The man looked at his cellphone, perplexed. He slowly placed it beside him on the bed and sat still, staring ahead, as he thought. After a time, he rotated his neck to loosen the muscles, then stepped again to the window and parted the curtain. He stood looking out and thinking.

THE SUN WAS NEARLY SETTING when Munoz passed through the entrance to the Los Angeles City Zoo. He followed the path around the Children's Area and took the fork to the right. A loud chorus of howls shattered the soft evening quiet. Continuing on he found his destination. The monkey cage. A sheer net, supported by a thin metal frame, rose some 40 feet into the air enclosing a heavy canopy of leafy trees. The tree branches were shaking wildly as black furred monkeys bounced on them as they shrieked. The ear shattering calls made the sign on the cage seem redundant. It read "Howler Monkeys."

On a bench to the side, Detective Joe Carter sat with his hat pushed back, his hands folded on his stomach, looking up at the monkeys. Munoz joined him.

"Some spot you chose, Joe," Munoz said.

"Yeah, ain't it?" Carter chuckled. "With me hanging around the DA's Office so much, my face is probably known to a few people. I figured they weren't the type that watched the Nature Channel."

"They probably see enough animals on the street."

Carter nodded in agreement then gestured toward the cage. "You know what's interesting? I was just talking with this zookeeper. He tells me that only the male monkeys do that yelling. They're the loudest land mammals in the world. The females just make this little bark."

"Well, it's sure not like that in my family," Munoz said.

"Right." Carter smiled. "But they only howl like that in the evening. It's to protect their territory. When rival bands call back it tells them how close they are. But see, there aren't any rival bands here. So the zookeepers broadcast these recorded howler sounds from a safe distance away, just like in the wild. Keeping things like they're supposed to be."

"That's interesting, Joe, but is that why you got me down here?"

"Not exactly," Carter said. "But first tell me. Do we still have our deal? Whatever I tell you or give you, my name stays out of it."

"Absolutely. You've got my word."

"All right," Carter said. He picked up a large manila envelope that lay on the bench beside him and handed it to Munoz.

"What's this?"

"That's the rest of the stuff we recovered from Hartman's cell."

"I thought we'd been given everything already," Munoz said. "That's what Taylor told the judge anyway."

"Yeah, I know. She was a little confused. Let's just say some of it fell through the cracks. I doubt it will do you any good, but now we're square."

Munoz met his stare and read between the lines. He opened the envelope and fingered quickly through the papers. Inside he saw a Public Records Request and numerous papers from the state in response.

"You know, Joe, I still don't get it. Why are you doing this?"

Carter smiled. "Hey, I'm just keeping things the way they're supposed to be."

"Right," Munoz said. "And we're a bunch of monkeys." He gave Carter a sarcastic look. "No, I mean it. Why are you doing this?"

Carter looked away and thought for a moment. "You remember that DA friend of mine? The one I told you about? The one the guards union ran out of office?"

"Yeah," Munoz said.

"Well, he told me when I first made detective that there was only one way for guys like him and me to last in this business. We had to play by the rules. No matter which way the chips fell. It was just easier that way, because we weren't smart enough to get away with doing it any other way." He chuckled softly and turned to face Munoz.

Munoz sat silently, sensing there was more to be said.

After a pause, Carter said, "And, I guess, if I'm being deep down honest, part of it is to cover my own ass."

Munoz was silent.

"See, if things ever went sideways, and there were questions whether this case was handled on the up and up, I'd be the first person my DA would throw under the bus."

Munoz nodded.

"You know what I think?" Munoz said. "I think you're starting to have doubts about Carlson's guilt."

Carter smiled wryly. "There's this old saying. If you hear hoofbeats behind you, don't turn round expecting to see a zebra." He paused. "Everything points to your gal, Manny. Sorry, but there's nobody else in the picture." He stood up. "Now I'm going to go look at a *real* zebra. Never seen one before."

The trial was scheduled to start on Monday, and Earl was riveted to his office chair. To go home would only invite a cold shower of guilt that he should be working on the case. In reality, he knew there was nothing further he could do, but he couldn't leave. Yesterday Munoz had given Earl a folder full of papers that had been taken from Hartman's cell. The rest of the material that Taylor had told the judge did not exist. Manny's "source" had said the failure to turn these over earlier had just been a "mistake," the result of some "confusion." *Yeah, right*, Earl thought. Taylor's only confusion was whether the rules actually applied to the prosecution. After all, she represented the forces of light holding back the darkness.

Hiding evidence from the defense was nothing new. But it always meant one thing to Earl. That the prosecutor thought the evidence was so helpful to the defense that withholding it was worth the risk of getting caught, so he had read through the papers with that in mind. None of it seemed to help his case. His only surprise was that Taylor had felt the need to hide any of it.

James McManis suddenly filled the doorway of Earl's office. His bushy eyebrows were white with age, but his eyes were as alert and penetrating as a hawk's. "When Manny stopped by yesterday and dropped off that new material, I took the liberty of looking it over. With your trial starting, I thought you might need a hand." He stood waiting at the doorway.

Earl could sense the old lawyer's hesitation. McManis' responsibility on the case had ended when he secured a change in the venue, but the victory had apparently rekindled his old competitive fire. It was heartwarming to Earl to see the old warrior unwilling to give up the chase.

"Thanks, James. I could use your insight." Earl understood that McManis needed to be invited back aboard.

McManis smiled, and took a seat.

"You know Manny wouldn't tell me where he got all this," McManis said, holding up a sheaf of papers. "Do you think we can rely on its authenticity?"

"If Manny says they're good, they're good," Earl said with confidence. "It's the bid package that PCA submitted to win the Haywood contract. I read through it and saw a clause in the contract that allows them to reject any inmate that has a serious medical condition. That would have supported our case that PCA and the union viewed Hartman as a threat, because he was building a case that PCA wasn't cheaper than state prisons. They were just cherry-picking healthy inmates, which would have given a boost to Kate's initiative. But without Polly...." His voice trailed off and he shrugged his shoulders.

"One thing did catch my eye," McManis said. "The guards union filed a letter of concern against a competitor of PCA, who was also bidding on the contract. General Corrections Corporation of America. The union attached an internal memo that GCCA sent to their outside attorney in connection with another matter. The memo is clearly an attorney-client communication, which means it's privileged and protected. Nobody else is supposed to have this. I can't figure out how the union got this."

He handed the paper to Earl.

GENERAL CORRECTIONS CORPORATION OF AMERICA

From: James Service, Corporate Counsel
To: Simel & Simmons
Re: Attorney-Client Communications
CC: All Wardens and Managerial Level Staff in Mississippi and Tennessee

Our internal investigation of inmate complaints concerning sexual and physical abuse by correction staff at our seven facilities in Mississippi and Tennessee has been completed. The conclusion reached in the report is that GCCA does have some exposure to both civil liability and possible criminal prosecution.

We have also been informed by the Prison Review Board of complaints lodged against us for providing substandard medical care. It is our official position that we have met our contractual obligation which is to provide treatment that meets the "industry standard."

In addition, we are informing you that we have been put on official notice that the Internal Revenue Service is initiating an investigation into whether or not GCCA has fully complied with its mandatory obligation to contribute to the Correction Officer's Pension Fund.

As our outside counsel, Simel & Simmons (S&S) is hereby instructed to provide legal advice and guidance to us in addressing these issues. The in-house report, along with any underlying data such as statements, notes or writings, has been sent to S&S as an attorney-client communication upon which we are seeking your advice.

S&S attorneys are instructed to conduct interviews of our staff and collect all relevant material in their possession that pertains in any manner to these complaints and any response to them by our staff. All staff has been ordered to fully cooperate with S&S and diligently search their records for any material you request and relinquish to you all originals, copies or notes. It is our understanding that all communications with and any documents provided to S&S will be protected under the attorney-client privilege and may not be discussed with any outside party. Our staff understands that any requests by third parties for statements or interviews must be referred to S&S.
James Service
Corporate Counsel

Earl read the memo and looked up.

"I saw this," he said.

"It's an old dodge in civil cases," McManis explained. "When a corporation gets itself sued, they hire an outside law firm. They park all their incriminating documents with the outside firm and have those lawyers take statements from any employee who might end up as a witness. Then the corporation claims that all this material is protected by the attorney-client privilege and the other side can't get to it."

"It's easier for some prosecutors on the criminal side. They just claim none of it exists," Earl said.

"But the whole reason a corporation does this is to be sure none of this gets out. So how did the union get this?"

"Beats me, James," Earl said, but his tone betrayed a lack of interest. He knew he should share the old man's curiosity but he couldn't and he knew why. It happened every time he was about to start a jury trial. The stress began to compress the world around him like a steel vise. It was as if he was looking through the wrong end of a telescope that concentrated his focus completely on the upcoming trial. His mind purged any thoughts except those about the case; how to skirt a rule of evidence, how to phrase a question, which answer would best fit into his argument. He recognized that the sleepless nights of worry were approaching.

McManis' paused, his alert eyes studied Earl "Lad, I can see you've got your hands full. Just give a shout if there's anything I can do."

"Thanks, James. That would be great."

CHAPTER 24

When Earl returned home Sunday night from the office, he first went to his closet to lay out his clothes for the coming day. His closet was divided between two opposing fashion camps. On the left were his custom tailored suits of English worsted wool, Italian wool and silk, and Irish linen, which he wore for brief court appearances and initial client interviews. No jury ever saw any of these. On the right hung his jury suits, off-the-rack wool suits in dark blue and grey. Serious, no-nonsense suits. The choice of a shirt was simple, he took the first off the top of a stack of identical white button-down dress shirts and added a dark conservative tie.

He slipped on a pair of jeans and went into the kitchen. He laid two pairs of identical leather shoes side by side on an outspread newspaper. Solid, dependable, black wing-tip shoes. Seated at the table, Earl applied polish with a black-stained cloth, then picked up a shoe brush. He stuck a hand inside a shoe and began to rhythmically buff it, periodically adding his own spit to achieve a high gloss. He held out the shoe at arm's length to admire the shine under the light, then moved on to the next. This was all part of the same ritual he performed the night before the start of every jury trial.

This attention to his dress was not to costume himself for some role he played in court, some false persona to appeal to the jury. Earl knew full well that would never work. Sooner or later, jurors always sensed if a lawyer was play acting. Earl was always himself in the courtroom; he could never do it any other way.

At the same time, Earl understood that jurors like everyone else, viewed people through a prism of prejudices. Opinions formed over a lifetime of experiences. Some juror might draw an inference about him based on a memory cued by the type of suit he wore or whether his shoes were polished. Assumptions which could hamper his ability to earn their trust or even damage his credibility. All this from perceived messages unintentionally sent. Messages he couldn't control. It was the same reason he was careful who he was seen talking to in the hallway or where he went to lunch. Earl wanted to appear to the jury as a blank slate, so their impression of him would be based solely on what he said and did within the four walls of the courtroom.

It always surprised him how little mention was made of the fact that there was not a single window in any courtroom in the country. It was more than an architectural artifice. It symbolized the principle that the intrusion of outside influences and opinions had no place in the business of justice. A reminder that decisions should only be based upon what transpired within the courtroom. It was an ideal, he knew more honored in the breach than the observance.

And, of course, he never forgot about luck. That was why his lucky tee-shirt waited on a hook in his closet. On its front was a reprint of the stripe-suited convict pictured on the Monopoly "Get Out Of Jail" card under which was printed "A Reasonable Doubt For A Reasonable Price." He had first worn it when he ran out of tee-shirts on the opening day of a murder trial. After his client was acquitted he had worn it on the first day of every trial since.

In the early morning, Earl abandoned any effort at sleep and drove downtown in the predawn darkness. He ate breakfast alongside the night crew from the produce market at Phillipe's "Home of the Original French-Dip Sandwich," and drank enough coffee to jack-up a cadaver, while he waited for the court day to begin. Earl was in the hallway when the doors finally opened at 8:30 a.m. He handed Mrs. Henshaw, the bailiff, a box of donuts for the staff and went into the court's lock-up.

Kate Carlson was pacing in her cell, dressed in the same Armani pantsuit that she had worn previously, but it hung even more loosely on her now-thin shoulders. Even ill-fitting, it was the look Earl had wanted. A professional woman. A successful lawyer. Someone with a lot to lose.

"How do you feel?" Earl asked pleasantly.

"I'm nervous," she admitted. "But I'm glad we're finally getting started."

"Good. So am I," he said with a smile. "Here's what will happen today."

Earl understood that while Kate was a lawyer, even a brilliant one, she was not a trial lawyer. To equate a tax lawyer with a trial lawyer was like saying an English soccer goalie and an American quarterback both played football.

"The judge will bring in about a hundred prospective jurors and spend the day questioning them to determine who can serve for two or three weeks. Hardship qualification. We'll begin picking our twelve from those left standing."

"Those without the brains or imagination to come up with a good excuse," she said.

Earl ignored her comment. He never allowed himself to look at jurors that way. Most jurors took their job quite seriously, so he preferred to treat them with respect, assuming that they were all on this journey together. Partners in the quest for the right answer, and he was there to help them.

"The point is our twelve are somewhere in that group. So you need to act, starting now, the same way you will when our jury is finally picked. Whenever we're in the courtroom, the jury will be watching you, sizing you up, trying to decide if you're the type of person who would do what the DA claims you did. Try to act natural, which I understand is almost impossible, with all that's at stake." He smiled sympathetically. "But try. And when we're out there never ever argue with me, don't tug on my sleeve if you think I'm making a mistake or if you want to tell me something. You'll have a yellow pad. Write it down. We'll talk about it when we get back in the lock-up and if we disagree you can yell at me in here all you want. But never, never in front of the jury." He eyed her with resolve. "This has nothing to do with my ego, it has to do with the picture the DA wants to draw of you as someone who thought she could outsmart the system. So don't look like you're in charge out there."

She looked intently at him for a moment. "Bobby, as you undoubtedly know by now, this whole ordeal has been extremely difficult for me. I don't just mean being in jail or facing a murder charge for something I didn't do. I mean us. Letting go. Putting my fate, my very life, in someone else's hands, someone else's judgment." She smiled. "I want you to know, I'm certain I made the right choice."

As he stepped back into the courtroom, Lauren Taylor was leaning against the jury box, lost in thought. Her blond hair was pulled back in a ponytail, which made her young face seem too small for her large, green-framed glasses. She wore a pale grey pantsuit, and no makeup. She seemed younger to Earl and less venomous. He hoped the jury was not fooled, but he had to admit it was a good move. That is if she could carry it off. Posing as an inexperienced young woman up against an older seasoned man might gain her some sympathy from the jury, perhaps even chalk up some shortcoming in her case to a mere oversight. But playing the coltish rookie seemed a hard fit for the Lauren Taylor *he* knew. He wondered just how long she could keep it up.

The bailiff brought Kate to the counsel table to join Earl, and the first batch of prospective jurors were crowded onto the spectator benches. Judge Parker ran through the offered excuses for not serving with the speed and decisiveness of a tobacco auctioneer. As the panel saw the normal excuses being rejected, a few hardy souls sought a reprieve based on creativity. One said she needed to be available to give her dog his antipsychotic medication while another feared being away from the work place she shared with her husband because he had just hired an attractive, much younger assistant. They drew some laughs but no sale with Judge Parker.

By the end of the day Judge Parker felt she had enough eligible jurors to begin the selection process, so they recessed for the day. Tomorrow the real game began.

"Your Honor," Earl said at the start of the next day's session. "Before the jurors are brought in and we call the first twelve into the box, I have a motion."

"I'll hear it," the judge said.

"The Los Angeles Superior Court has adopted a policy to refer to all jurors by the number on their jury badge rather than by name. I strongly object to this. The jurors may infer that this is being done to hide their identity because they are somehow in danger, and that Ms. Carlson is the source of that danger. An anonymous jury clearly violates the defendant's right to a presumption of innocence. There is absolutely no evidence that these jurors face any threat from any source."

"Your Honor," Taylor said. "The People request that the policy be followed and jurors be referred to by number."

"Do you have any reason to suspect the defendant constitutes any threat?" the judge asked.

"Not at this time," Taylor said reluctantly.

The judge looked bemused. "Still, I'm going to follow the policy," Parker said. "But I will inform the jury that this is a policy required in every single criminal case and has nothing to do with the defendant."

Earl rose from his chair at the counsel table to begin the day's *voir dire*, the questioning of the jurors. The *voir dire*'s supposed purpose was to determine whether a juror was capable of being fair and impartial, but everyone knew that was not what the lawyers used it for. Each side was looking for *their* kind of fair juror, that is, one who would decide the case their way.

The California legislature, at the behest of prosecutors, had given judges the authority to severely curtail the scope of juror examinations. The judge could limit the amount of time each side could expend; limit questions solely to determining whether the juror was personally biased against the defendant; or even require all questions to be submitted in writing beforehand. At a pretrial conference, Judge Parker said she would not put in place any prior restrictions on them and would "just see how it goes."

Rather than engage in a meaningless series of questions that only elicited monosyllabic responses, Earl tried to make the questioning take on the character of a conversation. Like friends talking, exchanging ideas and accepting the other's opinions with respect. What books were they reading, movies they liked, hobbies. He, of course, discussed the reasons behind the principles of Reasonable Doubt and the Presumption of Innocence, but then moved on to some of the issues in the case that he was anxious about. He wanted to get these thorny concerns out in the open where they could be talked about: jurors' distrust of lawyers; so-called "expert" opinions; "dangerous" prison inmates; prison guards' integrity, and so on. Each answer gave him a better feel for the juror's leanings.

Lauren Taylor had a different style. She worked hard at ingratiating herself, particularly with the women, sympathizing about juggling work and family duties, the challenges of raising teenagers. Even sharing a juror's confessed nervousness by admitting similar feelings of her own, as if this were her first trip to the plate and hoped she didn't embarrass herself. It was too early for Earl to judge the result.

When she finished, the chess match began. Each side had 20 challenges with which to excuse individual jurors without stating a reason, thus dismissing the ones they feared would vote against them. The goal was to get rid of the other side's jurors, while keeping as many of your own as possible.

Earl quickly saw that Taylor was good at it. She could smell compassion and spot critical thinking, both unwelcome traits in a prosecution juror. After exchanging a few challenges, it also became clear that she had adopted the thinking of some of her local colleagues. She wanted to play her tune to a jury using only the white keys. After excusing several seemingly acceptable black jurors, Earl asked to approach the bench. He argued that Taylor was violating a firmly established Constitutional principle by excusing jurors based solely on their race. Taylor offered some cleverly invented race-neutral reasons for each excusal. The judge gave her a skeptical look, but Taylor had said enough on the record to pass the test. Earl lost his motion, but from that point on Taylor was very circumspect in exercising her penchant for members of her own tribe.

At the end of two days, they had a jury. Earl surveyed them. It was a typical Los Angeles jury, as ethnically varied as the city's restaurants, a rich bouillabaisse of life experiences and social classes. Two African-Americans, two Latinos, five whites, an Asian and two indeterminates. Seven women, five men. A postal worker, two housewives, two teachers, a nurse, three clerical workers, a retired salesman, a bus driver and a dental technician.

It was a jury Earl could live with. He had to. The trial started tomorrow.

CHAPTER 25

Judge Parker strode onto the bench and seated herself. On the wall behind her was a large round emblem of the California State Seal. The single strand of pearls resting outside her judicial robe struck a contrasting note with the State Seal's depiction of the armor clad Roman goddess of warfare — Minerva.

The judge nodded to the bailiff, who ushered in the jury. The jurors filed out of their room and edged by each other in the box, taking care to reclaim their assigned seats like children on the first day of class.

"Ms. Taylor," the judge said. "Your opening statement."

Taylor and Detective Carter sat, as custom dictated, closest to the jury. She rose and went to the podium.

"I am here seeking justice for this man, Travis Elijah Miller." She clicked the pointer in her hand, and a photo of a smiling Officer Miller appeared on a screen against the wall beside the witness box. The jurors all shifted their gaze to the right. "He was a husband, a father and a Corrections Officer, who was murdered in cold blood. Gunned down doing his job. The job we all asked him to do. Keeping violent, dangerous criminals behind bars, in prison where they belong."

Earl could see that Taylor had abandoned her pose as an inexperienced novice. Her voice was strong and confident as she gazed steadily into the eyes of the jurors.

"Officer Miller was executed as he stood defenseless, by this man, Adam Hartman." Another click and a booking photo of a dazed Hartman replaced the smiling Miller. "Hartman was an inmate serving time at Haywood Prison for attempting to kill a man. He murdered Officer Miller during an escape attempt from that prison. An attempt planned and orchestrated by that woman, Kathleen Carlson." The juror's eyes all followed Taylor's outstretched arm as she pointed at Kate. Earl had warned Kate this would be coming and cautioned her to remain composed, and to meet Taylor's gaze. For his part, he tried to appear unfazed under their scrutiny, as if this was all to be expected. Nothing more than the usual courtroom theatrics.

"And why did Officer Miller have to die? For a fantasy. That's right. Kathleen Carlson had convinced herself that she was in love with a younger man and that he, in turn, was actually in love with her. This same young man. Adam Hartman. who murdered Officer Miller.

Now, Hartman was eligible for parole in seven years. So, you may ask, why not wait until he got out to start living this dream? True love can wait, right? But not this couple. You see, Hartman had done something — who knows what? — that angered a powerful and dangerous prison gang. There were death threats. So they felt they couldn't wait. So what did Kathleen Carlson do? She concocted a plan to help him escape."

Earl casually looked at the jurors. They seemed engrossed in her tale, following every word.

"First, she got a gun, one small enough to smuggle into the prison. Then she drove up to the prison on the appointed day, stopping on the way to test fire the gun." She clicked and a photo of the handgun appeared. "They met in the prison visitors' room, where you're allowed have contact with each other. That's where she secretly slipped him the gun. Hartman left that room and immediately used the gun to take the unarmed Officer Miller hostage. The plan was to force Miller to escort him to the vehicle yard and then drive him out of the prison. Carlson would meet up with him later and help him sneak out of the country, where she would later join him."

Earl could see from the corner of his eye that several jurors were now looking at Kate as if they had already found her guilty.

"But something happened they hadn't planned on. Hartman was confronted by an alert fellow officer, Clyde Rattner. So what did Hartman do?" Taylor's voice started to quake with emotion as she got to the killing. "Hartman calmly turned and shot Officer Miller. Shot him dead. And why? Because he was no longer of any use to Hartman, now that their plan had been discovered." She paused and stared at the jurors as if she were stunned into silence by this callous act of depravity. Finally, she drew a heavy breath and continued. "Luckily, Rattner saw his chance and jumped Hartman. They grappled over the gun and in that struggle Hartman was killed. As the author of this plot, Kathleen Carlson is legally responsible for both deaths. She was arrested driving away that day. She had gun powder residue on her hands from test firing the gun and a bullet cartridge was found in her car which she apparently dropped when reloading."

Earl knew he could object to these histrionics. Opening statements were not supposed to be an opportunity to argue your case, just an occasion to preview the evidence you plan to present. But Earl was reluctant to object; he didn't want to seem afraid of the prosecution case. So he had to sit and take it.

"Kathleen Carlson was a high-priced lawyer, a senior partner in a prestigious law firm, financially secure. Why would a woman like that do something like this? Maybe because she wasn't so content in that big corner office, working those long hours, constantly under stress. Maybe she also felt like a prisoner herself, trapped in a high-pressure life. So she started searching for a way out. First she tried politics and became the spokesperson for a controversial ballot initiative. But as she visited and corresponded with Hartman, she convinced herself she was in love. So in a sense, this evil scheme was really a way for *both* of them to escape."

Taylor paused and started gathering up her notes, then stopped. "My father was a Baptist minister. When he was once faced with this kind of inexplicable behavior, he told me something. He said people as they age sometimes lose certain attributes, women might lose their beauty, men their hair and others, unfortunately, their judgment." Taylor scanned the jury and turned toward her seat. Earl could see two women on the jury slowly nodding their heads.

Judge Parker rose. "We'll take a fifteen-minute recess." The jurors stood, exchanged glances and trooped into the jury room. The audience benches creaked as the onlookers got up and shuffled to the exit. Two reporters gathered up their coats, not planning to return. As with most criminal trials, this was the only side of the case they planned to report.

Earl turned to Kate, who sat silently staring straight ahead.

"Hey," Earl said. "It always feels this way when the jury only hears one side."

Kate turned to face him. "The trouble is, Bobby, I don't see where our side has much to offer." She got up, and the bailiff led her into the lock-up.

Earl stayed in his seat. Taylor had been good. More than good. She had given them just enough facts without getting bogged down in the details. He had underestimated her. He had been so incensed with her treatment of Sam that it had clouded his judgment and had convinced himself the jury would somehow recognize her deviousness, just as he had. But far from it, they had followed her lead.

"Mr. Earl, do you wish to make an opening statement?" There was no rule that required the defense to make an opening statement. The defense could postpone its opening until the start of the defense case or forgo it all together. But to Earl, waiving the opening statement was tantamount to waving a white flag. He was aware of studies that found many jurors actually made up their minds based solely on the opening statements and never changed them.

In most cases, the jury is presented with two contrasting accounts of what happened, one by the prosecution, another by the defense. The jurors then listen to the evidence to determine whether the defense version of events made sense, or enough sense to make them doubt the prosecution case. But he didn't have a defense story to weigh against the prosecution's version.

In its absence, he needed to encourage the jurors to adopt a particular point of view when examining the prosecution's case. In Earl's experience, most jurors adopt, early on, a distinct attitude toward their task; a way of thinking about the evidence they hear. Some jurors come to an immediate assumption of guilt, then listen for and only note the evidence that fits that conclusion. Others will at least entertain the idea that the defendant might be innocent and will occasionally mark facts that don't seem to support the prosecution case. A few adopt the Missouri State slogan of "show me," and demand the prosecution prove their case by providing enough solid evidence to overpower any other conclusion. That was the attitude he needed to foster in these jurors.

After Taylor's performance, he couldn't just sit there with the prosecutor's version still echoing in their minds or that would be the perspective through which the jurors would view all the coming testimony. They would be left with a paint-by-the-numbers prosecution picture onto which they would simply apply the evidence. With an equally predictable result.

"Thank you, Your Honor," he said and walked to the podium. He started speaking slowly, in a conversational tone, explaining the legal principles that protected defendants against the power of the state and why we needed them. Why the prosecution must produce proof beyond a reasonable doubt and how much evidence was required to get over that bar. How circumstantial evidence was different because it was susceptible to opposing interpretations. Then he got to the presumption of innocence.

"The prosecution has the responsibility of trying to prove Kathleen Carlson is guilty; we do not have to prove that she is innocent. Which means you must demand they answer certain questions, concerns that don't seem to fit this story they're peddling."

"Objection," Taylor scoffed.

Earl had wanted to goad her into objecting and got his wish.

"Opening statement, Mr. Earl," the judge admonished. "Not closing argument."

"Yes, your Honor," Earl replied. "The first question you need answered is *how*. How did Kathleen Carlson smuggle a gun into a high security prison? Before being admitted, every visitor to that prison is searched to prevent this very thing. They must go through a metal detector like at the airport. Now Ms. Carlson has a metal rod in her leg from a ski accident, so she was subjected to an even more rigorous procedure. First with a hand scanner to detect any metal and then a physical search by a prison matron. She was frisked, that is they ran their hands over her body to detect anything like a gun. And nothing was found."

Earl swept his eyes over the jury. They were listening. Some were even leaning forward, a good sign.

"And another *how*. How did she supposedly pass this gun to Adam Hartman in the visitors' room under the watchful gaze of the guard stationed there to prevent just such a thing? And how did Hartman walk out of the room with it? He was wearing a prison jumpsuit which had no pockets. Where could he hide it?" He paused, his face grimaced in skepticism.

"The third question is *why*. Why would Kathleen Carlson do something like this? The prosecutor supposes that Ms. Carlson, a prominent, well-respected lawyer had fallen in love with a prison inmate. So much in love that she would abandon everything for him, her law practice, her friends, her family, everything, to lead a life in the shadows with an escaped convict." He extended his palms out to the jury as if to say 'c'mon people.' "Your job is to demand *proof* of this torrid attraction."

"The reason none of this makes sense is that someone else was responsible for smuggling in that gun. Ask yourselves who benefits if Kathleen Carlson is convicted. Who profits from her downfall? Kathleen was the spokesperson for the Save Our Schools Initiative. SOS. If it passes, our tax dollars will no longer go to pay private companies to impose the punishment handed down by our justice system. No longer allow them to make a profit off imprisoning people. Private prisons will be put out of business in our State. That means the loss of millions and millions of dollars." He gave a knowing look at the jurors and nodded slowly as if they all understood what forces that prospect might set in motion.

"Who else benefits if the SOS Initiative is defeated? Fewer prisons means fewer jobs for prison guards. The Correction Officers' Union opposes SOS because fewer jobs means less money from union dues, which is the source of its political influence. That's the money they use to contribute to the campaigns of the very legislators who set their salaries. What better way to defeat the Initiative than to convict its spokesperson? And what surer way to do that than to use prison guards as the witnesses against her?"

Earl concluded his remarks and sat down. The judge announced the noon recess. As people filed out, Earl sat and took stock of where the case stood. He knew full well that his opening statement had not laid out a compelling case for the defense. It had merely raised questions that he hoped would lead the jurors to look behind the facts, because the facts were all in the prosecution column. Without some hard evidence to link PCA or the guards Union to the killings, the judge would not even allow him to bring them up at trial. They would join the Sharks on the sidelines, safely out of play.

But an opening statement was not the time to preview the shortcomings he saw with the prosecution witnesses. If he had detailed the flaws he perceived, it would have merely allowed Taylor to go to school on his remarks and prepare her witnesses for his cross-examination.

Without any defense witnesses, to punch holes in Taylor's case, Earl would have to rely on her witnesses. Somehow force those witnesses to admit facts that did not support the prosecution's version of events and acknowledge that those same facts might also lead to the conclusion that Kate was innocent. All this must be told through witnesses who were determined never ever to make such concessions. It was like putting on a play with actors who had to be trapped or tricked into saying their lines. Surprise was too great an advantage to forfeit.

The bustle and chatter behind him of the spectators leaving the courtroom shook him out of his brooding. He turned to survey the crowd. Among them was Jerry Reynolds, who had been with Buddy Wright when they first met. Reynolds stood up from his seat and remained in place, letting others in his row pass by. He fixed Earl with a probing look. His face was expressionless, as if he were dispassionately studying a problem on a blackboard. After a moment, he nodded to Earl as one would a worthy adversary and slowly followed the others out into the hall.

After the noon recess, Judge Parker took the bench.

"Call your first witness," she told Taylor.

Everyone was in their place. The jurors had been provided with notebooks, which lay open and ready on their laps. Earl's trial binders were within his reach, lined up along the railing behind him. Taylor's box of tabbed folders was on the floor next to Detective Carter's chair. Earl could feel the familiar sense of anticipation in the room which was present in every trial when the first witness was called. It reminded him of runners poised on their marks, anticipating the report of the starting gun, anxious to get the race underway.

Taylor stood. "The People would like to introduce as their first witness the statement of Officer Rattner that the court previously ruled was admissible."

"All right," the judge said and turned to the jury. "Ladies and Gentlemen, you are about to hear a statement read to you. The person who made this statement is unavailable to testify. You are not to speculate why that is the case. You should consider this statement in the same manner as any other testimony in the case and give it as much or as little weight as you feel appropriate."

"Thank you, your Honor," Taylor said. "I would like to have the statement read from the witness stand by a fellow officer."

"Proceed," Parker said.

"Call Officer Matthew Thompson."

A blond young man with a square jaw and blue eyes stood up in the last row. As he stepped forward, he carried himself with a military bearing.

In his freshly pressed Corrections Officer's uniform, with a stiffly starched shirt, perfectly knotted tie and jacket emblazoned with patches of authority, he was a commanding figure. When seated in the witness box, Earl expected to hear the strains of the Battle Hymn of the Republic in the background. Now Earl understood why Taylor had not shown the jury a photo of Clyde Rattner. Whenever they considered Rattner's statement they would now associate it with the solid, reliable face of Officer Matthew Thompson.

Earl had expected that Carter would read the statement, since he was the one who took it. Earl glanced over at the detective. Carter sat staring fixedly ahead, his arms crossed, his lips clamped tightly shut as if to prevent himself from voicing his opinion about Taylor's choice of a witness. He had apparently failed his audition.

"Officer Thompson, would you please read the statement given on the day of the shooting by Officer Rattner, a Corrections Officer at Haywood State Prison."

Taylor approached the witness box and handed him a copy.

Thompson turned to face the jury and began to read in a clear, firm voice. He used the first person in the narrative, which further enhanced the impression that this was his testimony. "I was called to assist as an escort for an inmate leaving the visitor's room and returning to the protective custody wing. When I got there, Officer Miller was with inmate Hartman, but something didn't look right. The inmate was too close to Officer Miller. Then I saw that inmate Hartman had a gun. When I called out, Hartman turned the gun on me. That's when Miller made a grab for it. So Hartman shot him. Miller went down. I jumped on Hartman and we struggled over the gun. Suddenly the gun discharged and Hartman fell. I called for medical assistance but Miller didn't make it."

Officer Thompson stood up and started to step down. One moment, Officer," Earl said. "If the court please, I have a few questions."

The judge gave Earl a questioning look but nodded her permission.

"Officer Thompson, do you work at Haywood Prison?"

"No, sir," Thompson answered.

"You know anything about these events we're dealing with here?"

"No, sir."

"You weren't there when any of this happened?"

"No, sir," Thompson said with a perplexed expression.

"You didn't take this statement from Officer Rattner, did you?"

"No, sir."

"You seemed pretty comfortable in front of an audience. What is your assignment?"

"I handle public relations for...."

"Objection," Taylor barked, interrupting the answer.

"Sustained," the judge said.

"So," Earl said. "You were just called here to read."

"I guess you could say that."

"Sort of like an actor," Earl said.

"Objection," Taylor said.

"Sustained," the judge ruled.

"What I mean is, you don't know if what you read is the truth or not. You're not vouching for any of it, are you?"

"Objection," Taylor pleaded. "Your honor?"

"Sustained. Move on, Mr. Earl."

Earl retrieved a photo from one of his binders and had it projected onto the screen. A sour faced Clyde Rattner stared out into the room.

"Do you know who this is?"

"No, sir."

"This is the real Clyde Rattner. You ever meet him? Know anything about him?"

"No, sir," Thompson answered.

"Since you weren't there, you can't tell us how Officer Rattner acted when he gave this statement, can you?"

"Of course not," Thompson said showing a little irritation for the first time.

"Whether he stammered, searched for words, acted nervous, was sweating, went back and corrected things. None of that?"

"No, I can't," he snapped.

"But the man who could, the man who actually took the statement, is sitting right here, Detective Carter. But he wasn't given a chance to tell us about it. Was he?"

"Objection," blurted Taylor.

"Sustained," the judge said firmly.

"Thank you, Officer Thompson. Nothing further."

As Earl sat down, Taylor shot him a sidelong scowl.

CHAPTER 26

"Call Captain Ernst Gunther," Taylor announced.

After Earl had exposed her attempt to personify Rattner's statement with the square-jawed Thompson, Taylor obviously wanted to end the day on a solid note. Give the jurors something to think about over the weekend.

On the stand, Gunther sat straight-backed, shoulders squared, his polished visor hat placed on the ledge before him. He looked comfortable in his crisp dress uniform; it was difficult to imagine him wearing anything else. Without sunglasses, his pale grey eyes swept the room in a confident, somber gaze, one meant to convey that he was a leader of men, those who walked the toughest beat in California.

Taylor walked him through the security procedure every visitor was subjected to at Haywood State Prison. He explained that all visitors had to pass through a metal detector, have their shoes and jackets x-rayed and no cellphones or briefcases were allowed inside. All this was designed to detect any possible weapon that might end up in the hands of an inmate.

"Now, what about the defendant? Did she go through this rigorous procedure on the day she visited Adam Hartman?" Taylor asked.

"No, she did not," answered Gunther.

"And why was that?"

"Ms. Carlson had presented us with a medical verification that she had a metal implant in her upper right leg. This would obviously set off the metal detector, so she was sent to our secondary inspection."

"What does that entail?"

"The subject is taken into a private room where a matron uses a hand scanner to detect any metal objects and then conducts a physical search which consists of the matron running her hands over the subject's body and possibly having her disrobe, depending upon the circumstances."

"Is this secondary inspection as effective as the normal security check?"

"Not really, because the metal implant is always going to set off the hand scanner, so a metal object hidden in the same vicinity might go undetected."

"A metal object like a gun?"

"Yes, like a small pistol."

Taylor's efforts to plug this hole in her case did not surprise Earl, but he had expected her to relish the opportunity to embarrass Kate by delving more deeply into the anatomical possibilities for concealment.

"The defendant met with Adam Hartman in the general visitor's room, is that right?"

"Correct," Gunther replied.

"Is physical contact permitted between visitors and inmates in that room?"

"Yes, it is."

Taylor showed a photograph of the visitors' room with its tables and vending machines that made it look about as closely supervised as a high school cafeteria. Gunther explained that the inmates were allowed to embrace their visitors and hold hands, so there would be ample opportunities to pass any small object which had eluded detection.

"What about lawyers? Do they use the same visiting room?"

"No," Gunter replied. "They use a different room which is equipped to protect the confidentiality of their communications."

Taylor showed a photo of the lawyers' visiting booths with their Plexiglas barriers and one-way phones. Gunther explained that these dividers prevented any physical contact and thus eliminated any possibility of passing anything to the inmate.

"The defendant is a lawyer. So were you surprised she used the regular visitors' room, rather than the lawyers' room?"

"I was," Gunther said on cue. "Until we searched his cell."

"Objection." Earl knew what was coming. The letters. He didn't want Gunther and Taylor to characterize them as love letters, as if that were the only way to read them. "Perhaps, Captain Gunther could merely tell us what was found without explaining what conclusions he wants us to draw from them."

"Sustained," Judge Parker said.

"What was it you found?" Taylor asked.

"A series of letters from the defendant to inmate Hartman."

Taylor had Gunther identify the letters as the ones from Hartman's cell. She projected the first one onto the screen for the jury and began to read it in a theatrical voice as if it were written by an enamored teenager.

"Objection, your Honor," Earl said. "As much as we might enjoy Ms. Taylor's performance, the letters speak for themselves and not necessarily the interpretation Ms. Taylor would like to read into them. The jury is quite capable of reading them."

"Sustained, but I must caution you Mr. Earl. Just state your legal grounds, don't make a speech."

"Yes, your Honor." Apparently, the judge had felt the need to rap his knuckles in front of the jury to remind him who was in charge.

Taylor concluded putting the letters up on the screen, then moved on to Adam Hartman's status in protective custody. Gunther explained that inmates in protective custody were isolated from the general prison population and housed only with other PC inmates in their own cellblock. They were even escorted by a guard whenever they left that cellblock.

"You mentioned that in order to be granted this protective status, an inmate must inform the prison authorities that he is under a credible threat to his life."

"That's correct," Gunther said.

"Who did Adam Hartman report he was threatened by?"

"The Aryan Brotherhood, a very violent prison gang."

"When you say violent, what do you mean?"

"The Aryan Brotherhood was responsible for several murders at Haywood Prison and dozens more in other facilities around the country. They have even killed correction officers."

"So if an inmate was being threatened by this Aryan Brotherhood, he might feel a real need to escape that danger."

"Objection," Earl said.

"Sustained," Judge Parker ruled. "Ms. Taylor, you seem to have forgotten that argument comes at the end of the case."

"Nothing further, Your Honor," Taylor said.

Even before the judge told him to proceed, Earl was on his feet like a boxer off his stool before the bell rang. "Captain, you said the secondary inspection wasn't as effective as the normal security checks. Is that right?"

"That's been my experience."

"Then you must have apprehended and prosecuted people who have smuggled contraband or weapons past this secondary inspection."

"That's our policy."

"So how many people have been prosecuted?"

"I don't have an exact number," Gunther replied.

"Let's put it this way. Has a *single* person ever been prosecuted for successfully smuggling a weapon through the secondary inspection?"

Gunther stared hard at Earl. "Not to my knowledge," he said finally.

"And if you suspected this secondary procedure was inadequate to prevent inmates from arming themselves and posing a danger to your officers, you'd do something about it, wouldn't you?"

"Of course."

"Have you made any changes in the secondary procedure since the shooting?"

"No," Gunther murmured.

"You testified that everyone without some medical issue goes through the metal detector. Does that include the guards?"

Gunther shot a quick glance at Taylor. "No," he said.

"Why is that?" Earl asked.

"It's financial. Their union contract states that their eight-hour shift starts the minute they enter the front gate. The gear they're required to wear would set off the metal detectors: steel-toed boots, belts with metal, communication equipment, that sort of thing. If each one had to strip down, it would take too long for them to reach their post and relieve the prior shift. We'd end up with a lot of overtime that we can't afford."

"So they get paid from the time they enter the facility until they actually reach their post. That's called walking time, isn't it?"

"That's right."

"What's to prevent a guard from smuggling something inside?"

"They're subject to random searches and checks," Gunther said.

"By random, you mean every once in a while one of them gets searched, just so long as it doesn't take too long and the rest just pass through."

"Objection," Taylor said. Earl wondered if the jury could hear the anxiety in her voice.

"Sustained," the judge said. "Move on, Mr. Earl."

"Let's talk about Officer Miller then," Earl said. "He was assigned to the sally port that day, wasn't he?"

"Yes."

"His duties required him to search each inmate when they returned from the visitor's room?"

"That's why he was stationed there," Gunther said.

"You told us that since Adam Hartman was in protective custody he was escorted by a guard whenever he left his cellblock, including to and from the visitors' room?"

"Yes."

"So Adam Hartman knew that Officer Miller was not going to be his escort when he left the visitor's room. He expected that someone else would be summoned to be his escort."

"I suppose so."

"Therefore it was no surprise to Hartman when Officer Rattner showed up."

"I guess you could say that."

"If Adam Hartman's scheme was to escape when he left the visitor's room, I guess he planned to form a two-guard convoy to get to the vehicle yard."

"Objection," Taylor said, unable to control the frustration in her voice.

"Sustained," Judge Parker said firmly. "Perhaps you also need a refresher as to when it's time for final argument."

"Sorry, your Honor." Earl paused. "Captain, why was Rattner chosen to be Hartman's escort?"

"He was on rover duty, so he was available."

"But others were available as well, weren't they? So why Rattner, why him?"

"I don't know what you mean."

Earl gave Gunther a skeptical look. "Didn't you tell me, when we spoke at Haywood Prison, that you chose Rattner because he was the only one who would work with Officer Miller?"

Gunther hesitated a beat as he stared hard at Earl.

"I may have," he said.

"And what was the reason your officers were reluctant to work with Officer Miller, an Iraq War combat veteran?"

"They thought he was soft. That he wanted the inmates to like him, so he let them get away with things. Which is very dangerous, both for him and anyone who worked with him."

"Actually, weren't there rumors that Officer Miller was working with the Attorney General's Office to investigate inmate abuse by his fellow officers. Isn't that the real reason?"

"Objection, your Honor. He's just throwing out baseless accusations."

The judge sat thinking, shifting her gaze from Earl to Gunther. "I'll let him answer. But move cautiously, Mr. Earl." She nodded at Gunther, who was looking up at her.

"Not that I'm aware of," he said with a shrug of his shoulders.

"Didn't the former District Attorney of Haywood County convene a Grand Jury to investigate that very thing? Guards abusing inmates at the prison?"

"Grand Juries are secret, so I have no idea."

"Weren't there allegations that you led a group of guards, called the Sharks, who inflicted this abuse?"

"Objection," Taylor said, attempting a tone of righteous indignation.

"Sustained, Mr. Earl," the judge said. "That's enough along that line."

"Nothing further, your Honor." Earl stole a glance at the jury, wondering if they understood where any of this was headed. There had been times in trials when he could feel himself taking command of a courtroom, controlling the witnesses, defining the issues. This had not been one of those times.

"Ladies and gentlemen," the judge said addressing the jury. "That concludes our testimony for today." The jurors energetically left their seats, excited to be released.

Earl turned to Kate whose face was pinched with concern. "Kate, we're just getting started. Remember, they can't get around the fact that they searched you before you ever got to the visitors room."

Kate didn't seem to hear him. Without replying, she got up and walked slowly to the door of the holding cell.

The evening lights were just coming on, bathing the marble stone of the State Capitol in a soft glow. Jerry Reynolds stood at the window on the top floor of the union's building and admired the view of the neoclassical structure with its eight fluted Corinthian columns. The illumination on the Dome had the gentling effect of candlelight, beckoning him to romanticize the Capitol as a citadel of democracy rather than the trading floor he knew it to be, the one where well-tailored lobbyists advanced the interests of the powerful few ahead of those of the voiceless many.

Reynolds' introduction to the reality of politics had come early in childhood when he listened to his father, a coal miner and union official, talk about the risk to their jobs and the possibility of no food on the table when these hardscrabble men went out on strike. He had stood with his mother and the other families to support the men as they tried to block the entrance gate against hired strike-breakers. Then he watched as the Sheriff's deputies and the company's hired thugs beat back his father and the other miners. Even at that young age, the lesson seemed clear. Politics was a game best played from the top down rather than from the bottom up. Get a firm grip on the reins of power, then stay conveniently out of sight as you pulled on them.

He stepped over to a wooden cabinet inlaid with tortoise shell and poured himself a drink. Alone in the office, he stared at the President's cluttered desk. Buddy Wright's chair was empty. It was a chair he had no desire to occupy. The strategy of the game was what he enjoyed, out-maneuvering opponents and muscling people into line. Let Buddy do the glad-handing. He went back to the cabinet to refresh his drink then sank into his accustomed chair, the one alongside the desk.

The office door burst open and Buddy Wright charged in dressed in a tuxedo. "Goddamn, I hate these monkey suit dinners. Why can't we just dress normal?" He flopped into his chair. "Get me a drink, will ya' Jerry? I gotta go to Senator Palmer's award dinner at the Knights of Columbus."

Reynolds supplied the drink. Wright took a large swallow and heaved a sigh with his eyes closed. "You made it back," he said.

"I took an early flight from LA, right after court concluded," Reynolds said.

"So how's little Miss Tight Ass doing?"

"Not bad. She's not the problem. It's that defense lawyer, Bobby Earl. Our original take on him was right. He's trouble."

"I thought you had this plan to take care of him," Wright said. "Something about making him look like a ding so no one would listen to him."

"Yeah, well, that didn't work out."

"Goddamn it, Jerry. You said you'd take care of this guy." He waited for Reynolds to offer an excuse. It didn't come. "So how much trouble is he?"

"Carlos Sanchez is on his witness list."

Wright looked a question at him.

"You remember. He's that Senator who was carrying the bill to do away with private prisons. The same thing they're trying with the Initiative. We killed it in Committee then ran somebody against him in the primary and beat him."

"Yeah, now I remember. We had to spend a shitload of money."

"Sanchez is there to do his prison-industrial-complex routine, which means Earl plans to show we're the ones really backing the opposition to Prop 52."

"Can he do that?" Wright asked. "I thought this was a fucking murder trial."

"Earl's trying. He wants the jury to get the idea we set up Carlson. The DA will try to keep it out, but you never know."

"Son of a bitch." Wright gulped down the rest of his drink and headed for the cabinet. "You gotta do something about this asshole."

"I did. He was stopped from going into that abuse investigation. The one where Miller was working undercover. The AG put the lid on his witness like we suggested."

"He better have, or our endorsement would'a found another home," Buddy snapped.

"But all this talk in Court about Prop 52 worries me. Right now the Initiative is dead. But the press is covering the trial. They're always looking for a new angle on a story. If they start focusing on us and put two and two together, it could put new life into the campaign. And if she gets acquitted...."

"Acquitted?" Wright spluttered, nearly spilling his drink. "You gotta be fucking kidding me. Is Taylor gonna lose this fucking case?"

"I don't think so. But she's punching way above her weight against Earl."

Wright returned to his desk with a fresh drink. He rubbed his face with a meaty hand then tipped back in his chair and stared up at the ceiling. After a moment, he asked, "What do you think we should do?"

"It seems to me the fact that Carlson was searched before she got to the visitors' room is going to hurt us. That's Earl's strongest point."

"Who searched her?"

"A matron named Denise Wallace." Reynolds reached into his briefcase and dropped a file on the desk. "That's her personnel file. No disciplinary actions. Single, two kids. Five years away from retirement."

"Did she really search that Carlson broad? Or did she do one of those matador passes?" Buddy asked.

"According to our people, she's pretty by the book. But, you know, a lot of women guards have trouble after a few years. The stress gets to them. So who knows?"

Buddy sat and thought for a while, then said, "Why don't you go talk to her. Like you said, being a woman in that job is awful stressful. I wouldn't be surprised if she qualified for an early disability retirement."

Reynolds stared off across the room and sipped his drink. He always preferred it when Buddy thought an idea had been his own. After a moment he turned to Wright. "That could work."

CHAPTER 27

"State your name and spell the last," the clerk directed.

"Robert Johnson, J-O-H-N-S-O-N."

"Officer Johnson," Taylor began, "what is your occupation and current assignment?"

"Correction Officer, Grade II, currently assigned to Haywood State Prison."

It was Friday morning and Taylor wanted to end the week on a solid note. Nothing did that better than photos of dead bodies. Johnson was the first officer to respond to the shooting. She would use him to paint a picture of the scene, Officer Miller on the floor, bleeding from a fatal gunshot, inmate Hartman gravely wounded, face down in a pool of blood, with Officer Rattner in control. And, of course, the small pistol next to Hartman.

It was clear to everyone in the courtroom that Johnson was nervous. This was obviously his maiden voyage on the witness stand. He concentrated on keeping his answers short and direct, just as Taylor undoubtedly instructed him. He kept his eyes riveted on her as if he were afraid to look away for fear she would disappear.

Like any prosecutor, Taylor was following the playbook that a successful prosecution needed to bring home to the jury the brutality of the crime. An angry jury usually found a way around any shortage of proof in their thirst for retribution. Johnson was the witness she was counting on to do just that, to paint a scene of bloody violence and senseless death.

Earl was sure that Taylor had diligently prepared Johnson for this testimony, rehearsing the questions she intended to ask and the responses she expected. Coached him on when and how to express emotion. At the same time, she had probably been concerned that he might unravel under cross-examination. Perhaps too concerned. Earl's guess was that among her instructions she had warned him to "not give Earl anything to work with," just answer the question and "don't talk too much." In the end it appeared this admonition became his only guide post.

On the stand, Taylor struggled to get him to emote for the jury. He was way too guarded. Rather than upset, he came across as flat. She dutifully served up the scripted launching pad questions about the shock of seeing the grizzly scene; the distress at losing a colleague; the fear generated afterwards among the unarmed guards. But each question received a monosyllabic answer.

Undaunted, Taylor turned to a more reliable source to kindle the jury's outrage. The crime scene photos. The lifeless eyes, blood soaked floor, dead bodies with limbs thrown askew. Earl had made a motion earlier to pare down how many of these Taylor could use. But after Earl's opening statement, Taylor had cleverly argued that the defense was disputing Rattner's account, thus making additional photos necessary to support her case. The judge returned several to her pile.

One by one, Taylor displayed the gruesome photos on the screen. She asked Officer Johnson to describe the scene they depicted. True to form, Johnson's description of the deaths of Officer Miller and Adam Hartman was as intimate and chilling as reading a commodity report on the day's price of corn. Taylor's frustration was evident as she abandoned her attempts to ignite his emotional pilot light and asked that hard copies of the photos be passed among the jurors and took her seat. Earl watched the juror's expressions as they examined the photos. Some studied them with no discernable reaction, others seemed jarred by the reality of violent death and quickly handed them on. A few jurors looked up at Kate as if seeing her for the first time, still others studied her in an effort to determine whether she was capable of unleashing such carnage.

"Mr. Earl," the judge said.

"Nervous?" Earl asked with an understanding smile as he rose. This was not a witness he intended to lean on or intimidate. He knew the jury saw Johnson as the guy who showed up for work every day and did his job. No fancy footwork, just one foot in front of the other. The kind of person who kept the wheels turning. "Just a few questions and we'll have you on your way."

"Yes, sir," Johnson answered stiffly.

"When you got to the screening room, both Officer Miller and Hartman were down and the gun lay on the cement floor."

"Yes, sir."

"You never saw a gun in Hartman's hand?"

Johnson hesitated, then said, "No, sir."

"Now, let me show you a photograph of the scene." Earl had selected a crime scene photo that was a close-up of Officer Miller's chest. One that Taylor had not used. He showed the photo to Taylor then showed it up on the screen for Johnson. "Is that the way Officer Miller appeared when you got to the room?"

"Pretty much."

Earl kept his place next to the witness stand and pointed at the photograph on the screen. "As you'll notice, his shirt is pulled open. So that's the way you found him?"

Johnson studied the photograph. "I don't know. The paramedics must have done that."

"But Officer Miller was pronounced dead at the scene. There were no efforts at resuscitation. Since you were the first on the scene this must have been how he appeared."

He glanced briefly at Taylor then said, "Yeah, I guess so."

"It looks like somebody must have ripped open his shirt before you got there in order to take something off his body, doesn't it?"

"Objection," Taylor exclaimed. "Calls for speculation."

"Sustained," the judge said.

"To your knowledge, did anyone ever search Officer Rattner that night? Go through his pockets, that sort of thing."

Johnson looked confused. "Gee, I don't think so."

Earl returned to the podium. After Johnson's lackluster testimony about the deaths, Earl did not want to fill the void with another graphic depiction.

"Tell me something, did you guys ever have trouble up there with visitors who managed to lock themselves out of their cars?" Earl asked.

"All the time. Some people," he said, shaking his head at such human folly. "I guess they're nervous or something. A lot of visitors are driving older cars and they're always locking their keys in their cars."

Earl took a moment as if reviewing his notes. The old adage in cross-examination is to never ask a question to which you don't know the answer. But Johnson's answer had provided an opening for Earl to take a chance. He remembered reading Rattner's personnel file that included an employment record as a tow truck driver and repo man.

"When that happens, what do you do?"

"We call Officer Rattner if he's available, otherwise the people have to deal with it themselves."

"And what would Rattner do?" Earl asked.

"He had this Slim Jim that he kept in his locker that he would use. He was really good at it. I never saw one he couldn't open."

Apparently being on familiar ground had loosened Johnson's tongue. "Tell us, what's a Slim Jim?"

"It's just a flat strip of metal with like a hook cut out at the end. He would slide it down between the window and the door frame and slip the lock."

Earl decided to stretch his luck and go for the final piece. He fixed Johnson with a look of concentrated curiosity, hoping to prevent him from glancing over at Taylor who would undoubtedly signal a warning. "Was Rattner good enough with that device to slip the locks on newer, fancier cars? Like a Jaguar?"

Taylor's chair squeaked as she got to her feet, but Johnson answered before she could stop him. "Oh, sure. It was harder with the new cars, but I've seen him do it."

"On the day of the shooting we've heard that Rattner was detailed as a rover. So he roamed around the facility, sort of wherever he wanted, right?"

"I guess you could say that."

"He could have stepped out to the parking lot with his Slim Jim, couldn't he?"

"I suppose, if there was a need."

"Maybe to open someone's car and put something in it?"

"Objection. That's just a fantasy in Mr. Earl's mind."

"Sustained, you know better than that Mr. Earl."

"Yes, your Honor." Earl paused a moment letting the testimony sink in, hoping the jury would make the connection. "Officer Johnson, did you ever conduct the random searches on your fellow guards when they came on duty?"

"Yes, sir. We all did. It rotated."

"We were told these searches were just pat-downs. Did you ever search their lunch pails?"

"Once in a while."

"Let me show you another photograph." Earl took a photo out of his binder, the one of Rattner's unopened cooler with his name scrawled on it with magic marker. Munoz took it when they were inside Rattner's house. Earl placed a duplicate on Taylor's table as he walked toward the witness stand.

"Do you recognize what's depicted in this photo?" Behind him, Earl could hear Taylor excitedly whispering questions at Detective Carter.

"Sure," Johnson said, smiling for the first time. He was back on familiar ground. "That's Officer Rattner's cooler. He lugged it everywhere."

Earl stepped back to his table and pulled out several more photographs. The ones which showed the hidden compartment. He placed duplicates in front of Taylor. She quickly glanced at them then leaped to her feet.

"Your Honor. This is the first I've seen of these. I don't know what Mr. Earl is trying to pull, but I'd like a conference in chambers."

In chambers, lifting each photograph from the group on her desk, Judge Parker examined them as impassively as if she were assessing new stationary samples. Taylor was unable to contain herself until the judge was finished. "I never received any notice of ...." she blurted out, but stopped short when Parker, without looking up raised a palm. After a minute, the judge put down the last photo and arranged the stack neatly. She finally looked at Taylor and nodded.

"I have never seen any of these before," Taylor said heatedly. "I was never given any notice the defense planned to use them. This is a clear violation of the rules of discovery. It is totally unfair. This is trial by ambush."

Earl, like Taylor, was standing behind one of the tall backed leather chairs facing Parker's desk. He met the judge's stare as she shifted her gaze to him. "This is cross-examination," Earl said calmly. "There is no rule of discovery that requires me to preview documents or photographs I intend to use. Surprise is one of the aspects of cross-examination that makes it such a valuable tool in the search for truth."

"Truth?" Taylor exclaimed. "This is a sideshow, a smokescreen. It has nothing to do with truth. This is…" she hesitated as if searching for a word. "This is ridiculous."

The judge sat quietly, letting Taylor wind down. "I believe Mr. Earl is correct. There is no obligation, on either the defense or the prosecution, to reveal material they intend to use in cross-examination."

Taylor tossed her head and rolled her eyes in frustration. "But…." she pleaded, before Parker interrupted her.

"However," the judge said, "I am concerned about the relevance of these photographs. Where are you going with this, Mr. Earl?"

"The People's theory is that Ms. Carlson smuggled the murder weapon into the prison and then passed it to Hartman. There is no direct evidence of this. It's all circumstantial. No one will testify they saw it happen. But it shows up right after her visit. So the prosecution argument is: how else could it have ended up in the sally port screening room?"

"That's not our only evidence," Taylor said desperately. "There's the bullet in her car, GSR on her hands, the letters. This is just a side show."

"Let him finish," the judge admonished.

"I am entitled to refute the prosecution theory by showing how another participant in the shooting, namely Officer Rattner, could have smuggled a pistol into the prison. Which is exactly what he could have done in the false bottom of his cooler."

"And it was the Rattner connection you were pursuing with your questions about his use of a Slim Jim."

"Yes, your Honor."

"It sounds to me," the judge said, "that you're attempting to show that Rattner is the real killer here. Which falls into the legal category of a third party culpability defense. The law is quite strict on that, as you well know. You'll need to prove a lot more than just the mere fact that Rattner had the opportunity to do it. I'm afraid that's not going to be enough to allow you to put on these photographs."

Taylor looked as relieved as a patient who just heard her tumor was benign. She vigorously nodded her head in agreement.

"But with all due respect, your Honor. I don't need to prove all that. Ms. Carlson is charged with felony-murder, based on a theory she smuggled a gun to Hartman who then shot Officer Miller. She didn't shoot anybody. I just need to raise a reasonable doubt that she played a part by providing the gun. Not what happened in that room or who pulled the trigger. Just an equally plausible explanation, based on the circumstantial evidence, of how that gun got there."

Parker held Earl's eyes as she thought. Finally, her lips curved slightly upward. "All right, Mr. Earl. It's a very narrow distinction and a bit sophistical, but I'll allow it."

"Wait a minute," Taylor said and turned to Earl. "Where'd you get these pictures? Who gave you permission to take them? That's private property. How'd you get access to it?" She turned back to the judge. "There's something not right here."

"Mr. Earl?" the judge said.

Earl took a moment as he thought. There were a number of ways to go with this. He decided to play it straight. "I entered Rattner's house without permission and found it there."

"That's illegal," Taylor exclaimed. "You can't do that. That's breaking and entering. Judge, I move to suppress the evidence. It's an illegal search and seizure."

"Look," Earl said. "I'm not proud of what I did. But I didn't have the power to get a search warrant like the prosecution does. I may have been trespassing, but that is not a legal basis to exclude the photos. The constitutional remedy of suppressing evidence is only available when the government conducts an illegal search. The sole recourse against a private citizen who trespasses is a civil suit."

The judge looked askance at Earl. "You may be legally correct, Mr. Earl. In fact, I know that you are. So I have no choice but to allow you to use the photographs." Taylor started to speak, but the judge raised her hand. Parker continued to stare at Earl. "I can appreciate the stress that cases of this magnitude put on lawyers. But I am surprised and very disappointed. I can think of no excuse for such conduct, but I'll leave it to the involved parties to address your behavior. I assume they will be notified." She dismissed the two lawyers with a wave of her hand.

As Earl stepped back into the courtroom, he could not help but feel a tinge of remorse over her disapproval. Over the years, Earl had been threatened and yelled at by some of the acknowledged champions of judicial intimidation. Men with reddened faces and bulging neck veins who spat saliva as they thundered down at him. Their vehemence had floated past him like elevator music. This was different. He respected Parker. But he quickly pushed aside his regret. He was representing an innocent person. Sometimes you had to take a hit for the good of the team, even if it meant leaning out over the plate. Taking his seat, he told Kate that everything was fine. Glancing down the table, Taylor fumed, ignoring Carter's agitated questions.

The bailiff brought in the jury, and Officer Johnson retook the witness stand. "Mr. Earl, you may continue," the judge said without any intonation. Earl was grateful she did not communicate her displeasure with him to the jury by using any of the subtle ways judges had of telegraphing their opinions.

"Officer Johnson, we were talking about this photo of Rattner's cooler." Earl put the image up on the screen for the jury. "Now, take a look at this next photo." He displayed a photograph that showed the cooler's false bottom." "Were you, or any of your colleagues, aware that it had this hidden compartment?"

Johnson stared as if transfixed at the image on the screen. After a long pause, he turned back to Earl with a lost look in his eyes. "No, sir," he said feebly.

"Is there a problem at the prison with cellphones being smuggled to the inmates?"

"Yes, sir."

"Did anyone ever figure out how it was being done?"

"Not really," Johnson answered.

"That small pistol that you said was lying on the floor, was it about the size of a cellphone?"

"I guess so," he said.

"Thank you, Officer Johnson."

When they returned from the morning recess, Taylor requested they quit early so she could consult with her appellate department about the legal soundness of the judge's ruling on the photographs. Earl explained to Kate that it was merely a tactic, like calling a timeout to "freeze" an opposing player before they attempted a crucial free throw, forcing them to ponder the consequences. He assured her that Parker was not one you could rattle into backing down; the points were safely on the board. Promising to see her Monday morning, he gathered his papers and left.

"Do you know who I am?" he asked.

"Yes, sir. Mr. Reynolds," she said.

"Do you know why I'm here?"

"Not exactly, sir."

The corner booth in the Half Moon Café was next to the kitchen door and furthest away from the front window. That was why Denise Wallace had chosen it. She had gotten the call last night, telling her to take a sick day and meet Jerry Reynolds that Saturday morning. She didn't know why, but it must have something to do with the shooting. Whatever it was, it wasn't going to be good. Everyone knew Buddy's Brain was the guy who delivered the bad news.

Reynolds removed a paper from his jacket pocket and slid it across the table. "Is that your report? The one about searching Kate Carlson?"

Wallace glanced down. The words on the paper were a blur as her mind jolted with alarm. "Yes, sir," she said, trying to sound normal.

"That's too bad," Reynolds said. "You've had a good career. Shame it has to end this way."

"I don't understand," she said.

"It's this prosecutor. She's saying the only way Carlson could have gotten that gun into the visitor's room was if she had help. Inside help. And since a pat-down should have found it. Well...." He shrugged and gave her a sober look.

"Me?" she yelped. "Oh, no. Mr. Reynolds, I would never do something like that. Never."

"I believe you. The trouble is it looks bad. Even if you're not indicted, the board is gonna say you were derelict in your duties. Not properly performing a security check, and as a result your fellow officer was killed."

"But I did. I swear to God. There's no way I missed anything."

"Maybe you did or maybe you didn't. Either way you're gonna lose your job."

"Jesus and Mary, Mr. Reynolds," she exclaimed. "I got two kids."

Reynolds sat silently staring at her as she bit her lower lip struggling not to cry. After a minute, he said: "There may be another way. But...." He trailed off, slowly shaking his head and wrinkled his face into a grimace, as if discarding an idea that had just occurred to him. "Never mind," he said finally.

"No, please," she pleaded. "What way? Tell me."

"I was just thinking, what if you didn't do such a thorough job. What if you were rushed or got another call? Maybe she begged to go the bathroom before you finished. I don't know, you'd have to search your memory."

Wallace stared at him as she struggled to comprehend his meaning. "But I wrote in my report that I did."

"Actually," Reynolds said, tapping the paper, "the report just says you followed procedure, it doesn't specify."

Wallace studied the report then looked up with a bewildered expression.

"Maybe you were afraid to admit you didn't do a full pat-down," he suggested.

"But wouldn't I still lose my job? Lying on a report and, like you said, not doing the inspection right so Miller got killed."

"You know we take care of our own, don't you, Denise?"

She nodded eagerly.

"I imagine working the tiers and walking the yard among all those animals is very stressful for a woman. All those comments and looks. The constant fear of being attacked. If you were to put in for a disability retirement, and the union backed you, I bet there's a good chance you'd get it. Which by the way makes your pension tax free. And if you were forced to retire because of stress, I don't think anybody would be looking at your job performance."

She sat, pondering his words. "You're saying," she said slowly, as if deciphering a code. "If I remember doing sort of a poor job of searching her, I wouldn't get in trouble. And the union would back me for an early disability retirement." She paused to search his face for confirmation. "Do you think the union would really do that?"

Reynolds gave her a patronizing smile. "Denise, you're talking to the union."

CHAPTER 28

Monday morning before court started, Kate Carlson paced the cement floor of the holding cell. Earl entered and she stepped quickly to the bars, gripped them and pressed her face closely. "God, that photo of Rattner's hidden compartment really hit home with the jury," she said excitedly. "I was watching their reaction. They really took it in. See, I told you. The bastards framed me." She was the most animated Earl had seen her, almost buoyant.

This roller coaster of emotions was something Earl had seen before when clients were put in the pressure cooker of a jury trial. They seemed to hang their fate on each succeeding witness, almost every question. This witness-by-witness assessment would either catapult them to giddy heights or drop them into despair, like patients who constantly took their own temperature. It was painful to watch, but a process in which Earl could not join. He had to maintain his distance, keep his focus on the cumulative effect of all the testimony and dispassionately assess which way the playing field was tilting.

"It was a good day," he said. "But the witness this morning is pivotal. It's their forensic expert. Fingerprints, ballistics, gunshot residue. The physical evidence is the real heart of their case."

Upon hearing this Kate's hopeful spirits evaporated. "But scientific evidence is unassailable. It's just physics." She pressed her hands to her head and stepped away to sink onto the cement bench.

"You're right about the science. But the conclusions to be drawn from it are not. The key is to accept the forensic evidence, but find a way to turn it around until it no longer points at you."

"And how could you possibly do that?" she challenged.

"I don't exactly know yet," he said.

Jacob Nishi did not look anything like what Earl had expected. The director of the Forensic Division of the Haywood Police Department was definitely not the pocket protector, slide rule in a holster, type. He had a round, full-cheeked face, black spiky hair and a trimmed goatee. His three button suit was avocado green with narrow lapels. A thin red tie rested on his mango colored shirt.

Taylor ran through his credentials then asked, "When and where did vou first encounter the defendant. Kathleen Carlson?"

"On the night of the shooting at 6:12 PM in the Haywood Police station," Nishi answered in a well-practiced professional voice.

"What if anything did you do at that time?"

"I rubbed each of her hands with several small plastic discs that were coated with an adhesive."

"What was your purpose in doing that?"

"To determine whether or not gunshot residue was present."

"And was it?" Taylor asked.

"It was, on both of her hands."

"What, if anything, does the presence of gunshot residue indicate?"

"By its presence, I can state with scientific certainty that the defendant recently fired a weapon," Nishi said in an authoritative tone.

Earl had to admit to himself that Taylor was doing a good job. Direct examination of an expert could be a ponderous slog. But she had made the choice to go straight to the bottom line so the jury would know in advance why they should listen to this testimony. Now she would backtrack and ask Nishi to fill in how he got there. If you did it the other way around, by the time you got to the expert's conclusion the jury's eyes would have already rolled back in their skulls.

"Now," Taylor said. "Let's go back. What is gunshot residue?"

"First, I'll explain how a gun discharges a bullet." He smiled indulgently at Taylor. "Put up the first chart," Nishi directed.

A schematic drawing of a revolver appeared on the courtroom screen. Nishi stepped down from the witness box, took a laser pointer from his jacket pocket and began to lecture to the jury as if this were a classroom.

"When the trigger is pulled on a gun it causes the hammer," pointing with his laser, "to strike the bottom of a cartridge. There is a sharp metal spike on the hammer, called the firing pin. Next chart," he ordered.

Taylor put up a drawing of a bullet cartridge with both a side perspective and one of the circular base.

"There is a small cap on the bottom of the cartridge called the primer." Pointing again with his laser "When the firing pin strikes the primer, it causes the compound inside the primer to ignite, which in turn causes the gunpowder in the cylindrical body of the cartridge to explode." Pointing to the side view. "This explosion propels the bullet at the front of the cartridge out the barrel."

"And is this," Taylor asks, "what produces the gunshot residue?"

"Just a moment," he cautioned Taylor for interrupting him. "The heat from this explosion causes a chemical reaction among the compounds in the gunpowder and the primer. The compounds vaporize then condense into microscopic particles or pellets. These particles are called gunshot residue or GSR."

"What happens to this residue?" Taylor quickly asked, trying to reassert control.

He ignored her question. "The burnt and unburnt particles are expelled from the weapon," Nishi continued, "just like the bullet. This is the smoke you see when a gun is fired. It escapes from the barrel and gets deposited on any nearby object. But it is also forced backward, out the cylinder that holds the cartridges, located near the revolver's handle. This residue gets deposited on the hand of the shooter."

Earl glanced furtively at the jury. They were paying close attention. Earl had prepared hard for this examination. But any successful cross-examination relied on more than just preparation, it depended on instinct. And Earl had learned to trust his instincts. So he studied Nishi as much as he listened to his testimony. He needed to understand the source of the confidence that allowed Nishi to step outside the starched shirt mold of his profession and strut like a peacock among black birds. That would be the key.

Nishi went on to explain that the adhesive patches were designed to pick up any GSR particles on Carlson's hands. These particles were then examined under a scanning electron microscope to determine if they had the requisite shape and then subjected to x-ray spectrometry to identify their basic elements. Based on these tests it was scientifically certain, Nishi concluded, that Carlson had GSR on her hands that was deposited there when she fired a gun.

"Did you also take samples from the body of Adam Hartman?"

"I did. I went to the coroner's office that evening and applied adhesive discs to his hands."

"And what was the result?" Taylor asked, turning to face the jury to receive the answer.

"Gunshot residue was detected on his right palm, establishing that his hand was in contact with a firearm when it was discharged."

"Nothing further, Your Honor," Taylor said and sat down with a look of triumph on her face. The judge nodded to Earl. Nishi sat with his hands folded in his lap and turned to face Earl with a look of indifference.

"Mr. Nishi," Earl said as he rose.

"It's Doctor Nishi," he corrected.

"You're a medical doctor?" Earl said with a touch of feigned surprise in his voice. "I'm sorry, I didn't know."

"I have a PhD in chemistry."

"Oh, a graduate degree," he said. "All right, *Doctor* Nishi." To Earl it was important with certain witnesses to immediately strike a tone that signaled to the jury his opinion of their trustworthiness. A warning against their being taken in. Nishi could not be treated as if his every utterance was delivered from a pulpit on high and endorsed by the amen corner.

"When a suspect is first taken into custody what is the recommended procedure to follow in order to preserve any evidence that they handled or fired a weapon?"

"I don't know the Highway Patrol's procedures," Nishi said dismissively.

"That's not what I asked you. What do the standard forensic manuals recommend?"

Nishi narrowed his eyes at Earl. "The recommended procedure is to bag the subject's hands in plastic."

"That procedure wasn't followed here, was it?"

"Not to my knowledge."

"The purpose of this bagging is to collect any of these particles, this GSR, before they fall off or get rubbed away. Right?"

"That's correct. But it made no difference in this case," Nishi said smugly. "The GSR particles were still present on your client,"

"But if these particles can be rubbed off then they can be deposited on or transferred to other surfaces, right?"

"It's possible."

Earl paused. He had figured out Nishi. It wasn't confidence he had, it was arrogance, which is often a screen for insecurity. Which meant Nishi would defend his opinions as if they were chiseled in stone, afraid to admit any doubt. To him, conceding even the smallest point in the defense's favor would be tantamount to admitting he had made an error. A foolish position for any witness to take, but most especially an expert.

"How small are these particles, anyway?"

"They are microscopic. They cannot be seen with the naked eye. That is why it is necessary to use an electron microscope." Nishi's tone was one you would use to explain the obvious to a child.

"So if these particles were transferred to another surface, nobody could tell. They wouldn't see them?"

"That's correct," Nishi said cautiously.

"Let's say an officer, like a Highway Patrol Officer, went to the shooting range and got GSR on his hands, those particles could be transferred to anything he touched, like his holster, his handcuffs, or his uniform. And he wouldn't even know it."

"I suppose that's possible, but hopefully even police officers wash their hands at some point." Nishi turned to the jury with a smirk, inviting them to share his amusement.

"Yes, but if they touch that equipment before washing, then came in contact with a suspect and used their handcuffs, isn't it possible some GSR could be transferred to the suspect?"

"Most unlikely."

"What about being placed in the back of a patrol car where other suspects have sat? Maybe suspects who have handled guns. Could someone pick up some GSR particles that way?"

"Very unlikely."

"You say very unlikely, but you have no way of knowing the history of that officer or his patrol vehicle, do you?"

"There was no need."

Earl stepped back to his table and glanced at some papers. "You said your first contact with Ms. Carlson was at the Haywood police station. There's lots of policeman there with lots of guns, right?

"Of course."

"Where was she when you took these samples?"

"She was seated in an interview room."

"I assume it was like we see on TV. She was seated at a table and her handcuffs had been removed."

"Your guess, for once, is correct."

"And I assume this room was used regularly to interview suspects. So lots of policeman and lots of suspects have sat at that table. Both groups who are likely to have handled or fired guns."

"I suppose so, dangerous criminals do get arrested," Nishi said. "We know that, don't we, counselor?" Nishi looked at Kate.

Earl ignored his taunt. "On what part of Ms. Carlson's hands did you find these particles?"

Nishi turned to his notes. "On the palms of both the left and right hand."

"Exactly where you would expect to find GSR if it had been deposited earlier on that table by some other suspect or police officer and she had placed her palms down on it." Earl held Nishi's stare as he stepped back and sat down, placing his hands flat on the counsel table.

There are moments one remembers when time stops. Like when a hunter sights a deer that turns and looks into his eyes, a moment before he pulls the trigger. Just before Earl asked his next question was such a moment. "Like this, Doctor Nishi?" Earl slowly stood up, pushing with his hands against the table.

Nishi paused as he shifted in his seat. "It's difficult to follow all these assumptions you're making."

"Well, tell us then, *Doctor*, on what part of the hand would you expect to find GSR if that person actually fired a gun?"

"I don't know what you mean."

"Oh, I think you do," Earl said.

"Objection," Taylor exclaimed.

Earl continued on, not waiting for the judge to rule. "Isn't it a fact that GSR would be found in the web between the thumb and forefinger or on the back of the hand?" Earl pointed at Nishi as if simulating a pistol.

"Those areas are possible, as well as others."

"In fact, the palm is the least likely location for particles to land because when a gun is fired the palm of that hand is gripping the gun's handle."

"Initially, but then she could have handled the gun after she fired it," Nishi said quickly as if relieved to come up with an answer.

"Did you find a single GSR particle anywhere else on her hands other than on her palms?"

Nishi took his time looking at his report. "I don't think so."

"There's no doubt about it, is there?" Earl said firmly.

"No," Nishi said flatly.

"So I guess your explanation is that Ms. Carlson must have washed the back of her hands but not the palms?

There was a snicker in the courtroom. Taylor jumped to her feet.

"Objection," she said. Earl snuck a look at the jury as the judge sustained the objection. Two members of the jury looked at Nishi with skeptical expressions. One leaned over to his neighbor and whispered.

"You say she might have handled the gun. Did you test the gun for fingerprints?

"Yes."

"Did you find any of hers?" Earl asked.

"There were a number of prints and smudges. The gun had been the object of a struggle so most prints were obliterated."

"According to Rattner's version, that is. But did you find any of hers?

"No."

"You also testified that GSR was found on the palm of Adam Hartman's hand," Earl said.

"It most certainly was," Nishi said emphatically.

"Since GSR particles can be transferred, if someone else had discharged the weapon, then placed it momentarily in Hartman's hand, couldn't that account for the presence of the GSR?"

"Only if you want to engage in fantasies."

"Or if you wanted to make it look like Hartman was the one who fired the gun."

"Objection," Taylor said.

"Sustained," the judge said with a hint of professional admiration on her face as she watched Earl's examination.

"Now, I understand a bullet was found in Ms. Carlson's car. Where was it exactly?"

Nishi turned to his notes. "On the floorboard, under the driver's seat."

"Were any of Ms. Carlson's fingerprints found on that bullet or on any of the bullets in the gun?"

"No, but she could have used gloves when loading the gun," Nishi said.

"Did you find any gloves in the car?"

"No, she probably discarded them."

"The prosecutor's theory is that Ms. Carlson stopped along the way, test fired the gun then reloaded it. Do you subscribe to that theory?"

"It seems to fit the facts."

"Cartridges generally come in a box, right? You find one of those?"

"No, she probably discarded it as well."

"All right, so let me see if I have this right. She cleverly used gloves when she handled the bullets, but not when she fired the gun. Then she discarded a perfectly innocent pair of gloves and a cartridge box to avoid any incriminating evidence, but didn't see fit to reach down and retrieve a bullet that she dropped?"

"I don't know what your client did."

"Or if she did anything at all, do you?"

"Objection," Taylor said desperately.

"Sustained," said the judge.

Earl stepped back to the counsel table and withdrew a photograph from a file marked *Rattner Car Crash*.

He stepped over to Taylor and showed it to her. Taylor merely glanced at the photo and got to her feet.

"Objection. The photo counsel proposes to use is totally irrelevant."

"Mr. Earl?" the judge asked.

"The photo deals with GSR. I'm merely testing the witness' expertise, which I am allowed to do." This was not Earl's real purpose. He just needed to get those photos into evidence on the chance he would later find a way to connect them to Rattner's murder. Luckily, the Evidence Code was crammed with exceptions, and Earl knew his Evidence Code.

"I'll allow it for that limited purpose," the judge said.

The court screen filled with a picture of the boulder that Earl and Munoz discovered across the ravine from where Rattner went over the cliff.

"Now, we've been discussing GSR, can you identify the discoloration on that boulder?"

Nishi looked warily at Earl, then down at the photo. "It appears to be the discharge from a rifle that was leveled on the rock. It's called a muzzle flash."

"Can you tell anything about the caliber of the rifle?

"From the size of the muzzle flash it would appear to be a large caliber high powered rifle."

Earl stepped over to Detective Carter and asked for the bullet casing they had turned over to the prosecution. It was the casing he and Munoz had found at the scene of Rattner's 'accident.' Carter turned to Taylor whose jaw was rigid with frustration. They huddled in whispered conversation until Carter shrugged and turned to search in a cardboard box on the floor. He handed Earl a plastic bag which Earl laid on the shelf of the witness stand.

"Can you tell me," Earl asked, "if this is the type of bullet that could have generated the muzzle flash that is shown in the photo?"

Nishi peered closely at the sealed cartridge. "This is a .338 caliber shell, slightly less than a .34. It is a high powered long range rifle cartridge."

"Judge," Taylor was on her feet. "We are now dealing with matters that have nothing to do with this case."

"Your Honor, I am merely going to ask the witness a hypothetical question to test his expertise."

"I'll hear the question," the judge said. "But let's not drift too far afield."

Earl put another photo on the screen taken from the vantage of the muzzle flash on the boulder looking out across the ravine to the point on the road where Rattner went over.

"Assume, if you will, that the distance from the muzzle flash on the rock across to the bend in the road is 500 yards. Further assume that an expert marksman is armed with a high powered rifle, say a Remington, series 700, and that the rifle is loaded with this type of bullet." Earl gestured to the cartridge in the plastic.

"Now," Earl continued, "could such a rifle fired from that distance with this bullet hit a target, say an inflated tire and penetrate it?"

"Objection. None of these facts are in our case," Taylor said with a tone of frustration.

"I assume, Mr. Earl, this will be your last question in this area," the judge said and fixed Earl with a stern look. "As such, he can answer."

"It would be an extremely difficult shot, even for an expert marksman. But yes, I believe it could deflate the tire, if that's what you're asking."

"Nothing further," Earl said and took his seat.

CHAPTER 29

During the noon recess, Earl was still riding on the adrenalin high from his examination of their forensic expert and filled with a craftsman's pride in a job well done. The import of the physical evidence no longer belonged exclusively to the prosecution. It was now in play and Earl planned to enlist it on the side of the defense.

Normally during the lunch hour, Earl would buy a sandwich at the fifth floor snack bar and retreat into the Attorneys Lounge. There, surrounded by his fellow defense lawyers, he could decompress in a lighthearted atmosphere where judges were bemoaned, prosecutors lampooned and colleagues gleefully skewered with good-natured derision. He sought this safe harbor as much for the camaraderie as he did as a precaution against being seen outside the courtroom by a juror who might be influenced by where or with whom he ate.

But not today. He planned to spend the hour in the court's lockup with Kate. He dragged the folding chair up close to the cell bars opposite Kate, who was seated on the cement bench and handed her a paper bag. Last night he had picked up two sandwiches from the Bay Cities Deli in Santa Monica. From his own bag he pulled out a Godmother with extra mortadella and took a generous bite.

"Good, huh?" he mumbled through a full mouth.

"It sure beats a slice of baloney between two pieces of dry bread," Kate said.

They ate in silence for a time, just relieved to be free of the pressure and scrutiny of the courtroom. Earl took off his coat, slid it onto the back of his chair and loosened his tie. He passed her a sheaf of papers through the bars. "Some lunch time reading," he said. "More material recovered from Hartman's cell. Includes the bid package submitted by PCA that won the state contract to house inmates at Haywood. I just wanted to make sure I didn't miss anything."

Keeping Kate occupied would give Earl the time he wanted to organize his thoughts. When the DA finished her case, they would be forced to make a decision — a big one. One that required a serious discussion with Kate, and he needed to settle on the best way to approach it. The question was whether Kate should take the stand in her own defense. He was still unsure, and time was running short. If she did, they would need time to go over her testimony and maybe bring in a colleague to do a mock cross-examination.

Putting a client on the stand was never an easy choice — even an intelligent, articulate, successful lawyer. Because telling the truth was no sure ticket to freedom. Some jurors professed a magical power that enabled them to assess a defendant's credibility, not from the substance of their testimony, but solely by how they acted on the stand. These soothsayers believed that only a liar would appear nervous testifying before twelve strangers who held your life in their hands; that only perjurers spoke hesitantly or blinked or needed a sip of water; that any truly innocent person would break down, cry, plead, supplicate.

Moreover, in Kate's case, there were those damning facts she would be asked to explain such as the coincidental appearance of the gun or the matching bullet in her car. And if she offered up that she was framed, it would sound so much like a tired Hollywood script that it would probably be viewed as a confession. And finally there were the letters that Hartman wrote to Kate, the overly friendly ones that the DA did not have. If Kate took the stand, the DA could demand they be produced.

"Oh my God!" Kate exclaimed. She suddenly lurched forward and gagged, nearly losing her mouthful of sandwich. She straightened up and closed her eyes as she slowly composed herself. "I don't believe this," she said as if overwhelmed. "Have you seen this memo? The one from PCA's competitor to their attorneys? The one about sexual abuses in their prisons."

Earl felt a cold wave of guilt. McManis had voiced puzzlement over how the guards union had acquired the damaging confidential attorney-client communication. By submitting the memo in support of the PCA bid, the union had enabled PCA to win the Haywood contract. Earl should have known better than to disregard a concern raised by McManis. The old lawyer's instincts had been honed by decades in the trial arena. It was like when a seasoned soldier senses danger, but can't quite put a name to it. Such hunches should never be ignored.

"What is it?" asked Earl.

"This law firm. Simel & Simmons. Leland Bain worked there before he came to H&C. It would have been about the same time this memo was written. I remember, because the younger lawyers were envious of his rapid advancement and referred to his former firm as the 'Simple Simon' firm. It was spiteful and demeaning, and Bain deeply resented it. But that's why I remember it."

"So you're thinking that Bain gave this memo to the union?" Earl paused as he considered the possibility. "Let's think about this for a minute. First of all, there's no proof of that. A lot of people probably had access to it. And even if he did, it may be a serious ethical violation, but I don't see how it helps us."

"Serious violation? It's the most serious ethical breach a lawyer can commit. Learning compromising information from a client is supposed to be protected by the attorney-client privilege! The lawyer can never divulge it. To turn around and use it against that client to benefit another client?" Her eyes were wide with amazement. "It doesn't get any more serious. He could lose his license." She waited for a response, then realized that Earl had missed the link. "Of course. You don't really know Leland Bain."

"So tell me," Earl said.

"There's something you have to understand about Leland Bain. Being the managing partner at H&C is more than a job to him, it's his life. It is the very essence of who he is. He has nothing outside of that. Being asked to resign and maybe lose his license to practice would literally destroy him. I don't think he could survive it."

Earl felt that somehow this might be important to the case. But right now he had something that was of a more immediate concern. In a few minutes he would be cross-examining a key witness --- the matron who searched Kate at the prison. He had to focus. There were no do-overs in a trial. Any brilliant question he thought of on his way home in the car would only serve to rob him of sleep.

"Kate, let me think about all this. But not right now. That matron is up next. I'll be down to see you on Saturday and we'll talk about this some more."

When Earl returned to the courtroom he was zeroed in. The testimony Denise Wallace would constitute the first solid piece of defense evidence the jury would hear. Earl had been looking forward it, but he also understood why Taylor was calling her. It was a smart move. Taylor could take some of the sting out of the damage by calling Wallace herself. Otherwise Earl would call her, and then Taylor would look as though she had tried to hide something. Taylor was undoubtedly upstairs right now preparing Wallace. He was going to enjoy this.

Seated at the counsel table, Earl swiveled around to survey the murmuring crowd. It had grown. There was a new energy in the room. A couple of grinning defense lawyers caught his eye and shot him a thumbs-up. This was finally starting to look like a contest.

The courtroom doors opened and Taylor walked in, escorting a heavyset woman in a guard's uniform. More solid-looking than fat, square built, like a walking Coke machine. The woman clamped her lips together and swept the room with small, mean eyes. Taylor nudged her indicating an aisle seat on one of the public benches which she lowered herself onto, darting suspicious looks at the people around her. Trailing behind them was

Jerry Reynolds, who took the seat beside her. No surprise there, Earl thought. He had been monitoring the trail since last week.

Earl studied Taylor as she took her place at the counsel table. She sat rigidly, staring intently ahead. There was a determined bearing about her, as though she had fixed on a course and was resolved to follow it. No matter what. After Nishi's performance this morning, Earl had expected to see her a bit frazzled. He was wrong.

The bailiff brought Kate out to join him. She smiled a greeting, still buoyed from the morning and their lunch time talk. The bailiff called the room to order and the judge took the bench. Earl noticed that Taylor was flying solo this afternoon as Carter was not with her. She must have sent him out on a salvage mission.

Denise Wallace took the stand, and Taylor walked her through that day. How she was called to search a female visitor. How Wallace had recognized her from the previous times she had visited Hartman. "Do you recognize that person in the courtroom today?" Wallace gestured in Kate's direction without looking at her, as if reluctant to meet her gaze. Wallace explained that each time Carlson came to Haywood she needed to be put through a special screening because she had a metal implant, and it was usually Wallace who got the call.

Taylor then asked her to describe what this special procedure entailed. How the subject was taken into a private room and a hand scanner run over their body. If the scanner alerted on the torso, rather than the extremities, the subject was required to disrobe and her clothing was examined. In extreme cases, even a body cavity search was required.

"Now, on the day in question, did the scanner alert on Ms. Carlson?" Taylor asked.

"It always did, because of her implant," Wallace said.

"Where on her body did the scanner indicate the presence of metal?"

"Like always, in the upper leg or groin area."

"And is this an area on the body where you have been trained that a metal object, such as a weapon, might be concealed?"

"Yes, ma'am."

Earl heard the courtroom doors open behind him, then he saw Carter quietly take his accustomed seat next to Taylor. She seemed surprised to see him. He shrugged his shoulders, then shook his head as if signaling he had been unable to accomplish her request.

Taylor turned back to the witness. "So did you conduct a further search as the protocol dictates?"

"No, ma'am."

"Was the defendant required to disrobe?"

"No, ma'am."

Earl felt as if he had been punched in the gut. Those rotten bastards, his mind screamed, they got to her. Earl stared hard at Wallace who refused to look in his direction. Kate gripped his forearm in alarm and dug in her fingers.

"Why didn't you conduct a proper search?" Taylor asked, pretending to be puzzled.

"I'm a single mom, raising two daughters," Wallace began. "One of my girls was home sick. I wanted to use my lunch break to run home to check on her. Cause' we live real close. So I needed to find my Sergeant for him to sign off on it before he left. His shift was ending and the Sergeant coming on don't really know me. So I was afraid he'd say no."

"So you're saying you would not have had time to conduct a proper search?" Taylor asked. "Why not?" She acted as though she were hearing this for the first time.

"Cause' she was wearing this fancy full dress, all puffy," Wallace said gesturing with her arms spread. "It woulda' taken forever for her to get it off and back on and a lot longer for me to search it." Wallace shook her head. "She usually wore pants like everybody else. But not that day."

"So it was unusual for her to wear that type of clothing?" Taylor asked, making sure the jury didn't miss the sinister implication.

"Oh, yes, ma'am."

"So what did you actually do?"

"I ran the hand scanner over her and it went off as usual. So I just waived her through." She paused, then said, "See I knew her. She and I used to talk, friendly like. I never thought she would do something like this."

"Objection," Earl said.

"Sustained," the judge said. "The jury will ignore the last portion of the answer."

Earl stared at Wallace, his face a mask of contempt. He wanted the jury to know what he thought of this. The trouble was that Taylor had coached her well, it was a convincing performance.

Taylor stepped to her table and picked up a paper. "After Officer Miller was killed you were asked to write a report about the search you conducted on Kathleen Carlson, were you not?"

"Yes, ma'am."

"And in that report you wrote," Taylor lifted the report to read, "that you had followed the proper procedure, right?"

"Yes, ma'am."

"But that wasn't true, was it?"

"No, ma'am."

Earl had to caution himself to remain calm. Taylor was really laying the wood to him now. He could tell she was about to take the air out of his cross-examination.

"So why did you write that, if you didn't really follow procedure?"

"I was afraid I'd lose my job if I told the truth. I got two kids to support. I know it was wrong. But I was scared."

"So why are you telling us all this now?"

"Cause' I feel guilty. I can't live with this no more. It's my fault Miller is dead. I can't keep working up there, knowing what I did. So I'm gonna resign."

Taylor took her seat, letting the words hang in the air. The judge looked at her with a pensive expression. "We'll take a fifteen-minute recess," she said. It was apparent this had caught him by surprise and she was giving him time to regroup.

Earl remained seated as he waited for Kate to be taken back to the holding cell. There was a shift in the mood of the courtroom. He could feel it. People were more subdued, thoughtful. Several jurors stared at Kate as if she now appeared more in line with their original expectations. Taylor was starting to prove her case.

Back at the holding cell, Earl took a seat next to the bars. Kate paced inside. "That lying bitch," she spat. "We were never friendly. Christ, she hated me. She relished the chance to search me." She stopped and clenched her fists. "Goddamn it," she said loudly. "That bitch searched me every goddam time. She loved it, the more humiliating the better." She glared at Earl. "I've slept with men who never touched me in places she did."

Earl went back into the courtroom to gather his thoughts. Off to the side, Carter and Taylor were conducting an angry exchange in throttled hisses. Taylor had her arms folded and her jaw set as Carter ranted at her. Earl turned back to his notes, his mind scrambling for a way to recover.

The judge retook the bench. Wallace returned to the stand. She shifted about in the witness box, hunched down like a large burrowing animal preparing to defend itself, staring out with her mean little eyes.

"Ms. Wallace," Earl began. "Let's see if we can agree on a couple things?"

Wallace made no reply, just gave an indifferent nod of her head.

"The first thing is that you're a liar," Earl said matter-of-factly. "Right?"

She looked confused for a moment then said, "I don't know about that."

"Well, either you lied when you made that report or you're lying now. One way or the other, you're a liar."

"I'm telling the truth now."

Earl paused and gave her a mocking smile. His estimation of her credibility needed to be reflected in the manner and tone of every question. He had to get to her. She couldn't be allowed to walk out unscathed.

"Before you made that report you were interviewed about how you conducted your search of Ms. Carlson, weren't you?"

"Yes."

"In fact, one of the people who interviewed you was Detective Carter here, wasn't he?"

"Yes."

"And you looked him square in the eyes and lied right to his face, didn't you?"

"I guess."

"By the way, when you're lying, do you have a certain manner or way of talking, so that the rest of us could tell?"

"Objection, your Honor," Taylor said.

"Move on Mr. Earl," the judge said with an almost-imperceptible smile.

"Now, you knew when you were being interviewed how important it was to be truthful, didn't you? Officer Miller had been killed. There was a big investigation. They needed answers. Truthful answers. Right?"

"I thought I'd lose my job."

"So no matter how important the occasion, you will lie if you think it's in your best interest. How about if someone's life may be at stake? Even that important?"

"I'm telling the truth."

Earl stepped back to the counsel table and tossed some papers about, hoping to convey his disgust with his body language. "Is this the first time you told this version to anybody?"

"You mean about what really happened? First was Mr. Reynolds."

Earl paused a moment in thought. Then he gave Wallace that mocking smile again.

"He works for your union, doesn't he?"

"Yes."

"When did this soul-cleansing take place? When did you tell him?"

"A couple days ago. He gave me the courage to tell the truth."

"Did he give you that courage by helping you figure out what was in your best interest?"

"I don't know, I just know I gotta resign."

"But what about your retirement?" Earl asked. "You guards have a very generous retirement plan, don't you? Can you still qualify for that?

"No. I ain't got enough time in. So I can't get no regular retirement," she explained.

"How about some other type of retirement? You discuss some other form of early retirement?"

"I don't understand."

"All right," Earl said. "Are you willing to swear right now, under oath, that you are not going to receive *any* type of pension from the state of California taxpayers?"

"Objection," Taylor said, "she's not an expert in those things."

"Rephrase, Mr. Earl," the judge said.

"Let me put it this way. Did you ever have a discussion with Mr. Reynolds about the possibility that you might be eligible for some type of retirement benefit?"

"I don't know," Wallace said. "We talked about a lot of things."

"An early retirement would certainly be in your best interest, wouldn't it?"

"Course it would. I got two girls."

"Yes, we've heard about your two girls. So when do you plan to announce this resignation?" Earl asked.

"Right after I'm through with this testifying."

"Of course," Earl said sardonically. "And under the watchful eye of Mr. Reynolds, who is seated right here in the audience." Earl turned and met Reynolds' cold stare. "Nothing further," Earl said.

Taylor spent her time on redirect by having Wallace deny over and over again that she had ever been promised any benefit for her testimony by any person on the face of the planet. Finally, with one last mention by Wallace of her two girls, she concluded. Then Taylor told the judge she needed time to line up her witnesses for tomorrow, so they recessed early for the day.

Earl had tried to steal looks at the jury as they gathered up their things to gauge how Wallace had come across. He couldn't read them. It was as if the jury had all joined some monastic order and taken a vow not to reveal their feelings. He worried that maybe he had been too abrasive with Wallace. Gotten ahead of what the jury thought of her and appeared a bully. He did notice one thing, none of the jurors looked at him when they were leaving. That was never a good sign.

Once outside in the hallway, Earl saw Taylor and Reynolds on either side of Wallace, escorting her down the hall. Each was gripping one of her arms as if hustling her away. Carter stood alone in their wake, calling out Wallace's name. They didn't turn or respond. Reynolds just raised one hand, and they kept walking. Carter turned back and saw Earl. Their eyes met. Carter's lips were clamped in disgust. He turned and headed for the elevators.

CHAPTER 30

Tuesday morning, the prosecutor's table was unusually silent. Carter and Taylor sat side by side, each staring straight ahead like two strangers on a train, both wanting to arrive at the same destination but for entirely different reasons.

The bailiff brought Kate out to join Earl. Her dark mood had carried over from yesterday's performance by matron Wallace. Right now, however, Earl could not afford to be diverted in an attempt to prop up Kate's spirits. He needed to focus on the apparent rift next door. Detective Carter was the next witness, and Earl now understood the real reason Taylor had asked for an early recess yesterday. She had not wanted to risk putting on a riled-up chief detective. Apparently time had not healed their dispute. Earl sensed a possible opening. But was it wide enough?

Judge Parker took her place on the bench. Carter climbed onto the witness stand, leaving his rumpled brown fedora under his seat at the counsel table. He was there to merely recite the "chain of custody" required to admit the physical evidence; where it was found, where it had been kept, who had handled it.

Taylor stepped to the podium and began her preliminary questioning. Her manner was stern and forceful, alert for any sign of defiance. Carter was composed and somber. He confined his responses to the exact scope of each question, never stepping outside those boundaries, just pitch and catch, call and response, nothing more. Yes, he was a detective with the Haywood Police Department. Yes, he was the lead investigator on the case. Yes, he had responded to a call from the Haywood State Prison to investigate the shooting deaths of a corrections officer and an inmate.

"In the course of your investigation at the prison" Taylor asked, "did you cause certain pieces of physical evidence to be collected?"

"I did," Carter replied.

Taylor held up the small handgun and in response to a series of questions Carter stated the gun was a .25 caliber, six-shot revolver, found with two expended cartridges, near Hartman's body. The serial number had been filed off, but acid had been used to bring up the numbers. Congressional legislation prohibits the establishment of a national registry for firearms, so there had been no way to trace the weapon's origin.

Taylor next picked up a plastic evidence bag containing a single paper and asked the Court that it be marked as an exhibit. "People's 5," the judge said, referring to a list she kept.

"Where was People's 5 found?" Taylor asked.

"Next to inmate Hartman's body."

Carter explained that the paper appeared to be a hand drawn map of the prison, which showed the visitors' facility and a circled area marked *vehicle yard.*

"In the course of this investigation, was Ms. Carlson arrested later that day driving in her car?"

"I was informed that was the case," Carter replied.

Earl knew he could object and force Taylor to bring in the Highway Patrol officer, but that would only give her a chance to clean up the questions raised about GSR being transferred to Kate during her arrest. With Taylor writing the script, the officer would probably remember he just had the interior of his patrol car steam cleaned with him inside.

Under her questioning, Carter testified that Carlson's car had been impounded and searched. An unexpended bullet was found under the driver's seat which was the same caliber and manufacturer as the cartridges found in the murder weapon.

When Taylor concluded, Earl noticed that she had not asked Carter to draw any conclusions from the evidence that pointed to Kate's guilt. Such testimony was objectionable, of course, but she had tried with her other witnesses to plant such seeds for her final argument.

The judge turned to Earl. "Any questions, Mr. Earl?" This was usually not an area that called for any cross-examination.

"Yes, your Honor," Earl said. His instincts told him there was an opportunity here, but he needed to tread cautiously, a step at a time, like inching out onto thin ice to see if it would support him. He had already taken enough cold baths in this case.

Earl stepped over to the Clerk's desk and retrieved the map in its plastic bag, then placed it on the witness stand. "Detective Carter, this map, People's 5, is it in the same condition now as it was when you recovered it?"

"Yes, it is," Carter said.

"I notice it's not wrinkled or torn, but it does appear to have been folded in quarters at some point."

"That's correct."

"It's about eight by ten inches, right? When folded in quarters would it fit in a shirt pocket, like the shirt pocket on a guard's uniform?"

"I'd say that's right," Carter agreed.

"Now, we've been told the jumpsuits worn by inmates did not have any pockets. So how do you suppose Hartman could have concealed this paper if he carried it out of the visitors' room? How could he have gotten it past the officer seated at the door?"

"Objection, calls for speculation," Taylor said.

Earl nodded in agreement at the judge. "Let me ask you this. Based on your experience as an investigator and your familiarity with Haywood's prison procedures, were you surprised about its condition?"

"Objection," Taylor said.

"Overruled, he can answer. He's qualified for this very limited purpose."

"I was surprised," Carter answered. "I would have expected it to be balled up in his hand or stuffed into his mouth. He could have concealed the revolver in one hand. It's small. But without wadding up the paper it's just too big. It would stick out."

Earl told himself, he had been right. He was on solid footing with Carter. The businesslike detective seemed determined to answer questions succinctly but honestly.

"By the way, were any of Hartman's fingerprints found on that paper?"

"No, they weren't."

"How about Ms. Carlson's?"

"No," Carter answered.

"Let's turn to another subject," Earl said. "You and I both attended the autopsy of Officer Miller, did we not?"

"We did."

"Did you notice anything unusual about Officer Miller's appearance?"

"What are you referring to?"

"Well, had the hair on his chest been shaved off?"

"Yes, it had."

"Have you seen individuals in the course of police undercover work to similarly shave their chests?" Earl asked.

"I have," said Carter.

"And why would they do that?"

"When you wear a secret recording device, or wire, it's often taped to your chest. Each time it's removed it yanks out some chest hair and eventually leaves a telltale bare patch that might look suspicious. So you just shave it all off."

"Was any recording device found on Officer Miller's body?"

"No, there wasn't."

"Did you have occasion to search Officer Rattner at any time that day?"

"No, we did not."

"Finally, Detective Carter, did you interview Officer Denise Wallace that night about the search she conducted on Ms. Carlson?"

"I did."

"Objection, your Honor," Taylor said in a strained voice. "That's beyond the scope of my direct examination."

Earl knew she was technically correct. Cross-examination was limited to those areas raised during the questioning on direct. "Your Honor," Earl said. "Not being allowed to go into it now, just means we would have to call Detective Carter as our own witness later on. The jury just heard from Ms. Wallace. For continuity's sake, they should be able to hear this now."

"I'll allow it, for the sake of clarity," the judge said.

"Detective, did you question her about the procedure she followed in searching Ms. Carlson?"

"I did."

"What did she say?"

"That she had the defendant disrobe then carefully scanned her clothing and searched her body."

"How did she describe the thoroughness of the body search she conducted?"

For the first time, Carter gave a slight smile. "She said that if Ms. Carlson woulda' had crabs, she could have counted them."

Someone in the audience chortled. The judge quickly silenced the audience with a stern look.

"Nothing further, your Honor."

As Carter retook his seat, Taylor leaned her head close to his and hissed under her breath between clamped teeth, and at the same time she struggled to keep her face expressionless in the vain hope her volcanic reaction to his testimony would go unnoticed by the jury. Carter appeared completely unconcerned as he tipped his head toward her as if listening to their plans for lunch.

"We'll take the morning recess," the judge announced to the jury. "Fifteen minutes."

"Mr. Earl, a word please," said Alice Russell, the Court Clerk. The courtroom spectators were returning from the recess. Earl had pulled files from his briefcase and arranged them on the counsel table. Last night he had reviewed his notes on the next scheduled witnesses, the police lab technicians. Taylor needed them to drop their customary mantle of infallibility in order to disabuse the jury of the notion, fostered by television programs such as *CSI*, that forensic science had almost mythical powers. Apparently the technicians were prepared to confess that it was unrealistic to expect them to provide the prosecution with any fingerprints or DNA that could connect Kate to the physical evidence. The science was just not there yet, except of course, for gunshot residue, which was as incontrovertible as the laws of gravity.

Earl walked over to the Clerk's desk. "At your service, Mrs. Russell," he said.

"I wanted to tell you that Ms. Taylor has asked for a hearing outside the presence of the jury. She's asking permission to call someone that is not on her witness list."

Earl turned and looked at Taylor who was seated at the counsel table, staring straight ahead, avoiding eye contact. "Is she now," Earl said.

"I assumed she had not informed you," the clerk said with arched eyebrows as she looked at him over her wire-rimmed glasses.

"We're currently experiencing a communication blackout, so thanks for telling me, Alice," Earl said with a grin. "Did she, by any chance, share the identity of our mystery guest?"

"No, it's apparently on a need to know basis," the Clerk said and rolled her eyes.

Earl thanked her again and returned to his seat. The bailiff brought Kate out and he explained this new development. She looked concerned, uncomfortable as always with any surprise. The judge took the bench and looked at Taylor. "You had a request, Ms. Taylor?" she said with a hint of impatience in her voice. Like all judges, she was anxious to keep the trial moving and sensitive to the jurors' perpetual complaint about "sitting around, wasting time."

"Yes, your Honor. I would like to call a witness who is not on my list."

"Who is it?" the judge asked.

"Leland Bain. It has just come to my attention that he possesses information that is extremely material to the People's case."

"Mr. Earl," the judge said. "What is your position?"

"A position of great disadvantage," Earl said. "We have not been advised of the existence of this witness until this very moment, and I have no idea what he's prepared to say."

"What is the nature of this proposed testimony, Ms. Taylor?" the judge asked.

Taylor explained, in the most general of terms, that Bain had a close relationship with Carlson when they were law partners. That Carlson had confided to Bain that she had a romantic relationship with Hartman. This testimony, Taylor argued, went to Carlson's state of mind and supported the prosecution theory of why the defendant was willing to help him escape.

Kate's hand clamped down on Earl's forearm. "That is a goddammed lie," she said in a voice loud enough for all to hear.

"Mr. Earl?" the judge inquired, ignoring the outburst.

Earl rose, placing a firm hand on Kate's shoulder. He argued vehemently about the unfairness of presenting a surprise witness on such a crucial question, particularly a witness whose testimony consisted entirely of hearsay, whether or not it fit under some exception.

When Earl concluded, the judge cupped her chin in one hand and stared down in thought. After some time, she straightened up and looked at Taylor. "I'm very troubled by the lack of notice of this witness. It places the defense at a great disadvantage. At the same time, I can see how important this testimony may be to the People's case." She paused, her lips pursed as she deliberated. "It is difficult to strike a fair balance between these competing interests. On the one hand, the People have a right to present their witness. Such a statement fits under the state of mind exception to hearsay of section 1250, showing her feelings toward Hartman."

Earl bound out of his seat but the judge cautioned him with an outstretched hand and a stern look. "On the other hand this catches the defense totally unprepared." She gave Taylor an accusatory look. "Therefore, in an attempt to offset the lack of notice, when your direct examination is concluded Ms. Taylor, we will recess early to give Mr. Earl an opportunity to consider this testimony. Tomorrow morning, we will address whether Mr. Earl needs any further time to prepare." She turned to the bailiff. "All right, let's bring in the jury."

Leland Bain took the stand, wearing his trademark red orchid in the lapel of a royal blue, perfectly tailored wool suit. He acknowledged the judge with a respectful nod, then turned and gave a brief smile to the jury as if to say he was one of them, just a good citizen doing his duty. Then he stared at Kate with the smug expression of a chess player who had just calculated that in the next few moves, his opponent would be inescapably in check mate.

"Mr. Bain," Taylor said, "two weeks before the killings at Haywood, did you have an occasion to encounter the defendant?"

"I did. At a Bar Association dinner."

"On that occasion did you have a conversation with her?"

"Yes, she had been a partner at my law firm for over fifteen years and had recently joined another firm. So naturally, I asked how she was doing. Kate said she was busy enough, but the new firm was not as warm and friendly as our firm. She said she missed her old home." He turned and gave Kate an understanding smile. Kate's face had a savage look, as if she wanted to claw his eyes out.

"And what did you say?"

"I remarked that I was surprised to hear that, because she looked so happy. I think I even joked that she looked ten years younger."

"Yes, go on," Taylor urged.

"She told me her good spirits had nothing to do with work. She had a completely new outlook. That her whole life had changed. She had met someone, a doctor, and she was in love. I said I was very happy for her."

"Did she mention the name of this doctor?"

"Just his first name. Adam, I believe."

"Nothing further," Taylor said.

Kate moaned under her breath, "Oh my God. It's all a lie. I would never confide in him. I loathed him. Sweet Jesus, Bobby." She shut her eyes and dropped her head in despair.

The judge turned to the jury. "We're going to recess a little early today as I have some matters to attend to. We'll see you back here tomorrow morning. Have a pleasant evening, see you on Wednesday."

Earl followed Kate back into the lock-up. He didn't trust himself to remain in the courtroom on the chance that Bain might walk near him. His anger was too close to erupting. Once inside, the bailiff locked her cell and left them alone. Earl stood at the bars as Kate paced back and forth, staring at the floor.

Christ, he swore to himself. Bain's fairy tale was just what Taylor had needed. It gave Taylor a "woman in love" motive that would explain away any seemingly irrational act attributed to Kate. What was the old adage, "love will cause you to do the craziest things." This would permit the jury to indulge their tabloid imaginations.

But why, Earl asked himself. Why would Bain insert himself in the case like this? And how was he going to be able to break down these lies when Bain could just make up whatever was needed to explain any shortcomings? This might force him to put Kate up on the stand. Earl kept telling himself not to panic, just get back to the office and focus. There had to be a way.

CHAPTER 31

To most inmates, the visitor's room at the women's jail took on a different atmosphere at night. It wasn't the lack of sunlight because without windows the florescent glare off the institutional green walls was as antiseptic as always. But they *knew* it was night, the end of the work day, the time when most people were home and all that meant; family, kids, cooking dinner, watching TV, in a word — freedom. It made being caged feel starker, more desolate. Kate Carlson was no different.

But tonight Kate felt an added sense of misery. Her inner walls were crumbling. The barriers she had erected against despondency and surrender, the ones that sheltered her resolve and hope, were giving way. She no longer had the strength to convince herself she had a chance. The sledgehammer blows from the lies of the prison matron and now Bain had taken their toll. She felt beaten down, barely hanging on.

"Chris, how nice to see you," Kate said, summoning up her inner core of civility, determined not to give voice to her wretchedness. "It's very kind of you to visit me."

Sitting across from Kate was Chris Kinder, Leland Bain's assistant. She had always been fond of Chris when she was at H&C, and at the same time, pitied her for the belittling abuse LB spewed at her. Everyone at the firm had been aware how her unflagging competence and tightlipped sufferance was rewarded with LB's derision.

"None of us thought you were guilty," Chris said with a sympathetic smile. "I'm sorry I haven't visited before."

"Oh, Chris. I understand. Just don't let LB know you came here."

"Oh, I'm way past worrying about that," she said with a dismissive shake of her head. "You knew how he treated me. I guess everyone knew." She looked at Kate for affirmation. "But you know what's worse? I'm ashamed of myself for taking it. I let him do it, that's the sad part. It's gotten to the point where I don't even remember who I used to be. He just kept grinding on me and grinding on me until something inside just wore down." She looked away as her voice trailed off. "My self-respect or something. I don't know. I'm just tired, tired of him, tired of the whole thing."

"Chris," Kate said earnestly, "we all knew about the situation with your mother. He knew you needed the job and took advantage of it. Everyone understood that."

"Well, not anymore. I've decided to quit. I have to."

"Chris, you know I would write you a glowing recommendation, but coming from me right now," she pinched the cloth of her uniform, "it probably isn't worth much. But I'm sure others will."

"That's not why I'm here. I want to get back at him. Hurt him if I can." She seemed to gather strength in saying the words out-loud. "We all heard how he testified against you in court. Made up some lie that you two were real chummy, when everyone knew you could barely stand to be in the same room with him. So I thought you might want to get back at him too."

"You mean the man who lied under oath to get me convicted of something I didn't do. So yeah. You could say that."

"So you understand how I feel. Good." Chris's eyes narrowed with conviction as she stared back at Kate. "So here's the thing. LB has been acting very strange lately. Not his usual arrogant self. And I think it's because he's involved in something shady. It may be something illegal or corrupt, I don't know, but it's definitely something that's not right. I don't think it involves your case, but it might be something you could use against him."

"All right, tell me."

"There's this man. He would call LB. He never gave his name, never identified where he was from. Just said tell LB his friend wants a word. LB would always take his call. This man had a very distinct voice, very calm, almost lifeless. Then everything changed a couple weeks ago. LB wouldn't take his calls anymore. And the man had changed his phone number. I know because LB wanted me to always keep a log of his calls in case he needed to call back or figure out who to bill for a call."

"Go on," Kate said.

"And LB started acting funny, sorta' jumpy. Whenever I told him the man was on the line, he got all nervous and refused to take the call. Then today the man called again and this time he left a message, which he'd never done before."

"What was it?" Kate asked.

Chris picked up a piece of paper. "I made a copy. He said, 'Meet me at the agreed location tomorrow at 10 p.m. or I will be forced to terminate our relationship.' He made me read it back and then just hung up. When I gave it to LB he really lost it. I've never seen him act like that before."

"What do you think it means?" Kate asked.

"I have no idea, but he had me cancel his driver tomorrow. He said he was going to drive his own car."

"Do you have those phone numbers?"

Chris held up the paper for the guard to see then passed it to Kate. "I wrote them both on this copy of the message."

"I don't know what this means either, Chris. But I know who can find out."

BACK AT HIS OFFICE, Earl dropped into his chair. He was tired. Bone tired. It was a different kind of tired than he felt after a long run. It was deep down. He felt drained. The strain of the trial was wearing him down. The intense concentration in court, the long hours of preparation, the sleepless nights, they added up. And now Bain had piled on.

For a moment, he let his thoughts find refuge elsewhere. He missed Sam. He missed seeing her smile with that little gap between her front teeth, missed talking with her about his case, missed holding her. It wasn't that he didn't understand the dilemma she faced. They were from two opposing worlds. He forced a rueful smile at the comparison that jumped to mind. They were like the couple in that old movie on Turner Classic Movies, *Adam's Rib*. Spencer Tracy and Katharine Hepburn, defense lawyer and prosecutor, except Spencer Tracy was good-looking. He decided to call Sam. Maybe just say hello, ask how Henceforth was doing. He picked up the phone and started to punch in Sam's number. Then indecision set in. He put down the phone. Maybe he should give her a little more time.

He was pulled back to reality when Munoz filled the doorway. "I've got everyone lined up, ready to go. Only one of them gave me any guff."

"Who was that?

"Well, when I told Ms. Taylor that we would need Captain Gunther back on the stand, she wasn't very ladylike about it. In fact, my granddaughter would have called her a 'potty mouth.' "

"I'm shocked," Earl said facetiously.

The phone rang. When Earl picked up, the operator asked if he would accept a collect call from the jail. He said he would and mouthed to Manny, "It's Kate." Earl listened as Kate described her visit with Chris Kinder, LB's assistant.

"What numbers did she give you?" Earl asked and listened as she read them off. "Wait a minute," he said and put down the phone. He stepped over to the book case and returned to his desk with a binder that he flipped open. "Read me those numbers again," he said and traced with his finger on a report.

"You said the meeting was at 10 p.m. tomorrow? Okay, what type of car does Bain drive?" He smirked. "Really? A light green Bentley. All right, Kate. We're on it." He hung up, and looked at Manny, his face lit with excitement. He felt energized, like a runner who just gotten a second wind. "I hope you have a night vision camera, because you're going to play a paparazzi tomorrow night."

WHEN COURT OPENED Wednesday morning, Earl sent word through the clerk that he first needed to recall a prosecution witness before deciding if he needed time to be able to deal with Bain's testimony. Judge Parker took the bench without the jury and, over Taylor's objection, agreed to permit it as compensation for the way Bain had been sprung on the defense. The judge reasoned out-loud that the witness would probably have been asked these questions earlier if Bain had been put on the witness list. Earl sat silently; he felt no obligation to correct this assumption. The bailiff brought in the jury, and the judge explained the change in the order of the witnesses.

"Recall Captain Gunther," Earl said.

Earl understood that, in any trial, it was important that the first witness for the defense be able to grip the jury. Rivet their attention. They had sat for days only hearing the prosecution side of things and now they expected some fireworks. Battle lines drawn. Fools exposed. Liars called to account. Unfortunately for Earl, today's lead off witness was not that "tip of the spear" type of witness. More like a batter who hits a sacrifice fly to move a runner over or a climber who hammers in a piton to enable those following to scale the cliff. Earl needed to establish a piece of information before the real contest could be joined.

Gunther took the stand, squared his shoulders and placed a sheaf of papers on the ledge next to his polished visor hat. His pale grey eyes fixed Earl with a self-assured look that said he was looking forward to their rematch.

"Captain Gunther," Earl said, "you maintain a list of all the guard's cellphone numbers, do you not, in case they need to be contacted?"

"We do."

"And at our request, you brought that list today?"

"I did," Gunther said with a hint of amusement at the harmless nature of Earl's questions.

"Would you please find Officer Rattner's number on your list?"

"It's here."

"Do you have your own cellphone with you?"

"I do," Gunther said cautiously.

"Would you please call that number?"

Taylor was on her feet. "Objection. Is this something for counsel's amusement? He knows Officer Rattner is not available."

The judge gave Earl a questioning look.

"The relevance will become apparent, your Honor," Earl said.

The judge stared thoughtfully at Earl, then turned to Gunther and nodded her approval.

Retrieving his cellphone, Gunther shared a disgusted look with Taylor and punched in the number. The still of the courtroom was startled awake by the strains of Dixie coming from the cardboard box next to

Detective Carter. He reached into the box and raised the offending instrument. He gave the judge an amused look, then fingered it into silence.

Earl stepped over to Carter and took the cellphone. "Captain, I think we can agree this is Officer Rattner's phone."

Gunther looked at Taylor who leaped up. "Objection. There's no foundation for where it came from."

"I don't think a foundation is necessary," Earl said. "I merely want to establish that this is Rattner's phone."

"Where is this headed, Mr. Earl?" the judge asked.

"Just one more question," Earl said.

"All right, one more," the judge said.

Earl stepped forward and handed the phone to Gunther. "Captain, please pull up Officer Rattner's call history and tell us the number of the last call he received."

Gunther pressed the call log icon. "213 966 3331"

Earl looked up at the judge. "Your Honor, before I proceed any further, may we approach the bench?"

"You may," the judge said and leaned to the side of the bench furthest from the jury, where Earl and Taylor positioned themselves.

"You have previously ruled," Earl said in a hushed tone, "that the jury was not to be told the cause of Officer Rattner's unavailability. To properly present our defense, it is now necessary to bring out the bare facts of his automobile crash."

"What? Taylor exclaimed. "That's ridiculous...."

"Keep your voice down, Ms. Taylor," the judge admonished.

"If necessary, I can make an *ex parte* offer in chambers," Earl said.

"Are you representing to me," Parker said with an exasperated look over another possible delay, "that the accident is material to your defense?"

Earl nodded. "I am."

"All right." She turned to Taylor. "I don't think the fact of an automobile accident will prejudice the People." She fixed Earl with a hard look. "But I am holding you to that representation, Mr. Earl."

"I will merely summarize the facts for Captain Gunther. Nothing further."

"Get on with it then," Parker said dismissing them.

As they walked away Taylor said over her shoulder, loud enough for the jury to hear, "Thank you, Your Honor," It was a sly trick to create the impression she had won the argument.

Earl returned to the counsel table. "Captain Gunther, are you familiar with the reason why Officer Rattner was not available to testify here in court?"

Gunther gave Taylor a puzzled look, then turned to the judge. "You may answer," the judge said.

"I am," he said.

"Is it true that Officer Rattner left his home, driving in his truck along a road cut into the side of a mountain when his right front tire blew out? And as a consequence, his truck plunged over the edge of the cliff and he fell to his death."

"That's my understanding," Gunther said.

Earl put on the screen a photo of the scene of Rattner's "accident."

"Is that the location on the road where Rattner's tire blew out and he went over the cliff?"

"That's correct."

Earl put up the previously shown photo taken from the muzzle blast boulder looking across the ravine. "Is that a view of the same location from a vantage point across the divide?"

"It appears so."

"Would you agree that the distance from that boulder to the road to be about 500 yards?"

"I suppose, more or less."

"Thank you. Nothing further."

The judge looked at Taylor to see if she had any more questions. Taylor smirked and shook her head.

"I'll see counsel at the bench," Parker said.

Earl and Taylor huddled at the side of the bench. Earl asked if he could start with Bain the next morning. What he didn't say was that he needed to buy time to let Bain's rendezvous play out that night. The judge was irritated and gave Taylor a glare for causing the delay. "Given the impact of Mr. Bain's testimony on the defense case, we'll recess until tomorrow morning." She excused the jury.

CHAPTER 32

Thursday morning. The front benches of the courtroom were full. The reporters were back. In their excited chatter, Earl could hear an undercurrent of anticipation, just like in the bull ring when the matador finally brings out his sword and *muleta*, the small red cape of death, the reporters sensed the end was near. They had the angle for their stories — a star-crossed love affair. Now all they needed was a tragic conclusion, the final fall.

The lock-up door opened, and the bailiff escorted Kate to her seat. "Why didn't you come talk to me?" she whispered urgently. "What do you plan to do with Bain?"

Earl had not paid his usual pre-court visit that morning. He had been up most of the night putting his thoughts in order. This was no time to be distracted. Luck had dealt him some cards, but success depended on how they were played. That meant keeping his head in the game. So, with an understanding hand on her shoulder, Earl signaled her to be patient. She clamped her lips shut in frustration and sank back in her chair.

Judge Parker took her place on the bench. Her single strand of pearls had been replaced by a Hermes scarf tastefully draped around the collar of her black robe. "Mr. Earl, are you prepared to proceed with this witness or are you asking for more time?"

"No, your Honor," Earl said with a confident grin. "I'd like to take a crack at him right now,"

"All right," she said. "Have the witness retake the stand."

The jury was brought in, and they found their assigned seats.

Taylor stood up. "If the court please, upon the conclusion of the testimony of Mr. Bain, the People will rest."

Such an announcement always produced a solemn atmosphere in a trial. It was as if the jurors realized that a milestone had been reached in their journey; the time was fast approaching when they would be called upon to sort out this jumble of contradictions and deliver a judgment. No longer would they be allowed just to sit back and experience the drama of a trial. A person's fate would soon be thrust into their hands.

To Earl, it signified something else. Taylor had made this premature announcement for a tactical reason. She was signaling to the jury that Bain's testimony about Kate's love for Hartman was the 'coup de grace.' The final blow. That there was nothing that Earl could ask or do that would alter the outcome. The case was over.

"Thank you Ms. Taylor, always good to look ahead," the judge said.

Out of the corner of his eye, Earl could see Taylor shifting nervously in her seat, like a ballplayer readying her body for a competition. Bain returned to the witness stand. He stared directly at Earl, with a challenge in his eyes, as if his look was meant to be a slap in the face. Earl met Bain's eyes, then his lips edged up slightly with a hint of a smile. The message was clear. They both knew what was at stake. This was to be a contest. A duel between the two of them in which there could only be one winner.

"Mr. Bain," Earl said, as if in recognition, as he rose.

"Mr. Earl," Bain replied with a nod.

They were like two boxers touching gloves to signal the start of a match.

"I gather," Earl said, "that you and Ms. Carlson were quite close. Socialized outside the office, went to dinner, that sort of thing?"

"Not really," Bain said. "I was quite surprised when she told me all that."

"Was anyone else present when Ms. Carlson bared her soul to you?"

"No, just the two of us. It was during the cocktail hour."

"You share any intimate details of your own life with her?"

"No," Bain said with a self-deprecating smile. "I'm afraid my life is rather boring. All I seem to do is work."

It was clear to Earl that Bain was intent on playing the role of an unbiased, even reluctant, witness put in this position by a coin flip of fate; not a combatant, just an innocent swept up by chance in Kate's malevolent wake. To a jury, such an image meant Bain should be treated like a football player who wears a red jersey during practice. You were not supposed to hit him. Earl had to strip him of this immunity.

"Now," Earl said, "you're quite familiar with this case, are you not? In fact, you appeared at a pretrial hearing in this very courtroom for your client the Prison Corporation of America, the people who own and operate the prison at Haywood."

"I did."

"But you waited until two days ago to mention this conversation to anyone?"

"I wasn't that familiar with facts of the case, you see. When I realized how important this conversation was, I felt obligated as an officer of the court to come forward." Bain turned to the jury as if knowing they would understand this responsibility.

"I see," Earl said with a skeptical smile. He paused to look down at the table and flip open his notebook. "Let's discuss this client of yours, PCA. They're your largest personal client, aren't they? In fact, they're your firm's most important client, worth millions of dollars in fees to Horgan & Cooley."

"Yes, they have detention facilities all over the country," said Bain.

"As their attorney, you must have drafted their bid to house State inmates at their private prison in Haywood?"

"Yes, I oversaw the package which successfully won that contract."

Earl held up a manila envelope filled with documents. "This is a copy of that bid package."

"Objection," Taylor said, "I've never seen those. It's a clear violation of the discovery rules."

"Your Honor, this is a copy of the documents that were found in Adam Hartman's cell. You can tell from the mailing address to Hartman on the envelope and that it bears the prison stamp of 'censored.' The court will recall that Ms. Taylor represented that she had provided all this material to the defense, so she must have just overlooked this."

Taylor quickly sat down.

"You knew that Adam Hartman had obtained a copy of this bid package, didn't you?" Earl asked.

"I heard something to that effect," Bain said with an indifferent shrug.

"Actually, as PCA's lawyer you were given a written notification by the Department of Corrections that they were mailing this material to Hartman, weren't you?"

"Yes, I believe you're correct," Bain said with a begrudging smile.

"Now, your client PCA was competing for that State contract with General Corrections Corporation of America, GCCA, another private prison corporation that also operates here in California."

"Yes," Bain said warily.

"And in this material that Hartman obtained was a letter of concern that the prison guards union filed opposing GCCA's bid."

"Yes, the union was concerned about some of GCCA's practices," Bain said.

"In fact, the union attached to their letter an internal GCCA memo written to their lawyers that revealed instances of physical and sexual abuse of inmates by their staff at their prisons."

"Something like that." Bain cleared his throat and shifted in his seat.

"Objection," exclaimed Taylor. "I thought we were trying a murder case."

"I'll tie it up shortly, Your Honor." Earl knew his assertion was the legal equivalent of '*the check's in the mail*,' but the judge nodded.

"All right," Judge Parker said. "I'll allow it for a time."

Earl marked the memo as an exhibit, gave a copy to Taylor and placed it before Bain. "In that bidding process I assume you worked closely with the union, because as a part of the PCA proposal they offered to only hire State correction officers from the guards union to staff their private prison."

"We thought the manner in which union guards were trained was more in line with PCA corporate values."

"This memo must have weighed heavily in PCA's favor in the decision to grant them the contract?" Earl asked.

"You would have to ask the Department about that."

"By the way, this memo from GCCA to their attorneys is clearly a confidential communication protected by the attorney-client privilege. No lawyer is allowed to share this confidential information. So do you know how the union came into possession of this memo?"

"No idea. I was told it was an anonymous source."

"Objection," Taylor said forcefully. "We are way off in left field."

"I don't know," the judge said, "if left field is a legal basis for an objection, but Ms. Taylor has a point. I'll need an offer of proof at this point, Mr. Earl." She turned to the jury. "Ladies and Gentlemen, just remain in your seats and talk among yourselves. We'll be back in a minute."

Earl picked up a file from his table and followed the judge and the court reporter into chambers. After several minutes the three returned and took their places. Taylor looked up expectantly at the judge.

"You may proceed, Mr. Earl," Parker said.

Taylor slumped back petulantly into her chair, grimacing in annoyance.

"Returning to this memo," Earl said. "Are you familiar with this law firm that represented GCCA?"

"I've heard of them," Bain said cautiously.

"Oh, you've more than just heard of them, Mr. Bain. You actually worked at that firm at the very time they received this memo from GCCA, didn't you?"

Bain narrowed his eyes into slits of resentment.

"That's correct," he said, biting off his answer.

"So you would have had access to this memo, wouldn't you?"

"As did all the other lawyers in the firm, as well as all the staff of the prisons to whom it was directed."

"Well, let me ask you this. If a lawyer who had worked at that firm *had* provided this memo to the union to use against his old client, wouldn't that be a serious ethical violation of the attorney-client privilege?"

"I'm no expert on legal ethics," Bain said dismissively.

"Neither am I," Earl said, "but isn't it pretty clear that a lawyer could lose his license to practice law if he took compromising information that he learned in confidence from an old client, then turned around and used it against that old client in order to benefit a new client?"

"You'll have to ask an expert about that," Bain said curtly.

Earl shrugged as if he thought the answer was obvious. "By the way, when you joined Hogan & Cooley, didn't they keep a conflict list, a sort of register of every client each lawyer ever represented, in order to avoid this type of situation?"

"Every firm does that," Bain said.

"In fact, these conflict situations are so important to your firm that a senior partner is in charge of this list, to insure the registration requirements are complied with. So you don't take on a new client who is competing against an old client whose trade secrets were known to you."

"Yes."

"He's called the Chief Ethics Officer, isn't he?

"That is true."

"So did you list GCCA as your former client when you signed up?"

"I don't think so. I must have forgotten, because I did so little work for them."

"Of course," Earl said facetiously. "But you did remember your old firm, when you learned Ms. Carlson was actually visiting Adam Hartman, didn't you?" Earl paused for a response. "You must have known she was visiting him. After all, Ms. Carlson was the spokesperson for an Initiative that would put your biggest client out of business in our State and she was visiting him in a PCA owned prison."

"I was aware," Bain said staring straight ahead, chaffing under the questioning, refusing to look at Earl.

"And I'm sure it occurred to you that the reason Ms. Carlson was meeting with Hartman was because he was housed in a private prison, and he might have information that she could use in her campaign against the use of private prisons?"

"Never gave it any thought," Bain said through clenched teeth.

"Weren't you concerned that Hartman might give this memo to Ms. Carlson as an example of how private prisons abuse their inmates? And that Ms. Carlson in turn might recognize the law firm in the memo as the one you came from and see that you had once represented a competitor of H&C's biggest client?"

"No," Bain snapped.

"If she had, you'd no longer be the managing partner with the big corner office at H&C, would you?"

"That's ridiculous," Bain scoffed.

"Really, let's consider this. You fail to report that you represented a prior client who just happens to end up competing against your current biggest client. Then this damaging memo from your prior client, written to you as a member of your former firm, shows up in your new client's bid package. Boy," Earl said arching his eyebrows, "if that ever got out it would probably make the firm's other clients think twice about staying with H&C. Double-dealing is not so good for a firm's reputation, is it? I would think your firm would have to give you the ol' boot."

Bain turned to face Earl with a murderous look and leaned forward by planting his hands on the stand. "I'm too damn valuable to the firm to worry about nitwit fantasies like that."

"Valuable enough for your partners to dig into their own pockets to repay all the fees collected from PCA over the years? Which is exactly what might happen in a conflict of interest law suit, isn't it? It's called a disgorgement remedy, as I recall."

"Listen, you...."

"All right, all right, Gentlemen," Judge Parker said. "Let's take the lunch break. I'll see you all back at 1:30, have a pleasant lunch."

After the lunch break, the atmosphere in the courtroom had changed. Apparently the word had spread throughout the courthouse that something remarkable was unfolding, something unexpected and quite extraordinary. The room was jammed.

Earl turned in his chair to survey the spectators. Several colleagues gave him grins of encouragement. In the back, Reynolds and Bowdeen sat like Roman patricians at the Coliseum, drawn to a gladiator contest. The reporters seemed pensive, as if no longer sure of their headline. The judge took the bench, the jury was seated, and Bain retook the witness stand.

"Mr. Bain," Earl said, "before the recess we were speaking of the amazing coincidence that a damaging confidential communication to you from an old client showed up to help your new client."

"Not as remarkable a coincidence," Bain shot back, "as a gun showing up right after your client visited Hartman."

"But that was no coincidence. Was it, Mr. Bain?" Earl paused and fixed him with sober look. "It was planned, wasn't it?"

"Yes, that appears to have been your client's plan. You should ask her to explain it to you, if she hasn't already."

"Let's see about that, shall we?" Earl put a photograph of Rattner up on the screen. "Have you ever had any dealings with this man?"

"Never seen him before in my life," Bain said, without looking at the screen.

"He's the prison guard who ended up with the gun that was used to shoot Officer Miller and Adam Hartman."

"The gun your client smuggled into the prison." Bain smiled smugly.

"That remains to be seen, doesn't it? Because he's also the guard who brought a lunch box to work that day with a hidden compartment. One that could accommodate such a gun."

"That means nothing to me," Bain said.

"Well, perhaps this will help," Earl said. "We've had testimony that Officer Rattner couldn't be with us because he died in a fatal crash when his front tire blew out, which caused his truck to go over a cliff. We also heard that just before that crash he received a call from a certain phone number. One with which I believe you're familiar, 213-966-3331."

"Why would I be? I've got better things to do than carry around phone numbers in my head."

"I understand," Earl said mockingly. "You're a very busy, important man. That's why you had your assistant keep a record of your calls, didn't you?" Earl held up a bound ledger.

"Yes," Bain said in a guarded tone.

"Well, that same number, the one that called Rattner, is also listed several times as calling you."

A glint of alarm flashed in Bain's eyes. "I talk to a lot of people every day."

"And this same person called and left you a message just two days ago, didn't he?" Bain sat as still as if he had just heard a warning shot. "Perhaps this will remind you." Earl held up a small piece of paper.

"Objection," Taylor said. "This is all hearsay."

"I'm allowed to present any material that might refresh a witness' memory, and it appears that Mr. Bain is in need of a little refreshing."

"Overruled," the judge said.

"This telephone message said to meet him last night at the agreed location at 10 p.m." Earl paused and stared at Bain. "Does that help you remember?"

"No," Bain said as his eyes burned into Earl's.

"Well, did you meet someone at 10 p.m. last night?"

"No," Bain snarled.

"Oh, but I think you did, Mr. Bain. Here, let's take a look at this?" Earl put a shadowy photo up on the screen of two figures apparently in an intense exchange.

"That's you isn't it, Mr. Bain? The one with that orchid in his lapel?"

As Bain stared in astonishment, Earl could tell he was furiously weighing his options. Should he just make up a story about the meeting or would that risk him getting caught in a further lie?

"I can't tell," Bain said in mock puzzlement.

"Perhaps Mr. Munoz, my investigator, who took the photo will be able to enlighten us. But let's speak about the other man in the photo, shall we?"

"Your Honor," Taylor said in an exasperated tone. "I must object. Where is this all going? It's totally irrelevant."

"Mr. Earl," the judge said. "I have been tolerant because of the circumstances you were placed in with this witness. But unless you can show me the relevance of this line of questioning, you'll have to move to another area."

"Judge, I'm getting there," Earl said imploringly. "If you will just give me five minutes, I assure you the connection will be clear. The last thing I want to do is waste the court's time."

The judge returned his stare while deciding whether to trust his assurance. After a moment she said, "All right, proceed. But let's see some progress."

Earl put up the photo of the muzzle blast on the boulder looking toward where Rattner's truck plunged off the road. "Mr. Nishi, the prosecutor's expert, told us that a high powered rifle made that mark and if fired from that spot could shoot out Rattner's tire, causing the accident. But it would be a difficult shot. Captain Gunther agreed the distance was about 500 yards." Earl put up another photo, one of the bullet casing found on the boulder. "Nishi also testified that this type of cartridge, which was found on that boulder, could have been used."

Another photo appeared on the screen, one of the marksman signing a paper target.

"Now, doesn't that appear to be the same man who appeared in the other photo talking with you?"

"I have no idea," Bain spat out.

"And if you look closely you can see the bulls-eye is shot out of the target and 500 yards is written at the top."

"Objection," Taylor said. "I fail to see what all this has to do with the murder at Haywood Prison."

The judge fixed Earl with a thoughtful gaze. "I think I see where this is headed, so I'll permit a few more questions. But if I'm wrong, Mr. Earl, that will be the end of your examination."

Taylor remained standing, looking puzzled.

"Now, here's the interesting point." Earl held up a report and stepped toward Taylor to show her. "You have a copy," he said and turned back to Bain. "Phillip Jones, a fingerprint expert is prepared to say that a partial print on the bullet casing found on that boulder matches the print left by the man signing that target. The same man caught in that photo talking with you."

"Object...." Taylor mumbled, then she slowly sat back down, a stunned look on her face.

"So let me summarize the evidence we have and see if you agree with this conclusion. It was you who provided the guards union with that damaging confidential memo from your old client. That memo insured that PCA was awarded the contract for Haywood prison and in return they became your client, which elevated you to managing partner of your firm. You learned that Hartman had obtained a copy of that memo, and you were afraid he would turn it over to Ms. Carlson. If she had recognized the name of your old firm and how you had concealed that your old client was a competitor of PCA, you would have been ruined. No more big-time lawyer, no more corner office." Earl paused. "Am I getting warm?"

Bain sat in shocked silence, as if staggered by a sudden blow.

"So you found this assassin," Earl continued, "who in turn hired Rattner to kill Hartman and frame Carlson. It was Rattner who smuggled in the gun in his cooler. He shot Hartman and had to kill Officer Miller because he was a witness. Rattner must have gotten nervous, and you were afraid he might expose your plot, so your friend set up a meeting with that last call to Rattner. That allowed him to be waiting on the bluff to shoot out Rattner's tire as he drove to this meeting, plunging Rattner to his death."

A boisterous clamor rose from the spectators as reporters struggled past people in their row to get to the aisle. The bailiff shouted for order. The judge pounded with her gavel. "This Court is in recess," she said loudly, then turned to Bain. "Perhaps you should see a lawyer, Mr. Bain. Return here Friday with counsel to inform me if you wish to invoke a privilege or continue testifying." Bain stared up at her with a dazed expression, like someone who had just stumbled from a collapsed building, unable to comprehend the calamity. He turned slowly to look blankly out at the spectators.

Reporters crowded the rail to vainly shout questions. "Are you going to take the Fifth? Did you order the killings?" Then they jostled each other to get out the door, talking excitedly into their cellphones. Reynolds and Bowdeen stood staring at Bain. Reynolds curled his lips in distaste, not at this display of moral depravity, but as if repulsed by such witless incompetence. Bowdeen's face was wooden, impenetrable, the face of a hangman. After a moment they turned their backs to him and joined the flow leaving the courtroom. Bain stared out with the look of a man whose fingers had just slipped off the gunwale of a life boat. He remained in the witness chair, frozen in disbelief, until the room emptied. Then he buried his face in his hands.

CHAPTER 33

When Martha buzzed on the intercom, it startled Earl out of his musing over the events of the day before. The judge had excused the jurors until Monday, but she had ordered the lawyers to return that afternoon, when she expected to hear Bain's decision. They would then discuss how to proceed. So Earl needed to look critically at the case as it stood now and ask how the jury was likely to see it. And just as important, how would Taylor try to explain it all?

Martha buzzed again, and Earl picked up the phone. "Mrs. Miller is on the line." Earl remembered Officer Miller's widow, but wondered why she was calling.

"Mrs. Miller," he said. "How's that boy of yours?"

"He's fine. But in a way, he's why I'm calling. I was going to take him out fishing like his Dad used to do, and guess what I found at the bottom of Travis's old tackle box? Those tapes you were asking about."

"You're kidding," he exclaimed. "That's great, Mrs. Miller. Those tapes will drop the hammer on those rotten guards up at Haywood. Call Frank Corbett at the Attorney General's Office right away. He'll know what to do with them."

"Already have. Those bastards mighta' took my Travis, but now they're gonna get what's comin' to them."

"I'm sure they will, Mrs. Miller. You can count on it."

"Anyway, I just thought you would want to know."

"Thank you for telling me. I hope this makes things a little easier for you."

Earl was convinced that Captain Gunther and his Sharks were guilty of a lot of things, but killing Officer Miller was not one of them. However, in an ironic twist, those tapes, by exposing the Shark's abuse of inmates, would also serve to advance the union's primary goal of increasing the state prison population. Unfortunately for the union, those additional numbers would come from the ranks of the Haywood Prison guards.

That afternoon, the judge felt the court session was best dealt with in her chambers and out of the public's eye. Scattered around the room, Earl, Taylor and Detective Carter faced the judge seated behind her desk.

"Let me introduce Mr. Madison from the firm of Cooper and Arnold," the judge said. "He is representing Mr. Bain, who has declined to be present."

A silver haired man in a chalk-striped grey suit nodded to the assembled room. Earl found it fitting that no one in Bain's own firm had stepped forward to represent him.

"Mr. Madison," the judge said. "Can I expect to see Mr. Bain back in my courtroom on Monday to continue his testimony?"

"I'm afraid not, Your Honor. The unfortunate allegations that have been raised against him, which we deny in their entirety, make it impossible. While we regard these groundless accusations as nothing more than scandalous lies, Mr. Bain has no alternative but to invoke his privilege against self-incrimination."

"It's hard to see," Earl interjected, "how these questions could, at the same time, be both groundless lies and calling for answers which might be used against him in a criminal prosecution?"

"I'm sure my colleague is aware," Madison said, "that even an innocent answer, under the right circumstances, might raise suspicions that eventually could lead to legal entanglements."

"Enough, gentlemen," the judge said. "I should inform you all that I was told yesterday that the Haywood District Attorney's Office has reopened their investigation into Officer Rattner's death and is obtaining Mr. Bain's bank records to determine if there were any unusual withdrawals. Consequently, I am going to permit Mr. Bain to invoke his Fifth Amendment privilege."

"If Bain is going to take the Fifth, I don't want it done in front of the jury," Taylor insisted. "It would just invite them to speculate about his motives for doing it. And as far as I'm concerned, this doesn't change anything in our case against Carlson."

"I'll have Mr. Bain exercise the privilege on the record, but outside the jury's presence. Which brings us to the next question. What do we do with Mr. Bain's previous testimony since he will be unavailable to either side to complete his examination? Are either of you asking that it be stricken and the jury be instructed to ignore it?"

Detective Carter interrupted by loudly clearing his throat and staring expectantly at Lauren Taylor. She stared sullenly back at him, then expelled a deep breath and said: "I'm reminded that yesterday Detective Carter took it upon himself to obtain a court order for the cellphone records of Officer Rattner and Leland Bain."

"I object," Madison said. "You had no right."

"That is an issue you can litigate at the appropriate time, Mr. Madison," the judge said. "But not now. I was the one who issued the order."

Carter handed the judge and Earl a copy of the records. "I have marked the calls between Rattner and the number attributed to the marksman, as well as calls from Bain to that same number. I was surprised they used their own phones, but I guess they figured the shooter's phone number would never surface."

Judge Parker continued to study the phone records. After some time, she looked up. "I assume, Mr. Earl, that you want these records admitted into evidence?"

"Yes, your Honor," he said.

"And I assume," she said turning to Taylor, "that Mr. Bain was your last witness?"

"That had been my intention," Taylor said. "But now I don't know."

"Well, I do. You are resting your case," the judge said. "You stated on the record you were resting your case after Bain testified and I'm holding you to it." Taylor pressed her lips tightly shut and stared hard at the judge.

"I will leave to another court," the judge continued, "the task of determining whether the guilt for the deaths of Officer Miller and Adam Hartman might lie elsewhere. My only responsibility at this juncture is to weigh the evidence against Kate Carlson." She turned to Earl. "I assume you have some witnesses to back up your cross-examination of Mr. Bain."

"Yes, your Honor." Earl quickly explained that Munoz would testify about recovering the bullet casing on the boulder with the muzzle flash, as well as identifying Bain in the photo with the marksman. John Shepard, the owner of the shooting range would qualify the video and acknowledge that the man on the video signing the target made those shots from 500 yards. Phillip Jones, would verify his report matching the partial print on the cartridge casing with those on the target. A lawyer from Bain's office would establish that he and Kate were not likely to share personal details as they were not even on speaking terms. And finally, Chris Kinder, Bain's assistant, would explain the phone calls from the marksman and the phone message about Bain's meeting.

"We'll put all that on before the jury on Monday. After which, given all this, plus the previous testimony, I don't see how I can allow the case to continue. I feel a reasonable doubt exists as to her guilt and consequently I am going to exercise my statutory prerogative and dismiss the case against her."

"You can't do that," Taylor protested.

"I can and I will," Parker said. "I am anticipating that Mr. Bain's bank records will also be made available to add to the evidence. When the defense evidence is concluded on Monday I will explain to the jury that their services are no longer needed."

Earl stepped back into the courtroom. His mind whirled over the sudden change of fortune. He felt a wave of relief wash over him, as if he had been pushing against a locked door that finally swung open to admit a flood of sunshine. He asked the bailiff to let him into the lock-up. Kate Carlson sat on the cement bench. When she heard the door open she sprang up and grabbed the cell bars with her fists.

"What did Bain say? Is he going to testify? Jesus, I still can't get over it. What a disgusting son-of-a-bitch. He makes my skin crawl. So what happened?"

"It's over, Kate. The judge has decided to dismiss the charges against you. The case is over."

"You mean we won?" she asked as if still unsure.

"Yes, we won. You're free."

"Oh my God," she said in a hushed voice and staggered back from the bars. She dropped onto the bench and closed her eyes. She hugged herself and rocked forward. Her shoulders started to shake as she began to cry.

The freeway was packed, but Earl didn't mind. He was exhausted. All those days filled with tension and worry and all those sleepless nights -- he felt like a wrung-out washcloth. Sitting in traffic was just fine with him. He had called Martha to tell her the judge's ruling and asked her to tell McManis. He said he would see them both on Monday and they should be prepared for a long lunch. Martha, true to form, protested against closing the office. "Very unprofessional, Bobby." But Earl merely explained what an unladylike entrance she would make if he had to carry her over his shoulder into the restaurant, then he hung up.

When he finally arrived at his house, he sat in the car for a long minute. How he wished Sam would be there to greet him, so he could gather her in his arms, smell her sweet scent, see her eyes ignite with affection and hear her voice trumpet with laughter. He crossed the front lawn, opened the front door and got as far as the sofa before collapsing. He was content just to sit, his mind a blank as if his brain cells had been drained like a lifeless battery.

A key rattled in the door. Earl forced himself upright. It was Sam. The door flung open as Henceforth pushed his bulk past Sam and charged across the room to hurl himself in a joyful greeting at Earl. The big dog's impact bulldozed Earl backwards onto the sofa where Henceforth slathered his face with a wet tongue. Earl pushed him off, bursting into laughter and wiped a hand over his face. God, he thought, it seemed a lifetime since he had really laughed. Seeing Sam made him feel jubilant, his mind buzzed with elation, like a hero returning home.

Henceforth gave Sam a chagrined look over his shoulder, embarrassed by his slobbery affirmance of loyalty to Earl, so he flopped onto the floor and promptly joined Beauty in a snooze. Sam joined Earl on the sofa.

"God, I was hoping I'd see you," Earl said happily.

"I came by to drop off Henceforth and congratulate you."

"Oh," he said and fell silent. Her tone was like a bucket of cold water in his face. A fierce dread took hold of him and sent him spiraling down. He felt so helpless not knowing what to say, as if he was trapped in an ink black tunnel, fearful of his next step. Steeling himself, he plunged forward.

"Sam, look." He drew a deep breath. "All I know is without you nothing ever seems complete. Like something's always missing. Even the color seems washed out of things, nothing's as bright."

She sat staring down. "It hasn't been easy for me either, Bobby. I spent most of the time away just thinking about us." She turned to face him. "You know, I love being a prosecutor. I still remember the first time my father took me to court. Watching him and how everyone respected him. So honest and fair. Being a prosecutor is all I ever wanted to be. Then you came along. Now it's as if I'm being pulled apart."

It was Earl's turn to stare off in silence and nod his head.

She reached over and took his hand in hers.

"But I don't want to give this up either. And I sure don't want to spend any more time agonizing over it. So let's live our lives and see where this goes. The Office will just have to get used to it."

Earl enveloped her in his arms, gently, gratefully, like a precious gift, then gave her a tender kiss. He finally pulled back and looked into her eyes.

"Besides," he said with a gleam in his eyes. "We don't have much of a choice."

"Really?" she said with a skeptical grin. "How is that?"

"We need to stay together for the sake of the children." He looked down at the sleeping dogs. "If you left, Henceforth told me he'd never be able to hold up his tail again. He'd be that depressed."

Sam gave him an appreciative smile. "I can think of a couple other reasons to put up with you, but I guess that'll do."

THE END
of
JUSTICE MAKES A KILLING

OTHER BOOKS FROM CHICKADEE PRINCE THAT YOU WILL ENJOY

THE STRANGE AND ASTOUNDING MEMOIRS OF WATT O'HUGH THE THIRD, by Steven S. Drachman
978-0991327409 and 978-0991327416

"NAMED TO KIRKUS REVIEWS' BEST OF 2011: [An] engaging tale of Western science fiction and amazing fantasy.... The cool hero's tale is told in charming, romping detail, from the magical adventurer's poor childhood in the Five Points and the Tomb[s], to his notorious, gun-toting dalliances in the Wild West and his wilder exploits through time itself .... Fast-paced, energetic and fun; a dime novel for modern intellectuals." — *Kirkus Reviews*

THE TENTH PLAGUE, by Alan N. Levy, 978-1-7329139-2-9

As global conflict engulfs humanity, should unspeakable means be used to prevent an unspeakable future?
"Debut author Levy sets the story in 2028, a world that's seen a brutal reprisal of the 9/11 attacks on America, ceaseless turmoil in the Middle East, and a bellicose Russia.... The prose is clear and crisp, and the action is relentless, fueled by a combination of brooding cynicism and the imminent prospect of catastrophe.... [A] bombastic and cinematic thriller ... fleet and dramatic[.]"
— *Kirkus Reviews*

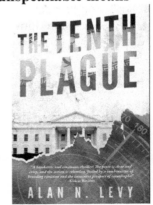

9 781732 913 9